SPECIAL MESSAGE TO READERS

This book is published under the auspices of

THE ULVERSCROFT FOUNDATION

(registered charity No. 264873 UK)

Established in 1972 to provide funds for research, diagnosis and treatment of eye diseases. Examples of contributions made are: —

A Children's Assessment Unit at Moorfield's Hospital, London.

•

Twin operating theatres at the Western Ophthalmic Hospital, London.

•

A Chair of Ophthalmology at the Royal Australian College of Ophthalmologists.

•

The Ulverscroft Children's Eye Unit at the Great Ormond Street Hospital For Sick Children, London.

You can help further the work of the Foundation by making a donation or leaving a legacy. Every contribution, no matter how small, is received with gratitude. Please write for details to:

THE ULVERSCROFT FOUNDATION,
The Green, Bradgate Road, Anstey,
Leicester LE7 7FU, England.
Telephone: (0116) 236 4325

In Australia write to:
THE ULVERSCROFT FOUNDATION,
c/o The Royal Australian and New Zealand
College of Ophthalmologists,
94-98 Chalmers Street, Surry Hills,
N.S.W. 2010, Australia

Sue Gee grew up on a remote farm in Devon, and in a Leicestershire village, before moving to Surrey and then London, where she now lives with her family. She is the author of six previous novels, including LETTERS FROM PRAGUE, serialised on BBC Radio 4's *Woman's Hour*, and was the winner of the 1997 Romantic Novel of the Year award. She is Programme Tutor for the MA Writing Programme at Middlesex University.

THIN AIR

In London, William Harriman, a retired civil servant, contemplates widowhood, estrangement from his children and the collection of antique china. In Shropshire, his lunatic trio of cousins eke out a precarious existence with numberless rescued dogs. The young Janice Harper — dog-walker, shopper-for-the-old and vegan cake-maker — is sent by them to lodge with cousin William and get a life at last. Meanwhile, floods, pestilence and disease are unleashed upon a reeling countryside.

Books by Sue Gee
Published by The House of Ulverscroft:

KEEPING SECRETS
LETTERS FROM PRAGUE

SUE GEE

THIN AIR

Complete and Unabridged

CHARNWOOD
Leicester

First published in Great Britain in 2002 by
Headline Book Publishing
London

First Charnwood Edition
published 2003
by arrangement with
Headline Book Publishing
a division of Hodder Headline
London

British Library CIP Data

Gee, Sue
Thin air.—Large print ed.—
Charnwood library series
1. Large type books
I. Title
823.9′14 [F]

ISBN 0–7089–9494–6

Published by
F. A. Thorpe (Publishing)
Anstey, Leicestershire

Set by Words & Graphics Ltd.
Anstey, Leicestershire
Printed and bound in Great Britain by
T. J. International Ltd., Padstow, Cornwall

This book is printed on acid-free paper

For Danusia, Hazel, Norah and Polly
in slightly different ways

Autumn 2000

I

Letters

1

The wind was getting up again, and William, tugging open the front door first thing in the morning and nearing — he knew, he could feel it — the closing years of his life, bent down for the milk on the top step and had his pyjama trousers whipped about his ankles. He straightened up, pulling his dressing gown to. Rain was blowing past the portico; it splashed on the steps and the unpruned rose at the gate, where a last, astonishing bloom collapsed. Glorious wet pink on soaking earth: he noticed that.

Below him, along the street, the first commuters banged their doors and fought with wild umbrellas. Dulwich to London Bridge: the 8.15. William had made the journey for over thirty years. Before him — standing there on the top step, clasping the bottle of semi-skimmed milk which his daughter had advised — were the tossing trees, the Impressionist umbrellas, silvered by the swirling rain. Behind, in the hall, the telephone was ringing.

'Hello?' On the hall table the milk bottle sank damply into the front-page photograph of floods.

'Global warming,' said Buffy, putting down her coffee cup in her flat in Notting Hill.

'What's that?' He sank into the chair by a tepid radiator, crossing his elegant legs. Eve had thought them elegant.

'This. This filthy wet. The floods, the storms,

the breaking banks. It's up to the first floor in York.'

William, cradling the receiver, looked down at the front-page photograph. Was that York? No — an ancient stretch of meadow, glassy and perfect, set with ancient trees. The water had risen around them, and now, as if waiting for the dove, was still and pure. The milk bottle had ruined it. Without his glasses, it could be anywhere.

'The world has changed,' said Buffy, pouring, he could hear it, another piping cup. 'The climate is in chaos — we've destroyed our *climate*, William. Nothing can ever be the same again.'

'You'd say that whatever the weather.' William ran his hand along the radiator, which, like him, was very cold. And less than tepid. 'It's our age, Buffy. Everything feels ghastly.'

'But this is *apocalyptic*. Your age,' added Buffy. 'I'm not in my dotage yet. What are you doing today?'

'Keeping to the house,' said William, swinging his leg for exercise and watching, against his ancient foot, the elegant flap of wine-coloured leather mules from Austin Reed. From Eve, one distant Christmas. They'd lasted well, as they were meant to. 'Phoning a plumber,' he added, feeling the chill at his back. 'And you?'

'It's Thursday,' said Buffy. 'My singing class.'

'That'll cheer you up.'

'It would if I could get there.'

'London isn't flooded.'

'It's only a matter of time. It's grinding to a

halt. I'm not going to stand in the pouring rain for a bus that never comes.'

'Get the Tube.'

'I hate the Tube. You know I hate the Tube. I hate everything.' There was a chink of the coffee cup. 'Sorry.'

'Poor old Buffy.'

'I hate being poor old Buffy.' A little pause, then: 'Sorry,' she said again. 'I shouldn't go on to you like this, William. You've got far more important things to worry about.'

'I've got the central heating to worry about, certainly,' said William, as the letterbox banged. He peered at the mat. Was that a square of white, among the bills? 'Tell you what,' he said, getting stiffly to his feet, 'when all this clears up, I'll take you to the flicks. How does that sound?'

'Very nice,' said Buffy. 'If there were anything one wanted to see.'

'Now come on — we'll find something. And anyway — ' He felt in his dressing-gown pocket for his glasses, which weren't there. 'I'll be seeing you on the stall on Saturday.'

'I know, I know, it's always fun. You're such a tonic, William, sorry to moan.'

'I'll see you very soon,' he said, craning his neck with the telephone lead at its fullest extension. 'I'd better get on now.'

The hall, lit only by the fading apricot silk of the table lamp, was darkened by the rain. He made his way past the curtained drawing room and bent to pick up the reminder for his TV licence, an envelope printed with violently coloured pound signs and, yes, a square of white.

Mr William Harriman, Esq — dear, dear. A wild hand, a cheap, thin envelope. He took it all, with the milk and paper, down to the kitchen, where Danny, still in his basket, opened half an eye. *Thought for the Day* was murmuring. William searched for his glasses, half listening to a soothing bishop from the studio in Bristol, where sandbags had been heaped along the Severn.

Here were the glasses, still on the morning tea tray. The phone rang again as he gazed at dreadful handwriting. Now what?

He climbed back up to the hall, sank into the telephone chair once more, peering at the postmark on his letter.

'Daddy?'

'Who do we know in Shropshire?'

'What?' Claire, as so often, sounded sharp.

'Shropshire. I've got a letter here.'

'I've no idea. I've rung about Matthew. It's Thursday.'

'So it is,' said William, thinking of Buffy's journey through the rain to sing Handel oratorios in a bright upper room of the Mary Ward Centre. And thinking, collecting himself, of Matthew.

'Is something wrong?'

Asking this, as from time to time it was necessary to ask — when a doctor or social worker or, once, the police telephoned or rang the doorbell — brought back, always, those days when they'd been forced to face it: that, yes, something was terribly wrong.

'What is it?' he asked steadily, as the dark rain lashed the world.

'Nothing's wrong with *him*, don't panic. But I should be visiting, shouldn't I? It's my day. And Geraldine's got an ear infection. We've been up half the night.'

'Oh, dear.' Dimly, he could recall such nights, waking at some god-forsaken hour to see the landing light on, and hear Eve's gentle voice, up on the top floor, with one of the children. Generally ears or sick bowls. Generally the sick bowl for Matthew, ears with Claire.

'Anything I can do?' He'd stagger up there, to pale, tear-stained faces; Eve, in her pink wool dressing gown, being sweet.

'No, no, darling, you go back to bed.'

He doubted that Claire said this often to Jeremy, no matter what kind of day lay ahead.

'Anyway,' she was saying, above a little wail, 'I'm taking her to the doctor and I'm keeping her off nursery. I'm not going to cart her off to see Matthew on a day like this when she's ill. Am I?'

'No, no, of course not.'

'So can you go?'

'Yes, yes, of course.'

'I mean,' said Claire, as the wailing increased in pitch, 'he probably won't notice either way, but — '

'Don't give it another thought. Poor little Geraldine.'

'We'd better get going, it's emergencies only.'

'Give her my love.'

' 'Bye.'

' 'Bye, darling.' But she had already rung off.

William looked at the rain, trickling down the

stained-glass panels of the front door, emerald and bottle green and violet. Would it ever stop? No matter, he'd get there. He went back down to the kitchen, where Danny was stirring, and about time too. 'We're going to visit Matthew,' he told him, putting the kettle on, and Danny, who knew that this word meant the acres of hospital grounds, and lots of racing about, thumped his dachshund tail and stretched. 'Out,' said William, unbolting the back door. 'Go on, make a dash for it.'

The wind and rain blew in as Danny made his reluctant exit, aided by William's slippered foot. He banged the door to, rinsed out the coffee pot. 'Shropshire,' he said again, looking at crazed uneven capitals. 'Oh, God, it's Mary.'

The last of the yellow leaves on the willow tree blew madly about the garden. William watched from the window above the sink. He and Eve used to have tea beneath that willow, on summer afternoons.

'*They fly forgotten, as a dream / Dies at the opening day* — ' he heard himself humming, as a minister pronounced on climate change from a radio car in central London and Danny scrabbled frantically at the door. William let him in, shook biscuits into his bowl, made coffee, put the toast on, slit open the thin white envelope. Of course it was Mary, who else would it be? 'I must be worse than I think,' he murmured, settling down, unfolding the cheap lined pages, with their startling hand. 'What on earth does she want?'

2

'You'd like it in London,' said Mary Harriman, stirring tea. 'Bit going on.'

'I expect there is,' said Janice, watching two more spoonfuls of sugar go into the Coronation mug.

'Not much going on here.' Mary dug out the teabag and hurled it into the sink. 'Suit you, down there.'

'Possibly.' Janice leaned back in the kitchen chair and watched the rain stream down the little windows. At the front, the towering hedge obscured the lane, and most of the light, further obscured by the rows of china dogs. At the back, a disconsolate fowl was huddled on the sill, muddy white, with a drooping comb. Mary gazed, as Janice gazed, at the broken cement and churned-up mud in the yard, with its chicken-wire pens and flung-together coops and kennels, from whose open doorways the dogs stood staring out. It had rained for three days.

'Mind you,' said Mary, drinking, 'I haven't set eyes on William since I don't know when. Mother's funeral, I think.'

'Fifteen years ago,' said Janice. 'I know. You said.'

'And he's only a second cousin,' said Mary. 'Or third. Not as if we'd keep up much anyway.' She put down her tea. 'Sure you won't have another cup?'

‘Certain,’ said Janice. ‘I should be on my way.’

‘Can’t go in this.’

‘I know.’

Early this morning the rain had been light; it had stopped for over an hour, and the sky had cleared. During this lull, Janice had set out to do her deliveries, the bicycle panniers filled with the shopping of three households. She went slowly at first; as the load grew lighter, and she approached her second drop, she picked up speed, spinning along between the hedges, glimpsing the misty hills through field gates. Then, as she came to the Dog Museum, it had started to chuck it down again.

‘Been waiting for you,’ Mary had said at the front door, taking the carrier bags of tins and sliced white Mother’s Pride. ‘Come along in.’

Across the yard, the rain was beating down on Ernie’s caravan. Janice could see him, morose and smoking, at his table by the dingy Perspex window. Broken guttering let down a stream of water, just above his front door. It would rot the steps.

‘Those dogs will go mad if they don’t get out soon.’

‘I think it’s easing off.’ Janice got up, and peered out of the window at the front. Her bike leaned dripping against the gate.

‘You need a van.’

‘I know. One day.’

‘Make a lot of money in London.’

‘Doing what?’

Mary didn’t know. She finished her tea. Sophie came in from the snug.

'What do you want?' asked Mary.

'We've visitors,' said Sophie, in her pink-and-blue print pinafore, and spaniel hair slide.

'Where?'

'Down the lane.'

Mary and Janice went back to the window, to look. A family of three in cagoules and wellingtons was approaching the gate: middle-aged parents with a plumpish boy. They stopped at the sign, and looked at the house. The man walked on a little, passing the kitchen window. He stopped again, and beheld the rows of china Alsatians, terriers, poodles with curly china topknots, greyhounds with red china ribbons, eager Labradors. He saw Mary and Sophie and Janice looking back at him, and started. Rain dripped from his hood.

'Come in out of the wet,' shouted Mary, banging on the window. 'Only a pound.'

Janice watched them all confer. Then they clicked open the gate. Somebody usually did.

'Fancy going for a walk in this,' said Sophie.

'An ill wind,' said Mary, going to the back door. 'That's three pounds we've got here.'

'Two-fifty,' said Sophie. 'Family membership.'

Mary gave her a look.

'I must be off,' said Janice.

'I'll let you know when I hear,' said Mary. 'I'm sure William will put you up.'

'Thanks.' Janice nodded to the visiting family as she zipped up her jacket, pulled down her knitted hat and strode across the yard. They were gazing bemusedly at the sisters: Sophie in her pinafore, chopped-off hair held back with the hair slide, and Mary in pond-green cardigan, drooping skirt and ankle socks, their sixty-year-old faces as fresh and scrubbed and pure as Blyton children.

Mary held out the Jubilee tin. Across the yard the dogs had come out of their sheds and were up by the chicken wire, tails beating hopefully in the wet. Janice saw the boy's eyes widen as he took in their number, the ranges of breeds, and half-breeds.

'Are they all yours?'

'They are,' said Mary. 'Rescued, every one. Rescued from terrible homes and looking for good ones.' She shook the Jubilee tin. 'Do you like dogs?'

'Some dogs.' He went towards the wire.

'Martin,' said his mother, her voice uncertain, as Janice climbed on to her bike.

'They're good dogs,' said Sophie, peering from the dim-lit porch. 'They won't bite.'

'Some will,' said Mary. 'Any dog will, when roused.'

'Martin — '

Martin's father took control. 'Martin, come here. What kind of museum do you have?' he asked Mary, feeling in his pocket, as she rattled the Queen about.

'A Dog Museum,' she told him, prising the lid off.

'It says so at the gate,' said Sophie. 'On the notice.'

'I know, but — '

'Two pounds fifty,' said Mary. 'Family membership.' She nodded towards more creosoted huts, set at some distance, with cobwebbed windows. 'Everything's in there.'

'Would you like a guided tour?' asked Sophie, giving her little laugh.

Nobody took any notice.

'That's fifty, three pounds, and two is five.' Mary was firmly counting out change.

'Thanks. Well — we'll go and have a look.' He turned to his wife and child. 'All right?'

'What do we get for family membership?' asked Martin.

'Entrance,' said Mary, observing him with dislike. 'Entrance to the museum.'

'Do you have a newsletter?'

'That's a good idea,' said Sophie.

'No, it isn't.'

'Can I Adopt a Dog?'

His parents were shifting from foot to foot.

Mary's manner changed. 'What kind of dog would you like? We've terriers, lurchers, greyhounds — greyhounds make lovely pets, very gentle. We've whippets and cross-bred Labradors and spaniels — '

'We'd love to have a dog.' The boy turned to his mother, as the rain splashed down. 'Wouldn't we? You're always saying, because I'm an Only Child.'

'Yes, but — '

'But it's out of the question,' said Martin's father.

'We live in London,' explained his mother sadly.

'London?' said Mary. 'Do you, now?' She looked towards the gate in the hedge, but Janice had long since gone.

There was a sound from within the rain's swift pattering. Ernie had opened his plywood door and was standing on the top of his caravan steps, holding a roll-up in yellowed fingers.

'You stay there!' yelled Mary.

* * *

William, after breakfast, found a plumber in the Yellow Pages and phoned him. He ran a tepid bath, he dressed, came down again, drew back the drawing-room curtains. The windows at back and front were high, almost floor to ceiling, and in summer the room was filled with graceful light. It was one of the things they'd fallen in love with, looking for somewhere to settle and have a family, all those years ago. The house, then, had needed much doing to it; over the years they had had things done. Now they needed doing all over again, and he hadn't the heart. Mrs T., on her one day a week, almost a part of the furniture, kept dust at bay and silver polished. That was quite enough. He drew back the heavy old velvet curtains Eve had found in the sixties, their rust brown faded to mushroom in the folds, their calico lining in ribbons. He unlooped the tasselled silk ropes she had found in the Liberty sale, tied the curtains back, and stood looking out, down through the front garden to the wet black railings and the rainswept street.

'Lucky you caught us,' the plumber had said. 'We was just on our way to a call.'

Now he stood reading his letter again.

It's ever such a long time since we were all together, William, wrote Mary, dotting her capital Is and looping extraordinary Ts. *I think it must have been at Mother's funeral, God rest her soul. She did suffer, William, it was a Blessing in the end. We are all keeping well and the Dogs are a Comfort. We have a girl who does the shopping who wants to come to London. Going to waste, up here. I thought you might know of a Job and Lodgings. You are always welcome here yourself, of course, if you ever fancy a visit. Ernie I know would be glad of a Visit. Looking forward to hearing from you soon. The girl is called Janice Harper, she is twenty-three I think and Tall and Fit.*

A van turned into the street at the far end and came along slowly. William waved.

'That was quick,' he said, opening the front door to the two men climbing the steps. Beside him, Danny shimmied about.

'Morning, mate. Morning, sausage.'

They wiped their feet and tramped in.

'I'm Jim and this is my boy Darren. What's the problem?'

William indicated the stairs down to the kitchen, the boiler. They dropped their bags and stood before it, awestruck. Danny gazed up with them.

'What's that, circa Domesday Book?' asked Jim. He got out a screw-driver and attacked the casing. Falls of soot came away with the front.

'Dear oh dear oh dear. How long since you had a service?'

William couldn't remember.

'Dangerous. People die from less.'

Darren sniffed, pushing back his baseball cap. 'Wunsamunf,' he said, twisting his earring.

'I'm sorry?'

'That's what we was told at college. Check it out wunsamunf.'

'Once in a very blue moon, this looks like,' said Jim. 'Pass us that spanner.' Danny was nosing in the bag. 'Nothing in there for you, mate.' He stroked his ears. 'Bright, aren't you? Bright as a button. Getting a bit grey round the chops. How old are you, then?' Danny licked his horny hand.

'He's very old,' said William. 'Like me. He was really my wife's dog.'

'Is that right?' Jim straightened up, and turned back to the boiler, now exposed. Soot clung to every visible surface. 'You was lucky,' he said. 'Got a dustpan?'

⋆ ⋆ ⋆

Martin and his parents entered the first of the museum huts and fumbled for the light switch. A single naked bulb hung from a frayed flex in the centre, spotted with long-dead insects.

'Gordon Bennett,' said Martin's father, pushing his hood back and looking about him. 'Fucking hell.'

'Derek!' said his wife.

'It's *sweet*,' said Martin, approaching the first of many booths. Within, a team of stuffed huskies strained at the leash towards him. They were made of fake fur, and wore fierce expressions, felt tongues lolling over plastic teeth, glass eyes bright in the gloom. Behind them, next to a sled heaped high with parcels, an Eskimo just a bit taller than Martin stood stiffly in his fake fur suit, smiling broadly. From one gloved hand hung a whip, from the other a brilliant fish, its papier-mâché body marked out with felt-tip scales, its mouth agape. As backdrop, on the three tall walls of the booth, a painted scene of pinned-up lining paper depicted dazzling snow, a polar bear, a fiery melting sun. A small Eskimo child bent over a pool in the ice with a fishing rod, where a seal had obligingly popped its head up. A little puff of blue smoke rose from an adjacent igloo.

'They *made* this?' asked Jenny, leaning closer to gaze at fake-fur seams. 'Martin, don't touch.'

'But they're sweet.'

'I know.'

Derek was taking a look at the booth next door.

'Blimey oh flaming Reilly.'

'What? What?' Martin went to see. A vast St Bernard with a dear little keg of brandy round its neck was nosing a prone figure in a fantastic heap of snow. Martin gingerly put out a toe and a million grains of polystyrene shifted.

'Martin!'

'Sorry.'

The man in the snow wore climbing boots and held a pickaxe. A wicked coil of rope was clipped to his waist and a great big bloody gash ran down his cheek. But he was still breathing, you could tell. St Bernard had got there just in time. Beyond them, on the pinned-up paper walls, the mountains of Switzerland rose in jagged peaks, their snow-topped summits lit by a blood-red disc.

He could do pictures like this, he could get a job here.

'I could get a job here,' he told his parents.

'You don't have to be barking mad to work here, but it helps,' said his father. 'Ha, ha.'

Martin looked at him pityingly. Jenny giggled.

'Is it all winter dogs?' she asked, feeling the half-term holiday perk up. It could be hell, with just the three of them.

'What other winter dogs are there?' asked Martin, moving along the aisle.

Nobody knew.

'Look!' he said suddenly. 'Come and look!'

Derek and Jenny, united as they had not been for days — well, ages, really, thought Jenny — followed to where their only child was pointing.

A mighty waterfall roared down a great ravine. African animals prowled in the burning distance, beneath an African sun. And here, in the tumbling darkness of the pool, a child was drowning, a white child, brought here no doubt by her missionary-explorer parents, circa 1870. But help was at hand, for while her parents were off with their Bibles, heedless of Africa's teeming dangers, the family dog, a yellow retriever, had leapt into the boiling pool and was tugging the little girl to safety. Flaxen hair streamed out behind her, her ribboned hat bobbed wildly, a pale little hand was flailing in the foam. But the dog had her blue-and-white dress in his grip, and the rocks were but feet away.

'Fantastic,' said Derek, wiping his glasses. 'Bloody fantastic.'

Martin, gazing into the distance beyond the top of the falls, made out a cheetah, a wildebeest, a rhino. He could have done that rhino, easily.

'What are they called, these things?' he asked.

'Dogs,' said Derek, putting his glasses back on.

'No, stupid, the things — the — ' He made a gesture to embrace it all, each scene, each recreation.

'I suppose they're diorama,' said Jenny, who'd been a primary-school teacher before she had Martin, and often wished she was still. 'Aren't they?'

'What's a diorama?'

'A prehistoric grass-eating animal.' Derek blew his nose.

'You think you're so funny.'

'I know.'

'But they *can't* have done all this,' said Jenny, as they wandered on. 'No one could do all this.'

'Not so much could, as why.'

'Why not?' asked Martin, and there they could not answer him.

And so the soaking-wet morning passed. In hut after hut they marvelled: at hunting dogs, bringing limp game across autumn fields; at Lassie, leaping a ravine; at guide dogs, in the second hut, leading blind men through the traffic; dogs for the deaf alerting deaf housewives to the phone; circus dogs leaping through hoops, beheld by lions on stools, while scarlet-coated moustachioed ringmasters cracked their fearsome whips. Finally, and perhaps most magnificent of all, were the hounds streaming after the outstretched fox — 'I think that's a real fox,' said Martin, and it was — while the painted hunt leaped over the five-barred gate. It was a toss-up between this and the panting Border collie, crouched low before his swirling flock of sheep. He was pretty good, and the sheep were real wool.

'Enjoying yourselves?' called Mary, as they stepped over puddles to the last hut. Rusting bits of cars were heaped up by the fence that bordered the field; a dismal-looking hen was crouched beneath a mudguard.

'It's wicked,' said Martin.

'What's that?'

'Don't bother,' said Derek, as Jenny began to explain. He held the hut door open for her. 'Shall we have lunch in the pub?'

'What about Martin?'

'There'll be a games room somewhere.'

He smiled down at her; she smiled up at him, feeling so much better than this morning. She followed their only child inside, to shelf upon shelf of Dinky Toys.

* * *

Janice, on leaving the Dog Museum, cycled between high hedges to her last delivery: Albert Page, living alone at 3 Rushock Bank with his cat and his arthritis, living on Winter Vegetable soup, struggling with the ring-pull.

'You could try packets,' said Janice once, watching him.

'Packets? Packet soup? What do you think I am?'

'Or those cartons,' said Janice. 'They're nice.'

'What's that, then?'

'Carrot and coriander. Vichyssoise.'

'How much do they want for that?'

She told him, setting down tins and Rich Tea biscuits. Why did you have to be over ninety to enjoy a Rich Tea biscuit?

'Because they're cheap, that's why,' said Albert, stirring at the stove. 'How much did you say them cartons were?'

She told him again.

'One pound *eighty*? One pound eighty for a carton of soup?'

'I know,' said Janice, 'but they are nice.'

'I should think they blooming are. One pound eighty. I should cocoa.' He tipped the cat off his chair and sat down, trembling.

'It's never going to stop,' he told her today, as she set the carrier bag down on his table.

'What's that, Albert?'

'This rain. Do you think it's ever going to stop?'

'I think it's clearing,' said Janice, glancing through his kitchen window, which, like Mary and Sophie's, was in need of a good clean. 'Want me to do your windows for you, Albert?'

'Why? Short of a bob?'

'I'll do them for nothing,' she said, folding the

carrier bag. 'I like cleaning windows.'

'You're a good girl' he told her, as she sprayed out a cloud of Mr Muscle. 'Isn't she, Tibs?'

'Only people on the telly have cats called Tibs,' said Janice, rubbing with the duster. 'People in adverts.'

'Old crocks like me,' said Albert, stroking Tibs's magnificent head. 'You're doing a good job there.'

'Can you tell?'

'Don't be cheeky.'

Janice rubbed away the last smears, and stood back. The duster was black. 'That's better. Now you can see when the sun comes out.'

'It won't.'

'It might. Right, then, I'd better be off.'

'Where you off to?'

'My other job.'

Albert gave a filthy laugh.

'Do you mind?' And she was gone, leaving him in his snug little kitchen, with the chill of the unheated cottage, in which nothing had been changed or touched since 1959, all around him. The garden at the front was nice, though, a proper cottage garden, which he still managed himself, though now it was a sodden mess.

She cycled away with a farewell ring on the bell, tyres whirring splashily, rounding the corner to where the road began to climb. She settled to it, head down, bike lighter with the last load gone, panting but determined. Three bends to go. The land on either side, glimpsed here and there through gates, stretched over soaking fields and clumps of woodland to fall away down to the valley, dotted with sheep, and rise again to the far wooded hills of Leinthall Ridge, brushy and autumnal, with great dark patches of fir. The storms had done dreadful damage, they'd been talking in the pub about it, and here, as she rounded the last bend, up on her pedals and gasping, a ripped-off branch was lying halfway across the road. She pulled up, wet brakes squealing. When had this come down? Somebody could have been killed. And here, in the middle of the morning, somebody still could be. She laid the bike down on the verge and walked up to the fallen bough.

The rain had stopped, but was still in the air, and it was windy up here, always. She felt the cold, driving across the valley and churned-up fields, stirring in the bare branches of the oak at the gate, where a great yellow gash showed where the limb had been torn away. A crow, drinking from a puddle, looked up at her sharply, then bent to drink again. Janice put her gloved hands round an upper branch and tugged. A few remaining leaves shook on the twigs, and twigs crunched underfoot. The bough was enormous: how come no one had reported this? She heaved and pulled and at last got it moving, inch by inch, over the road and on to the verge, where it was harder to move for the last pull, dragging on the bumpy wet grass, and she had to stop and draw breath. Phew. She clapped her gloved hands, flexed her fingers, tried again. There. Done it.

She walked back to the place where the bough had lain, and kicked away the last long bits of branch. That crow was up on the gate now, watching her, beady old thing, and in the silence of the morning, disturbed only by the rising wind, she heard the sudden chatter of a couple of magpies, hopping about in the oak. Their glossy green-and-purple plumage was caught in a fitful, unexpected glance of sunlight, gone as quickly as it had come, but still — two for joy, that was something. And here, coming up the hill from the far side, was the yellow council lorry: she waved, and it drew up beside her.

'Had to pull it out of the road myself,' she told the young man leaning out of his cab window. She gestured down the road.

'Did you, now?' He glanced to where the huge bough lay. 'You must be strong.'

'I am,' said Janice, sniffing in the wind and feeling for a hanky. 'Lucky, isn't it, or someone might've been killed.'

'We've had that many calls. Can't do everything at once.' He grinned down, meaningfully, and she blew her nose with some force. She walked alongside as the driver put his foot down again, and when they drew up by the bough said, 'Right, I'll leave you to it, then,' and crossed to pick up her bike, as they parked and got down, lifting out the power saw.

'Where d'you drink, then?' called the young man, as she got on.

'That'd be telling,' she said, and rode away, on the flat at last, with the wind on her face, and the whining saw behind her, and the smell of the wood, and the sawdust — a good strong cheerful smell, which made her think cheerful thoughts. Could do with a few of those.

* * *

This was the pattern of Janice's week. Deliveries in the morning to a load of old lunatics and loners. Once she'd done a couple, word had seemed to spread — the first was just as a favour, a friend of her gran's, then it was a friend of the friend, then the friend's neighbour, and so on. Three pounds a week she charged them, saving all that effort in town. Peanuts, but cash. In the afternoons she worked in Cloud Nine, the café up on the hill, where she'd had her first weekend job while she was still at school, and where she might as well stay on, really.

'What's the matter with you?' her dad demanded, when she went down to the Jobcentre and came back saying she didn't fancy anything much. 'Nice bright girl like you. You should be working in the bank.'

'No I shouldn't,' said Janice, sixteen and horrible to live with. They both said so.

'You need to go to college, get your A-levels,' said her mother, watching the toaster.

'Why?'

'So you can go to university.'

'I don't want to go to university.'

'Turning your nose up. Wish I'd had the chance. Get a proper job, then, something in Shrewsbury.'

'There's a nice pet shop in Shrewsbury,' said Janice, who'd hung out in the back streets when bunking off. 'White doves, fantails. And exotics. Perhaps I could get a job there.'

'Work in a pet shop? What d'you want to do that for?' Her mother took out hard white toast.

'You do it too high,' said Janice, taking her slice. 'You should set it at three, I keep saying.'

'There's children in Africa,' said her mother, pulling her chair out.

'I know.'

Anyway, she hadn't gone to work in Shrewsbury, neither in the pet shop nor the bank. Nor had she gone to college, to do her A-levels, though she went on reading, like she always had. She just did deliveries and dog-walking. Her parents had gone on and on till she said she'd leave home, and they said good riddance, and then they all got fed up with this; so long as she was paying her way, which she just about was, making a contribution, anyway. Later, she thought she might like to go to horticultural college: she wasn't bad in the garden. Sometimes she did the old lunatics' gardens, when they were getting past it.

But now she was twenty-three, and getting nowhere. Bored with it all. Bored with eking out a pint and wispy roll-ups. Fed up — you could say that again — with living at home. Thirty-three Curlew Gardens, a 1950s estate out the back of the bypass. Why didn't it just fall into a hole in the road?

One day, something would happen.

Not if you don't make it, said a voice inside her, as she stopped outside Cloud Nine, saw it was empty, and wheeled the bike round the back. There was a garden here: in summer, customers sat outside at the picnic tables, looking out over the hills, scattering cake crumbs for the birds. Janice made the cakes — at least she could turn her hand to things, her mother said, defending her at home when necessary. She did a nice lemon drizzle, coffee-and-walnut, good plain fruit and a delectable chocolate.

'Should be working in a hotel,' said her dad, wiping his mouth. 'Should have done Hotel and Catering.'

'I'm happy as I am,' said Janice. 'I like my independence.'

'I suppose the next thing you'll be saying is you don't want to get married.'

'Who's there to marry, round here?'

'Other people manage. Look at Tracy Keenan.'

'Please.'

Janice, outside the back of the café, opened her pannier and took out the last remaining item, a double tin (Oxfam, £1.20) with chocolate in the bottom and iced jam sponge on top. She carried it up the path to the side door, and let herself into the kitchen.

'That you?' Steve, proprietor of Cloud Nine and proud of it, was behind the counter.

'All right?'

'Quiet,' said Steve. 'Not a dicky bird.'

In summer, walkers strode over the hills and cluttered the café with rucksacks. Carloads of families bought endless cans and crisps, lesbian teachers read paperbacks in corners. In autumn the walkers kept up; by now, mid-November, weekday customers were like winter migrants:

nowhere to be seen.

'Cuppa tea?'

'Please. And I'll make a sandwich.' Janice took her things off, hung them on the hook on the kitchen door and rummaged about in the fridge for her own supplies. There was a stove in here, a mottled old grey thing which ran on Calor gas and reminded her of something she'd had in her doll's house, now up in the loft. There was a kettle, which sat on the top. But Steve, behind the counter, had a fantastic tea urn, his pride and joy, which simmered and hissed and sent clouds of steam boiling romantically about his cropped blond head, and the heads of his customers, waiting for their good strong pot, or herbal tisane. Rows of sickly smelling, sweetly coloured boxes stood on the shelf: bilberry and blackcurrant, lemon and tangerine, raspberry leaf.

'I prefer PG Tips myself,' said Janice, adding her soya milk.

'Most normal people do.'

Steve's urn had been given him by his mother, when the Ludlow WI were having a turnout. He, having been to university, told Janice it came from the pages of a novel by Virginia Woolf.

'Which one?'

'*Jacob's Room*. It's always hissing away. It carries clouds of eternity within.'

Janice had read *Mrs Dalloway* and some of the *Diaries*. At least she read, said her mother. She reads too blooming much, said her dad. Why hadn't she gone to university, if she liked reading so much?

'Because I was a free spirit,' said Janice, pulling her jacket on.

'What's a clever young man like Steve Bounds doing running a café?' asked her mother.

'Because he likes it. Anything wrong with that?'

'Why isn't he teaching?'

'He doesn't like teaching.'

'Why isn't he married? Why don't you marry him? You're always up there, you might as well.'

'Because he's gay,' said Janice. 'Why do you think?'

She heard her father groan.

The pot of tea was waiting on the counter when she carried her sandwich through.

'Thanks.'

'Good morning?' asked Steve, joining her at a corner table.

'Same as usual.' She told him about the family, arriving at the Dog Museum in the downpour, looking aghast.

'I'm not surprised,' said Steve, pouring two large mugs. Janice, tucking into her peanut-butter and soya spread sandwich, realised she was starving. All that exercise.

'Mary Harriman thinks I should go to London,' she said, between mouthfuls.

'London? Whatever for?'

'Work. Stimulus. Not to mention money.'

'You can't go to London.' Steve was adamant. 'How would I manage?'

'There's nobody here in winter. It's hardly worth keeping it open.'

'Yes it is. People come. You know they come. It's a service, up here, people are glad of us. And in summer I really need you.' He looked at her, across the red-checked tablecloth. 'Please don't go.'

'Well,' said Janice, finishing her sandwich. 'I don't suppose I will.' She sipped her tea. 'God, I needed this.'

'What does old Mary know about London, anyway? I shouldn't think she's ever been there.'

'Neither have I. She's got a cousin there, or something. She's written him a letter.'

'Can she write?'

'Sort of. A bit.'

'Well, anyway,' said Steve sadly, 'I don't want you to go.'

The clock on the wall chimed once, melodiously. The deal in winter was that Steve did mornings, and Janice afternoons.

'I'm going into Welshpool,' he told her. 'You'll lock up and everything?'

'Will do.'

When he had gone, she settled herself with more tea and another sandwich. She got out her roll-ups, and smoked with her tea, and her book, a second-hand collection of Emily Dickinson which she'd found, as it happened, in Welshpool, in the bookshop down the alley behind Iceland.

It's all I have to bring today —
This, and my heart beside —
This, and my heart, and all the fields —
And all the meadows wide —

Sometimes she thought that she should have been someone like Emily, brilliant and alone and yearning.

Out of sight? What of that?
See the bird — reach it!
Curve by Curve, Sweep by Sweep —
Round the Steep Air —
Danger! What is that to Her?

The café door swung open, striking the bell. Janice looked up. The rain had quite cleared, and in forgotten sunshine the glass door was shining with drops. A young man stood there, his motorbike helmet under his arm, his leather jacket zipped to the top against the wind. He wiped his enormous boots, put the helmet on a table, and went up to the counter.

'It's me,' said Janice, getting up. She lifted the flap and went behind. 'What can I get you?'

He unzipped his jacket, and ran his eye down the chalk-written board at the back.

'I'll have a tea and a toasted ham-and-cheese, on brown.'

'Come far?' she asked him, slicing granary bread.

'Just Ludlow.' He had a light growth of dark stubble, and his eyes were very blue. As water hissed into the china pot, steam hung about him like a nimbus.

'Been working here long?' he asked her, as she reached in the fridge.

'Too long.' She closed the fridge door and unpeeled the packet of ham. 'I'll bring this to you, if you want to sit down.'

He went to the table where he'd parked his helmet, glancing at her book as he passed. She took him his tea, and then the sizzling sandwich.

'Mind — it's very hot.'

She went to the door and breathed in the freshness of it all: the sky rinsed clear and the distant clouds sailing over the hills like departing ships. His motorbike was parked on the verge, a metallic green, gleaming. A jackdaw was perched on the telegraph wire, preening wet feathers.

'What are you doing tonight?' he asked her, when she went back inside.

3

William walked up Denmark Hill. The rain had blown away after lunch, which he'd eaten on a tray in the drawing room, listening to *The World at One* while the men went on banging about. They finally left at two. William wrote out a cheque for a hundred and thirty-five pounds and said he hoped that would be it for a good long while.

'Like I said,' Jim told him, pocketing the Coutts cheque. 'You're lucky to be here, mate.'

'Wunsamunf,' said Darren, stroking Danny's ears.

'Once every six, that's for sure,' said Jim. 'Lucky you didn't have to have a new boiler. Expertise, that's what you got here.'

William thanked him, and saw them off on the steps. The sky was still cloudy, but light and high. He wrapped up, and fetched Danny's lead. 'Right, then. We're off.'

Still windy. Wet leaves blew along Denmark Hill. November, thought William, approaching the hospital. London in November. The place and month had always held for him a particular light, a particular sensation: as a boy, playing on the Dulwich rugby pitch; as a young man at UCL, hurrying across the quad in the fading afternoons; as a civil servant, looking out from his Treasury desk along Whitehall; now, in widowhood, in his life's winter. Such a strange, undefinable feeling, every year: the sky smoky; the bus such a clear bright red; the air, like a piece of music, melancholy, shot through with something sharper.

At the hospital gates he stopped to let an ambulance pass, then walked slowly across to the glass doors. He tied Danny up to the hook. 'Shan't be long.' People were coming and going: doctors with clip-boards, women with flowers. He hadn't brought anything today. Inside, in the shop, he picked up the *TLS* and a Twix. One could only try. He made his way down the endless corridors.

John Ogden had been in here once. No, twice. As he often did, William imagined Ogden's huge bulk and trembling fingers coming to rest before the piano, pulling the stool out, starting to play. He imagined Beethoven and the showers of Schumann, the Brahms, spilling out into the grounds from open windows. Hours passed in a trance; then he slept.

William and Eve used to listen to Ogden; before his breakdown, they'd gone to hear him: at the proms, at the Festival Hall. They used to put him on in the drawing room, settling down with an LP after supper.

* * *

Matthew was in the day room, staring at a quiz show. William tapped on the glass. One or two people looked up through the clouds of smoke, and looked away again. He pushed the door open, and coughed.

'Hello, Matthew.'

Matthew turned. His face was pallid and expressionless; there were soup stains down his jumper. William had thought on his last visit that he needed a haircut; now it was worse.

'Hello, darling. Want to come out for a bit?'

Matthew turned back to the screen. Enormous scores were flashing in white and gold, and a gong sounded.

'Danny's outside,' said William. 'We could go for a turn in the grounds.' He felt in his pocket and pulled out the Twix. 'Do come.'

'I'm wearing pink knickers today,' said Patricia, who often told people this. She gazed up at him from her plastic armchair, a long snake of ash on her cigarette just about to fall.

'Are you, now?' said William. He put an ashtray under her hand, and she winked.

'You're a very nice young man.'

'I was once.' He waved at the smoke, and went over to Matthew. 'Have a bit of choc.' Matthew took the Twix very slowly, and held it. The doors to the garden were closed, but unlocked. Beyond them, a man walked up and down, deep in conversation with an invisible companion, gesturing. Beyond the cedars a bonfire was smoking. November, thought William again, feeling a tug at his heart.

'I can't stay in here,' he said, through the clouds of cigarettes. 'Do come outside for a bit.' He felt in the other pocket. 'I've brought the *TLS*.'

Matthew sat with the Twix in his lap. William coughed again, and opened the door to the garden. Heads turned. He stepped outside on to the terrace, leaving the door open, and he walked up and down, smelling the bonfire and the autumn air. Clouds blew over the cedar trees. The eloquent man disappeared. After a while, Matthew got up, and came out.

'Shall we fetch your coat?' said William, kissing him.

He found a nurse, who unlocked the coat room. 'Having a walk with your dad?' he asked Matthew. Matthew held out his arms and allowed the coat to be pulled on, and a scarf to be put round his neck. 'Don't you look nice.'

They went round the front for Danny. 'Claire couldn't come today,' said William, undoing the lead. 'Geraldine's got earache. She sends her love.'

Matthew nodded. They returned to the huge expanse of grounds. Matthew threw a stick and it landed at his feet. William threw another and Danny went tearing off. The windy sky was full of racing clouds.

'I had a letter today,' said William, tucking Matthew's ungloved hand through his arm. 'From batty old Mary. Remember her?'

Matthew shook his head, frowning.

'We went there a couple of times when you were small. You and Claire used to chase the hens.'

There was a little smile. It always gave William hope.

'Fierce old cousin Edna,' he went on. 'The mother. Remember?'

He could feel the struggle, the swim through layers of time.

'Never mind,' he said after a little while, and patted the hand which once held a bow and soared through Schubert. 'I sold a rather nice old serving dish last week,' he told him, changing tack, keeping to everyday things. 'Mason's Ironstone. Fetched quite a bit.'

4

On Saturdays, William and Buffy had a stall in Camden Passage. They'd had it for years: since Eve's death, and long since William's retirement. Buffy had also retired. 'Thank God, thank *God* for that,' she'd said on her last Friday, in 1988, tipping the rubber bands and paper-clips and bits of fluff into the wastepaper basket, heaving the awkward drawer into the filing cabinet for the last time. They took her out to lunch and gave her a polyester scarf.

'How *could* they have thought I'd wear that?'

She gave it to Oxfam. 'At last I can do what I like,' she said on the phone to Eve, her one remaining schoolfriend. But then she got bored and lonely. She missed the ringing phones, the wasted-looking temps and Mr Lawson. Computerisation was coming in: she knew she could never have coped. 'Windows are what you look out of,' she said, when they sent her on a course. 'A mac is what you wear in the rain.' The time had come. She was glad the time had come. And yet —

'Not much fun,' she said to Eve on the phone. 'Bit miz, really. Didn't think it would be, but it is.'

She gazed from her third-floor sitting-room at the pigeons on the rooftops opposite; at her bright window-box geraniums.

'How come Buffy never married?' asked

William, at supper, when Eve told him about all this. He poured them each a glass of Chablis, unfolded his napkin, and sniffed as Eve lifted the lid.

'She just didn't,' said Eve, ladling the chicken casserole. 'Some people just don't.'

'No one does, nowadays.'

'That's different.' She passed him his plate.

' "My partner," ' said William, thinking of Claire and Jeremy. 'Partners are people you set up a firm with.'

'You sound like Buffy.'

'Poor old Buffy. I wonder why she didn't. Marry.' He spooned out new potatoes. 'She isn't — '

'No.'

'Well, that's something.'

Later, when they were having coffee in the drawing room, Buffy rang again.

'I've had an idea,' she said.

Eve listened, the phone crooked on her shoulder while she carried on with her tapestry. 'That *is* a good idea.'

'What is?' asked William, looking up from his book.

'William's asking what the idea is,' said Eve to Buffy.

'Tell him,' he heard Buffy say. 'See what he thinks.'

He thought it was brilliant. Pottering round the country sales, bringing the stuff back. Just china, said Buffy. China and glass. They should specialise. 'We could do it together,' said Eve.

'I'll join you,' said William. 'Now I'm retired I

can do as I like.' Forty years in the Treasury: enough for any man, and now he had his pension. 'Sounds like fun.'

It *was* fun. Looking through *Country Life* and *Miller's Guide*, setting off early on Saturday mornings with rugs and a flask and Danny in the back. They became experts, turning over Coalport plates and Minton coffee cups, checking for chips and rivets, learning the manufacturers' marks from Cushion & Honey's *Handbook*: that was a world in itself. They wandered round marquees, set out on the lawns of listed houses, they bid in dusty salesrooms, they loaded it all into boxes, wrapping each piece in *The Times*.

'Another thing that isn't what it was,' said William, thinking of his own long-dead father, and breakfast in the morning room.

At first, they had a stall in Portobello, because it was close to Buffy's flat. It had all been her idea in the first place, and you could make a fortune there, not that William and Eve were in need of that. 'But I need every penny,' said Buffy, and anyway, it was fun being there, quite a different part of London; it did them both good to leave the sedate acres of Dulwich, where William had, after all, lived all his life.

They set off at the crack of dawn, much as if they were going down to a sale in Wiltshire or Gloucester — just to get across London, but you had to, on Saturday, just to get a parking space. They set out the stall and sat, on summer afternoons, listening to extraordinary music — heavy metal, said Buffy, who had been forced, through proximity, to learn this — and watching anorexic young women, still out of their heads from last night's substances and sex, wander dreamily in and out of the traffic, on and off the pavement, trailing silk and velveteen. 'Don't they get awfully *hot*?' asked Buffy. Wide-eyed American tourists gazed after them, then came, with some relief, to the antiques.

'Worcester,' said Buffy firmly, watching manicured male hands hover above a fruit bowl. 'Royal Worcester, 1870s.'

'Is that so? Honey? Honey, come and take a look . . . '

And Honey came. 'How about these little coffee cups?' she asked.

'Those are Royal Doulton,' said Eve, with her sweet soft smile. 'Pretty, aren't they?'

'They certainly are. Do you take American Express?'

It was all most satisfactory.

Not everything they bought and sold was of this class, of course. Amongst the triumphant finds in the sales, and special pieces bid for at the auctions — 'You can do the bidding, William,' said Eve, and he did it to the manner born — there were plenty of things which they bought just because they loved them: unmarked blue-and-white eggcups; a little blue-and-white tea set which might have been Copenhagen but wasn't, though quite as pretty; any number of cups and bowls and single serving dishes. Tureens. Tureens with ladles. And then there was the glass, which became Eve's passion, and the Spode, which became Buffy's.

'I don't think I can bear to part with this,' she said, cradling a breakfast cup and saucer, circa 1830 and without a chip. Its perfect diameter was a full six inches, a serious, proper breakfast cup, with a heavenly handle. They were down at a sale near Cirencester, a liquid spring morning bedewing the grounds beyond French windows, the trestle tables nicely spaced, a buzz in the air.

'Keep it,' said Eve, watching her. 'You deserve it.'

And so Buffy's collection began. The whole enterprise was going swimmingly. They joined the Antique Collectors Club, took out subscriptions to specialist magazines, couldn't have enjoyed themselves more.

Then Matthew came home with a first from Durham, and shut himself into his room.

* * *

'Darling? Matthew? Are you coming down for lunch?'

'Matthew? Want to pop out for a drink?'

At first they thought he'd had his heart broken.

'You can tell me,' said William, sitting on the edge of the bed. 'I can remember. Just.'

'Fuck off,' said Matthew.

He lost a stone and the house stank: of his unwashed body, his cigarettes.

'He's ill,' said Claire, furious. 'Surely you can see he's really ill.' She sat with him while they rang his tutors, who had all gone off for the summer. They rang the university counsellor and got an answerphone. When the counsellor picked up the message and rang, she said that Matthew had been in to see her a year ago, but it was confidential. She did say that the classic age for a schizophrenic breakdown was between sixteen and twenty-four. Matthew was twenty-two: he'd had a gap year, teaching in Ghana. He'd come back strained and silent. Had it begun then? I think it began when he was in his teens, said Claire, only *you* two never noticed.

Matthew went into hospital on a perfect September morning in 1991, the trees in the grounds just turning crimson and ochre, the air invigorating. William and Eve held hands, fighting back their tears. Matthew sat on the edge of his bed, his head cocked, his eyes glazed.

'We love you so much,' said William. 'You'll soon be home.'

'We'll come tomorrow,' said Eve. 'We'll come whenever you want.'

'Fuck off,' said Matthew.

'You're crowding him,' said Claire, and stalked outside.

In the carpark they clung to one another.

'He'll be all right,' said William, wiping his eyes. 'They'll pull him through.'

Eve wept. 'Poor little Matthew. He looks so — '

At home, William poured them each a brandy.

'How is he?' asked Buffy, phoning that evening.

'Not very good,' said Eve. 'I'm not sure about the stall this week. I'm so sorry.'

'Don't give it a thought.'

Two weeks later, Eve went for a routine mammogram with the NHS Mobile Screening Service, set up in the carpark in Lewisham Hospital. She came out to where William was waiting in the car, listening to Mozart from St John's, Smith Square. She was later than he'd expected, since there'd hardly been a queue. 'People don't show up,' said the receptionist in her cubby-hole. 'They really should. Anyway, you're here, dear.' She ticked off Eve's name on a list and gestured to a curtain. 'Undress to the waist. You can keep your jewellery on.'

'I feel like a gypsy,' said Eve with a little laugh. 'I've always wanted a caravan.'

'Have you really?' asked William, and then, as she disappeared, 'I'll be waiting outside.'

Eve, when she came out at last, looked pale.

'Everything all right?'

'I think so. They took a couple of shots more than once.' She put her hands over her navy wool jacket, and the crimson and cream and indigo scarf which he loved.

'Bit sore?' he asked her, kissing her cheek. It sounded ghastly, he couldn't imagine it.

She shook her head. 'It'll wear off. Let's go.'

Ten days after that she had a letter, and went, without telling him, he later realised, down to the surgery.

Three months later, she'd gone.

'She won't see the baby,' Claire sobbed. 'She won't see the *baby*.'

'I will,' said William, 'I'm longing for that.'

Matthew, at the funeral, stood like a ghost, pale and vacant. He let William kiss him, and didn't tell anyone to fuck off, but they said that he shouldn't come home. Not yet. After a while, they let him.

He wandered in and out of rooms. He cradled Danny for hours, sitting in Eve's place on the sofa, watching television. He did not go near the piano, or pick up his violin.

'Shall we have that off for a bit?' asked William, as daytime soap followed daytime quiz. His head felt as if it would burst. 'How about a bit of music?'

He switched the television off, put on Schubert's Piano Trio No. 1, found himself in tears. Matthew got up and went up to his room, right at the top of the house.

* * *

'Please come down,' said William, reliving the sickening misery of when it had all begun. Eve had been there then, they had had one another. 'Come down and have a spot of supper.' Danny gazed up at him; beneath the bedclothes his tail began to thump. 'See?' said William. 'Danny wants supper. Come on, old chap.' Matthew turned away. William sank down on the edge of the bed and put his head in his hands. Matthew kicked him off. William went out, and down to the kitchen, Danny following. He held him in his arms and sobbed.

Dreadful, dreadful days.

After a little while, Matthew perked up. He came down to breakfast and looked at the paper. He started to talk about the news. William found he was having a conversation. His heart began to lift, as if someone had unloosed a great weight — he found himself watching, in some obscure place within, a kite, bobbing about in the clouds above the common, while he and Matthew, as a little boy, watched it, hand in hand.

'He's getting better,' he told Claire on the phone. 'I really think he's turning a corner.'

A day or two later, he came into the drawing room to find Matthew laughing wildly at a nature programme. Lemurs clambered about in swaying trees. They made William smile, but they didn't make him clutch his sides. He looked at Matthew and a little rivulet of anxiety ran through him. That night he woke to a fearful crashing about downstairs, and realised, as he ran down there, that Matthew had perked up because he'd stopped taking his pills.

'Oh, Christ,' he said, as the dining-room glass went splintering. The door was open: inside, he saw a madman. Then Matthew turned, and his face was murderous. He came towards him, his hand upraised, holding one of his grandfather's heaviest silver candlesticks. William fled. He ran upstairs and dialled 999. Then he barricaded himself into the bathroom, hearing the dining-room table overturned, waiting for the sirens, and the flashing, sickly blue.

* * *

Matthew went back to the hospital, raving, and was put out for hours. Next day, when William and Claire went to see him, he could not speak.

Gradually, he got better. Months later, with the promise of a visit from the district nurse each day, William had him back. It was pretty grim. They played draughts, where they used to play chess. They played Chinese chequers. Each game took hours. The television roared. Matthew, between games and programmes, wandered about. William thought he was looking for Eve. He could sense how much it disturbed him being back here, even on the medication.

After a while it was decided that, until he could cope on his own, Matthew should be based in the hospital and come home now and then, for as long as they both enjoyed it.

This, for a long time now, had been the pattern of things.

* * *

And later, much later, when Buffy cautiously suggested that perhaps — only when he felt up to it, of course — they might resume their old activity, and have a little stall, William said he would like that, and yes, it would probably do him good.

But not in Portobello. Would she mind that dreadfully? It was just the thought of travelling right across London, it was just the thought of being there, where Eve had been — was he being terribly selfish?

Of course not, said Buffy, it would do her good to have a change of scene: she'd been thinking about it herself. How about Camden Passage, a good halfway place for the two of them, and a very good pub for lunch. People came flocking on Saturdays. And Wednesdays.

'Let's just say Saturdays for now,' said William, refilling her glass. 'Would Saturdays suit you?'

'Very well indeed,' said Buffy, who by now had long since booked herself into the Mary Ward Over-Sixties Club.

'My dear,' she told the receptionist, 'I'm over seventy.'

'That doesn't matter at all, my love.'

'My name is Buffy Henderson. Please don't call me love.'

She went to the choir and the art class, she even did a little training on the Internet.

Life had begun, at last, to look up again.

It had begun to look up for William, too. And this, for a long time now, had been the pattern of things.

5

Now, on a November morning, he set up the Camden Passage stall with Buffy. It was bitter. Danny was curled up in an ancient anorak beneath the trestle; Buffy, in her fingerless gloves, unwrapped a Staffordshire teapot, and put it next to an unmarked milk jug, patterned in green and blue.

'What do you think?'

'Perfect.' William was unwrapping the newspaper from six little Victorian glasses, engraved on the rim with a garland of grapes.

'You did wash them?'

'Of course I washed them.'

They sat sipping coffee from Thermos cups, waiting for the crowds.

'Five weeks to Christmas,' said Tom, on the next stall. 'Things should pick up a bit now.'

'That's a nice little set of spoons,' said William, having a look.

'Seventeen-ninety,' said Tom. 'Very nice.'

'You should be inside, with something like that,' said Buffy. 'You should be in the Arcade.' She finished her coffee and got out her lipstick. 'You're getting too classy for us.'

'It's the overheads,' said Tom. 'It's the overheads, or I would be.'

'I like those earrings,' said William, noticing, as Buffy looked in her little mirror.

'Liberty sale. You've seen them before.'

'Have I really?' He watched her pursing her lips. Tendrils from her bun were escaping a knotted scarf; the fingers in fingerless gloves were blunt and reddened; a trellis of broken veins embroidered her nose and cheeks beneath visible powder. She was wearing the deep-pocketed, hairy grey jacket she always wore in winter: it made him think of yaks, and stony paths. Sometimes, watching Buffy set things out on the stall, he thought of the careful way Eve had unwrapped and set things out — not that Buffy was ever clumsy, it was different, that was all. Eve's touch was delicate, Buffy's workmanlike — professional, perhaps, was the better word. In quiet moments he'd find himself moving from the memory of Eve's hands, and the sheen of her nails, to her pink-and-white skin, its softness and opacity, her silken white hair, the scent she wore, whose name he could never remember, and which he had to ask Claire about each Christmas.

'Why don't you write it *down*?'

After Eve's death, when he tried, once, to go through her clothes, a drawer he pulled open released a ghostly cloud of that scent, clinging to petticoats and stockings. That had been one of the worst days. Now, on the whole, in daytime, he tried not to think of any of this.

The traffic on the Essex Road was building up. A hesitant sun shone briefly on the plate glass of Waterstone's, behind the Green. Pigeons conversed on the top of the war memorial; the sun touched the six Victorian glasses, set out in a circle.

'Those will have gone by lunch-time,' said Buffy, settling back in her fold-up chair.

'Have I told you about my letter?' asked William. 'I seem to be telling everyone.'

'You haven't told me.'

'From my second cousin in Shropshire,' he said. 'Second cousin twice or thrice removed, if I remember rightly. She's a rather extraordinary old thing — well, they're a pretty rum lot.' He stopped, remembering cousin Edna's funeral, held in St Michael of All Angels, up in the hills. It had rained then, too, blowing in great windy gusts across the churchyard, where the little group of mourners had assembled round a precipitous grave while the vicar struggled with his surplice. Claire and Matthew had not been among them, could even then remember Great-Cousin Edna only dimly, from the one or two visits when they were little, when she had shouted at them.

'Anyway,' said Eve, making arrangements for them to stay overnight with schoolfriends, 'they're far too young to attend anyone's funeral.' So he and Eve had gone up there, and stood beneath his black umbrella on one side of the grave while Mary, Sophie and Ernie, Edna's children, stood on the other. What a strangely affecting sight they made. It seemed probable that none had visited what one might call a clothes shop for many years: their buttoned-up, belted overcoats, in murky shades of flecked maroon and camel, the sisters' pulled-down berets and Ernie's knitted scarf and hat, all looked as if they had drooped from hooks on the crumbling plaster of the kitchen passage since circa 1959. Sophie had wanted to wear Mother's court shoes, bought some years before from the Sue Ryder shop in Oswestry, but Mary, looking out at the rain as the hearse drew up at the gate, had bullied them all into wellingtons, now thick with Shropshire graveside mud.

In the chill of the church, they had sung *Abide with Me* in mournful whispers; watching them clutching their hymn books, William wondered how on earth they would all manage, released from Edna's maternal grip, which had been fearsome. Ernie's long yellow fingernails picked at a thread in his greenish scarf; his wispy untrimmed hair straggled here and there from beneath the woollen hat; he had not, for a long time, met anyone's eye.

Afterwards, William drove them all back to the house, the three of them squeezed in the back, seeing, through the swishing wipers, two trudging figures arriving at the gate.

'That'll be Win,' said Mary, leaning forward. 'And Johnny.'

'They should've come to the church,' said Sophie, shifting. 'They was good friends to Mother.'

'People don't like funerals,' said Ernie, the first remark he had made throughout the journey.

Indoors, greeted by two lurchers and a rheumy-eyed spaniel, they assembled in the kitchen, beneath a slatted airer hung with strange-looking underwear and a quantity of socks.

'Your health,' said Johnny, raising his teacup.

'She was a good strong woman, your mother.'

'She did suffer in the end,' said Mary. Ernie gazed out of the window at the ceaseless fall of rain. Sophie passed round a plate of ginger nuts and another of digestives. Win had made a fruitcake.

Describing all this to Buffy, as the market began to fill up, and one or two people paused to consider her 1940s Dartmouth Pottery tea plates, William wondered how, indeed, the cousins had all continued to occupy that long, half-lived-in house, where paper peeled in damp shards from every upstairs room — he knew, he'd been up to the icy bathroom, had a look into desolate bedrooms — and nowhere, surely, was bearable in winter except the kitchen. Christmas cards over the years had told him that Ernie now lived out in a caravan in the yard, and that they had taken in more dogs. Beyond this, he knew nothing.

'Now Mary's written out of the blue. Can I help a young woman who wants to come to London,' he said. 'She wants a job and lodgings, as Mary puts it.'

'Bit of a tall order.'

'Do you think I should have a lodger?' He moved his cold feet to embrace the sleeping Danny.

'Not someone you've never met.'

'Claire thinks I should sell, and buy a flat. She's always saying it.'

'I must say,' said Buffy, 'I don't think I could cope with anything more than a flat, now. On the other hand — '

'Quite,' said William, who knew that they would have to carry him out of that house, in which everything in his life that had ever been important had occurred.

'But I do sometimes think I should have someone about the place,' he said. 'I mean — you never know.'

Buffy's attention had been diverted to the middle-aged woman in a raincoat whose eyes were on a 1920s cow creamer, and also a very pretty butter dish, patterned in Marguerite.

'May I?' She made to lift the lid, and realised it was Sellotaped.

'I'll show you, if I may.' Buffy turned it over. 'Winton.' She indicated the mark. 'Nineteen thirties. Rather nice, isn't it?'

'It's sweet.' The raincoated woman put on her glasses, and peered at the label. 'Does that say sixty-five pounds?'

'It does.'

'And the creamer?'

'That we can do for thirty-five.'

'Oh, isn't Christmas dreadful? All so tempting, but — '

William pointed out the ceramic toast racks. 'These make nice presents. And they won't break the bank.' He lifted one whose sections were gently scalloped. A little sprig of juniper was painted on the front, and the end had a stripe of juniper green. 'Now this is also Winton, but we could do it — ' He picked it up, and looked at the label. 'Well, it says twelve pounds, but I'm sure we could knock something off for you.'

The woman put her glasses on again, and had

a look. 'It is quite sweet. It's just that the creamer is *so* sweet.'

Buffy and William waited. A young couple stopped to look.

'Oh, those are nice,' they said, looking at the toast racks.

In the end, they sold the creamer to the woman in the raincoat, knocking off £6.50, and a 1920s shell-design toast rack to the couple.

'You were saying,' said Buffy, as they disappeared into the throng. It was getting quite busy now, and also quite a bit colder.

'Where was I?' William turned up his collar, round his sea-green woollen scarf.

'Contemplating a lodger,' said Buffy. 'That colour does suit you, I must say.'

'The thing is,' he said, contemplating the sound of a key in the lock at the end of the day, and a friendly drink by the fire now and then, 'the thing is Matthew, of course.'

'Is he coming home for Christmas?'

'I hope so. He does find strangers unsettling. I don't think it would really do.'

'Perhaps in the New Year.'

'We'll see.' William leaned back in his chair. 'One day, of course, I hope Matthew will be home for good. That's the plan.'

Buffy didn't answer. Then she said, 'What about Claire? Would she like a lodger? Au pair, sort of thing. Does she like children, this girl?'

'I have no idea. And you know what Claire's like — especially with the children. She has her own ideas; she doesn't really like suggestions.'

'Oh, well, just a thought.'

'Rather a good one. Any more coffee?'

Buffy poured out the last cupfuls.

'What are you doing for Christmas?' he asked her. 'Any plans?'

'Not quite sure yet,' said Buffy, moving a couple of candlesticks. She finished her coffee, and stood up. 'Time for a little wander.'

6

'I'm going out with a tree surgeon,' said Janice.

'That won't do you any good,' said Mary.

'It might.'

Sophie was unpacking the groceries; tins of bulk-buy mushy peas were piled upon the table. Outside, the holm oak in the sodden field behind the museum huts was tossing in the wind. Inside, a heap of dogs lay snoring in front of the range.

'Perhaps your young man could come and do some surgery here,' said Sophie. 'If that tree comes down we'll be ruined.'

Janice glanced across to the back window. Ernie's caravan, parked alongside the field fence, was, she realised, really quite close to the oak. She said so.

'That tree,' said Mary, stirring in three spoons of sugar, 'has been there since I was a girl.'

'I was a girl then, too.' Sophie's fingers strayed to her hair slide, this morning a small enamelled sheepdog, black and white and friendly, with a nice red collar. 'Does he work for the council, your young man?' she asked Janice.

'No,' said Janice, remembering the bloke in the council lorry that day she'd pulled half a tree across the Ridge. Was he a tree surgeon? If so, she might have met two in one day, something of a first. 'He works for himself,' she told Sophie. 'He's called Eric. I'm not sure — '

Did a drink after work, a dizzying ride round

the lanes on his bike, and a sudden, liquefying kiss, back in the pub carpark, make someone your young man? They were seeing each other again tonight. She thought of his stubbled cheek grazing hers, beneath a stormy sky, and had to put her mug down.

'What you need,' said Mary, 'is a change of scene. Bright young woman like you.'

'You sound like my mother.'

'Mother knows best,' said Mary, and Sophie's gaze, which had been upon the last lumpy carrier bag, strayed to the photograph upon the mantelpiece, next to the Coronation tin. On the other side of Mother, Charles and Diana smiled down from their transfer-printed mug, on the day of their engagement. What a dreadful business that had been. That poor, poor girl.

'What *I* need,' said Mary briskly, 'is help with walking these dogs. Does he like walking, your Eric?'

'He rides a Harley-Davidson,' said Janice, thinking of her cheek pressed against his leathered back, her arms tight round his waist. 'Anyway,' she said, looking out once again at the weather, 'if I'm going to walk them now, I'd better get going.'

A tail thumped behind her. 'He heard us,' said Mary. 'Didn't you, Ned? Off you go, then.'

'You haven't heard from your cousin, then?' Janice got up. 'In London.'

'I haven't, but that doesn't mean to say I won't. He's a good man, William.'

'Blood is thicker than water,' said Sophie, and started to tell Janice just how William and they were all related, on their mother's side. Janice rinsed out the mugs at the sink, pretending to listen.

'Walk,' said Mary to the heap of dogs on the hearth-rug, and the kitchen was suddenly filled with swirling chaos. From outside in the pens came a manic barking.

'Quiet, you hounds!'

Mary opened the back door: they all streamed out, and the pens went wild. Sophie gave Janice a handful of leads from the passage hooks. Outside, she bent to fasten them. The windy morning air was filled with yelps and yaps and howling; the sky, after last night's downpour, was full of high, fast-moving cloud. Everything felt bright and clear and hopeful.

'Right, then.' Mary unbolted the gate, looking up the lane for visitors. You never knew. Janice was dragged through by two straining Labradors, a whippet, a greyhound and three collie-cross. Up in the hills she could let them off. 'Have a good time,' shouted Mary.

'Heel!' shouted Janice.

The lane was full of soughing trees and gurgling ditches, the wind was whipping across the fields. More rain was on the way, they all knew that.

* * *

William was having Sunday lunch with Claire and the family.

'Sit down, please, Hugo,' said Claire. 'Geraldine, please sit down. Where's Piers?' She went to the bottom of the stairs. 'Piers!'

Jeremy was lifting a cast-iron casserole from the hotplate to the table. 'Mind! Hands off the table, please, Geraldine.'

Piers came down the stairs and into the kitchen, looking flushed and hot.

Claire sat down again. 'About time, too.'

'Hello, old chap,' said William, reaching out an arm.

'Hello.' Piers slid into his seat.

Rain was streaming down the window behind the settle.

'Now, then.' Jeremy lifted the lid. A heavenly smell wafted into the air: chicken, tarragon, white wine, cream. Courgettes and parsley and slivers of carrot were all detectable as he ladled out the first helping, and Claire prepared to serve potatoes from a stoneware dish. Everyone perked up.

'That smells *yummy*.' Geraldine half rose from her seat to look and was told to sit down again.

'How's that poor old ear?' William asked her, unfolding his napkin.

She looked at him blankly.

'That was ages ago,' said Claire. 'She's forgotten all about it.'

'I'm glad to hear it. Oh, look who's here.'

Danny, until now being good in a cardboard box by the Rayburn, had, with the lifting of the casserole lid, begun to take an interest. He came trotting up.

'Danny!' said Hugo. 'Danny! Here, boy.' He bent down from across the table and peered beneath, patting his leg. Danny was there like a shot.

'Hugo!'

'Oh, come on, he only wants a little bit, can't he have just a little bit?'

'No.' Claire glared at William.

'Come on, Danny.' He bent to look beneath the table. Danny, sitting firmly between Hugo's feet, looked back at him unflinchingly. 'Come on,' said William again. Hugo's feet tightened their grip. Plates were going round the table. As William pushed his chair back and bent down farther, he caught the edge of the cloth, and a splash of the glorious-smelling sauce fell on to it.

'Daddy!'

'Oh, dear, I'm so sorry. Now, Danny, come here at once.' He reached across and took hold of his collar. Danny yelped, and stood his ground. Hugo was shaking with laughter.

'Hugo!'

Geraldine bent down to see what was going on. 'Oh, look at him, he's so *lovely*. Aren't you, Danny?'

'Geraldine!'

'What's he doing?' asked Piers, moving his bit of the cloth aside.

'Children!' Claire was going pink. '*Will* you all behave? We're trying to have *lunch*.' She looked at their father. 'Jeremy!'

Jeremy had set down the ladle. 'I'm certainly not going to serve any more until everyone's calmed down.'

'Thank you. Now, Daddy, will you please take charge.'

'Of course, of course, I'm so sorry.' William, now on his hands and knees, took hold once again of the collar, and Hugo at last gave in. His feet suddenly moved apart, Danny came skidding across the hardwood floor, and as William released him he went on skidding, flying past the Rayburn, until he hit his box.

The children were helpless.

'Look at him — *look* — he's like a *cannonball*!'

Danny righted himself and shook himself violently. He looked across at them all, and gave a little bark.

'He wants you to do it again. Oh, go on, Grandpa, do it again.'

'I'm not sure he does,' said William, conscious of Claire's fury at his elbow. 'And I think it's time we all enjoyed this delicious lunch, don't you? Now, basket, Danny. Basket!'

Danny got into the box, and looked out sorrowfully.

'Poor Danny.' Hugo was gazing at him. 'I *wish* we had a dog.'

Claire's hand came smartly down on the table. Pepper and salt pots shook.

'If I hear one more word . . . Will you *please* all settle down.'

'Why are you always so *grumpy*?' asked Hugo.

'I'm not.'

'You are.'

'I must say, this looks like the best lunch I've had for a long time,' said William, and meant it. Cooking for one — it was pretty dismal. Even now. Perhaps Buffy was right — a lodger might be a good idea. Then again — he certainly wouldn't want to be cooking all the time, and laying tables. There was something to be said for a tray in front of the television.

'Have I told you about my letter?' he said to Claire. She didn't answer. 'Darling?'

She was scarlet, tight lipped. Tears spilled on to the tablecloth.

'Darling — ' he said again, and put out a hand. She shook it off.

'Oh, dear.'

Silence fell round the table.

'My fault,' said William. 'I shouldn't have brought him.'

'This is going to get cold,' said Jeremy, helplessly. 'Perhaps you could pass the potatoes.'

* * *

'Anything I can do?' asked William, later. The rain had stopped; they were walking across the park. Ahead, the children were hurling sticks for Danny. Jeremy, due in court first thing tomorrow, had stayed behind.

'Do you mind?' he'd asked them, as they put on their macs in the hall and the children had a skirmish about who should clip on Danny's lead. 'It's the one chance of a quiet hour.' Already, he was straying towards the stairs, and the desk in their bedroom, piled high with briefs and files.

'Of course not,' said William. 'You go ahead.'

'Do whatever you like,' said Claire, wrenching open the front door. Danny strained towards it, panting. 'Out!' she said to them all.

The street was full of the silence after the rain, the quietness of a Sunday afternoon in London.

The children and Danny swiftly broke it, racing towards the park gates. The trees dripped; deep puddles lay everywhere.

'Not that I want to interfere in the least,' William went on carefully. Oh, how careful one had to be with Claire — more so than with Matthew, he often felt, in spite of everything. Even Eve had had to tread round her sometimes, and still had her head snapped off. And then, when she died, Claire had been inconsolable, and sobbed after Piers was born as if her heart would break.

'I want her to *be* here, I want her to *see* him — '

Gradually the weeping stopped, and the mantle of motherhood settled on her shoulders. She drew it tight around her. She trained to be a counsellor with the National Childbirth Trust, trained to be a breast-feeding counsellor, decided, after all, not to return to the solicitors through whom she had met Jeremy, and who had given her maternity leave.

'The law can do without me. We can manage. My place is here,' she told William, come to admire his grandson on a summer afternoon. Danny sat in the shade at a required distance; Piers lay in his grandfather's arms, gazing up at him. Gazing back, flooded with mingled love and grief, William listened, or half listened, as Claire talked of Winnicott, and bonding, and feeding on demand. He tried to remember whether Eve had gone on in quite this way, at quite such length; could only remember the two of them watching Claire sleep, saying how perfect she was. And so had Matthew been, and who could have ever predicted what hell lay waiting for him, as summery light and shade played over his pram beneath the trees?

'Claire?' he said to his daughter now, watching the children racing about with Danny in the cold damp air.

'What?'

'As I say,' he said, skirting a puddle, wishing he could take her arm and the two of them could walk companionably, father and daughter talking things over, on a Sunday afternoon. 'I don't want to butt in — '

'Then don't,' said Claire briskly. 'I'm just a bit overtired, that's all.'

'It's a lot for you,' said William, watching Piers and Hugo haring over the soaking grass, with Danny leaping joyously after them. Geraldine was struggling to keep up, shouting, 'Wait for *me*!' Eternal cries of childhood, and that was one of the most potent.

'Boys!' called Claire. 'Hugo! Piers!'

There were other families, other London dogs, let off the lead, claws clicking along the wet black paths, lifting their legs on empty flower-beds, sniffing elaborately at one another, shouted at. It was starting to rain again: umbrellas went up.

'God, will it ever stop?'

'I've had a letter from mad old Mary,' said William, trying again, putting up his own umbrella. He held it over his daughter and she didn't move away. He started to tell her about this missive, as the rain began to fall faster, and then gave up, as everyone fled for the trees and bandstand. The children grabbed Danny and climbed the steps; half a dozen Dulwich families stood in its shelter, gazing out across grass and tarmac at the downpour. Teal and mallard quacked from the lake; Claire saw a mother she knew, and began a conversation about school governors. William picked up Geraldine, whose hand he found in his.

'What do you want for Christmas?'

'Danny. I wish he could live with us.'

'I'm afraid I'd be rather lonely without him,' he said, and in the chill of the darkening afternoon, with the rain falling like a punishment, on and on and on, had a sudden glimpse of how true that was, the big house cavernous around him. He gave a little shake: this wouldn't do.

* * *

'What were you saying about Mary?' asked Claire, getting the tea. They'd come back soaking, everyone making a dash for it across the park, and the hall was full of wet shoes. The children were all watching television, Danny snuggled in among them on the sofa; Jeremy had shown his face and taken it away again; the kettle was simmering on the hob.

William told her, watching her move about the kitchen, competent and unhappy. It was so: clearly it was so.

'Buffy had a thought,' he said, leaning back in his chair.

'Don't do that.'

'What?'
'Lean back on your chair — I'm always telling the children. You can break the chair and you can break your back. Jeremy had a client that happened to: no insurance, nothing. What was Buffy's thought?'
William tipped himself forward again, and told her. 'You know, mother's help. Sort of thing. Perhaps if things are getting a bit on top of you — '
'They're not.' She went out to the bottom of the stairs.
'Jeremy! Tea, if you want a cup.'
'Shall I take it up to him? I know what it's like when you're deep in something.'
Claire looked at him. 'He still has the use of his legs.'
William gave up. He took the cup that was offered to him, beheld his son-in-law, grey about the gills with overwork, come down for his, and retreat once more; he listened to the synthetic chirrup of cartoons from the sitting room.
'There's no real drama on any more,' said Claire. 'Nothing of substance.' She sat down, and reached for the paper, turning the pages of the Culture section, sighing. William picked up the travel pages, and ran his eye over Christmas breaks in the Seychelles. Parakeets skimmed the treetops, silvery fish leapt from ink-blue waters. If Eve were still here, they could be planning things.
Next door, the cartoons came to a violent conclusion. Channels were flipped, and voices

rose. Claire got up and went through. From somewhere in Tunisia's New Year weekend for two, William became aware of discord: Sunday night homework still to be done, general insubordination. Voices grew louder, Danny came through.

'Hello, old chap.' He reached down to fondle his ears. Claire reappeared, and drew the curtains on the rain-soaked afternoon, now turning into a filthy wet evening.

'Time we were off,' said William, rising. 'Thanks for a lovely lunch.'

'That's all right.' Claire put the teacups into the dishwasher, where the lunch things waited. Danny, sniffing the remains, went after her with interest. 'Nothing for you,' she told him sharply, and went to the bottom of the stairs. 'Jeremy! Are you coming to say goodbye?'

In the hall, with his coat and scarf and umbrella, and Danny clipped to his lead once more, William kissed the children in turn, shook hands with Jeremy and brushed Claire's cheek, which was all that seemed possible.

'Think about it,' he said, and opened the front door on to sheets of rain and darkness. 'Someone to help you out a bit.'

'Help you do what?' he heard Geraldine asking, as he made his way to the car beneath their streetlamp. Silver rain drummed on the roof. 'Nothing,' said Claire. 'It's bathtime.'

''Bye,' he called to the closing door, getting his keys out, and sensed, as the door banged to, family life closing in on itself, his visit over and done with even before he drove away: on with the next thing, and then the next. Another day over. Was this how Claire wanted to live?

He started the car and pulled out, the wipers at full tilt. The street was curtained, porch lights shone through the drowning world.

'God Almighty,' said William aloud, all at once washed through with desolation. He hadn't felt as bad as this for a long time.

7

'He says he doesn't know. He says something might turn up in the New Year.' Fountain pen flowed across creamy pages; Mary put the letter down, next to its thick lined envelope. Sophie turned it over wonderingly.

'This looks nice.'

'William's always done things nicely.' Mary looked across the table at Janice, rolling up a few shreds. 'Do you good,' she said. 'Bit of class.'

'I've got that already,' said Janice, thinking of last week. Eric lived up in the hills, in an abandoned shepherd's hut he rented from a farmer. The beam of his Harley-Davidson headlamp cut through the driving black rain and showed, on the winding road, a one-storey dwelling of stone and patched-up slate set among boulders and empty sheep pens. Miles from bloody anywhere. They got off the bike, and she ran for the door and stood shivering while he wheeled the bike under a lean-to of galvanised iron. When he switched off the ignition everything went pitch black. She heard the rain soaking into the turf, and battering the slates; she heard his footsteps squelching up to the front.

'Don't you have a torch?'

'Don't need one when I'm on my own. Know it by heart.'

He unlocked the door and felt for the light switch. 'This is it.'

Janice blinked. 'It's nice.'

One room: table and a couple of chairs, open fire, sink, cooker. Bed. She hung her soaking jacket and woollen hat on the back of the door; he put down his helmet, lit a candle in a bottle on the table, and nodded towards a door. 'In there, if you want it.'

'I'm all right for now.'

Eric poured whisky into a couple of tumblers. 'Cheers.'

'Cheers.'

He lit the fire and they sat drinking. The wind rattled the door and windows, the rain came down in torrents, they heard a slate shift on the roof.

'That's another one gone,' said Eric. 'I'll have to get up there.'

'Not now.'

He looked at her. 'No.'

When they'd finished their whisky he got up and kissed her. They took each other's clothes off and lay before the fire. The floor was stone flags, with a couple of rugs.

She shut her eyes, thinking about it. She'd thought of nothing else for days.

'Look at you,' said Mary, putting the letter from London back in its envelope. 'Fit for nothing.'

'Oh, I don't know.'

Janice gazed dreamily across the kitchen. It wasn't raining; in fact it was brightening up. Across the yard she could see the door of Ernie's caravan pulled open, and then he appeared on the steps, having a bit of a look-round. Poor old bugger.

'If it stays fine, we might have visitors,' said Sophie, stirring her tea. 'We might do a Christmas party.'

'And pigs might fly,' said Mary.

Ernie was coming down the rotting steps. One day he was going to break his leg. He stood sniffing the sky and the dogs in the pens came forward: Janice watched him go over and greet them. Their tails wagged wildly, they licked his hand through the wire. That was the good thing about dogs, they didn't care what you looked like: she supposed that was half the point.

Ernie was crossing the yard, skirting the puddles so as not to let in the wet. Where were his wellingtons, silly old fool? The wind blew his jacket and scarf about, wisps of hair straggled out under his woolly hat. Dreadful. She heard him open the back door and slip off inadequate footwear. Then he came creeping up the passage.

'What do you want?' demanded Mary.

'Just looking in. Bit brighter today.' He padded over the kitchen flags, long yellow toenails poking through his holey socks. 'Any tea?'

A tail or two thumped on the hearth. He bent to give his greetings. 'Good boy, there's a boy. Any tea?'

'It's gone cold,' said Mary.

'I'll make a fresh pot,' said Sophie, rising.

'Nice and strong.' He straightened up, and beheld Janice, drinking and smoking her roll-up. 'I'm right out of baccy,' he told her.

'Is that right?' She reached for her Rizlas and tin.

He watched her prise it open. 'Good little tin, that.'

'Much the same as yours, isn't it?'

'Mine's old. Like me. And empty.' He shuffled to the chair by the hearth and eased himself on to it, rubbing his hands. 'Christmas is coming. Ta very much,' he added, taking the wafer-thin roll-up. 'Got a light?'

'Always cadging,' said Mary, as Janice passed him her lighter. 'Always on the scrounge.'

'If it wasn't for me,' said Ernie, inhaling happily, 'there'd be no museum, no income, nothing.' He pulled a shred of tobacco from his lip.

'That was a long time ago you did all that.'

'Lasted, though, hasn't it?' He watched Sophie stirring the pot. 'Still pulls the crowds. Any biscuits?'

'You old bugger,' said Mary, levering open the tin.

'How many visitors have you had this year, then?' asked Janice, remembering the dismal trio who'd been there the previous week.

'We had a good summer.' Sophie gave Ernie his mug. 'We've entered it all in the book.'

'You mean I have,' said Mary, getting up and fetching it from the back windowsill. 'It's me who keeps the records.'

'You was always the learner,' said Ernie.

'You *were* always the learner,' Mary corrected him.

'No I wasn't. I was always the one at the back.'

He gave Janice a dreadful wink. 'It was my art that saved me. Saved the family fortunes.'

Mary pulled out the last of a little row of scarlet Woolworths exercise books, wedged between years of *Yellow Pages* and a shelfful of 1950s *Dairyman's Days*.

'Who did those belong to?' asked Janice, noticing them for the first time.

'Them was Father's.' Ernie sipped his tea. 'He was dairyman to Broxwood Hall for years.'

'That's how he met Mother,' said Sophie reverently. 'When she were in service.'

'Was in service.' Mary sat down again, smoothing out lined pages.

Janice looked at the deep-scored Biro, the columns of dates and figures, and at the letter from London, with its exquisite hand. She felt a stirring of curiosity, of interest even. Did such a hand betoken such a life? Was bossy old Mary right — should she stretch her wings next year? Just as she and Eric . . .

Just as she and Eric what?

The fact was, she hadn't seen him since the soaking-wet morning which followed that wild, soaking-wet night. He'd driven her down from the hills and left her, that was the fact of the matter, back in Cloud Nine, where Steve gave her a quizzical look.

'Mind your own business,' she told him, wiping down the counter. The Harley-Davidson had roared away, and it hadn't roared back again. Not once, in a week. Pretty poor show, her dad would have called it, had he the chance.

'And where were you last night?' her mother

had demanded, as she reappeared for her microwaved tagliatelle for three. Ugh. God, what was she doing still living at home? She might be up in the hills, in a shepherd's hut, spread-eagled before the fire at the hands of a tree surgeon. An expert in the field, as it were.

Cut to the quick though she was, Janice heard herself give a sudden bark of laughter.

'Whatever's got into you?' asked Mary, looking up from her counting. 'I make it fifty-five to date, with July and August the peaks.'

'Summer holidays,' said Ernie sagely. 'That's what brings them.'

'You don't say.'

'And how much money has that made you?' asked Janice, returning herself to the present with a wrench. 'If it's not rude to ask.'

'Almost a hundred pounds. Family discount is what brings it down.' Mary pursed her lips.

'But it is an attraction,' said Sophie. 'You can't deny it.'

'Was it your idea?' Janice asked her, sensing the glow of pride.

Sophie gave a modest little smile. She was wearing one of her prettiest hair slides today, a pair of leaping dolphins in turquoise blue, smiling benignly down on pudding-basin trim, green turtleneck and a pinafore patterned in floral pink and red. Little daisies, or marguerites, perhaps. A bias-binding trim.

'Where do you get those slides?' asked Janice.

'In Healing Arts, down behind the cathedral,' said Sophie promptly. 'They do a lovely range.'

'Frippery and con tricks,' said Mary. 'One-to-one herbal teas. Reflexology. Psychodynamic star signs. Counselling.' She gave a violent sniff. 'Holistic beeswax.'

Ernie snorted.

'Well, they do very nice hair slides, anyway,' said Sophie. 'And they're always very kind to me, I must say. I'm hoping to pick up something nice for Christmas.'

'Bit late for that,' said Ernie, pulling tobacco shreds off the tip of his tongue. 'Now if I had my time again — ' He cast a meaningful look at Janice, and flicked the tobacco towards the hearth. It landed on a greyhound, and stayed there. There was a little, irritable twitch of skin.

'Your time came and went and nobody even noticed,' said Mary, closing the museum accounts in an access of irritation.

'Not even me,' said Ernie. 'Heh, heh. Oh, well.' He drained his Charles & Diana mug with a flourish. 'Didn't do them two much good, neither.'

'*Either*.' Mary stood up. 'If you want to make yourself useful you can get in the back parlour and do some de-fleaing. Otherwise, out you go.'

Ernie rose resignedly. 'Where's the powder?'

'Out on the passage shelf, where it always is. Now bugger off.'

He shuffled out, returned with a giant tin and moth-eaten brush and waved it at the hearth. 'Come on, now. Then it's a walk.'

They leapt and shook themselves. Claws clicked over the flags. Ernie lured them through the back parlour door and closed it. There was a sudden cacophony.

'Quieten down! Quieten down, you curs!' His voice when raised was like a punctured organ pipe, whistling and wheezing, with sudden forceful peals. 'Down, I say!'

'Holy Moses,' said Janice. She packed up her papers and tin, put her mug down next to the letter. How could there be a commonality of blood between the erudite, elegant William Harriman and this trio of Harriman crackpots? How distant could cousins be?

'Did Ernie really do all the dioramas?' she asked, pushing her chair back, thinking of straining huskies, racing across the sunlit snow, and brave St Bernards, beneath the mountain peaks.

'He did,' said Mary, passing the empty mugs to Sophie and gesturing at the sink. 'He did have a way with it all, I'll give him that. Not that it lasted, but for a while it kept him busy.'

'It kept him very happy,' said Sophie, rinsing the mugs beneath the brass cold tap. She put them on the draining board, alive with silverfish. 'He was at his best, in those days. We put up the huts with Mother's legacy and Ernie filled the lot.'

Janice pulled on her woollen hat. 'And does it run in the family? I mean — ' She indicated the letter, with its glimpse of another world. 'I mean, is your cousin William artistic?'

'He's clever,' said Mary. 'He's a civil servant, or I should say he was. Very clever with money.'

'Was it the Post Office he worked in?' Sophie

asked, setting down the last cracked, tea-stained mug. 'Was that it?'

'The Treasury, you fool.'

'The Treasury,' sighed Sophie. 'Isn't that a lovely word?'

* * *

Oswestry was Christmassy, with lights around the lampposts. Puddles reflected red and green and gold, the windows of Past Times were full of amber silk cushions and goblets engraved with holly leaves and Latin. Janice met Tracy Keenan coming out of Lo-Cost with feverish toddlers and a pushchair.

'And another on the way,' she said, nodding down at a bright acrylic bulge.

'Well done,' said Janice. 'Fantastic.'

'It's hard work,' said Tracy, 'but it's worth it.'

Janice knew how she herself must look — like a biker, which she was, in one aspect of her being: tall, lithe, irresponsibly selfish and carefree, in her black Lycra leggings and Doc Martens, her zipped-up jacket and nifty close-fitting woollen cap. She clapped the ringless hands of singlehood and beamed down at the infants, who shifted from foot to foot with streaming noses.

'What do you want for Christmas?' she asked them, and they began their frightful list. Perhaps it was different if they were your own.

'What about you, then?' asked Tracy, moving them all aside for an old bat on a Zimmer frame. What was she doing out here in the cold and wet? Perhaps she'd like some Christmas shopping done. Janice found herself checking this thought abruptly. Enough of old bats with their tins and Rich Tea biscuits. Enough of serving toasted sandwiches and walking packs of dogs. Was this all that the millennium had had to offer her?

Something's happened to me, she thought, standing among the milling shoppers, hearing the Rotary Club rattle its Rotary Tin and churn out 'Hark the Herald' from its Rotary Camper Van. In 2001 it's tree surgeon or bust.

'What are you up to, then?' asked Tracy, whose mother used to hang out with Janice's mother, in distant, unimaginable days when both were girls with hippie beads and joss-sticks.

'I'm still working in Cloud Nine and all that,' said Janice. 'You know. Shopping. Dogs. Same old things. I'm going out with a tree surgeon,' she added, hoping it was true.

'Get you,' said Tracy. 'What's his name?'

'Eric.' Janice thought of Keith, Tracy's electrician husband, with his funny teeth and coils of flex in the van. 'He's ever so good looking,' she said cruelly.

'Not Eric Lammering,' said Tracy. 'Not that Eric Lammering with the bike.'

'Why? What's wrong with him?'

'Oh, nothing. Just he's a bit of a one, that's all.'

'I like a bit of a one,' said Janice, possessed by unstoppably sickening feelings. 'What do you mean?'

'Oh, nothing. You know how these things get

around. Just he's a bit of a . . . well, like I say.' Beside her, the children were starting up. 'Mum, Mu-um.'

'I'd better go before they catch their deaths,' said Tracy, beaming. 'It's ever so nice to see you again. Ta-ra, see you later, merry Christmas.'

She wheeled the pushchair around and disappeared into the throng.

'Ta-ra,' said Janice, watching her go.

Well. Well, how about that, then? What was a bit of a one when it was at home? She stood on the main street as the light began to fade, and the rain to fall once more, swirling past the Christmas lights in pretty colours. 'Hark the Herald' had turned into 'We Three Kings'.

One in a taxi, one in a car, she heard within herself from irreverent schooldays. Now it sounded somehow rather plaintive.

One on a scooter, blowing his hoo-ooter . . .

I've given myself to a love-rat, thought Janice, with not an item of shopping done, Christmas or otherwise. She turned up her collar and strode into Lo-Cost, as dismally fluorescent a shoppers' hell as anyone could wish for. There might indeed be something to be said for a total change of scene.

* * *

'What did you say you were doing for Christmas?' William asked Buffy the next weekend. They were sitting at the stall, where holly and mistletoe had been placed cheerfully here and there in little sprigs and vases. Danny, curled up on a folding chair, had a scarlet ribbon tied to his collar. This alone, William knew, enabled him to put an extra five quid on every single thing on the stall.

'Oh, isn't he *sweet*?' said every single punter.

'I didn't say,' Buffy answered, moving a set of eggcups. 'What about you?'

'Oh — ' William let his response die unfinished. He thought of Claire and Jeremy, the fury across the turkey, the children overwrought, ignoring him. He thought of his darling boy, vacant before Christmas television, the two of them pulling a hopeless cracker. Dismal. It shouldn't be, but this year it was. Had he been in denial, all the other Christmases since Eve had gone? Why should this one feel so especially terrible?

'Don't suppose you'd like to come over to me?' he said, watching the careful arrangement of bone china. Not very practical, for eggcups. 'We could light the fire, raise a glass. Even a couple of glasses.'

'Oh, William.' Buffy's hands, in their fingerless hairy gloves, hovered like moths above the stall. 'Would you really — '

'I'd love it,' said William. 'Do come. Only if you're free, of course.'

'Since Mother died in 1989 I've been freer than I care to remember,' said Buffy, recalling the fall of the Berlin Wall and she before the television, suddenly horribly loud, as November afternoon drew in to November night. 'It would be heavenly, William.'

* * *

Christmas came and Christmas went, and was infinitely more enjoyable than William had imagined. The house was warm, the boiler roaring. Buffy arrived on Christmas Eve with a basketful of parcels, including a pudding, which she had made herself, listening to *Any Questions*, and a tin of mince pies, likewise, but with *Home Truths*. He met her at the station and held his umbrella over her all the way down the street, awash with the worst downpour for days. Fairy-lit trees stood in rain-lashed windows, the gutter gurgled.

'I tell you, William,' said Buffy, shifting her basket from one arm to the other, while he carried her overnight bag, 'I tell you, your grandchildren will live to curse us.'

'Don't say that.'

'But it's true. Our sins and foolishness visited upon the heads of generations. A hole in the ozone layer the size of Timbuktu, rivers foaming with detergent and dead fish, the globe warmed up to boiling point.'

'Oh, come, come.'

'Desertification. Rainforests ruined. Oestrogen in the drinking water, men no longer men . . . ' A great lake lay before her in the dip in the pavement.

'Here, take my arm,' said William, guiding her into the streaming street.

'You see? We can't even walk on the *pavement*. Floods, William, floods and pestilence lie ahead.'

'Well, Noah got through it,' said William. 'Now do buck up.'

Indoors, he took her soaking coat and fake-fur Russian hat, and hung them to drip in the hall. Danny got up from his place by a crackling fire, which she glimpsed through the open door of the drawing room. At once, she began to feel better.

'Now you settle yourself in that chair,' said William, 'unless you want to spend a penny first — '

'Well, perhaps I'll just pay a little visit.'

In the downstairs cloakroom Buffy took out her tortoiseshell combs and put them in again, and pursed her lips over the last — the very last — of her Lizzie Arden Petal Pink. There. She powdered her nose, took one last look. Well. Too late to do much about it now.

'Come and have a drink,' said William, as she returned.

Decanter and glasses winked in the firelight; there was an enormous bowl of nuts.

'Heaven,' said Buffy, settling down with her whisky mac, and Danny at her feet.

'Cheers,' said William.

'Cheers, William. And thank you so much.'

'Absolutely my pleasure. You've saved the day.' He eased himself into his own chair, on the other side of the hearth. Buffy knew that they now occupied the positions which he and Eve had held all their married life, when they weren't hand in hand on the sofa watching television. Oh, dear. Oh, well. She raised her glass again.

'What have you done today?' she asked him.

'This morning I got in a quantity of drink and

a small organic bird. This afternoon I listened to the *Nine Lessons and Carols* and made some chestnut stuffing.'

'I say, did you really? How glorious.'

'It was very pleasant.' William did not add that he had wept with the very first notes of 'Once in Royal David's City', dissolving with that pure sweet treble and the thought of Matthew, who'd sung in the school choir so beautifully and whom music now left cold. He'd pulled himself together with the first lesson, then sobbed aloud through 'O Little Town of Bethlehem', Eve's favourite. Had he not had the prospect of Buffy arriving at the station in the wet at half past five, he didn't know what he'd have done. Phoned the Samaritans, perhaps: he found himself thinking this, and then felt ashamed, when he had so much to be thankful for.

'How would you feel about midnight Mass?' he asked Buffy, refilling her glass.

'Oh, stop, William, I shall be drunk as an owl,' she said happily. 'Well, it's entirely up to you, dear. I'd like it, of course, provided I'm not legless by then.'

'Let's see what the weather's like. Not if it's chucking it down. Now then, supper. I thought we'd have something light. I've got in a bit of wild salmon . . .'

How delightfully the evening passed. Supper. *Christmas from Around the World*. And the rain eased off, miraculously, and at a quarter past eleven, drunk and warm and purposeful, they staggered down the steps and off to St

Matthew's, which was packed and full of bonhomie.

'The only thing is,' said William, as they found two places near the back, 'I'm afraid I might get a bit tearful. It's that treble solo that does it — those first six notes of 'Once in Royal' and I'm a goner. If it happens, you must take no notice: I'm just a sentimental old fool.'

'Join the club,' said Buffy, and held herself erect. It was a long time since she'd allowed herself a good cry, and she really, really didn't want to make a fool of herself now.

In the end, tears streamed down both their faces as the choir processed by candlelight, the cross held high and gleaming. Then they'd recovered, and got into the spirit of things, and Buffy, her voice well exercised by the Mary Ward Over-Sixties choir, sang her heart out.

As they made their way out up the aisle, greeting people William had known all his life, he suddenly saw Jeremy, whom he had missed entirely, standing right at the back, looking tired and legal.

'Hello, old boy!' William clapped his arm. 'Good to see you.'

'And you,' said Jeremy, moving with them through the throng to the porch and the smiling deacon. 'Claire said I might see you here.'

'She's home with the children. Of course. Do you know Buffy Henderson, my old friend and fellow stallholder? My son-in-law, Jeremy Wright.'

'Of course. We've met several times.' Leather

glove met knitted glove in Christmassy enthusiasm.

'Have you really met? I must be losing it,' said William. 'Anyway, looking forward to seeing you on Boxing Day, old chap, if that's still all right?'

'Yes, yes, of course.'

They were out in the churchyard, where recorded bells were ringing and the rain was falling fast. Up went everyone's umbrellas.

'Matthew's joining us tomorrow,' said William. 'I expect Claire's told you.'

'Yes, indeed. Hope it all goes well. And happy Christmas.'

And he shook hands again and loped away.

'What a sad-looking chap,' said Buffy, as they made their way home across the common. 'Whatever's happened to him?'

'Don't know,' said William. 'Don't quite know. The stress of modern life or something more sinister. I'm trying not to think the worst.'

'One should never think the worst.'

'Thus speaketh the prophetess of doom.'

'That's different. Global disaster is not on a par with domestic distress.'

'Oh, I don't know.'

* * *

But Christmas Day passed happily. Bacon and eggs for breakfast, presents by the fire. Buffy gave William a Friends of the Earth calendar and a tea towel with a scarlet border and a Christmas goose in the snow. Also a bottle of Scotch, and a packet of chocolate Canine Treats.

'I say, Danny, have a look at these.'

He needed no second bidding.

William gave Buffy the millennial edition of Lyle's *Antiques Review* — 'Oh, how splendid, I shall pore over this for hours' — and a Crabtree & Evelyn casket of Elizabethan Garden soap and foaming bath oil. 'Oh, what luxury. And there's a *mitt*, look.'

'Good gracious.' He gazed at it, china blue and rather on the small side. 'Do you use mitts?' he wondered.

'I do now.' She got up to kiss him. 'Thank you, William. Lovely, lovely.'

'You've been much too generous. Look at this Scotch. Do you think — ' He glanced at the carriage clock on the mantelpiece.

'We can't start drinking at half past *ten*,' said Buffy.

'Are you sure?'

By the time they came to put in the bird they were well away.

'I must sober up,' said William. 'I'm fetching Matthew at twelve.'

'Have a black coffee. I'll do the sprouts.' Buffy put on last year's Greenpeace apron, which she'd brought for this very moment. The previous night, unpacking in the spare bedroom, which Eve had made both restful and full of charm, she had thought herself a mad old fool, bedecking her bosom in sperm whales and ice floes. But better than a floral pinny, surely. She hung it up next to her dressing gown, made, incredibly, from the hair of the Pyrenean mountain dog and dyed powder blue. That morning, the apron came into its own, perfect for peeling and basting and steaming, over her Jaeger jumper from the previous year's sales.

'Don't worry about a thing,' she told William, pouring coffee into a Copeland Spode mug for him. 'This is pretty.' She had a closer look: Spode blue watering cans, trowels and rollers. Even a little fork.

'Their Gardeners range,' said William, taking it from her. 'My birthday present from Claire.'

'She has taste.'

'Oh, Claire has always had a good eye. The house is perfect.'

'Something wrong there. A house with three children shouldn't be perfect. Is it three?'

'It is.' He drained scalding coffee and rose from the kitchen table. 'See you about one o'clock.'

'We should have waited. With the presents? I have got Matthew something.'

'No, no. It's too much for him, all that carry-on, we've tried it before. Much better to keep it simple. A couple of little things by the fire at teatime — he'll love that.'

⋆ ⋆ ⋆

Matthew came up the steps on William's arm. Around them the garden dripped and somewhere in the street a blackbird was singing, joyous and pure.

'Listen to that,' said William. 'Here we are, then.' He fished out his keys on the top step and unlocked the front door. A delicious smell of roasting bird came wafting out to greet them. 'Buffy!' he called, and turned back to a still and silent Matthew. 'Come on in, darling, welcome home.'

Matthew stepped into the hall, and looked about him. Holly hung over the pictures, drawing-room firelight leapt. 'Danny?' called William. 'Look who's here.'

Danny came trotting out, saw Matthew and rushed to greet him. Matthew gave a slow, sweet smile which tore at William's heart with love and hope. 'Well, well. Here we all are. In you come by the fire; let me take your things.'

Matthew's hands went up to his scarf and stayed there. Buffy came up from the lower depths. 'Here we are,' said William again. 'Matthew, do you remember our friend Buffy?'

'Hello, Matthew.' Buffy was flushed from the oven, still wearing the sperm whales, her hair drifting out of her combs and bun. 'Happy Christmas. How nice to see you again.'

Matthew's hands were still on his scarf, his coat damp.

'Come on through to the fire,' said William, leading him gently by the elbow. 'You can take your things off there. Buffy — '

'I'll join you in a moment.'

Progress was infinitesimally slow. It took ten minutes to get Matthew into the drawing room, allow him time to gaze round and issue, once more, that heartbreaking smile of recognition, take off his gloves and his scarf and coat, hang them up, return to find him still in exactly the same position, lead him to a fireside chair and settle him with a glass. He looked at it, holding it before him in mid-air, perfectly still.

'Nothing alcoholic,' said William. 'It's called Norfolk Punch. Lots of herbs and spices. Rather good.' He went to the door. 'Buffy!'

'Coming!'

They raised their glasses. 'Happy Christmas.'

'Cheers.'

'Happy Christmas, darling.' William's glass touched Matthew's. 'Going to try a drop?'

The Norfolk Punch went slowly to his lips. He sipped minutely, then again.

'Thought you'd like that. Thought so. Just the ticket, eh?' William heard himself, being hearty and going on. If Claire were here, there'd be a sharp reproof. Well, she wasn't. Face all that tomorrow. 'Cheers,' he said again, and then: 'How are things below deck?'

'Coming along nicely,' Buffy told him, without turning her gaze from Matthew, who was inching his Norfolk glass towards the fireside table. Then she came to, and said brightly, 'I'll summon you both in a bit.'

'Anything I can do? I don't want you slaving away.'

'I'll call you to take out the bird.'

* * *

Lunch was perfect: the bird sweet and tender, the sprouts crisp, potatoes just right with all the scrunchy bits, the stuffing, though he said it himself, magnificent. Buffy's gravy slipped down like wine, which was scarcely surprising, since that was mostly what it was, thick with giblets and mushrooms. William poured claret into lead crystal glasses, and white Amé for Matthew, and prepared to feel Christmassy and content, his old friend at the other end of the polished dining table, laid with silver candlesticks and holly, his dog by the fire, his son come home.

'Wonderful to have you here,' he told him. 'Wonderful to have you both.'

Matthew nodded. It took him half an hour to eat half a potato, two sprouts and a sliver of bird. Between each of these mouthfuls he laid down his knife and fork and gazed before him — at the candles, at china, at a speck of dust, spinning in the heat from candlelight.

'Try a little bit more,' said William. 'Just a little bit.'

It took him back to the days in the high chair. Claire had eaten every scrap, thrown rusks about with abandon. Matthew had picked.

'Not enough to keep a bird alive,' said Eve, white with anxiety. 'How will he grow?'

Had it all started, even then? A turning away from food, from life, retreating into another kind of world? When he started school it got better. Soon he was eating like a horse. They forgot all about those crumbs of meals, until he came home from Durham.

'Matthew! Lunch-time! Are you coming down?'

A dreadful silence.

Watching him now, staring at specks of nothingness, spearing a sliced mushroom in infinite slow motion, William asked himself, for the millionth time, whether it still had to be like this. Was it the illness, or was it the drugs? Was Matthew, without his medication, still capable of murder?

* * *

'He's drugged out of his skull,' said Buffy later. 'I'm sorry to say so, but it's true.'

'Ssh!'

'My dear, he can't hear you. I'm not sure he can hear you when he's awake.'

It was late afternoon. Lunch had at last been completed, with crumbs of pudding and teaspoons of cream for Matthew, who'd gazed at the flaming brandy as if at the Holy Grail. They'd had coffee by the fire, and the tail-end of the Queen's Speech before presents. Matthew had fallen asleep, while letting William help him unwrap a pair of leather gloves with fleecy linings.

'For winter walks,' said William, indicating the dog, the winter sky beyond the window. Matthew nodded, and did not raise his head. Gently William took his present away, and eased the head into a comfortable position against the wing of the chair. 'Have a good sleep, old chap,' he murmured. 'Do you good.'

Now it was almost dark, the blackbird, incredibly, starting up once more, but closer, perhaps even in his own front garden.

'Listen to that.'

'I know,' said Buffy. 'The most beautiful of all the songbirds. Almost the last — we're poisoning our wildlife. When did you last hear a song thrush?'

William couldn't think. He looked at sleeping Matthew. 'Do you think I should wake him? Or perhaps he needs his sleep.'

'He's drugged out of his skull,' Buffy said then. 'Surely you can see that, William. I'm sorry to say so, but it's true.'

William winced. 'Ssh. *Sotto voce.*' He looked at his son, his once fine features — the Harriman nose, the generous, sensitive mouth, Eve's delicate brows — blurred with years of suffering.

'He could have been a professional,' he said quietly. 'He could have had anything he wanted. He went to Durham on a music scholarship.' His voice broke.

'I know,' said Buffy gently. 'I know. I'm so dreadfully sorry.'

William shook his head. 'Do you really think he's overdosed? I mean, that they're overdosing him?'

'It doesn't seem right.' Buffy put down her empty coffee cup. 'He moves like — ' She stopped herself saying it, undead. 'Like a robot,' she said carefully. 'He hardly speaks. I mean, surely in this day and age — '

'They have tried, though. Over the years it's all gone up and down. Sometimes he's been a bit better, but if they lower it too much he gets so restless and unhappy. He doesn't sleep, and that makes everything worse, and then — ' He broke off. 'Oh, I don't know.'

'Why don't you have another word with them?

In the New Year. See if they can't try just a *little* less.'

'I will,' said William. 'I'll ask for a review. The whole team. We haven't had one of those since . . . since I don't know when. I do wonder if perhaps it's all taken for granted now. Long-stay patient, no trouble, you know.'

'Yes,' said Buffy. 'I should have a word. Now, shall I make a pot of tea?'

'I will.' William rose. 'You've done more than enough. Have we room for Christmas cake, do you think?'

'Sinful,' said Buffy. 'Why not? And what about this dog? Shouldn't he take a turn or two before tea?'

'He should.' William whistled. 'Come on, old chap.'

Dog and master made their way to the lower depths. She heard the door to the garden pushed open with difficulty, warped with wet weather, and then banged to again. Distantly she heard the kettle filled, and then, from the front garden, the blackbird's song, renewed once more, soaring into the winter afternoon.

Buffy got up. She went to the huge high windows and looked out. There he was, on the topmost branch of the magnolia, perfect from tip to tail, a bird out of every book of her childhood — singing through A.A. Milne and E.H. Shepard, dark amidst the apple blossom; warbling in James Reeves's water meadows, on Grahame's riverbank. Oh, how thrilling and sad it felt.

'You're beautiful,' said Buffy aloud, as the last

of the Christmas light drained from the sky and rain trickled down the darkening glass. 'You're everything you should be.'

Behind her came a little sound. She turned and saw Matthew, awoken, gazing at her. 'Come and listen to this,' she said, and went to take his hand. He let her. Slowly he unfolded his long, once elegant limbs — his father's limbs, well made and perfectly proportioned — and let her lead him to the window. And they stood there, as the blackbird's liquid voice explored the trill, the rill, the fluty phrase, the whole full-throated miracle.

'You're musical,' said Buffy, at last, turning to Matthew. 'Your father says you're very gifted.'

'I was musical once,' said Matthew slowly, the most lucid and complex sentence he had uttered all day. She realised his hand was still in hers. This was what it might have been like, to have a grown-up son you cared for.

William's son.

She checked the thought before it even formed itself, turning as he came in with the tea tray, seeing his look of astonishment and delight, as the blackbird opened his throat in a last abandoned ascension of joy, and darkness fell.

2001

II

Visits

8

And then it stopped raining, and the big freeze came. Just before New Year William woke to a different light, felt stillness all around him, and drew back his bedroom curtains on to snow. Garden and rooftops and trees transformed: he stood there, thinking of Monet and Pissarro, whose paintings of *Winter at Giverny* and *South Norwood under Snow* had been reproduced on several Christmas cards that year. He thought of the children, in years when it had seemed to snow more often, out there building snowmen, racing down the street and through the park, pelting him and Eve with snowballs, shrieking. When was the last fall?

He stood there in his dressing gown, counting years — not a good thing to do at his age. Where had they gone, and how had they gone so quickly? But he counted back and thought that the last time when snow — real, proper snow — had fallen in London was in January 1990, when Eve had been dead two months and Piers, his first grandson, was not yet born. So this must be the boy's first sight of it — extraordinary. His own childhood seemed always to have been filled with snow, every winter.

It began to fall again, light but insistent. How entirely beautiful it was, and how fortunate that he had had the boiler fixed. Time for breakfast. Put something out for the birds. Perhaps later he'd take Danny up to the hospital, get Matthew out in the grounds, in his Christmas-present gloves. White fields. Snow light. Good for the soul.

For a moment, watching the tumble of flakes — thicker and faster now — work their other-worldly magic on the garden, William remembered the look on Matthew's face, lit up on Christmas Day by the blackbird's stream of song. My love, he thought, with a little twist of longing. We'll have you right again.

Down in the kitchen the kettle boiled. Upstairs the paper fell on the mat. Out in the garden Danny was sniffing the air, excitedly shaking off snowflakes. The willow tree, each branch outlined, was exquisite. As always — in boyhood; with his own children; on every occasion except in the black year after Eve's death, when Matthew had tried, incredibly, to kill him — William felt with the snow a lift of the heart, a sudden rush of hope.

* * *

By New Year the country was in the grip. The television showed stranded cars in Northern Ireland and Glasgow; in London the temperature had dropped ten degrees below freezing; blizzards were sweeping in from the west. The news every hour grew worse: patches of freezing fog, black ice, stretches of the motorway closed.

'Thank God we're not going anywhere,' William said to Danny, turning the boiler up. 'That's one good thing about getting old: you don't have to go anywhere.' He lit the fire and poured a large measure of Buffy's Christmas Scotch. 'Cheers, old boy. Happy New Year.'

He rang the family: Claire answered.

'Happy New Year, my darling.'

'Oh, hello.'

'How are you all getting on?' he asked her, and thanked her again for Boxing Day, which had been a strain.

'You don't have to keep thanking me,' she said.

'What are you all doing tonight?'

'People are coming in for drinks. Most of the terrace.'

'That sounds fun.'

She didn't answer.

'Claire — '

'What?'

'Just . . . happy New Year,' he said again, hesitantly. 'I mean — I hope it's a really good year for you, darling. Less . . . well, you know — '

'Less what?'

'Well, fraught,' he said, and saw in his mind's eye a wintry skater, venturing much too close to the Danger sign.

Claire said tightly: 'I do wish you wouldn't. I do *wish* you wouldn't. If I need your platitudinous words of wisdom, I'll ask for them.'

William watched the ice beneath his skater crack, over terrible blackness. For a moment he couldn't speak.

Then he said quietly: 'Very well.' He wanted to speak to Jeremy, to wish his son-in-law, for whom he and Eve had always been thankful, and of whom he had grown genuinely fond, a very good New Year, but he knew that he mustn't ask for him. In any case, he did not trust himself to utter another word.

There was silence. Then Claire said: 'Well. Happy New Year. I must get on,' and put the phone down.

William replaced the receiver, trembling.

* * *

Buffy rang just after ten. 'I'm not staying up until midnight,' she said briskly. 'Had to do it last year, had to see the wretched millennial thing. This year I'm bedding down at a sensible hour.'

'Quite right.' William, still shaky, leant forward to turn down the television.

'What are you watching?'

'I really couldn't tell you.'

'William? Is everything all right? You sound a bit — '

'I'm fine,' he said, as firmly as he could. 'Let me wish a happy New Year to a good old friend.'

'And a very happy New Year to you, William. And thank you again for Christmas — it was perfect.'

'It was good, wasn't it? Did me a power of good. We must do it again.'

'Well — lovely.' Buffy's voice was cautiously warm. Why the caution, he wondered, but hadn't the strength to enquire. 'And how are the family? Have you spoken to Claire?'

'I have.'

'William? Something's wrong, isn't it? Tell me.'

'Oh — you know. Families.'

'You mean Claire.' Buffy was brisk again. 'Now what's she done? She's hurt you, I can tell.'

William leaned back in his chair and closed his eyes. He felt tears rise — good God, he was getting like a girl, waterspouts at the slightest thing. He swallowed hard, cleared his throat.

'William?'

'Just a little tickle.'

'That girl,' Buffy said forcefully, 'needs a good hard smack. I'm sorry, dear, I don't mean to interfere, but I don't like to think of you upset.'

'It's all right.' He wiped his eyes. 'I expect it's the time of year. A seasonal disorder. Everyone's too emotional. Or hormonal. You know. Women's sort of thing.'

'I'm a woman, but I don't think I've gone around upsetting people in quite the way Claire manages. She needs a counsellor or something.'

'UHT, perhaps.'

'That's *milk*, William. You mean HRT. Honestly.' She gave a snort of laughter.

William at once began to feel better. He blew his nose and chucked another log on to the fire. 'Do let's change the subject. Isn't the snow glorious?'

'It's bloody cold.'

'I thought you said we were warming up. Globally.'

'Don't mock. You're burying your head in the sand.'

‘Or the snow,’ said William wittily.

‘It isn’t *funny*.’

Sometimes she sounded like Claire. But different. Buffy had a bedrock, always had done, he knew that. Claire, who looked as if she was embedded in every kind of rock on earth, lived, he now realised, above a morass of violent misery.

But why? Did she not have everything she had ever wanted?

* * *

Janice sat up in her bedroom in 33 Curlew Gardens. The room was small and, in winter, stuffy. She propped her pillows up against the wall and leaned against them on the narrow bed, writing a letter. It was Sunday afternoon, and downstairs the telly was roaring. Outside, the New Year snow had muffled everything, and it felt as though no one in the entire world would ever do anything, ever again.

Dear Mr Harriman, she wrote, *I wonder if you can help me. I am thinking of coming down to London, in order to change my life*.

She crossed this out at once.

Dear Mr Harriman, If I don’t get out of this place I shall go —

How on earth should she write? Probably she should go through it all with Steve, but the Ridge was impassable, the café shut up, and Steve gone off for a week to Marrakech. All right for some.

Dear Mr Harriman, We have never met, but I think your loopy old cousin has written to you about me. I am thinking of coming to London, and —

And what?

Dear Mr Harriman, I hope you won't mind me writing when we have never met, but your cousin Mary kindly suggested that you might be able to help me.

There. That sounded pretty normal, didn't it? She was pretty normal, wasn't she?

Janice put her pen down and gazed out of the window. God, it was dead out there. No hum from the bypass, no sheep on the hills. Perched on the bed like this she could see only the snow-covered tops, beneath a relentless opaque grey sky. Somewhere in a fold beneath was Eric, in his shepherd's hut, toasting his feet in thick wool walkers' socks before a fantastic fire.

She ripped the sheet from its pad and tore it into pieces.

9

Everything slowed down with the snow. The skies, after the first fall, were dark and low; the milk came late, likewise the paper. The post barely came at all. For two or three days, in freezing weather, William kept to the house, feeling himself in shut-down mode, not minding. He put out some food for the birds, lit fires, played Brahms and Schubert. He stood browsing at the bookshelves, pulling out forgotten volumes. Recalling Monet and Pissarro, the morning he had awoken to a new white world, he dipped in and out of the art books on which he had, in his time, spent a fortune. For a whole afternoon he sat reading a life of Matisse, who, during a youthful illness, distraught at the prospect of life as a small-town lawyer, was given a box of paints by his mother.

'*From the moment I held the box of colours in my hand, I knew this was my life . . .*'

William turned the pages, losing himself in windows on to the sea, the shaded garden; in scarlet, green and Prussian blue interiors — rugs, screens, samovars; he gazed at women in silken patterned robes, or naked on daybeds, naked beneath the trees. Here was the shimmer of lemons in a blue-glazed dish; here was the Cartier-Bresson photograph everyone knew: Matisse in old age, in a corner of his sunlit studio, glasses upon his nose, cap on his head, tranquil dove in his hand while he drew. The dove's companions, released from their cage, sat watching, murmuring. Old age; a contented morning; working until the end.

When William looked up, he saw it was almost dark, the snowy trees ghostly in the fading afternoon, everything muffled and still. Not a bird, not a footstep. He got up to draw the curtains, looked out on the empty street. Matisse's radiant interiors receded: this was an oil from a London painter, whiteness smudged into grey in the dusk, here and there a lighted window. *Winter Street*, something by one of the Camden Town Group, perhaps — London in the twenties, in a muted palette. Whistler would have dissolved it all, to black and white and gold. I might have been a painter, William thought, recalling lost afternoons in classes, decades ago, before he was told to concentrate on serious subjects. I might not just have looked at everything, I might have picked up a brush. And he stood where Matthew, at Christmas, had stood, briefly transfigured by the blackbird's song, letting the depth of the afternoon sink into him.

That evening, he sat at his desk — his father's old desk — in the corner of the drawing room, and wrote to Matthew's consultant, asking for a meeting. The letter began as a brief request, and became an impassioned plea — for a young life going to waste, brilliance occluded, gifts which must be rediscovered. He read it through, remembering how busy he himself had been, in the old Treasury days, wanting letters and memoranda to keep to the point, to let him get on. For a moment he considered tearing it up, writing just a brief note. Then he signed and sealed it, and gave it a first-class stamp.

Leaning back in his chair — his father's old chair, a Windsor — tapping his fountain pen against his lips, hearing the fire crackle, and Danny sigh before it, he wondered whether to write to Claire. Would that make things better between them?

I don't want to intrude, my darling, but I'm here if you need me, I'm always here, for both of you.

No. He could feel her irritation even as he considered it. Let her be, let her come to him, when she was ready. That was best.

Over supper, soup on a tray, he realised that he had not spoken to anyone for two days, and had not minded. The snow had done that: falling like a meditation, enclosing the house, and him. In bed, in the dark, in utter silence, he closed his eyes on Matisse's windows, Matisse's women — fully aware of their beauty, keeping it to themselves. It had been a long time since William had thought of female beauty — of skin, unclothed, of a glance, a touch — in relation to anyone but Eve, who all his life had made him happy, just to look at her. In bed he was almost always aware, still, of her absence, of the place where she should be, beside him, feet tucked beneath his feet, arm round his middle as they fell asleep. Now, on this winter night, he began to contemplate not her, not even an individual, but an idea of something perfect — a room, a figure, clothed or naked, an arrangement of colour.

I have been nourished, he thought, his hands behind his head, listening to the tick of the clock. Perhaps these tranquil, unexpected moments, after all the emotion of Christmas and New Year, were what was meant by the accommodation of old age — and reached without speaking to a soul.

In particular, he had not spoken to Claire. Was this why such calm had come upon him?

Have I lost her? he wondered, turning over, pulling the pillow down. For so long he had felt he had lost his son — but his love for him had remained, grown deeper even: pure, piercing, unswerving. With Claire — how hard she was to care for. As he sank into sleep, the images of remote, secret but untroubled womanhood swam once again before him. Claire, in new motherhood, had briefly had something of these qualities — a certainty about her place in the world, about her physicality. Now . . . He sank into sleep, before he could work it out.

* * *

Next morning, the skies had cleared: by the time William had done with the paper, over a late breakfast, the snowy garden was lit by brilliant sun. He finished his coffee, made a shopping list, took down the lead from its hook.

'Walk,' he announced, as if he needed to, for Danny, at the first chink of the chain, was racing up the stairs.

The hall was full of light, streaming in through

the lintel glass and through the stained-glass panels, coloured lozenges falling on to the tiles. Picking up his letter to the consultant from the table, William, in his winter coat, caught sight of himself in the mirror and thought, for a startling moment, that he had seen his father. He almost greeted him aloud — Father? Then he stood there, taking a good look at himself, as the dust in the flooding sunlight danced against the glass.

Thinning white hair but a well-made head — he'd give himself that. The Harriman nose, strong and bony; eyes a faded blue, with the pale circle round the iris which everyone developed as they got older — once it came, that was it: you knew you were on your way. But still — he wasn't there yet, and, like his father, had in old age a decently handsome face, he allowed himself, tucking his scarf in, pulling on his gloves.

Danny was gazing up, alert and waiting.

'What do you think?' he asked him. 'Still pass muster?'

Dachshund tail beat on Victorian tiles. William reached for his hat on the hook, glanced back in the mirror. 'Hello,' he said, to his father's eyes, and saw his father smile. Beside him, there was a little bark of anxiety: how much longer could this take?

'Right.' Hat, shopping bag. 'We're off.'

Snow was already melting on the steps: he took them carefully, clipping on Danny's lead at the gate. The air was invigorating, but very cold: he took a deep breath and at once began to cough. Better take it slowly: he set off, wondering whether he should have a flu jab, something he had always resisted, as a mark of frailty, when he was still active and fit.

People were out and about in the streets, setting off for the shops, like him, scraping snow from garden paths. There was Edith Horsley, at number seventeen, doing just this, in her woollen gloves and wellingtons. He raised his hat, and they agreed that it was a beautiful morning. The sound of shovel on stone rang through the air, a train came into the station and doors slammed. William walked on. The scarlet of the post-box on the corner was still trimmed with white: he posted his letter to the consultant, and thought of Matthew, in the overheated day room, turning — he hoped — from the television to gaze out at the stretch of grounds, firs dark against the glittering white.

He had reached the main road. The 14 was rumbling through the slush; the queue at the bus stop moved forward quickly; people were hurrying in and out of the shops in the cold. How busy everyone was. After his days of seclusion he found himself wondering whether he might see anyone he knew. He went to the bank, where Danny was allowed, and to Spar for basics, where he wasn't, and thence to the delicatessen, which a dachshund always found interesting, even from his hook outside.

Full-roasted coffee was grinding; the ham slicer slid smoothly back and forth. Time for an interesting lunch or two, a bit of company again, a root about in the sales. Time for a concert, a visit to a gallery. William, in the queue at the counter, wondered that the smells of coffee, marinated olives, salami and cheese and fresh bread could so quicken the blood, but so it was: he made his purchases, including a carton of spinach-and-nutmeg soup for lunch, and a small pannetone cake in a blue-ribboned box for tea.

Who might join him for tea? Or supper, come to that?

If Buffy didn't live right on the other side of London; if he were able to drop in, now and then, on his daughter and grandchildren, as one might hope to do, without it being always the wrong moment; if Matthew, darling Matthew —

He tucked his wallet back in his inside pocket and made for the door. Danny, on the pavement, leapt up in an abandonment of joy. And William, greeting and unhooking him, running gloved hands over beloved glossy head, felt again the sudden, unexpected prick of tears.

Now what? Where was the tranquillity of his retreat, where the joyous quickening of the blood?

I am alone too much: he almost said it aloud.

Life had its routine, and its satisfactions. The china stall was the heart of the week, the outings to sales delightful. There were times — he had just had one — when solitude was divine.

But with the children lost to him —

He straightened up, blew his nose, gathered himself and his shopping together.

'We need something to happen, old boy,' he said, as Danny looked brightly up at him. 'Not giving up yet.'

Then he set off home, down the street where

the thaw was just beginning, the snow on the pavements pockmarked with drips from the trees, the railings black again, and shining; and let himself into the empty house: finding, on the mat, a letter.

* * *

Dear Mr Harriman . . .

He stood with his back to the empty grate, the sun-filled drawing room smelling of cinders and wood ash. The letter was on good paper, in a pleasing, youthful hand.

Dear Mr Harriman,

I wonder if you would be kind enough to help me. I know we have never met, but your cousin Mary has said you might know of a job. I am twenty-three and though I have no proper qualifications I am able to turn my hand to most things. At present I am working as a dog-walker, shopper and general help. I have been shopping for the Dog Museum for about three years. I also work in a café, and make good cakes, though I say it myself, though I am not really a cake-making sort of person, to look at.

Although I do not know London, I think it is time I did. Mary and Sophie have talked about you, and although I have never met anyone like you I don't know where to begin, or anyone else to ask. If you know anyone with a spare room who needs some general assistance, perhaps you could tell me. I am practical but not brainless.

I hope you are well, and look forward to hearing from you.

Yours sincerely,

Janice Harper

William, in his long winter coat, in the great high space that was his drawing room, filled with books and paintings, china in alcoves, and a walnut desk, the light from the thawing snow pouring through high windows, read this letter twice.

What was a Dog Museum? What, in God's name, could it be, and why would it need shopping done for it?

Ill-written words from another letter, arriving before Christmas in floods and driving rain, came all at once to mind.

The Dogs are a Comfort, Mary had written, capitalising at will.

He had assumed, not really thinking about it, that she meant the two or three living beasts last seen after Edna's funeral, but they must be long since gone. Had she had them stuffed? Or was this some other place entirely, a Heritage Britain venture of some kind? He shook his head, trying to imagine it.

More to the point, here was this young woman. Living in Curlew Gardens — how charming.

He tried to imagine her — someone who did not look like a cake-maker and who, he recalled, Mary had in her letter described as Tall and Fit. And clear minded — he felt that from the letter he now held in his hand: someone who knew herself, and knew how to get what she wanted.

Well.

Danny was sitting at the front window, in the fall of sun on pale worn carpet and Persian rug, looking out at the street and garden. Small though he was, the window was low enough for him to do this, and now and then his ears pricked up, as something of interest appeared. The possibility of cats was essentially the focus, but today, William knew, he was aware of the change in the weather, enjoying the intriguing little falls, now and then, of clumps of melting snow, from the magnolia tree and the extravagant stems of unpruned roses. Up went the ears, this way and that, out went the eager nose, and in the sunshine his chestnut coat gleamed like a polished antique.

'What do you think?' asked William, walking across the room in his unbuttoned coat, laying the letter on the open walnut desk. Danny turned to glance up at him, then looked back at the garden, where a blue tit had suddenly arrived, and was swinging on the last of the bag of nuts. William stood watching it too — such a beady, compact, bright little bird — trying to imagine, in his house, a lodger, an energetic young woman breezing in and out, turning her hand to things, chatting away, while the smells of baking wafted up from the kitchen.

'Oh, God, I don't know.'

On the one hand the prospect of companionship, conversation, help when needed. But with what? He didn't need help — not yet, not really.

Shopping was perfectly manageable, a focus to the day. Twice-weekly mornings with Mrs T. had for years kept the domestic wheels oiled. The house was dilapidated in corners, but clean; his shirts were ironed, the silver polished. And anyway, Janice Harper was not offering herself as a cleaner.

It wouldn't do, it wasn't suitable.

A lodger was one thing, coming and going, with a job outside the house. An ever-present young woman: no. Someone wanting to talk, while he wanted to read: no.

Had he grown selfish, living alone all this time?

'Can't get it right,' he told Danny, and it was true. He swung from contentment to loneliness, unstable as an adolescent.

Well — this was life without Eve. Even now, even after all these years. If you were essentially monogamous, this was widowhood: nothing ever quite right.

Perhaps he had better just accept it, live with it. A lodger could only bring complications.

And anyway — there was Matthew. Up at the top of the house was his old room, along the upper landing from Claire's; there were his books and music and violin, shut in its case. One day, when he was well enough, he'd be back here — that, at William's time of life, was who should be living here.

So they'd have to see. Any other arrangement now could only be pro tem.

The blue tit flew up from the last of the nuts and was gone. Danny, bored now, looked round, awaiting instructions.

'Lunch-time,' said William, and they made their way out to the hall, where the bag of shopping, including the very good soup, was propped against the table, while Janice Harper's letter lay on the antique desk in the sun, amongst old fountain pens, and letters from the past.

10

'He's written back,' said Janice, heaving in provisions. She set the bags on the kitchen table, and numberless dogs on the hearth got up, stretched, and came to have a look.

'William?' asked Mary, turning from the sink. Enormous and impenetrable heaps of washing filled it; her sleeves were rolled up to her elbows, her pinafore soaking.

'Yes. You need a machine,' Janice added, nudging away three hairy lurchers and the red-eyed bassett-hound. She unpacked the tins of Saversoup, and flimsy economy packs of toilet rolls: she stacked up tins of Chum. 'No one on the planet washes by hand any more.'

'More fool them.' Mary held up a pair of Ernie's trousers. Pitch-black water streamed from the turn-ups.

'Ugh,' said Janice. 'Yuk. How can you?'

'Pounding and beating,' said Mary, flinging them back in the sink. 'That's what gets the dirt out, and we can't afford a machine.'

'Rubbish.' Janice piled up the tinned steamed puddings, put the bags of dog biscuits in their corner, pushing away a narrow-nosed collie. 'I've told you a million times you can get them on instalments. Argos. Curry's. Anywhere, for God's sake.'

'Hire purchase.' Mary was full of distaste. 'The beginning of the end.'

'You don't even have to pay interest. Not any more.'

'Why don't they give them away, then?'

Footsteps sounded on the creaking boards above, and came down the stairs, with their dangerous carpet, rodless and frayed. The latch on the bottom was raised with a click: dogs padded over at once.

'What have you been doing up there all morning?' demanded Mary.

Sophie closed the door and smiled sweetly at Janice, from within the circle of hounds. She was wearing a sky-blue nylon polo neck beneath a pinafore trimmed in purple, and her hair was hooked up with a cheerful new slide on which two cockatoos with vast yellow combs swung on a perch beneath an arch of brilliant foliage.

'You look nice,' said Janice, taking out custard creams and Bourbons.

'Titivating.' Mary sloshed violently in the sink. 'Preening in the mirror. Who cares? Who cares what you look like? There's work to be done down here.'

'You could have a washing machine and time to titivate, too.' Janice shook out the last of the carrier bags and folded it.

Mary sniffed. 'It's been a long time since I sat looking in mirrors.'

'Just as well.' Ernie's sepulchral voice sounded from the passage. A blast of snow-laden air blew behind him and all the dogs rushed towards it. He banged the door to.

'Oh, let them out,' Mary shouted, and yanked up the plug from the sink.

'Good day for washing, I must say.' Ernie came padding across the floor as the dogs all raced past him.

'Why don't you do it, then?' she asked him, wrenching on the taps. They leapt about unnervingly.

'Why don't you buy a machine?' asked Janice again.

'Debt!' yelled Mary, and they all stepped back. 'Debt and the poorhouse!'

Sophie's hands went to her mouth.

'What's this?' asked Ernie, making for his chair.

'Mother,' said Sophie, biting her lip. 'Mother taught us never, never — '

'Never to get into debt,' said Mary, and turned off the gushing taps with determination. 'And she was right.'

'She was.' Ernie settled into his chair and those dogs remaining, a small brown creature of indeterminate breed, and Flossie, the ancient spaniel-cross, settled down at his feet with a sigh. 'When we want, we wait,' he told Janice.

'The credit card is not for us,' said Sophie, eyeing the Bourbon biscuits.

'Neither a borrower nor a lender be.' Mary turned back to her rinsing with finality.

'Don't suppose you've got any baccy,' Ernie enquired of Janice.

'No,' she said, tugging open the ill-fitting drawer in the kitchen table, stuffing the folded bags inside. 'I don't suppose I have.'

London had got to be better than this.

* * *

'Doesn't anyone want to hear about my letter?' she asked, a little later, when everyone had calmed down. The house dogs were outside, sniffing about in the patches of snow, nosing up at those in the pens, skimpy little old ones shivering inside the porch. Beyond the fence, the field was a map of white and green, the last snowy islands shrinking beneath the morning sun.

In here, the tea was made, the range refilled, and Sophie had swept the floor of dog hair. The desperate heaps of washing lay inert in the sink and Mary was at last sitting down, reaching for the sugar. Janice had given Ernie a shred or two of Golden Virginia, so he was happy now. She felt in her pocket and pulled out the letter from William Harriman.

'*Dear Miss Harper,*' she read aloud, and they all settled back to listen. She had at once a vision of them all as children — a state of being curiously close to them still: three pre-war children, stuck out here in the back of beyond without even any electricity, sitting round the table — could it have been this table? — waiting for bread and jam, and being good.

'*Thank you so much for your letter, to which I have given much thought.*'

What a lovely, graceful line. It fell upon the snow-lit kitchen, and upon the strangeness of the lives within it, like a phrase of music.

'*I should very much like to be able to help you, and since I live alone, in a roomy old family house, and am not as young as I was, it would make perfect sense for me to have a lodger . . .'*

'There!' Mary was triumphant.

'A roomy old family house,' murmured Sophie, gazing about her.

'Bit different from this one, I expect,' said Ernie. He rubbed his knees. 'It's freezing, out there in that trailer.'

'Don't start.' Mary looked at Janice with flinty bright eyes. 'Carry on.'

'*However,*' read Janice, wondering again how Ernie did, indeed, survive in his leaky tin dwelling, '*I have to confess to some mixed feelings. Chiefly, these relate to my son, Matthew, whom my cousins may remember from one or two childhood visits.*' She looked up, enquiringly.

'Dear little boy,' said Sophie.

'Him and his sister.' Ernie blew smoke into the air and watched it dissolve, and vanish.

'*Since the death of my dear wife, Eve, Matthew and my daughter and her family have become the chief focus of my life, and about Matthew I have particular anxieties. He suffered a breakdown some years ago, and has for a long time been in hospital.*'

Janice looked up, to see the effect of this news, and was met with total incomprehension all round. 'Hospital,' said Sophie sadly, at last, and touched the two bright cockatoos on her slide, swinging on their perch.

'Go on,' said Mary, reaching for the teapot.

'*He still is not well enough to live on his own,*' read Janice. '*My hope and dream is that one day he will come home, and if that were to happen I don't think I should want to have to worry about anything else. On the other hand, I have, as I say, plenty of space here now, in which I rattle about, with my wife's little dog, Danny. Like me, he has seen the last of his youth, but I think there is life in both of us yet.'*

'There was always life in William,' said Mary.

'He sounds a dear little thing,' said Sophie. 'Danny. What breed, I wonder?'

Janice turned the page. The handwriting was like no other handwriting she had ever seen — it made her think of museums, and manuscripts, and shafts of light.

'Dachshund,' Mary said briskly. 'That's what I seem to recall. Smooth-haired.'

'*I am not without interests*,' the letter continued, '*as you yourself clearly are not. (I do like the sound of your cakes.) I run an antiques stall — china and glass — with my dear wife's oldest friend, which is great fun. I read a great deal, and am thinking of taking up painting. I see my grandchildren as often as I can. In other words I am not, I hope, someone who needs to 'get a life', as I think the phrase is nowadays.*'

'More than you can say here,' said Ernie, stubbing out the last shred of roll-up on the hearth with the heel of his stockinged foot.

'Don't do that!' Mary was on to him at once. 'No wonder they're all in holes.' She turned back to Janice. 'So what's the top and tail of it, then? What's he decided?'

'*So what am I saying?*' Janice read out, each of them hanging on every word. '*I think the position is that I could offer you temporary accommodation, while you find your feet in London. You could stay in the spare room, for minimal rent, for, let us say, a period of three months. I should expect you to look for a job — I did have something in mind, with my daughter's family, but my daughter must speak for herself, and I don't know if it would suit either of you. Essentially —'* Here there was a long, elegant dash. '*Essentially I am used to having the house to myself, and am perhaps a little cautious at the idea of sharing it. So if this does not sound too unwelcoming, and you would be happy to settle for bed and breakfast and supper on occasion — I could give you your own kitchen cupboard, of course — then by all means do come and stay.*

'*I shall wait to hear from you, and, if all this sounds acceptable, I look forward very much to meeting you. I am really a very friendly person, and Danny is certainly a very friendly dog. Yours sincerely, William Harriman.*'

'There!' Mary said again, and put down her mug. 'Just the ticket.'

'I don't know why you're so anxious to be rid of me,' said Janice, laying the letter down. 'Who will do all your shopping?' She pictured them, standing at the bus stop in all weathers, in their belted coats and ancient headwear; trudging through Oswestry or Shrewsbury with plastic holdalls, hauling sacks of dog biscuits. Poor old bats. And all that dog walking: how would they manage that?

'There's a PS,' she added, and read it out to

them. '*Do tell me — what is a Dog Museum?*'

Sophie was filled with wonder. 'To think he doesn't know.' She turned to Mary, fingering her slide. 'Didn't you tell William? When you wrote? Doesn't he know what we do?'

'He knows we have dogs,' said Mary shortly. 'I can't remember what else I've said.' She got up, and went to look out of the back window, where snow was sliding in clumps down the corrugated-iron roofs of the huts, shut up for the winter. No one came in winter, ever: couldn't expect it. But in the spring —

The dogs outside sensed her presence, and came over, in twos and threes. They stood in the snow beneath the window, looking up at her. Flossie barked. She was a poor old thing who'd had too many litters. Mary had found her shut up in a barn on old Jim Walsh's land — he was a wicked old bugger. She'd been out with the pack on a summer afternoon in 1997, and heard a whining. When she broke into the barn she knew at once there were puppies, could sense it, and saw them all, right at the back without even a piece of sacking, and the bitch sucked dry and thin as a bone. 'You come with me,' said Mary, and took the lot of them, the puppies in her holdall and the bitch called Flossie — she generally knew their names as soon as she saw them — slipping in at once with the pack, her tail between her legs, drooping dugs swinging back and forth, pattering weakly down the lane. The sun was high and the air still; the lane was full of cowpats. Mary led them all home and gave Flossie a vast bowl of milk. The four pups were almost beyond saving, but she saved them, all except one, which Ernie buried. He was used to that, though he didn't like it. She found homes for two, and the last was here now: Jip, with his mother, just as it should be, both with their operations done, and that cost a fortune, every time. But this was her life's work, the work of all of them, and she wouldn't have it any other way.

'We'll manage,' she said to Janice, turning to look at them all, two weaklings, both a bit soft in the head, and a fit young girl. 'You get a life,' she told her. 'Seize your chances.'

* * *

Janice went walking, up in the hills. Her black woollen hat was pulled down as low as it would go, her scarf wound tightly round her mouth. She wore two pairs of gloves, and a vest, T-shirt and two jumpers under her army surplus jacket, lined with dung-coloured fleece. It weighed a ton. There were two pairs of socks inside her walking boots, one thin, one thick. She knew how to dress for the country, for walking this lot: she was boiling now, though high up the snow was still thick and looked likely to freeze tonight. The dogs were off their leads, which she'd slung round her neck, or stuffed in her pockets. They'd gone streaming off in all directions, and though one or two little ones wanted carrying she wouldn't give in, not yet — they needed exercise, do them good, bit of snow wouldn't hurt them.

In summer, the problem was always the sheep.

Mostly, the dogs were well trained and not all that interested, but there were two or three you had to keep an eye on all the time. No question, with any of them, of going through the fields, lambs or no lambs, but up here it was generally OK. A couple of heads would come up in the bracken, or you'd round a corner and hear them, cropping the turf. They'd take one look at the dogs and scatter, bouncing off up the slope, or down into a dip. Janice would whistle and shout, the dogs would wheel round to her, and the ewes would pick up grazing as if nothing had happened. Now they were almost all down on the lower slopes, or inside for lambing, though now and then you'd suddenly see a tough old blackface with tight horns and mad yellow eyes come looming out of the snow at you. She supposed there might be one or two buried in drifts, but the thaw was on its way: they'd come out, look around, and trot away, as if nothing had happened. Thick. She knew about sheep, like she knew about old people, now.

Some old people, anyway. This lot. Her gran, and her gran's friends. Albert Page. She didn't know about William Harriman, who had seen the last of his youth but still had life in him. She strode along the hillside track, the letter in its vellum envelope tucked back inside her trouser pocket.

I should very much like to be able to help you, and since I live alone, in a roomy old family house . . . I am a little anxious at the prospect of sharing it . . .

Was that what he had said? Something like

that. She realised that though she did not have the letter quite by heart, already his style, and the rhythms of his prose, had begun to feel familiar, though she knew no one else who wrote, or spoke, like that. Steve, when he flew back from Marrakech, was probably the only other person she knew who would appreciate it.

Since the death of my dear wife, Eve . . . I run an antiques china stall, read a great deal, and am thinking of taking up painting . . .

A voice from another age, urbane and courteous. A fountain pen, flowing over the creamy pages, from his roomy London house. Something which Janice had not known was missing from her life was answered by all of this. She strode along the wintry track, watching the dogs race up and down the slopes, slipping in falls of snow, barking and shaking themselves, and turned over well-made phrases in her mind.

And what did you wear in London? she wondered, boiling in her layers and fleecy lining. Not army surplus, that was for sure. Would she look a right idiot down there? Would she sound a right idiot, every time she opened her mouth?

The sky was cold and clear, though cloud was gathering. Janice rounded a bend and stood looking down the hillside.

Ah. There it was.

Preoccupied as she had been with the prospect of another life, it had not escaped her attention that she was in the folds of the hills of Wenlock Edge wherein lay Eric Lammering's shepherd's hut.

There it was, nestled in the snow, with his bike

parked under the lean-to.

She could see, from her vantage point up here, the rising plume of smoke from the chimney, set on the sloping patched slate roof. He was there, the bastard, there by the roaring fire with his glass of whisky and who knows what poor fool of a girl, taking her clothes off on a winter afternoon, thinking the snow and the firelight so romantic, just as she, Janice Harper, idiot, had thought the drumming rain and howling wind.

She bent down, and from the melting snow picked up a stone. She rubbed it against her jacket, and then she hurled it, up in an arc, and watched its distant, symbolic fall on the lower slopes.

'So much for you!' she shouted, and at once the dogs were all round her, barking, looking out to the place where the stone had fallen and back at her, tongues hanging out, eyes eager.

Serve him right if she unleashed the lot of them down there. Set a pack of dogs on him, that's what she should do.

Instead —

'Come on,' she called to them, and turned, whistling them to heel, not looking back. They all swerved to follow, and then race past her, as she bent and threw another stone, as far as she could, back along the way they had come, back towards the museum. Off they all went after it, except for little Pip, Ernie's Yorkie, who stood there trembling in the snow, looking up at her beseechingly.

This time she took pity, bent down and picked him up, wrapping him deep inside her heavy jacket, striding after Doberman and Dalmatian-cross, collie and lurcher, greyhound and spaniel and God knows what, streaming away through the Shropshire hills as the winter sun slipped down.

* * *

That night, in her stuffy bedroom, with its Anaglypta wallpaper, Marks & Spencer tie-back curtains and louvred cupboards from Homebase, she wrote to William Harriman, thanking him for his kind offer.

I will look for a job and try not to get in your way, she wrote. *PS The Dog Museum is run by your cousins as a charity to support their work with rescued strays. It is probably unique. I will tell you all about it. PPS I am a vegan.*

* * *

'I've done it,' William told Buffy. The snow had gone, the rain had returned, they were sitting at the stall on Saturday morning. Things felt pretty much back to normal.

'What's that?' asked Buffy, unscrewing the Thermos.

'Arranged for the lodger. The Shropshire lass.'

'Oh.' Buffy poured scalding coffee into the plastic beaker with concentration. Her grip was not as it used to be. She passed the beaker to William. 'Well. There's a thing. And when's she coming?'

'In a couple of weeks — I expect she's got

things to sort out up there, and I'll have to get ready, too. Clear out the cupboards and things.'

'Yes, yes, of course.' Buffy sat back with her cup. The stall was a little thin today, and the market quiet. No one was spending much after Christmas and then the sales. And now the bloody rain again. Even Danny, curled up on William's old jacket on the fold-up chair beside her, looked a bit glum. She gave him a little pat.

'Which room are you giving her?' she asked, thinking of the pretty spare room where she had spent Christmas, with its soft satin eiderdown, and curtains from Ruffle and Tuck.

'Claire's room,' said William, stretching his long legs out beneath the stall. 'I think that'll do. I want to hang on to the spare room, just in case, and of course she can't have Matthew's.'

'No, of course not. Claire won't mind, will she?'

'I shouldn't think so. Why should she?' William put down the beaker, and looked at Buffy. 'Do you think she will? Do you think I should make it the spare room?'

'Oh, William. No. Do what you want, dear, it's your house. Claire has her own life now — how could she possibly mind?'

William was silent. 'I'd hate to upset her again,' he said at last.

'You won't,' said Buffy firmly. 'And anyway, it's not going to be for ever, is it?'

'No, no, it's a temporary arrangement. I've made that quite clear. Just while she finds a job and gets settled. She won't want to hang around with an old codger like me once she's got into the swing.'

Buffy touched his hand, with her fingerless knitted gloves. 'No one,' she said, 'in a million years, could ever call you an old codger.'

He gave her his meltingly beautiful smile.

* * *

A week later, Janice said goodbye to Steve, back from Marrakech and perky, until she told him.

'You can't,' he said. 'You haven't even given notice.'

'I'm giving it now,' said Janice, lighting up. The snow had all gone and now it was raining again, great dark sweeps of it blowing over the Ridge. The windows of Cloud Nine were almost black, and the tea urn had never hissed more comfortingly. 'Let's face it,' she said, inhaling deeply, 'no one is going to come here for weeks. You don't need me. You do not need me,' she said again with emphasis, seeing his face. 'If you can't make tea and sandwiches twice a week you're not fit to call yourself proprietor.'

'The cakes,' he said sadly. 'What about the cakes?'

'There's two in the fridge.'

'I've never really understood,' he said, suntanned and gorgeous beneath spiked hair, 'how you could be a vegan and make them. Cakes are the hardest thing. There's no substitute for eggs, in a cake.'

'Tell that to Albert Page,' said Janice. 'He lived

on dried egg through two world wars.' She had felt sorry, saying goodbye to him.

'I might never see you again,' he said, trembling at the door.

''Course you will,' she told him, giving him a peck on his papery old cheek. 'And the social worker will be in tomorrow.'

'Social.' He snorted. 'I don't want no social. They'll put me in a home.'

'No they won't,' said Janice, knowing they probably would.

'Dried egg is still egg,' said Steve. 'How can you cook with eggs and dairy foods and call yourself a vegan?'

'Vegan is as vegan does.' Janice sipped her tea. 'I don't *eat* all that stuff. It does not pass my lips.'

'Not what I call proper vegan.'

'I have to live, don't I? Stop going on about it. Who did you meet in Marrakech?'

'No one.' He took her hand. 'Please stay.'

Janice looked at the hand. 'I thought you were gay.'

'I am. I just like you, that's all.'

'I like you too, and I'm going to London.'

* * *

She said goodbye to Mary and Sophie and Ernie, and that was hard.

'But you're doing the right thing,' said Sophie bravely. She was wearing the dolphins today, leaping joyously out of crested waves. 'You'll have a good time, I expect.'

‘’Course she will,’ said Ernie. ‘Don’t get too posh.’

‘She’ll do what she wants,’ said Mary.

They all crowded into the porch. Rain dripped from the tiles, the dogs stood looking out. Janice counted nine heads, poking their noses in the gaps between pinafore and frayed tweed jacket.

‘Goodbye and good luck,’ she said quickly. ‘I’ll probably be back in a week, let’s face it.’

She turned and ran ducking through the rain to her bike, and rode away in great sprays of water.

* * *

‘Dulwich?’ said her mother. ‘Who lives in Dulwich?’

‘William Harriman. He’s a retired civil servant. From the Treasury. He has a dachshund and two grown-up children and collects old china.’

‘And how did you find him?’

Janice explained and her parents whitened.

‘A relative of those barmy old — ’

‘He’s different,’ said Janice. ‘He’s completely different and I’m going and that’s that.’

They saw her off at the station, on a windswept afternoon. Rain blew in drifts from the platform roof and dripped from the baskets of trailing ivy. Janice, on her Apex single ticket, sat in a corner of the only smoking carriage, and waved with the greatest sense of relief she had ever felt in her life.

11

'Now, then,' said Buffy, starting the day. 'Now, then.'

What a business it was, getting going. She sat on the bedroom chair, and tugged.

The thing was to keep to a routine: she'd realised that years ago, almost as soon as she'd retired. While you were working, the prospect of unfettered days, with a lie-in whenever you wanted, was perfect bliss. It hadn't taken long to realise that lie-ins, and laxity, were a great mistake. She looked back on those early days — gazing mournfully out at the traffic, and pigeons on rooftops, tending her window-box geraniums as if they were the only thing that mattered — with something approaching horror. The china stall had saved her, a whole new lease of life begun, and the Mary Ward Over-Sixties Club had been a revelation.

Had she wanted, she could have filled every day with activities in Queen Square: Keep Fit, Computer Skills, Sculpture, Writing for Pleasure, Making Music, Circle Dancing. There were even trips to Paris. She opted for Choral Singing, and for Computer Skills — which, had she had them, might have delayed her retirement, but she'd felt such a fool, in the office, peering at the screen, trying to click in the right place and always missing, while people sighed, and said they must go to lunch. Once she could go at her own pace, with none of it mattering, not the way it did when you were getting paid for it, she found she was rather a whizz. Well, she could do it: get on to the Web, type things and print them, set up files and even send attachments, though this last was of minimal interest: she had nothing to attach, and no one to send it to anyway. She did, however, now have an e-mail address: buffy@hotmail.com. At first, she used this for very little, opening it up in the computer room at Mary Ward on Wednesdays and finding nothing there except, now and then, an encouraging word from her tutor.

Good morning, Buffy. Nice to have you with us today.

It was meant very kindly, but she had hoped for more. Who from? Who might she send to? No one she knew was on e-mail at home, and although once or twice she had triumphantly sent word to the office, where everyone now sat gazing all day at their screens, and though Mr Lawson sent back *Hello, Buffy! Wonderful to hear from you electronically! How is retirement?*, she knew she must let them get on. Nothing worse than clinging like a mollusc: once you had gone, you had gone. That was work for you. Forty years, and nobody gave a damn. Anyway, e-mail was just for fun, she didn't *need* it.

Then, one afternoon, just as she'd got home from the Mary Ward and was putting the kettle on, the telephone rang.

'Good afternoon. Is that Miss Henderson?'

The voice was young, and rather nice, and male.

'Who's that?' asked Buffy, her mind racing.

'This is the Friends of the Earth,' said the voice. 'My name's Nick, I'm calling from our fund-raising department. Is this a convenient moment?'

Buffy looked at the receiver, just as they did in films. Now she knew why.

'How did you get my number?' she demanded.

'From the phone book,' nice Nick said mildly.

'What do you want?'

'I was coming to that. We're looking for new subscribers, people who really care about the environment and want to make the world a better place. Do you know about our work?'

Buffy said: 'This is outrageous.' She could hear the kettle coming to the boil; she was dying for a cup. 'What do you mean, telephoning people out of the blue, intruding on people's privacy?'

'I'm dreadfully sorry,' said Nick. 'Would you prefer to have something sent in the post? It's just that people get so much mail these days — sometimes they prefer a personal call.'

'Well, I don't,' said Buffy, hearing the kettle click. 'I think it's a nerve. It's like those people selling double-glazing, or damp-proofing, who ring just as you're getting the supper. 'We're in your area, this is a courtesy call.''

'That's different,' said Nick, in his nice young voice. 'This is something important.'

And she knew, all at once, that it was.

That had been the beginning. Before she knew it, Buffy, who for much of her life had felt on the edge of things — working at jobs she didn't much care for, helping her mother look after her father, then looking after her mother — found herself with interests and a cause. Packing up her mother's flat, washing and putting the china in boxes, she had realised that china was something she had always really loved, and the idea for the stall had come to her, just like that. Now she knew all about Spode. At Mary Ward she found she could click a mouse, and sing. She came home humming Handel, let herself go in the bath with Hubert Parry, learned to like Britten.

Then, with Friends of the Earth, her eyes were opened. What use to sing, when the songbirds choked on pesticide? There was lead in petrol, there were oil spills in oceans. The hole in the ozone layer was growing larger, chemicals seeped into the soil from which harvests grew. Even bread was risky.

She threw herself into it all.

Caught up with campaigning, collecting on corners and leafleting every household in W8, had saved, if not the world, then Buffy herself, in the long dark months after Eve's so sudden, dreadful descent into illness and death. Poor Eve, sweet Eve — her oldest and most loyal friend. Poor, poor William, who, at the funeral, with that broken boy beside him, and Claire sobbing her heart out, had looked quite haunted. His companion of a lifetime gone — there had, for William, never been anyone but Eve. Fortunate Eve, Buffy allowed herself to think later, as she had thought on their wedding day, throwing confetti after the departing car, going home for tea with Mother. And poor me, she thought, though she hated self-pity.

But without the cheery Saturdays in Portobello, without the drives out to the sales, boxes and hamper in the back — how bleak the week felt now, all of a sudden. There was nothing like old friends. There was nothing like finding, on some dusty trestle, a perfect Minton bowl without a chip. 'I say — do come and look at this.' So companionable, such fun. Of course, she could run the stall by herself, but it wasn't the same: she tried it, and it felt quite horribly lonely, packing up afterwards, carrying boxes back to the empty flat.

Environmental campaigning saw her through. As secretary to her local FoE group, she was in touch with other groups, on mailing lists for meetings. When she opened up her e-mail, there were lots.

Looking back, Buffy thought now that those days in the eighties had been quite innocent, compared with what went on now. She had joined Friends of the Earth before Genetically Modified was — as it were — on anyone's lips; before BSE; before Dolly had been cloned or the weather, so unnervingly, had begun to change.

'We're ruining the *climate*, William,' she told him. Why couldn't he see?

* * *

Recently, however, it was not just — just! — the ceaseless rain, and the television pictures of storm-lashed coasts and burst embankments, which kept Buffy awake at night. Her body, to which, for decades, she had given little thought, was making itself known to her in divers troublesome ways. Even without a hot drink last thing — and she missed the comforting cocoa — she was forever getting up in the night. Staying with William at Christmas, she'd had to stumble along to the bathroom in the small hours, wondering whether she was waking him with the flush: not once, but twice. So embarrassing, though of course he was so well bred that he would never have mentioned it.

Now — horrors — she seemed to be suffering from constipation. She had never thought she might gaze at a bottle of Senakot as if it were a friend, but so it was. Even this didn't always do the trick. And her clothes felt uncomfortable, in more than the usual after-Christmas way. She found herself wearing her skirts unbuttoned at the waist, and, on coming home after classes, desperate to put her feet up. Her feet weren't quite right, either — even K shoes needed stretching. She felt the cold much more: sitting at the stall on Saturdays required layer after layer, and a rug right over her knees. And her knees weren't right — oh, what an effort to climb the stairs to her singing class, to climb the stairs to the flat.

In short, my dear, she told herself this morning, struggling into her tights, in short you are not as you were. Not that that had ever been anything much to write home about.

She got to her feet, heaving up M & S sixty-denier over her bulging bottom. The curtains were still drawn; the bedside lamp cast its glow upon the room, reflecting, in the wardrobe mirror, the heap of quilt, the tea tray, *Antiques Review* and cold hot-water bottle, and Buffy, getting dressed. She caught sight of herself, and was, for a moment, horrified. Surely she didn't really look like that. Surely her tummy had never been — and wasn't now — so vast. She moved quickly to open the wardrobe door, to take out her skirt and Jaeger cardigan. Generally speaking, she considered this mirror her friend. Certainly, it showed her, in the familiar privacy of her bedroom, an infinitely kinder version of herself than the one you were liable to behold in the all-round glass of a John Lewis cubicle, where, frankly, until you had the garments on, it was better simply not to look. To see oneself at every *angle*, beneath that unforgiving neon —

Buffy zipped up her skirt, as far as it would go. No question of the waistband button — *how* had she got so fat?

'I think of myself as medium-sized,' she said aloud, and put on, over her thermal vest, her pin-striped shirt, and grey cashmere cardigan. Then she swung the door to again, and had another look. There — that was better, that wasn't too bad at all. Couldn't go wrong with cashmere, couldn't go wrong with grey, and silver earrings. She brushed her hair into its knot, with its tortoiseshell slide, put on her strand of pearls, worn every day for perhaps a dozen years — it didn't matter, it was a classic, classics were a part of you — and put in her earrings. When she'd done her face, she could face the world. Do it after breakfast; she could feel her tummy rumbling.

She drew back the curtains, looked out on to the rainswept road. Half past eight on a Wednesday morning, and London going to work, as for forty years Buffy had done, queuing at the bus stop, fighting through the Tube — never, never again — buying her poppy-seed cream cheese rolls in the sandwich bar at lunchtime, eating them at her desk with Anita Brookner — *that* was someone she would never read again — clattering away for years on Remington, Adler, Olivetti, in the days before Olivetti sounded like something you'd have for lunch in Islington. Taking down shorthand and typing it up again, for all those men — surveyors, solicitors, property developers, insurance brokers. Not one had asked her out. No, that wasn't true. There had been birthday lunches — their birthdays — and sometimes a quick drink at the end of the day. On the whole, though — no. Mr Lawson, to whom, for her last ten years in the saddle, she had been quite a good PA: he had been kind, the only one ever to ask when *her* birthday was, though he had forgotten the very next year. But he himself led a less than vigorous life, she could tell. Up and down for thirty-five years to Haywards Heath: what kind of life was that for a man?

Anyway, it was all long since behind her now, and watching the scurry of Notting Hill below her, the snow all gone and the rain just pouring down, Buffy was glad. She watched the mad dash from the newsagent's, the rush down the steps of the Tube, the soaking-wet wait for the bus, and then she took her tray and cold hot-water bottle through to the little kitchen, put on the wireless and boiled herself a very nice free-range egg.

* * *

Wednesday was Choral Singing: heaven.

'Blest pair of sirens, pledges of heav'n's joy . . . ' sang Buffy, washing up.

The class began at two, and when it had finished they all had tea downstairs. Surely the graceful, interconnecting houses in Queen Square which made up the Mary Ward Centre gave room to one of the happiest places in London. From the art studio on the top floor to the ground-floor vegetarian café, it was alive and bustling with activity. In the writing class you could hear the choir; on the stairs — broad, shallow, but an effort, it had to be said — you could smell oil paint and baking. In the spring you glimpsed people with learning disabilities contentedly potting petunias; in summer, with the windows open wide, you could hear, as you walked through the square, the drifting notes of piano and recorder. People learnt French and Italian; you could do TEFL and ESOL and TESOL, and receive free legal advice. The girls on the desk were kind and smiling, the tutors cheerful.

Now and then a melancholy stray student or two wandered in for a meeting: these came from a nearby college of London University, where they took things more seriously. One of the most lugubrious-looking men Buffy had ever seen in her life turned out, at the Christmas party, to be studying Psychoanalysis & Literature. He started to talk about Freud, and she hurried away.

'Where the bright Se-ra-phim, in burning row, / Their loud, up-lifted angel-trumpets blow . . . ' she sang now, washing up the breakfast things. She put away eggcup and saucer, and went into the sitting room.

A mailshot awaited: the desk was piled high, leaflets on one side, envelopes on another, stamps, and the long list of names and addresses, in the middle. That would keep her busy until lunch-time, and no mistake. After which, rain or no rain, she would set off.

She tidied up a bit, and settled down.

Greenhouse gas emissions — do you care?

Buffy sat licking and sticking, in her small west London flat, in her lamplit sitting room, with its walls of antique rose, and plumped-up cushions. The bedroom wasn't large, and the kitchen and bathroom bordered on the poky, but the sitting room, with its comfortable sofa before the television and china wall plates, with Mother's inlaid desk, and the Sutherland table up against the wall — things in here, thought Buffy, writing out an address in Shropshire, certainly could be worse.

The excessive burning of oil, gas and coal is raising our planet's thermostat to unacceptable levels . . .

Would they realise, in Shropshire, just how bad things were? Buffy wondered, putting the envelope on to the pile. In Herefordshire, the floods had been fearful — two years ago a whole pig farm had been drowned. But Shropshire? She pictured a place a little less dramatic, softer, less ancient, and more prosperous.

The battle against the carbon-belching corporations has begun . . .

Buffy reached for the next envelope, crossed off the last address. Now where was she? Northumberland. Bare craggy hills, sheep huddled in snowdrifts, grey stone farmhouses, thick-walled barns. That was the pleasant thing about mailing lists — you could, in a more frivolous frame of mind, travel all over the country in a single morning.

The rain splashed into her window boxes, where the first shoots of crocuses and narcissi were nosing up.

'Hymns devout and ho-ly, devout and ho-ly psalms,' sang Buffy, and picked up the ringing phone.

'Good morning, Buffy.'

'William.' She put down her pen. 'How nice to hear you.'

'Filthy morning.'

'Isn't it? I'm doing a mailing list, about greenhouse gas emissions.'

'Ah. I'm interrupting you.'

'No, no,' she said quickly, 'I didn't mean that at all. How are you?'

'Fine. Very well. I thought I'd let you know she's arrived.'

For a moment, her mind full of fossil fuels and the Kyoto Summit, Buffy couldn't think what he meant.

'The lodger,' said William. 'The Shropshire lass. She got here last night. I rather like her.'

'Oh.'

'She's absolutely not a London person, but I think she'll fit in quite well. Danny likes her. She says she's used to dogs.'

'Oh. Good.'

'I'll probably take her out and about a bit later, so she can get her bearings.'

'That's a good idea.'

She pushed her pen back and forth on the blotter, letting all this sink in. 'Tell me a bit more about her.'

'Well,' said William, with some enthusiasm, 'she's quite nice to look at. Tall, and pretty supple, I suppose. She's done a lot of cycling. Short dark hair, nice country skin — I don't know what else. But easy on the eye, in a boyish sort of way.'

'Boyish,' said Buffy.

'Sort of. Perhaps that's not the right word — she's certainly not what I'd call masculine.' He gave a little laugh. 'If Claire were here she'd say I was obsessed with gender.'

'Is that the kind of thing she says these days? No wonder she's unhappy.' Buffy could hear herself sounding sharp.

'Are you all right?' asked William.

'Fine.'

'Only you sound a bit — '

'I'm fine. Perhaps I'd better get on — I've got to get this in the post, and it's my singing this afternoon.'

'What a busy person you are — I'll let you go.

See you on Saturday. I've found a rather pretty little jug and sugar bowl.'

'Very good,' said Buffy, and put the phone down. She picked up the next leaflet.

The icecap in the Arctic Ocean is melting fast . . .

She stuffed it into the Northumberland envelope, and put on a stamp. The glue was beginning to make her feel queasy — she should have one of those little sponges in a dish. Well, she hadn't. She turned in her chair, to take a breather. The rain was falling faster and the sky was black as pitch. She'd put another light on. Lights on in the *morning* — what a waste, and it all contributed. The icecap was melting, and she, who cared, was using electricity in daylight. It was all a vicious circle.

Buffy got up, and switched on the lamp by the sofa. That was a bit better. But oh — how quiet it was, up here. Only the falling rain, the tick of Mother's carriage clock. She looked at her desk, with its heaps of dreadful news. Walking back to it, she caught sight of herself in the mirror over the Sutherland table, saw such a grey-looking person without her lipstick, someone to whom you wouldn't give a second glance. She licked her lips, which were dry with stamp glue.

'I was feeling quite happy,' she said aloud.

* * *

'Where the bright Se-ra-phim, in burn-ing row, / Their loud, up-lift-ed an-gel Trum-pets blow . . . '

Their voices rose into the brightly lit upper

room; the piano was triumphant; the rain was blowing away across Queen Square.

'Oh, may we *soon* a-gain re-*new* that *song*, / and *keep* in tune with Heaven . . . '

Michael, their young conductor, was in rapture, urging them on.

'To live with *Him*, and sing in *end*-less morn / of light . . . '

But this, like the beginning, was in eight parts, and Buffy found herself stumbling.

'To live with *Him* . . . '

An A sharp or A natural? Whatever it was, she couldn't get it.

And she gave up, and let the voices all round her soar confidently and joyously towards the ceiling.

'And sing in end-less *morn*, in *end*-less morn, in / *end*-less *morn* . . . '

'Right!' said Michael, looking at his watch. 'That's it — well done, see you all next week.' And they all trooped down to the café.

'Such a *tonic*,' said Sylvie Strauss, standing next to Buffy in the queue at the counter. 'Don't you just love Parry?' Sylvie was from New York, had come to London when her husband had relocated his business, in the seventies, and just fallen in love with it. Poor Ray had passed away in 1992, but she had made a good life for herself here, and hardly thought at all about going back.

'I do like it,' said Buffy, picking up a piece of carrot cake, 'but I'm afraid I'm not quite up to the eight-part sections.'

'You're a second alto? You know, I think that's harder. Up at the front with the firsts — I think we're that little bit stronger in numbers. I'll have an Earl Grey, please,' Sylvie said to the girl at the counter. 'Just a dash of milk, that's perfect, thank you so much.'

They carried the trays to the last remaining window seats. Dorothy and Stanley were already there, their macs slung over the chairs; all around them, the tables were filling up, and they could hear the front door bang open and shut, and the thunder of feet up and down the uncarpeted stairs. Stanley, who used to work for Camden Council Parks and Gardens, was staying on for Circle Dancing; had already, in the morning, done Life Drawing with Elsbeth Fermor, who'd trained at the Slade. He opened his shoulder bag, laying it flat on the table to put away his music. Buffy glimpsed within it a tin of pencils, a recorder, a pad of drawing paper and a heap of cassettes. He zipped it all up with a flourish, and took it away from the teacups.

'Such a dear old boy,' Buffy had said to William, describing the various members of the choir at Christmas, as they'd walked up the street after midnight Mass, under his umbrella. 'Left school at fourteen, all his life out in all weathers, never married, never done anything much — and now: he's an inspiration.'

'Sounds splendid,' said William, unlocking the front door. 'Rather like you, dear. How about a nightcap before we turn in?'

They'd sat before the banked-up fire with their brandy, yawning.

Oh well, thought Buffy now, shaking her sweetener into her tea. Oh well. Never mind.

The rain had gone but the light was fading: she sat looking out at the darkening square, and the toings and froings of students in the street. A group of young Italians was smoking out on the steps: they were lissom and dark and stylish, casually draping their arms over one another's shoulders, stubbing out their cigarettes, leaning against the wet railings, laughing.

'Are you all right?' asked Dorothy, the oldest soprano in the choir.

Buffy turned to her, saw a kindly look.

'Not quite yourself today?'

'I'm absolutely fine,' said Buffy, pulling herself together, and she was, why ever shouldn't she be? 'And I must give you all one of these.' She rummaged in her bag for the leaflets, and put them on the table, brushing crumbs away. 'Do take one — I'm on a new subscription drive.'

Amidst the tea cups a fierce plume of burning oil rose into the sky. Choking dark smoke blew over a tiny moon.

12

He had met her on the platform. She knew him at once, as the train pulled in: the tall, greying, well-proportioned man in his winter coat and stylishly knotted sea-green scarf, waiting in the grey afternoon with the bright little dachshund on his leash. And William, as the doors banged open and shut, saw a lean young woman in jeans and black woollen hat heave out a nylon grip and come striding down towards him — and of course this must be her, who else? He waited, the nervous excitement he had felt all morning subsiding suddenly as a lifetime's courtesy took over.

'Miss Harper?' He held out his leather-gloved hand.

'That's me.' She was fresh faced and fit, and she shook hands properly, not like some limp-wristed girl.

'William Harriman. How do you do.'

'I'm fine, thanks,' said Janice.

'May I take your bag?'

'No, no, that's OK, I'm used to lugging things about.'

She looked down at Danny, alert and bright eyed. 'Hello.' She bent down to give him a pat, as people moved past them to the gate, and the train pulled out again. 'You're nice.' Danny's ears were up, and he barked, once.

'He loves visitors,' said William, 'but he's not a yapper.'

'That's good.' She straightened up again, and they walked along the platform. 'Where I come from, there's quite a bit of yapping.'

'You have dogs at home?'

'No, no, there's only my mum's goldfish. I mean at the Dog Museum. Your cousins.'

'Ah, yes, indeed,' said William. 'This I must hear about.'

They came out of the station, and walked along the tree-lined street. Janice looked about her, taking in the tall, well-presented houses, with their tiled paths, window boxes, well-painted, solid front doors. She opened her mouth to say it was posh here, and shut it again.

'And that's us,' said William, nodding towards the cross-street at the end. Janice beheld the glossy row of arrow-head railings, the flights of steps, the wintry lilac and tulip trees.

'Wow.' She couldn't help it.

'We're the black front door, and the magnolia.' William was tugging Danny to heel. 'That's quite a sight, in the spring.'

'I bet.'

The January afternoon was growing darker; lights were coming on.

'Time for tea,' said William, getting his keys out.

'That sounds good.' And it did — not just the prospect of Earl Grey in bone china; she knew that was what it would be — but the phrase itself: orderly and graceful. She could hear her mother yell out across the back garden — 'Janice, your tea's on the table!' She could see Mary Harriman stirring the brown enamel teapot amidst the tins of Chum. As they climbed the steps she caught sight, through a gleaming high window, of firelight and a vast gilt mirror, deep in an endless room.

'Do you like muffins?' asked William, unlocking the door.

* * *

He showed her to her room, and explained that it had been his daughter's, that both the children had been up here, at the top of the house, once they were out of babyhood.

'Claire has her own family now, of course,' he said, opening white-painted cupboard doors. 'But she still keeps a few things here.'

There was a little shelf of books, and another of dolls in costume — a flamboyant Spanish dancer with a fan, a Highlander with bagpipes, kilt and tiny sporran. 'I remember buying that,' said William, following Janice's gaze. 'On her tenth birthday — we stayed in a house on a loch on the West Coast. Lovely summer — except for the midges, of course.' He closed the cupboard doors. 'Hope you'll have enough space for everything. Come down when you're ready — no rush.'

'Thanks.' Janice heard him go slowly down again, and along the broad landing where, he had shown her, were his room, the spare room — 'my wife used to sew in there' — and the bathroom. 'There's a cloakroom downstairs,' he added, 'so we won't be too much on top of one another.' She heard him murmuring to Danny, and then she couldn't hear anything, as they descended into what at home they'd have called a basement, but which William had described as the bowels of the earth.

She stood in the attic room and took it in. He had put a little bunch of snowdrops on the chest of drawers: she sniffed them and was at once transported to Shropshire woodland days. There was a nursery rug by the bed — heavy cotton in pale blue and white, with a border of animals, going into the ark, over and over again. The bed itself was white and narrow, set beneath the sloping ceiling with a pale blue quilt and a bedside lamp on a white-painted locker. A china Benjamin Bunny was on the windowsill, in his Tam o'Shanter and red spotted handkerchief, with his string of onions. Beatrix Potter had been part of Janice's childhood, too. The window was curtained with more animals: pandas chewing bamboo on sky-blue chintz.

Janice, twenty-three years old, a country girl of independent spirit but limited experience of travel, stood in the room of someone else's childhood and wondered that William had put her in here, rather than the spare ex-sewing room. How strange, to give a stranger your daughter's old room, when you didn't have to. Perhaps he thought it would be comforting. You shouldn't need comforting, at twenty-three. But it sort of was.

She went to the window, overlooking the street. The sky was quite dark now, and she could see in it, everywhere she turned, the sodium glow of the city. In winter, when she looked out of her room in Curlew Gardens, she could see only the blackness of the empty fields across the road, and sometimes starlight. The bypass beyond was unlit at night, and the Shrewsbury streetlamps distant. Here, even in this secluded patch, the vast stretch of London pressed upon you.

Could you hear it, too, the city? She opened the window, and leaned out. Only a train, rattling away from the station: when it had gone, it was dead quiet. Except — she listened. Yes, there it was again, the soft, hollow hoot of an owl. A London owl, but that did feel like home. She listened, but he didn't call again, and it was getting cold. She shut the window, drew the cheerful pandas, unzipped her nylon bag, and put her Lycra leggings and walkers' socks into Claire's old chest of drawers.

* * *

They had tea by the fire, and the muffins were served in a proper silver muffin dish with a lid.

'Just for fun,' said William. 'I don't live like this every day.'

'No. Right. Thanks.' She helped herself, sitting on the edge of a fireside chair whose springs had long since gone and whose loose covers were frayed and worn. This was the only thing about the house which put her in mind of the cousins, though the covers here had clearly once been very good. She spread strawberry jam and sat back a bit, looking around. Being tall, Janice generally felt pretty large indoors — they were always standing back for one another in Curlew Gardens, and the lounge with the three of them in it always felt crowded. In Eric's shepherd's hut . . . She refused to think of this. At Albert's she had to duck in the doorways; in Cloud Nine the kitchen was tiny. At the Dog Museum — well, it was full of dogs. But here —

'No butter?' William asked.

'I'm a vegan, remember,' she said. 'That's why I said no milk.'

'Oh, dear,' said William. 'Oh, dear. I'm afraid I don't know much about vegans. I'd rather put this aspect of things to the back of my mind.'

'Never mind,' said Janice, wondering whether the muffins had whey in them. Well, she couldn't ask to see the packet now, not when she'd just arrived. 'I'm sure we'll manage.'

'But — ' He watched her, sipping milkless Earl Grey tea, from a pink-and-green Minton cup: his favourite tea set. 'How are we to — ' He'd have to think about every ingredient. What was he to do about supper? He'd been in the kitchen all morning, and a liver-and-bacon casserole had just gone into the oven. 'I'm getting old and forgetful,' he said. 'I pretend it isn't so, but I'm clearly losing it.'

He looked so distressed that Janice said quickly, 'Please — please don't worry. I'm not expecting you to cook for me. And I've brought some stuff to start me off.'

'Stuff?' wondered William, reaching for the teapot.

'Soya milk. Soya protein and spread.'

'But isn't it all — ' He poured them both more

tea, thinking all at once of Buffy. 'Isn't it all genetically modified?'

'Not *all*. It says on the labels, doesn't it: GM free. Where's your nearest health shop?'

William had no idea.

'I'll find it,' said Janice. 'There's bound to be one somewhere.'

'The certainty of youth.' He lifted the lid of the muffin dish, as his mother had done all through his own youth. 'Do have another.'

'I'm fine, thanks.' She leaned back in the chair, surprisingly comfortable, and tried to take in the room. Fitted bookcases, crammed with hardbacks; gently lit alcoves of china cups and saucers, jugs and coffee pots; a carved oak corner cupboard, overflowing desk, worn sofa, the fireplace with its clock, and candlesticks, dark woven rugs on old pale carpet, the flickering fire, the heavy curtains — and the height of those windows, the space of it all. She could see herself walking slowly from one end to the other, stopping at a bookcase, reading on the sofa for whole afternoons, space and quiet all about her. She could feel how you might, in such a room, expand your whole sense of yourself, in ways which until now she had only ever glimpsed when cycling over the hills in summer, the valley stretching away below and the sky magnificent. She put down her cup, and felt suddenly excited.

'More tea?' asked William, watching her.

'No, I'm fine, thanks,' she said again.

Between them, on the hearth-rug, Danny gave a little twitch in his sleep, and then another. She reached down to pat him, and he opened a contented eye.

'Seems funny having only one dog.'

'Now, this museum,' said William. 'Tell me.'

So she did. She told him about the dilapidated huts, with their extraordinary interiors: the scenes of hunting, of dramatic rescues and domestic help; the vivid painted backdrops in the booths, and stuffed-toy enormities of dog and handler: huntsman, housewife — deaf housewife, she added — ringmaster, Eskimo. She described the vast St Bernard, with his felt tongue, furry ears and keg of brandy, guarding the fallen climber in a heap of polystyrene snow; and the burning African veldt, beyond the drowning daughter.

'And *Ernie* did all this?' asked William, putting down his teacup. '*Ernie*?' he said again.

'He did,' said Janice. 'A long time ago. Now he lives in a manky old caravan out in the yard.'

And she told him about the pens, the makeshift kennels, the countless dogs up at the wire, whom she took walking, with the house dogs —

'*How* many?' William interrupted. 'How many all in all?'

'About forty? Fifty? It changes all the time, they come and go, they're always looking out for homes, they have an ad in the *Shropshire Star* every week, in the Pets column.'

'Who pays for that?'

'God knows. Scrimps of pension, I suppose, with the three of them. And in summer they do get visitors. We have an ad for them up in Cloud Nine.'

'Cloud Nine?'

So she described the hilltop café, too, but briefly because he was naturally more interested in the poor old cousins, who at this moment would be shutting up the hens for the night, and taking the house dogs out for a last run down the lane.

'You don't walk all those dogs all at once?'

'No, no, in shifts.'

'And they're all strays.'

She could see him trying to imagine it all. 'Pretty much. Some were born there — it's expensive getting them spayed, and besides — ' She stopped, remembering a morning the previous spring when Ernie had come out to greet her with two soft-faced puppies nestling inside his jacket. She had never seen him look so happy.

'They can't resist the puppies?' William guessed. He shook his head. 'Well, well, well. And what's the house like these days?'

Janice had never been upstairs, could only wonder about the bedrooms, didn't want to think about the bathroom. She painted a picture of the kitchen, the heaps of dogs snoring on the hearth, Mary washing extraordinary garments at the sink, Sophie mopping the tiled floor. The walls were bulging and the paintwork gone; now and then you met a hen, nesting on a heap of local papers, and the draining boards ran with silverfish.

'Good Lord,' said William. 'Dear, oh dear, oh dear.'

'Sophie's tried to explain how you are related,' said Janice, stroking Danny's haunches with her foot. 'I couldn't quite get it.'

'You're not alone there,' he said. 'Some distant ancient alliance — I've never really focused on the exact connection, I'm afraid. But anyway — ' He looked at her, from across the fireside, and gave her a little smile. 'Here you are, my dear, by a strange concatenation of circumstances. And what shall we do about supper?'

* * *

Winter. Whole blimming world shut down by teatime. Ernie, out in the trailer, lit the paraffin lamp and stirred his enamel mug. Both objects had been in the family for generations: his dad and his granddad had swung that lamp in them pitch-dark lanes, setting off for the milking at some ungodly hour, tramping through iced-up puddles and frozen mud with its beam going this way and that before them; hanging it up on the hook in the Broxwood milking parlour and a lot of other cowsheds, too: they'd had to go where the work was, though Dad had been lucky to settle at Broxwood in the end, good steady job to finish up with. But blimming heck, what a life, week in, week out in all weathers.

> Oh, the country, the country,
> The country gets you down.
> There's nothing like the country
> To make you want the town . . .

Good little song, that, though he couldn't think where he'd heard it. Something on the wireless, no doubt, and he reached out and turned it on, waiting through some daft short story for the news, smoking and sipping his tea. Must be forty years old, this mug, carried with the sandwiches down to the farms, going up to the house for a fill. 'Thank you very much, ma'am.' They'd manners, in them days.

Beneath the table, Pip lay at his feet, and took the chill off; through the window he could see across the yard to the house, where a single light was on in the kitchen, and old Mary was at the table, scraping out tins into bowls and shouting. They'd all be round her, and supplies was getting low. He watched her shake out scraps from a pan, eking it all out till they got into town again.

Have to do it all themselves, now. None of that cheerful ring of the bike bell coming up the lane, none of that striding into the kitchen with the bags. None of that chat, the sharing a bit of a smoke.

'What did she want to go and do that for?' he said, nudging Pip with his foot. 'We was going on all right.'

* * *

William had the casserole, Janice had wholewheat pasta. He opened a bottle of wine; they ate in the kitchen.

'Would you mind if I smoked?' she asked him afterwards, as he poured coffee beans into the grinder.

This was something else he had not considered. Had she mentioned smoking in her letters? He folded down the packet of Dark Italian Roast, and put it back in the tin — a rather nice tin, black and gold and Chinese red. 'I'd rather you didn't smoke in the bedroom.'

'Oh, I won't,' said Janice, who had imagined just that — a long quiet unwinding with her tin and her book, on the blue-and-white quilt. 'I won't smoke now, if you don't like it.'

'No, no. Go ahead. Please.' He found her an ashtray, switched on the grinder. The room filled with the pleasantly mingling smells of the casserole, the last of a very good claret, freshly ground coffee, and cigarette smoke. He watched her lean back in her chair, inhaling on a roll-up, taken ready made from her Golden Virginia tin. She looked completely at home.

* * *

'And what are your plans?' William asked her, as they sat over tiny Coalport coffee cups, last used at Christmas, with Buffy and Matthew, sitting at the polished dining-room table, in the candlelight. Janice held hers with enormous care: this was pleasing, and she had good hands, he noticed, strong and slender, with flat, well-kept nails.

'I'm not sure yet,' she said, putting the cup down. 'It's rather early days.'

'Yes, yes, of course. No rush. But is there anything you'd like to do tomorrow?'

'Get my bearings a bit? Have a look round the

shops?' She yawned. 'Sorry. I suppose I should look at the papers. Find some kind of agency.'

'Agency,' said William. 'The papers. Yes — I suppose that's right. I wonder if perhaps my daughter . . . well, we'll see. More coffee?'

'I think I'll turn in, if that's all right.' Janice took a last puff, and stubbed out the roll-up. 'Can I wash up?'

'No, no, we have a machine.' He watched her pick up her tin, and get to her feet. 'I'm sure you'd like a bath, after your long day. Do help yourself to things up there. Did you find the towels?'

'Yes, I did.' She gave him an easy smile. 'Thanks for everything. It's all great.'

'Very nice to have you here. Sleep well.'

Upstairs, Janice lay in a foaming scented bath and watched the clouds of steam rise past painted tiles. The soap lay in a scallop, on whose edge knelt a smiling cherub. Sprigged wallpaper was peeling away from the corners, and the white-painted bookcase next to the towel rail was full of the kind of old green and orange Penguins you found in the second-hand bookshop in Welshpool: here, they looked as if they'd been untouched for decades, their spines stained with steam. Part of the furniture, like the white wicker chair; part of Claire and Matthew's childhood, she supposed.

Apart from the brief introductions to the costume dolls, they had hardly talked about William's children since her arrival. There were photographs in the drawing room, but she had not taken them in, and he had not shown her.

They had talked, in fact, almost entirely about people he had not seen for twenty years, and whose strangeness he must be struggling to imagine.

After less than twenty-four hours, she found it hard to imagine them all herself.

She swished hot scented water around her. Whose scent? She looked through the clouds of steam at the pretty glass bottles on the corner of the bath. An old bath, with limescaled taps and chipped enamel. And rather old bath oil, now she came to look at it, the labels faded, and the bottles almost empty. Could they have belonged to William's wife? Hadn't she died years and years ago?

Getting out, drying herself on an enormous lavender towel, Janice knew that the bottles must, indeed, have belonged to Eve, who, like William, had clearly known how to buy things that aged well, that lasted.

But fancy keeping your wife's old bath oils. Did he — no, surely he didn't — he didn't use them, did he? Flushed with her hot bath, the towel wrapped around her, Janice bent to look at the bottles more closely. Their glass stoppers were tight; she had taken one out with some difficulty, she recalled. No — he wasn't using them, just kept them to look at, and remember.

How touching.

How fantastic, to love someone like that.

She pulled on her nightshirt, brushed her teeth, brushed her damp hair, rubbed away the film of steam on the mirror, and looked at herself. She looked completely different from how she looked at home.

* * *

Some time later, after he had done all his jobs — loaded the machine, booted Danny out into the garden, put out the milk bottles, whistled Danny in again, locked up, raked the fire, put the guard up; God, what a lot you had to do, just to go to bed — William slowly climbed the stairs, switching lights off. He stopped on the landing, suddenly assailed with memory and longing.

Darling?

He almost called out, but he didn't, just stood there, while Eve, years and years ago, had her bath, the wireless murmuring, her bath scent wafting out, drifting, like her laughter at a play — in the days when there were plays you could laugh at — along the landing, into their bedroom, where he got undressed, and pulled on pyjamas and dressing gown and went along to brush his teeth and sit on the bathroom chair, and chat.

Oh, sweetheart.

He closed his eyes, as the last threads of steam, filled with roses and lavender and something indefinable, entire unto itself, floated through his house in winter, and disappeared.

13

Within three days, Janice had found a job. She was working in a wine bar in the Village, where, as chance would have it, a Polish girl called Danuta, who wanted to make experimental films, had been taken on by a small independent production company the very week before.

'Too good a chance,' the manager told Janice, when she had her interview. There'd been a notice for part-time staff in the window. I could do that, thought Janice. Easy. And in she walked, and got it, just like that. 'They're called Egret Films,' said the manager, a woman in her forties called Sandra, who had smoked and drunk too much all her life. You could see, soon as you saw her — open pores, bags beneath the eyes. 'Have you ever heard of them?' Janice said she hadn't. 'Very hip,' said Sandra darkly. 'I expect she sees herself at the London Film Festival, with some erotic little short.' Janice didn't know what she was talking about. 'Anyway, she was off, with two days' notice. In the week it's not so much of a problem, but the weekends — ' She blew out smoke expressively, indicating crowds and drama. 'What do you know about wine?'

'Not a lot,' said Janice, 'but I'm a fast learner. And I've got a lot of experience of restaurant work. I'm good with customers. All sorts,' she added, for it was true.

'References?'

'On their way.'

'P45?'

'What?'

'P45 — from your last employers.'

'Oh, right, yes, of course. I've been self-employed, on the whole.' And she gave an edited version of her working life to date, highlighting charity work, and volunteering. And that was that. Friday to Sunday, lunch-times and evenings. And Tuesday and Thursday evenings, when it wasn't so busy. 'We're closed on Mondays, and the lunch-times I can manage, on the whole; it's pretty quiet. On Wednesdays I have a young man. As it were. Good.' She held out her hand, bedecked with designer steel. 'See you tomorrow. In at the deep end, but you look pretty competent.'

'I am,' said Janice. 'Is this your own place?' she asked, as they walked out of the smoke-filled back office, across the hardwood floor. There were little marble tables, each with a slender vase, and a spray of white freesias, and the bar was high and swish looking. Everything was neutral, or white on white, and the chairs were black and chrome.

'It is now,' said Sandra, pausing to straighten a chair. 'I bought it with my husband, but he left me for a girl of twenty, the bastard. I made sure I got this in the settlement, though he got the flat, the shit. Now I live over the shop.' She yanked open the plate-glass door. 'He was always touching up the staff. Danuta told me he'd tried it on with her, once, but she's a tough little thing, got her eyes on something a bit more than a failed actor.' She stepped aside for the first lunch-hour arrivals. 'Be with you in just a moment. She flashed them a smile. 'Anyway, good riddance, that's how I feel now,' she said to Janice. 'Thank Christ we had no kids.' She looked at her, about to reimmerse herself in the cold, pulling on her black woollen cap once more. 'He'd have had more sense than to try it on with you.'

'Yeah, well, right,' said Janice, not sure how she should take this. 'See you tomorrow.'

''Bye now.' And Sandra closed the door.

Janice went off through the Village. She bought a spinach-and-onion samosa and a small bar of Green & Black vegan chocolate at the health shop, and she went to the library and asked how to enrol, and whether they had books about wine, which they assured her they had. She walked home, eating the chocolate.

'I've got a job,' she told William, at lunch-time. 'And can you sign this, as a proof of address?'

'How clever you are,' said William, putting his glasses on. 'And this is for the library?'

'I've finished *Great Expectations*, and I've got to find out about wine.'

'Wine,' said William, happily. 'Now there I can tell you all you need to know.'

* * *

Within a week, a routine, and a way of life, were established. Janice stocked up her shelves in the kitchen cupboard, which William had cleared of a quantity of long-forgotten jars of Marmite, ancient stock cubes, curry powder, jams with a growth of pale furry mould. 'Good Lord.' He chucked it all away, and asked Mrs T. if she wouldn't mind getting up on a chair and giving the whole thing a good scrub. He thought there were weevils.

'There would be,' she said, clambering up for a look. 'I'd be surprised if you didn't have mice.'

'All old houses have mice,' said William firmly, making her tea. 'It's part of their character.'

Now the shelves were full of packs of organic raisins, wholewheat noodles, bags of soya mince, chick peas, lentils, and tins of beans. This last, at least, he recognised. His semi-skimmed milk stood in the fridge beside cartons of soya milk enriched with vitamins and calcium. A box of sunflower spread, a cheerful yellow, rested on top of soya sausages, in Country Herb and Tomato & Garlic guises. A Cranks wholemeal loaf was in the bread bin, and the vegetable rack was fuller than it had ever been. He'd never seen so many swedes and parsnips. As for the fruit bowl —

'I must say you do look well on it all,' he told Janice, over their breakfast of coffee and toast and fresh orange juice.

'It's a very healthy diet,' she said. 'People don't realise.'

'But the iron,' he muttered, thinking of his liver casserole.

'There's loads of iron in spinach.'

He thought of Popeye, and the children rolling about.

'You must meet my daughter,' he said, reaching for the coffee pot. 'And my son.' What a lot there was to arrange, and think about. 'And one day you must come and visit the stall. You'd love it. And we must show you something of London, after all.'

After breakfast, they went their separate ways, though on the first weekend they'd gone together to the park, for Danny's constitutional. 'Now you know where it is,' said William, throwing a stick, 'you might like to bring him here yourself, when you feel like a breath of fresh air.'

'I thought I'd put my dog-walking days behind me,' said Janice, bending to pat Danny's eager little shape, as he came running back. But she did take him now and then, needing to stretch her legs after the unaccustomed days spent reading, or working in the wine bar. She strode beneath the trees in her zipped-up navy jacket, leggings and vegan-version Doc Martens, her hat pulled down, Danny's expensive lead in her gloved hands.

'You can get fabric leads,' she told William, on her return. 'They don't have to be leather.'

'I'm a leather sort of person,' he said, with finality, and that was that.

He spent two evenings telling her about wine, pulling down books about French vineyards, the wine-growing regions of Italy, the soil, the sun. Of course, he told her, there were fine Australian and Californian wines, no doubt about it, but the European wines — now there, there was *history*. And he told her about summer holidays with his wife, motoring down to the Auvergne, staying in sun-baked villages, lunching for hours; about the cheeses, the old boys playing boules beneath the trees, the peeling, faded blue shutters. 'I'm sorry,' he said at last, closing the books and throwing a log on the fire. 'I'm getting carried away.'

Once Janice started working, they pretty much stopped eating together. She came down late, long after William had breakfasted with the paper, and taken Danny out to the shops. On Wednesday he was on the Camden Passage stall — you could come then, he said, since it's your day off, and she said that she would, one day, and he sensed that he might be crowding her, and left it for a bit. But he came home from the stall that evening to find the house full of an interesting smell, and put down his boxes of china in the hall and went down with Danny to find Janice in the kitchen, and the red-checked tablecloth laid for two. A pan of parsnip soup stood piping on the stove, and a dish of pasta was in the oven. 'Well, well,' he said, pulling the cork of a bottle of 1998 Beaujolais, 'this is a bit of all right.' He told her about the stall, and the sale of a 1976 Denby thatched cottage for £65.

'Sounds like the kind of thing my gran used to have,' said Janice, ladling the soup, which he found perfectly delicious. After that, she cooked a vegan supper for him every Wednesday. They settled down, and it felt as if he'd always known her.

* * *

And then, at last, he had a reply from Matthew's consultant, apologising for the delay, offering an appointment at the end of February. He looked at the calendar. Then he rang Claire, to tell her — something specific to talk about, so it didn't seem as if he was pestering. He realised, dialling the number, that they hadn't spoken for almost three weeks. Good Lord.

'Hello, darling.'

'Oh. Hello.'

'Just thought I'd ring for a chat. How are you?'

'Fine. How are you?'

'Very well,' he said, and meant it. 'Very well indeed. Couple of bits of news.' And he told her about the hospital letter, reading it out to her as he sat in the hall, swinging his foot. 'I don't suppose you'd like to come?' he said tentatively. 'Someone else in the family — give a proper picture of how Matthew used to be.'

'They know how he used to be, you've told them often enough.'

William took a long, deep breath.

'What other news did you have?' asked Claire. 'Only I've got to go out in a minute.'

'I've got a lodger,' he told her, as the key turned in the lock. Ah, here she was, coming in with Danny close behind, and an armful of library books. And here, right behind her, came Mrs T. puffing up the steps. Quite a houseful.

'What?' She was suddenly alert.

'I've got a lodger,' he said again, smiling at everyone, as Janice went on up the stairs with a cheerful nod, and Mrs T. and Danny went down to the kitchen. And he told her all about it. 'Remember the mad old cousins?'

'Yes,' she said curtly. 'I do. And where's this girl sleeping?'

He felt a little twist of anxiety. 'I've put her in your old room,' he said brightly.

'What?'

'It's so nice and sunny up there. You know what the spare room is like. Those rooms at the back never get the sun.'

'They get plenty of sun. That's my room.'

'Oh, darling — '

'Don't darling me. How dare you let my room without permission?'

'Oh, come, come — '

'Come, come nothing. It's *my* room.'

William, though it was barely lunch-time, felt the strong urge for a glass of Scotch. And for conversation with Buffy. 'That girl,' he could hear her saying briskly, 'needs a good smacked bottom.' He'd ring her at teatime.

'It's only for a little while,' he said to Claire now, keeping his voice steady.

'What's a little while? A lodger's a lodger. Has she got a job?'

'She has, as a matter of fact.' He started to tell her about the wine bar, but Claire cut him off.

'She's obviously *dug in*. If she comes from those crackpots in Shropshire we'll never get rid of her.'

This, William realised, with a different kind of painful little twist to the heart, was the first time for years that he could recall his daughter conjoining them with this pronoun. We, he thought longingly, swinging his foot more slowly now. How long is it since we've been that?

'I'm coming over,' said Claire. 'I'll come after lunch and meet her.'

'I thought you were going out.'

'This is more important. I'll come before picking up Geraldine.'

'How is she?'

'Perfectly well.' And she put the phone down.

William went into the drawing room, and poured himself the Scotch. The room was full of pale February sunshine, wintry but lighter, definitely lighter, and he realised it had not rained for days. Or had it? He hadn't been so much aware of the weather these last few weeks. He held up his glass to the light with a trembling hand.

'You *mustn't* let her get to you,' he could hear Buffy saying, but how could he help it? Your children were your children — everything they did was important, everything mattered. And if they turned against you —

'Mr Harriman? Fancy a tin of soup?' Mrs T. was in the doorway. She was wearing a knitted maroon cardigan today, with a cable-knit front, and pockets. She'd always been a terrific knitter; she and Eve used to discuss patterns, polishing the silver together.

He put his hand across his eyes.

'There's winter veg or tomato,' Mrs T. went on, impervious.

'I think — ' He knew there was fresh leek and potato, made by Janice yesterday, with coriander and dill snipped in, but he hadn't the energy or heart to say so.

'Anything.' And he took his glass to the

window, turning his back.

For a moment Mrs T. was silent. Then she said, 'We'll have the tomato, then,' and stumped off.

* * *

He rallied. Scotch always helped. At lunch, he announced to Janice, taking her leek-and-potato soup from a blue Cornish Ware bowl, and to Mrs T., dunking her bread in the Heinz tomato, 'Claire's coming over this afternoon.'

'Is she? That's nice.' Mrs T. wiped the bread round her empty bowl, and got up. 'Cuppa tea, anyone?'

'Not for me, thanks.' Janice reached for the fruit bowl. 'She doesn't mind me having her old room, does she?' she asked William.

'No, no, of course not — ' For what could he say? 'Why ever should she?'

'She might. People have special feelings about childhood rooms, don't they?' Not that she'd care who had her room in Curlew Gardens, they were welcome to it.

'Do they?' He supposed they did. Certainly he would never have considered letting Matthew's room, but that was different, Matthew was coming home one day. Oh, dear, how thoughtless he had been about Claire — no wonder he drove her mad.

And did she speak the truth, about their family? Was it really possible that he hadn't known Matthew at all? Was that really why he —

'Anyway, I'm glad I'm meeting her,' said

Janice. 'Then I'm going out.'

'Where?' Oh, dear — how rude that sounded.

'Think it's time I crossed the water, saw the sights.' She was munching on an organic apple. 'They'll never believe at home that I've been to London, otherwise.'

'How are they all? At home? Getting on all right without you?'

'Oh, yes.'

They'd spoken once, on the phone.

'What's it like?' Her mother was breathless with anxiety.

'It's great, it's really nice.' She was standing in the spacious hall, light flooding through the stained-glass panels. 'It's . . . I'll write and tell you.'

'He isn't mad? He isn't like — '

'No,' said Janice. 'He absolutely isn't.'

And looking at William now, across the kitchen table — a little out of sorts today? — she thought how clever old Mary had been, to know that she'd like it here, and would, improbable as it seemed, fit in.

* * *

The doorbell rang just after two.

'Want me to get that?' shouted Mrs T., still in the kitchen.

'No, no, it's all right.' William, bracing himself by the fire, got to his feet. He supposed, if Claire and he had been closer, she'd have had a key — she did have one, surely she did; when Eve was alive she used to come and go, letting herself in, hugging her mother in the hall. 'Sorry I snapped.' 'Darling, it doesn't matter, I understand. You've got a lot to think about.' She hadn't even had the children then.

He was in the hall; he could see her square, determined shape at the door.

'Darling, come on in.'

'Hello.' She was brushing past him, looking around. She was wearing a grey jacket, and a long grey scarf — a good scarf, perfectly good, but it made her look like a schoolgirl, somehow, or at least a student, though the rest of her looked like exactly what she was: a clever, nicely heeled middle-class mother, just past her best. Hard to remember what Claire's best had looked like, quite — for a wild, disloyal moment, following her into the drawing room, he found himself thinking of Clare Short, then checked this at once. But certainly she had nothing of Eve's delicate bones, or pink-and-white skin, or gentle manner. Matthew had the Harriman height, the nose. Before he was ill, he had had the charm — still had it, buried somewhere, visible now and then with that sweet, vague smile.

But Claire —

'Well?' She was looking around the drawing room. 'Didn't you say I was coming to meet her?'

'She's upstairs — I'll call her.'

'She's in my room.'

'Oh, darling — ' He strode back into the hall. 'Janice! Janice, can you hear me? Do come down for a minute.'

'Coming!' yelled Janice, who had been opening the window to get rid of the smell of cigarette smoke. Had it done the trick? She left it open, the early afternoon sun, infused with just the faintest hint of spring, falling on to the blue-and-white bed, the blue-and-white animals, going round and round the ark. It was the kind of thing you might put by your own child's bed, having loved it all through your childhood, made up names for the animals, knelt on it to say your prayers, if you said them. But Claire had left it here.

'Coming!' she called again, with a last wave at the lingering Golden Virginia, and she ran downstairs.

* * *

Bloody hell, she looked just like Mary.

'My daughter Claire,' said William, his hand hovering behind her shoulders. 'Claire, this is Janice Harper.'

'How do you do?'

'Fine, thanks,' said Janice, stepping forward. She shook Claire's hand in the firm and friendly fashion which was partly instinctive and partly intentional, in that she knew it won her over to people. 'How are you?'

'Oh — I'm well, thank you,' said Claire.

There was a little pause, in which the sharp smell of Flash came powerfully into everyone's consciousness, as Mrs T. did her stuff downstairs. They could hear her, pulling chairs out, sloshing away.

'Well, now,' said William. 'Well, now. Coffee?'

'Not for me, thanks,' said Janice.

'You won't be able to make it, will you?' said Claire. 'Not with Mrs T. down there. Anyway, I've just had some.'

Janice regarded her sharp brown eyes, her furious tension. Mary to the life.

'It's ever so nice of your dad to let me stay here,' she tried, and meant it. 'Can't be easy, sharing the house when you've been on your own a long time.'

'It's doing me a lot of good,' William said warmly. 'Very nice to have a young person about the place again.'

'I hear you're working locally,' said Claire, still in full override mode, still looking at Janice.

'Yeah, that's right. In this wine bar. It's good.'

'In the Village? Not Drake's?'

'That's it. Do you go there?'

'Very occasionally. You don't go to wine bars much when you have three young children.'

'No, I bet.'

They were all still standing in the middle of the room. Down in the lower depths, Mrs T. had started singing.

'Oh, I want to be alone, oh I want to be alone, / Oh, I want to be alone with Mary Brown . . . '

'Goodness,' said William, 'that's going back a bit. I can remember my father singing that in the bath.' He looked at the two women, the one so square and fearsome, the other tall and leggy, so full of youth and promise.

'When I *see* her in the park, when I *kiss* her in

the dark, / Then I tell her she's the nicest girl in town . . . '

Mrs T. was in full throttle.

'We used to play that on seventy-eights,' he said wistfully. 'Don't suppose you'd have met a seventy-eight,' he added to Janice.

'Bit before my time. We're all digital now.'

'Are we really?'

'Oh, for God's sake,' said Claire, but she sounded just marginally less violent, and looking at her sudden, softening smile, Janice was put in mind of Mary in milder mode, patting one of the smaller dogs, or greeting them all when they came home for walks.

'Hello, my beauties, that's it, wag, wag, wag.'

'I say, do sit down everyone,' said William, coming to. 'What are we all doing, standing about?'

'I told you I was just dropping in,' said Claire, her eyes on Janice. 'My father says you're renting my old room,' she went on, but though William inwardly flinched at what this might turn into, her tone was less querulous and shrill. Janice had this effect on people, he realised, hearing her easy 'Yes, that's right'. I felt at ease with her at once, she's a good fitter-in.

'Must seem a bit funny,' she went on. 'Do you want to come up and see it? I've not changed anything, just sort of put my things there.'

'As one would,' said Claire kindly. She looked at her watch. 'I'm picking up my youngest in half an hour.'

'How old's your youngest, then?'

'Just four. She's still at nursery, going into

reception in September.'

'That's nice.'

'Geraldine,' said William. 'Lovely child. And how are the boys?' he asked Claire, then rather wished he hadn't, as she launched into a full account of SATs, standards, underlying anxieties manifesting themselves in rudeness, calling on all one's parental skills.

God, had there ever been such mothers as there were now? When he and Eve had been young parents they'd never gone on like this, he was sure of it. School was school, and home was home, and that was it, wasn't it? What a fuss these days.

And *that* was why Matthew broke down, he could hear Claire accusing him, over and over again. Because *you* never noticed *anything*.

'I told you I'd heard from Matthew's consultant, didn't I?' he said absently, staunching the flow.

'Yes, you did, you know you did, and no, I don't want to come to a meeting at the moment.' She turned back to Janice, who had been listening politely. 'Right, then. Let's have a look.'

'After you,' said Janice, stepping aside at the door.

'No, go ahead — it's your room now.'

'Not really.'

'Well, you know what I mean.'

Somehow they entered the hall.

'On Ilkley Moor bah't'at,' sang Mrs. T., lugging the Hoover upstairs. 'Oh, hello, Claire, haven't seen you for a long time. Going on all right?'

* * *

They climbed the stairs, with their worn eau de Nil carpet beneath brass runners. The walls were hung, all the way up, with watercolours, little oils, sepia family photographs. 'This is my father, just after he was called to the Bar,' William had told Janice, taking her up through them all one evening.

'After what?' she said, looking at the weird white wig and cravat.

'Ah,' he said, with his nice kind smile. 'A different kind of bar from the one you're working in, of course,' and he explained, in the nicest way. Anyone else might have made you feel an idiot.

'And this is Eve's grandmother . . . ' He pointed to a delicate young woman with her hair piled up, in a beautiful dress, all soft and cloudy. 'Chiffon — those were the days. I don't suppose any of you young things wear it now.'

'No,' said Janice, in her Lycra jacket with the yellow stripe. 'Not really.'

There were no photographs of the cousins, and she had remarked on this. William shook his head. 'Don't know why. I'm sure we had one of Edna somewhere . . . Edna's their mother, of course,' he added.

'Yes,' said Janice, recalling the fearful, hatchet-faced visage on the museum mantelpiece.

And had there been pictures of Edna, or of her curious offspring, she realised now, following

Claire up to the top floor, then William might have noticed the unmistakable family resemblance between Mary Harriman and his daughter, now she was grown up. In childhood, of course, it was hard to tell just who anyone was going to turn out like. Which perhaps was just as well.

'Gosh, what a climb,' said Claire, on the top landing. 'We used to race up and down these stairs.' The winter afternoon sun was spilling from the open door of Janice's room on to the carpet. Claire glanced at Matthew's room, the door of which was closed. For a moment, Janice detected a fleeting, quite different expression on the well-defined features — a sadness, a tenderness, and something indefinable, which was at once shut down as she gestured to her own long-uninhabited bedroom.

'Go ahead,' she said, with a little twisting smile.

And Janice went ahead, and pushed the door wide, and held it aside — what a lot of this there was today; she couldn't remember feeling so self-conscious, so mindful of her manners — and Claire crossed the threshold.

For a moment she did not speak. She stood looking about her: at the shelf of Beatrix Potter books, and Ardizzone's *Little Tim*, at the costume dolls smiling blankly into the sunlight, at the rug with its ark and animals, the open window on to the town garden, and the blackbird's song, which downstairs no one had noticed, what with Mrs T., though Janice had become aware of his visits, his perch high up on the magnolia, set amidst mossy flags.

'Well,' said Claire at last. 'Well, at least you haven't ruined it.'

'I hope not,' said Janice carefully. She saw with Claire's eyes the heap of books on the bedside table — Emily Dickinson, brought from home, and *Great Expectations*, likewise, and the Dulwich library books — Peter Ackroyd's *London*, and *Hawksmoor*, and William's books on wine, which he'd lent her, and which, she knew, she was the first person to open for years and years. The ashtray had been washed, and slipped into the drawer, and there wasn't the faintest trace of smoke. She saw Claire's eyes flicker over the spines of the books, the jackets hung on the back of the door, her hat on the top hook, the trainers and boots in the corner, a few papers on the desk, and really nothing else to see, was there? She'd hardly been in the place five minutes.

'All right?' she asked, and Claire said quietly, 'Yes, of course, it's fine.' She walked across to the narrow bed, and made to sit down, then quickly drew back. 'Sorry, what am I thinking of?'

'It doesn't matter. It's fine, really.'

But Claire was looking at her watch again. 'I must be going. I hate to keep Geraldine waiting.'

'Must be a lot of work,' said Janice politely. 'Three children.'

'You can't imagine. I must say, I had no idea.' Claire was at the casement window, looking down. 'There used to be bars on here, when we were little,' she said. 'I made them take them off, when I was ten.' She leaned out, past Benjamin Bunny, shining in the sun with his red-spotted handkerchief. 'It's quite a drop, I must say.' For a second her voice held a real chill; then she had moved away, was back in the middle of the room, and smiling at Janice, warm and direct.

'Thanks for letting me have a look. Old times' sake and all that.'

'It's a pleasure,' said Janice. 'Any time.' Beyond the open window, the still winter air and quiet, empty street were filled with the blackbird's song — gosh, but that bird could sing, she hadn't imagined a London bird could sound so —

Claire was at the door, checking the time again. They went back down the stairs.

'I don't suppose,' she said, as they came to the lower landing, 'that you'd ever be free for some baby-sitting? I expect that wine bar keeps you pretty busy.'

'It does,' said Janice, rounding the corner. 'But yeah — one day, why not?'

* * *

Her heart leapt when she heard his voice.

'My dear. How nice to hear you.'

'Hello, Buffy,' William said again, warmly. 'Hello, old girl.'

She did wish he wouldn't call her that.

'How are things?' she asked him, leaning forward to turn the television down. It was the wildlife slot: zebra were thundering past a crouching lion, to ghastly technomusic. In a moment, they'd show the whole kill, she knew it: the rending of limbs, the shriek, the rolling eye — sometimes it looked as if they'd planted a camera right under the lion's chin. She wouldn't put it past them. In the old days, with David Attenborough, they used to cut away at the kill, move to flamingos or something. Gnus. And the music was proper music, too. Now you had to see every dreadful moment, all with this awful hiss-buzz-buzz, as if you were in a club.

'What did you say?' she asked him, one eye on the screen.

'I said things are pretty good,' said William, and she could sense he was holding a glass, as she was. She raised it to him.

'Cheers.'

'Cheers.' He did sound bright. 'Just thought I'd give you a ring — had quite a day.'

'Oh?' It was Monday, Mrs T.'s day, if she remembered rightly. What sort of a day could you have with Mrs T.? Something to do with that girl, she thought, the Shropshire lass, and braced herself.

'Claire came over,' William was saying. 'She'd got in a frightful state on the phone, you know what she's like — thinking of you, old thing, was the only way I got through it.'

Still have my uses, then, thought Buffy. And she cradled her drink, as jackals crowded round the carcass, and looked away, and listened.

'She's quite a girl,' said William, finishing the story. 'By the time Claire went she was a different person, quite won over. Even kissed me goodbye.' In truth it had been the merest brush of the lips, barely a peck — but still. This was progress — this, considering the phone call, was something of a miracle. He'd stood on the step, watching her hurry out of the gate and get in the car, turning to raise her hand and nod, before she drove away. And he went on standing there, as the light began to go, hearing the blackbird, liquid and exquisite, with Danny beside him on the step. From deep in the house came the sound of the Hoover, and footsteps, running down the stairs. It almost felt like the old days — everyone getting on with things, civilised and affectionate.

Was that how it had been?

'I'm off now,' said Janice, and he turned to see her, pulling her gloves on in the hall.

'It's getting dark,' he told her, putting out a hand. 'Surely you don't want to go up to town in the dark.'

'Oh, I shan't be long, I don't suppose. I would've gone earlier, but — '

'We delayed you. I'm so sorry.'

'No, no, it was great. Right, then.' She bent to give Danny a pat.

'I'll walk you up to the station,' said William. 'He's longing for a little turn, aren't you, old chap?'

'There's no need — '

'It's no trouble.' And he took down the lead, and his things from the coatrack, and off they set, the blackbird singing his heart out behind them, and the lights everywhere coming on for tea.

'Should get the three forty-five,' said William

checking his watch. 'I was hoping to show you some of the sights myself. What are you going to do?' For she was, after all, a young woman of twenty-three, and he mustn't fuss round her, mustn't feel anxious about her, setting off into the city, as darkness fell.

'Just thought I'd look round, really.'

'A splendid skyline from London Bridge,' he told her. 'St Paul's, the NatWest Tower. And the Millennium Bridge, of course, not that anyone can use it.' And he started to explain: about the disconcerting creak and sway, the sudden closure.

'Gosh,' said Janice, and then: 'Look! There's a train! 'Bye!' And she ran off like a hare, up the last stretch of the street and through the station gate, and was gone.

'Quite a sprinter,' he said to Buffy now, reaching for the whisky. He leaned back in his chair. The fire was lit, and the house smelled pleasingly of furniture polish.

'We're out of Hoover bags,' Mrs T. had told him, taking her money.

'I'll get some tomorrow.' He saw her off with a cheery wave.

Buffy had gone rather quiet, he noticed, refilling his glass. 'Hello?' he said to her.

The wildlife programme was over, and now it was *Panorama*: that theme tune, Wagner at his most stirring. Quite unexpectedly, her eyes were full of tears.

'Buffy? You still there, old girl?'

'Yes,' she said quietly. 'I'm still here.'

* * *

And the next thing was Matthew. William thought about the hospital meeting with another lift of the spirits. Snowdrops were everywhere in the garden — in clumps beneath the magnolia at the front, between the flagstones; in corners beneath the trailing dark ivy on the walls, and in the rose bed; in heart-stopping drifts across the grass at the back, and there, just there, at the foot of the willow tree. He couldn't remember the last time they had looked so dense, so white and green, so snowy. He bent down to pick them, running his finger over the pure perfect drops, the petals still tightly furled; he watched them come out, in the warmth of the house, the outer petals like wings around the tiny bell of the centre, edged with two delicate little green hearts, conjoined.

Sitting at his desk, gazing at them in the fluted glass vase he thought he had found in a sale, but which might have belonged to his mother, he found himself reaching for pencil and paper, making a drawing. He propped it up against a pigeonhole full of bills. Not bad. Rather pretty, though he said it himself.

Should they be pretty? Mackintosh would have stylised them into something austere. And Dürer — ah, well, Dürer.

Perhaps he would be better painting them. Where were his water-colours? He opened drawers, found files and newspaper cuttings, and the children's school reports, tied up with pink solicitor's ribbon. No paints, no brushes.

Perhaps he might buy some, next time he was in town — call in at Cornelissen's, what a treat, while he was taking Janice to the British Museum.

Did she want to go to the British Museum? He sat there, half listening to *Composer of the Week*, making a list of all the things she might want to see, all the things she should see. British Museum, V & A, the Tate. He stopped. Not 'the Tate' any more. Tate Britain — he thought that was probably for him. Tate Modern — probably for her. He still hadn't been.

Wallace Collection, National Gallery. The Courtauld: he pictured them walking across the frosty courtyard of Somerset House, the fountains splashing on to the cobbles, him taking her arm. They'd spend the whole morning with Cézanne, Monet, Pissarro; then they'd have lunch, walk by the freezing river, come home for tea.

He sat there, tapping his pencil against his lips.

It was a Tuesday morning, and Janice was walking Danny in the park. No wine bar today: when she came back, they'd have lunch, and then —

Greenwich Maritime Museum, he wrote down, and found himself thinking of the Dog Museum, so truly strange.

'I like walking Danny,' Janice said. 'It brings it all back, keeps me in touch with the whole canine experience.' She flashed a smile, taking down the lead.

What could he show her that wasn't about dogs?

The *Cutty Sark*, he wrote, keeping close to home. Those jars of ship's biscuits. Scurvy. The Dome. He crossed this off at once: it was up for sale, it should never have happened. 'I knew,' he'd said to Buffy many times, 'I knew it would never work.' 'And why is that?' she asked him, Sellotaping the lid on a butter dish, stacking art deco tea plates.

'Because a dome,' said William, 'sits on top of something. That's the whole point. It surmounts. It's the crowning glory; the architectural summit, as it were. It's a miracle of arches, tension, buttresses. St Paul's. Wren.' He waved his hands. 'Brunelleschi, Florence, Prague. St Petersburg. A *dome*, for God's sake — a gilded dome. How can it squat on the ground? With all those silly things sticking out, like a flying saucer. It's ludicrous.'

'You're absolutely right,' said Buffy.

Right, then. No Dome. Good riddance.

Chris de Souza was murmuring on the hi-fi in the corner. The morning concert: what had they got today? There was the usual tuning up, and settling down, the coughs, de Souza burbling on, and then the sudden applause, his voice rising above it, as the conductor entered, and —

And all at once the winter room, with the leafless trees beyond the high clear glass, was filled with unutterable beauty.

William leaned back in his chair at his desk, and closed his eyes, and let the Kreutzer Sonata flood him.

He saw himself and Eve, at autumn concerts; he saw Matthew, at his music stand, here, in the middle of the room, his face intent, his long hand on the bow, graceful and exquisitely articulated, fingers running over the strings, the phrases soaring.

He sat there until the end of the first movement, and then, in the pause, the renewed coughs and rustling, wrote down: the Wigmore Hall. Purcell Room. Festival Hall. He thought for a moment, then added the Proms. Well, why not? If she stayed, why not?

Was she musical? Well, if she wasn't, he would teach her. He would take her to concerts, and play her things, and teach her.

And Matthew —

I have been a fool, thought William, as the second movement opened. I have colluded in this — this apathy, this half-deadness, this entirely lost persona. I have gone up to that bloody hospital, and dragged him down here, and never once, not for years, have I ventured farther. There's a world. There are galleries and concerts. I shall take him with me — I shall reawaken him. I shall take them both —

The key was in the front door. He looked round from his chair as she came in, fresh from the cold and full of energy, letting Danny off the lead to run and be welcomed home. The music was —

'I must introduce you to Matthew,' he said. 'We can't delay.'

III

Intimations

14

'Valentine's Day,' said Ernie, stumping round the shops.

'Blimming Valentine's Day.'

Sophie's hand fluttered over her hair slide, a keen young pointer, with jewelled yellow eyes.

'Forget it,' said Ernie. He shifted a five-kilo bag of dog biscuits from one hand to another. 'Don't even think about it.'

Inside the post office, he slipped out of the queue and had a look at the card racks. He gazed at cushiony satin hearts, ran his eyes over elaborate verses. What about the rude ones? The rude ones were all right. He found them further down, and stood there pulling them out, one by one, and laughing.

'Stop it,' said Sophie. 'People are looking.' She tugged him back into the queue.

'I could write some of them verses,' he said, fingering his wispy beard. 'Easy. I could do some of them drawings.'

Sophie took no notice. She waited for the nice voice to tell them it was their turn at last.

'Cashier number six, please!'

'My sister couldn't come today,' she said, pushing Mary's pension book beneath the glass.

'What a shame,' said the woman cheerfully. She counted out £68.34 and stamped the book. 'There you go.' And she pressed her buzzer.

'Cashier number six, please!'

‘’Bye,’ said Sophie. ‘Thanks ever so much.’ She counted it all out into her purse.

‘I’ll look after that,’ said Ernie.

Every week they went through this. Two of them came into town on market day, and one had to stay and look after the Museum.

‘It can never be left unattended,’ said Mary, and they knew she was right. Each week one of them signed the pension book, giving permission for another to collect the funds: Mary in her wild, capitalised Biro, Sophie with her enormous looped S and H, and Ernie in his good clear hand. Ernest William Harriman, read Ernie’s signature, and you’d think that behind it stood a person of some education, an architect, perhaps, or an artist.

‘Which is what I am,’ he said, from time to time. ‘I should have gone to college. Should have gone to the Royal College of Art, in London.’

‘They’d never have taken you, you old crackpot,’ said Mary.

Today it was she who was minding the house. Generally the sisters took it in turns: with Janice gone, Ernie was needed to carry the bulk. He and Sophie went back outside, and stood in the freezing-cold high street, ticking off their list. Biscuits for human and canine consumption. Tea bags. Toilet rolls. When things got tight, they made do with torn-up pieces of the *Shropshire Times*, just as their parents had had to, during the war, when they were children. Not all the pieces flushed away: sometimes Ernie, having a pee in his Elsan, would find himself peering at a bit of a headline, mad odd words still floating in the pan. In his time, he'd peed on Livestock, Red-Handed, Fifty Happy, Toddler.

Now they ticked off beans, Saversoup, Mother's Pride and Chum. Cheese, streaky bacon, cookers. Light bulbs. Washing powder. Mushy peas. Sugar. Sardines. Spotted dick.

Even in Lo-Cost there were Valentines.

'Mind out,' said Ernie, pushing his trolley at a pair of giggling girls. 'I said mind out the way.'

They turned and stared at him, then turned back to the cards, in fits.

'I'm going to have a look-round,' said Sophie, up at the till.

'Oh no you're not.' He stacked tins on to the conveyor belt.

'I am,' she said stubbornly.

'You'll have us all in the poorhouse.'

'I've saved up every penny.'

This conversation took place every few weeks. In the intervening period, the jam jar on Sophie's dressing table filled up with tiny bits of change.

'Go on, then,' said Ernie, outside in the cold again. 'I'll get my baccy.'

'See you at the bus stop.' And she was off, away from the main streets and into the cathedral close, past all the tourists, and the jackdaws on the grass; bobbing at the clergy; smelling, on the other side, down in the tucked-away alley, the heady mix of lavender and tea tree, old rose and rosemary, sandalwood and myrrh.

She pushed the door open and breathed it all in. Healing Arts. Lovely.

Crumbling joss-sticks stood in little brass holders; there were boxes of soaps, racks of sensual oils: everything in here was healthy and healing and kind. She stood there, in her belted green coat and mud-brown beret, taking it all in.

Natural loofahs, dried flowers, natural peppermint foot cream. Soothing tape recordings, helpful books. Stress, Deep Massage, Bio-Massage, Anxiety and Depression, Phobias, Herbalism, Crystals, Star Signs. Homoeopathy. Aromatherapy. Bio-energetic Therapy. Eating for Life. You could cure yourself of anything in here.

And there, on the counter, were all the little pretty things: lavender bags, lucky ladybirds, stick-on glittery moons and stars. The cards of hair slides.

'Good morning, Sophie.'

Oh, they were so nice in here.

'And how are you today?'

'Keeping well,' said Sophie, as one or two people moved away. 'Mustn't grumble.' Her fingers in frog-green knitted gloves hovered over the slides, went back to her lips, returned decisively. She could feel her heart begin to race. No other shop in the world had things like this. Poodles and boxers and a fabulous great Dane. He was new. Her fingers trembled. He was splendid: from the top of his sleek grey tail to his brilliant ears, muscles rippling beneath the mushroom sheen — what a magnificent beast.

'Have you seen the birds?' asked Daphne behind the counter, in her warm, expensive voice. 'We've had some new ones in.'

Sophie looked. Not just cockatoos and parrots

and budgies but swooping swallows and cooing white doves. Pairs of darting bluebirds — lovebirds. Was that what they were? She peered.

'Aren't they pretty? Specially for Valentine's Day — we've sold quite a few.'

'Bit late for me to think about Valentines,' said Sophie, facing facts.

'Oh, don't say that. It's never too late for love.' Well-kept hands took the card down from the rack; silver-ringed fingers removed elastic thread. 'There. Why don't you try them on?' And she placed the pair of lovebirds in Sophie's outstretched hand. They lay on the frog-green bobbles like spirits from another world.

* * *

'What did you get?' asked Ernie, smoking in the market bus shelter. The winter air was full of the smell of sheep and cattle. Bits of straw, chip papers and cigarette butts blew about in the icy wind; they could hear the clanging pens, the shouts, the lowing and bleating. Tom's Trailer was serving hot teas and soup, but they hadn't a farthing left.

'Well,' confided Sophie. 'It was a toss-up.'

Ernie snorted.

'A Great Dane or lovebirds,' she told him. Oh, how she lingered over that Great Dane. 'I'll keep him for you, if you like,' said lovely Daphne. 'You can buy him next time you're in.' And she put him in a paper bag and tucked him beneath the counter. Sophie knew that Mary would look on this as on a par with Credit, but how could she refuse?

'I got the lovebirds,' she said, and reached into her pocket.

'Show me on the bus,' said Ernie, as it rumbled towards them.

They clambered on, heaving up bag after bag. It started to rain. A tin rolled out on to the ground.

'That Janice,' he said. 'That blimming Janice Harper.'

She had sent them a beautiful card of the Tower of London.

'I'm waiting for my Valentine from that girl,' he said, settling into his seat.

The wipers began to swish back and forth across the muddy windscreen; Sophie pulled out the birds, in their tissue-paper wrapping, and showed him.

He raised his eyes to the heavens. 'Long way they'll get you.'

'Did you get anything?'

'I might have done.'

'What? Go on, I won't tell.'

But he pulled out the paper, and buried himself in the market prices.

All the way home, looking out through the streaming windows at the sodden, grey-green fields, she thought about the choice she'd made, fingering iridescent blue wings and tenderly entwined beaks, recalling powerful shoulders and hindquarters, a noble head.

He was a prince, and that, when she got him home at last, was what she would call him.

* * *

It rained for the rest of the day. Ernie, after a lunch of cut-price cream crackers, mild Dutch Edam and a mug of tea, locked his ill-fitting front door and settled down. The paraffin stove was lit, and a nice fug was building up. He sat at his Formica-topped folding table by the window, and opened the brown paper bag.

There. Just the ticket.

The Yorkie at his feet turned round twice, and settled. He started to snore. Ernie ran his fingers over the shiny tin lid. Quite a good size, quite a bargain. He lifted it, with his yellowing fingernails; he drew a little breath.

Yes.

Ultramarine. Cerulean. Moss green. Winter green. Pillar-box red, blood red, amber and umber and ochre. Blackboard black. Chalk white.

And here, in the shiny tin groove at the front, two brushes.

If Ernie had gone to the Royal College of Art in London, he'd have had squirrel, he knew it. Squirrel or even sable, for the really delicate stuff. He'd done out the huts with a job lot of Dulux — no choice, working on such a grand scale, what else was he supposed to use? But now —

He picked up the slender red handles, and ran the brushes between cracked finger and thumb. Soft as a smooth-haired puppy, soft as a puppy's ear. He peered. Probably synthetic, probably nylon, the world was going to the dogs — ha.

Never mind. It would do for now.

From the other recycled brown paper bag he slipped out the pad. It wasn't the quality art paper he deserved, but it would do. For what he had in mind, for starters.

Ernie stood at his sink, and rinsed out a jam jar. The sink was made of stainless steel, but you'd hardly know it. About once a year Mary came across the yard in a fury, bearing a tin of Vim and a scouring pad. Generally in the spring: there was generally a bit of a turnout all round in the spring. He looked out of the back window on to the rainswept field: come April it brought a bob or two, with grazing. He'd be bringing in a bob or two himself, come summer, once he got going. He could see it now, a nice little show in a teashop somewhere, called on by all the nobs.

Ernie wiped the jam jar on his sleeve and took it across to the table. For a moment, sitting there with everything before him, all set out and ready, he knew the purest pleasure. He reached for his baccy tin, rolled up, lit up; he closed his eyes. An image of Janice Harper swam before him, the only smoking companion he'd had for years, coming in so bright and cheerful — breath of fresh air. Every dog in the place perked up, even an old dog like him. Ha. He felt himself begin to drift, came to with a practised start. Fall asleep in here with a cig and you'd be done for.

Right, get a grip. There was the paint-box, there were the brushes and paper and water. Just like the old days. The very old days. Puffing on his roll-up, looking at it all, Ernie beheld a long-forgotten scrap of a boy, up at the front in the art class, the radiators banging away, the schoolroom crammed with kids and smelling of sweat and farmyards. Powder paints and primary colours — mix 'em, that was the thing.

Mix 'em up and make green and gold and purple. All around him kids were sniffing and kicking each other, slopping the water from 1940s jam jars and being told off. Up at the front, high on the teacher's desk, draped in blackout cloth, stood a jar of catkins, and a jug of buttery daffodils. Spring had come at last. Pale sun shone through the schoolyard windows, a thrush was up in the apple tree, they had half an hour till the dinner bell. He dipped his brush, he peered at the jug, the jar, the catkins: he began.

When was the last time he had been so happy?

Rain drummed on the caravan roof; beneath the fold-up table Pip sighed and snored. Ernie reached down from his chair, pulled him out, set him upon the window seat.

Wake up, he told him, you've got a job to do. Now, look at me.

* * *

Sunday morning. The rain had blown away, the day was brighter, church bells rang. In the old days, with Mother, they'd always gone to church. Before Father passed away they'd all gone together, regular as clockwork, walking down the lane in order: them two at the front; then Ernie; then she and Mary, holding hands, keeping an eye on Ernie. At this time of year it would still be parky, but you'd hear the lambs, stop to look at them through the gates, see an early bird or two with a bit of hay, bit of twig, darting in and out of the hedges. And the bells were lovely, hopeful and happy. Not like those dreadful funeral bells that had tolled for Father, then Mother. You wouldn't want to hear those again.

But with Mother's passing, the going to church had passed, too. Not straight away. No one really talked about it, or decided, but there were always jobs to be done from the week which now they could do on a Sunday. Cleaning out the pens, cleaning the huts — that was a job and a half. The dogs could be walked on a Sunday morning, as well as the afternoon: they could do shifts. She'd been the one who'd wanted to keep up the churchgoing, but somehow they just . . . stopped.

It was the hymns she missed the most.

Sophie sat up in her bedroom, before her dressing table. This, like much of the household furniture, was postwar utility, made of varnished plywood. Over the years, some of the varnish had worn away, leaving thin furrows. Sometimes these made her think of a ploughed field, sometimes of a desert after a sandstorm, the sand whipped into ridges, which she had seen on a poster, once, in the window of a Shrewsbury travel agent, beneath a lovely sunset. Sometimes, as she dreamed away up here, the scratches put her in mind of the sand on a beach, the ridges left by retreating waves, hard on bare feet as you ran. It was a long time since Sophie had run anywhere, but as children they had once been taken by Father and Mother on a seaside holiday: it had left a lasting impression. She remembered the sand, and the leathery dark purse of a dogfish, lying upon it; she remembered the mysterious depths of a rock pool, and the fronded, sucking mouth of the sea anemone, wherein she had not dared to place her finger, in spite of Ernie's urgings, and Mary's scorn. She sometimes thought, still, of her ruched bathing costume, which had been very pretty, and of Mother yanking down her white rubber bathing cap, the painful stuffing up of her hair beneath it, the tightness of the strap and buckle beneath her chin.

Somewhere in the house was a photograph album, with tiny black-and-white photographs of this holiday in gluey paper corners. There they all were, lined up and smiling into the sun with Rover, their very first dog, eating their sandy sandwiches.

They'd had a good time, then.

Sometimes, sitting before her mirror, Sophie would run the point of a nail file over the varnish, scraping it away still further, making lakes and lagoons, and foreign countries. Mary, coming in once and finding her, miles away, scraping back and forth, had accused her of vandalism, and idleness, and shouted. Since then, Sophie had tried to desist. It was, after all, her favourite piece of furniture, something she felt had been made exclusively for her.

There was a three-fold mirror. Plain as it was, the glass fixed to the plywood back by rusting clips, this felt like luxury. To see oneself from every *angle* — to look this way and that to see if things were right, without having to crane, or peer, or ask someone else to hold a mirror behind you: it was like being a film star. There was also the endlessly interesting activity of angling the side panels so that, when you leaned in and looked to left or right, your reflection went on and on, endlessly repeated. She had done this when she was little, and she sometimes did it now, setting the panels and leaning forward, turning her head, and — there! Sophie after Sophie after Sophie returned her gaze, stretching back and back — as if to the very place where she, Sophie Harriman, had begun.

What a peculiar thought.

The dressing table had two levels, and was in three sections; this, too, felt like something of a luxury. In the lower, middle section, she had arranged her hairbrush, comb, and a small Pyrex bowl with a lid, in which were kept hairpins, buttons, suspenders, poppers — anything still waiting to be reunited with its place of origin. On the raised sections on either side, each with a little drawer, were her jam jar of change, and the small china boxes, collected over many years, and each with a distinct personality. These were for the slides, and one held brooches.

Bells were ringing; somewhere along the landing, something dripped.

'Dear Lord and Fa-ather of Mankind, / Forgive our foolish ways,' Sophie sang quietly, lifting the lid of the china box, patterned in pink roses. This was where the birds were kept, and now she had a new addition. Lovebirds — what a lovely word. Just to think of it made you feel happy. She picked them up tenderly, held them in her cupped hand, stroked their blue-blue wings. How they swooped and darted, how they billed and cooed. Lovebirds. Bluebirds. Both such pretty things.

'Re-clothe us in our right-ful mind, in purer lives Thy ser-vi-ice find . . .'

She unfastened the clip, leaned forward, and slipped the slide into a strand of dark hair. Wonderful, really; she hadn't gone grey. Still young at heart; still a girl, at heart.

She pressed the clip shut, tidied a few strands of hair; she leaned into the depths of the three-fold mirror. And there she was, retreating with the birds into infinity, reflected over and over, on and on, going deeper and deeper, far, far away, but never — no, never; she felt a sudden racing of the blood, a rush of terror — vanishing into thin air.

* * *

Janice was seeing the sights. On her first trip she had taken herself to London Bridge — a wonderful place to start, as William had indicated, if you wanted to soak up the new Thames atmosphere. London! She wasn't in Oswestry, or Welshpool, or in a council estate on the back of the Shrewsbury bypass, was she? She had left home. At last, thank God, at last.

It was already dark. She stood outside the station beneath a streetlamp, her head bent over the *A — Z*. She was between two monumental buildings: Guy's Hospital, sprawling hugely across the road, and Southwark Cathedral. Well. She wasn't going to go prowling round a hospital, was she? Even if it was famous. Nor did she fancy, in the darkness, entering a cathedral. Choral singing by candlelight? No thanks, not today. Anyway, it would probably be locked. What else? The Old Operating Theatre (Mus). Instruments of torture, no anaesthetic — please. The Clink Prison? What had she stepped into?

But all along the Embankment suits were hurrying into pubs and wine bars, getting out of the cold. She took another look. Shakespeare's Globe. Ah. Steve would like to know about that. But it was quite a walk, and anyway . . . She had a sudden vision of herself, in jacket and jeans and vegan-version Doc Martens, striding into a foyer filled with posh people, all dressed up and talking about Shakespeare. Perhaps another time. As she heard herself think this, she knew it was just the sort of phrase which William used. She could hear him saying it, with a little smile.

Right, then. What should she do?

'Got a light, love?'

Janice looked up at the balding man before her. He grinned, in a horrible, intimate way, and she said coolly, 'No, I haven't, and don't call me love,' and stood there, willing him to go.

'Be like that, then, you fucking cow.' And as he walked off she knew in a concentrated instant exactly why her mother had not wanted her to come to London. But he'd gone, and she could hack it, she'd be OK.

And she turned, and walked down to the river, which took her through side streets, but she made sure she always had people in view. And when she leaned on a railing and looked out over the water, where lay the illuminated hulk of HMS *Belfast*, she began to breathe steadily again, and to feel in control of things. She felt in her jacket pocket for her tin, and lit up. That was better. Barges chugged to and fro, and the water washed against the wall beneath her; the moon was rising, the Thames was silver and black. And to right and to left it was magical. William was right. The floodlit dome of St Paul's, the skyscrapers and arches of the bridges — and there, far down to the right, was Tower Bridge. This picture-postcard sight, familiar from every book about London she had ever opened, now filled her with excitement and satisfaction. She was here, she'd seen it. The mighty stone walls of the Tower itself were bathed in floodlight — God, this was fantastic.

And she leaned on the railing, letting it all sink in, the smoke from her roll-up drifting out across the water and a river-boat hooting, deep and sonorous, into the London sky.

* * *

Where next?

'I'd like to take you to the Dulwich Picture Gallery,' said William. 'I'd like to take you to the Horniman Museum, when it's a bit warmer — lovely gardens. Wonderful glasshouse. We could have tea.'

'That'd be nice.'

They were having a drink by the fire. Janice,

used to halves in the pub, and a game of darts, was beginning to get used to William, on the evenings she was at home, lighting the fire at about six, having a look in the drinks cupboard, bringing out a couple of glasses.

'Whisky? Sherry? Do you young things drink sherry? Or would you rather have a glass of wine? There's a rather nice Chablis in the fridge, if I remember rightly. Or a little Beaujolais Nouveau?'

'Not all wine's vegan, you know,' said Janice, and explained about blood, and eggs, and cochineal, made from crushed insects.

'Good Lord.' He watched her, sipping her whisky and ginger, rubbing her foot along Danny's spine, before the fire.

'There are all the concert halls,' he said, setting non-vegan wines aside. 'What I really want to do, when it brightens up a bit, is take you and Matthew to a concert. Of course' — he gave a thoughtful smile — 'I'll have to introduce you, first.'

'That'd be nice,' said Janice, again. 'I don't know much about music,' she added. 'Not classical music, not really.'

'Well, we can put that right.' He got up, went over to the hi-fi, ran his fingers over the shelves of LPs.

'You can't buy those any more,' she told him. 'Don't you have CDs?'

'A few. But I love my old collection. Eve and I used to listen all the time — some of these recordings go back decades. Nothing wrong with that. Some of them are famous — von Karajan,

Kurt Masur, Lorin Maazel — great names.'

She'd never heard of any of them, but it didn't matter. That was the thing about William: he made everything easy; you felt you could say anything, pretty much, and he'd take it all in his stride.

'What sort of music do you like?' he asked her, but she knew, as she started to tell him, that he wasn't taking it in.

'Now,' he said, slipping an LP from its sleeve and setting it on the turntable — it was like the Ark here, 'what do you think of this?'

The first few phrases sounded, piano and violin, and a ripple ran through her. In part this was recognition — had she heard this before? Must've done — Steve often used to put on Classic FM in the Cloud Nine kitchen. She leaned back in the chair, let it wash over her, heard it begin to soar —

God. Yes — yes, she had heard it before, she remembered stopping washing up, or whatever, and listening to this fantastic music, looking out over the sunlit hills, where swifts were wheeling and —

She shut her eyes.

'The Kreutzer Sonata,' said William quietly, going back to his chair, and then: 'Matthew used to play this.'

God, did he really?

The violin was a living thing, exquisite, tender and wild, like rain on a river, like —

For the whole of the first movement they listened together in silence, something Janice had never done before in her life, never even thought about doing, though it felt quite natural now. Then, when the last notes had died away, she opened her eyes and saw William watching her, as the firelight played over the scattering of ash in the hearth, the fender, and the sleeping dog.

He raised an eyebrow. She nodded.

'Yeah, it's great.'

'You're musical,' he told her, leaning forward to throw on another log.

Well. That was something else she hadn't known.

Then the next movement began.

* * *

Within a week he had taken her to the Dulwich Picture Gallery and the National Maritime Museum at Greenwich. At the Dulwich, reached by a pleasant walk through the village, they tied Danny up to a ring outside.

'This is the first purpose-built art gallery in England,' William told her, straightening up. 'Designed by Sir John Soane in 1811. So now you know.' It was cold, and Danny, sensing abandonment, began to whimper. 'We shan't be long, old chap.'

Janice was glad to hear this, and William sensed it.

'I know,' he said, ushering her through the blue-painted door, set in its pale stone arch. 'Galleries can be exhausting. We'll just have a look at one or two things. Now then — ' And he had picked up a plan at the desk and was leading her into the first room.

Polished floors and gilded frames: she looked about her, half listening to William talking of Canaletto, Watteau, Poussin — painters she had never heard of, and none of whom did it for her, with their great dull buildings, overstocked flower-beds, soppy girls in gardens, and over-sized nymphs and river gods, draped in pink and blue.

'No?' asked William, seeing her face.

'No,' she said. 'Sorry.'

'No need to be sorry. See what you make of the Dutch. I think they'll be more to your taste.'

And he was right. For a start, she'd seen some of these on birthday cards: huge great soaring skies reflected in the still waters of the dykes in that flat, flat land — you'd have to be dead from the neck up not to like those. And the quiet courtyards in faded brick, the women with their plain black dresses and neat white caps, talking together: you could almost hear their voices, as they went about their work, sweeping and washing and sewing in the sun.

'Better?'

She nodded.

'Let's have a look at the Rembrandt, and then have lunch.'

The Rembrandt he showed her was called *Girl at the Window*. It was dark, and painted in close-up, the girl with her untidy hair and plain cotton blouse and jacket taking up almost all the canvas, as she leaned from a shadowy dark background on a rough stone windowsill. She was — what? Fifteen? Maybe a bit more. She was completely human — not like those simpering girls and nymphs, but sturdy and practical. There was also something about her which Janice couldn't quite put her finger on, but was to do with the way she was lit, from that shadowy background: made to look both ordinary and special.

'I thought you'd like her,' said William.

⋆ ⋆ ⋆

At the National Maritime Museum they let Danny off the lead in the hilly grounds and threw sticks. He went racing after them, until they reached the bottom. It was still cold and pretty windy: clouds raced over the rooftops and a fitful sun played over the pillared façades and struck the glass Observatory.

'Now that,' said William, 'is what I call a dome.'

They crunched across the gravel, and tied Danny up once more. This time William had put his dachshund coat on, and he fished out a dog chew from his pocket. Danny ignored it, and barked until they were out of sight.

Inside, in the vast main building, they wandered through rooms full of models and maps, sextants, uniforms, flags. They went to the exhibition of polar expeditions, and Janice, who had, with her father, watched an amazing programme about Shackleton and the *Endurance* the previous autumn, now gazed at the photographs again: the skeletal, ice-encrusted masts and rigging, the frostbitten men and the husky puppies, born at sea, gambolling over the snowy wastes.

'God,' she said suddenly. 'You know what this makes me think of?'

'What's that?'

'Ernie,' she said, and began to laugh. 'One of the huts. The Eskimos. I told you about them.'

'So you did. What would old Ernie make of this, I wonder?'

'Can't really see him here, somehow.'

But how strange, she thought, as they walked on, to think of these separate but similar Harriman passions — museums, galleries, pictures, in their oh-so-different guises.

'The Observatory?' asked William, as they left Scott and Shackleton behind. 'Have you the strength for the twenty-eight-inch telescope and Meridian Line?'

'Just about.'

They unclipped Danny, and walked him across to the Observatory building, leaving him outside once more. Inside they beheld the Line, walked over it, walked back.

'Do you realise,' said William, reading from the guide, 'that until the late nineteenth century a cup of tea at half-past four in London might be taken at five in Norwich? With nothing and no one to put you right.'

'How weird,' said Janice, imagining the strange disharmony of bells and chimes throughout the land. Mind you, the Dog Museum would always be out of step.

'Whereas now,' said William, 'all is in order. More or less.' And he reset his watch, on its pigskin strap, with its plain white face, Roman numerals and fine gold hands and rim. 'My father's,' he told Janice, watching him. 'I must have changed the strap a good few times, but I've worn this watch since the day he died. Day after, anyway.'

He glanced at her wrist, where her digital watch from Argos kept perfect, pulsing time.

'Doesn't it wear you out?' he asked her. 'All that flashing?'

'No, not really.' She had never given it a thought.

'I'd find it very tiring. Let's go and have some tea.'

⋆ ⋆ ⋆

The days went by. She was getting to know her way around. Up in her bedroom, at Claire's white-painted desk, she made a list of other places to go to, north of the river.

Tate Modern. The London Eye. She pictured herself and William, slowly revolving through the cloud-filled sky.

15

Valentine's Day: the whole country on alert. Few, apart from brazen schoolgirls, admitted this, but it was true. Hope dies hard, and even in old people's homes there was a little joke, a little flutter of the heart. Would there be — could there be — one for me?

William and Eve had rarely sent one another Valentines, but he had always bought her flowers, and taken her out, and generally marked the occasion. After her death, he had found the day so painful that he had, in a sense, abolished it, quickly turning the pages of the paper past the columns of sentimental gush and mild pornography which these days passed for romance. After a while, the abolishing was so successful that he rarely gave the day a thought, except to use it to put the prices up on the stall. Marvellous how a scarlet satin ribbon could lift the dullest jug, or sell a stack of rather ordinary saucers. Tie them up, cut the price tag into a heart, and bob's your uncle.

'Go on, make her happy,' he urged with a winning smile. 'Just the thing to put under flowerpots.'

A romantic to his bones, William generally put a flowerpot on the stall, planted by the Dulwich florist with miniature daffs or narcissi — heavenly scent of spring, cheering everyone up, worth at least a couple of quid on everything. Romance without a head for business — where did that get you?

'There we are,' he said to Buffy at the end of the day, divvying up the takings. 'Not a bad day's work.' He carried the boxes to the car and drove her home. But although they certainly had, after Eve's death, shared many a supper, they did not, she noticed, do so on Valentine's Day. He carried her china up the stairs, he stayed for a drink, and then he had to be off, baby-sitting for Claire and Jeremy, in the early days, or just . . . going.

Buffy had never had a Valentine in her life. She told herself she had long since come to terms with this, no longer gave it a thought. This year —

This year, in the days of the run-up, she gave herself up to mingled misery and hope. The night before, she sat knitting before the television. She brought through a mushroom omelette and a glass of Sauvignon on a tray, and left most of the omelette; she had a hot bath and read, in bed, two chapters of *The 1940s House*, which she and William, at opposite ends of London, were both enjoying, on the screen and on the page. And all the while there ran through her bloodstream the insistent, hopelessly insistent, little line of enquiry. Would there be — could there be — might he, perhaps —

She fell into a restless sleep, waking at two with a heavy head, and went urgently to the bathroom. The heating was off, of course, and it was bloody cold. Everything, at two in the morning, in the middle of February, felt completely bloody.

* * *

'How is it,' William asked Janice, as the day approached, 'that a nice young girl like you has no boyfriend?'

They were having a late breakfast: she was off today. He looked at her over the top of the paper, wherein he could beat a retreat if he had overstepped the mark.

'Young woman,' said Janice, slicing a banana on to her bowl of high-fibre cereal. 'No one's a girl any more.'

Was this really so? How dreadful. He lowered the paper, frowning.

'Unless,' she said, licking her fingers, 'you're talking girl power, of course.'

'And what is that?'

'Power,' said Janice, getting up to drop the banana skin in the bin. She came back, and sprinkled on brown sugar. 'Doing what you want. Not taking no for an answer. Getting what you want. Like, always.' Not that there had been an enormous amount of empowerment in Shropshire. Not so as you would notice.

'An enviable state of affairs,' said William. He looked at her, fresh skinned and still a bit sleepy, munching away. It was true — she wasn't a girl, not what he understood by the term. Girl was — how could he put it? — girl was romantic, wore dresses, was light on her feet, was like — he searched his memory — the girls in blue muslin running along the pier in that painting by Philip Wilson Steer in the Tate. Tate Britain, rather. Girl was like those young things laughing and holding down polka-dot dresses in a seaside summer breeze in that wonderful fifties photograph taken by . . . taken by —

He gave up, and looked at the young woman before him, tipping up her bowl to finish the soya milk, sensible and organised, eating a healthy breakfast.

'How is it that a young woman like you, if I may so rephrase it, is without a boyfriend?'

'Search me,' said Janice. 'Toast?'

'Let me — ' he made to rise.

'It's all right, I'll do it.' She got to her feet, and opened the bread bin. 'One slice or two?'

'Two, please.' He watched her wield the bread knife. 'Was there perhaps some young man in Shropshire?'

'Like, mind your own business?' said Janice, and dropped two slices of Honey & Sunflower Stoneground into the toaster.

William retreated to the paper, as men, throughout the ages, have been wont to do.

After breakfast, they went their separate ways.

* * *

Upstairs, in her bedroom, she sat at Claire's old desk and took out the Valentine's card from the paper bag. She drew it out of its Cellophane and looked at it. It was the coolest she had been able to find: just dead plain white, with a single word, in small red letters: Hello? Inside, it was blank, except for the smallest red heart. She took out a stamp and stuck it on the envelope. That was the easy bit. Then she picked up her Biro. Of course, people were probably e-mailing Valentines these days, from some cool Internet café, or loft, or office desk. No one she knew at home was on e-mail, but it was only a matter of time. Everyone here was, except for William, of course. Sandra, in her office at the back of the wine bar, was forever scrolling through messages and swearing, puffing away.

'What's he on about, the fucking idiot?'

Would Sandra get a Valentine?

Would Janice?

Her fingers hovered, over the letter E. E for Eric. Not much call for e-mail, up in a shepherd's hut, or up a tree.

Should she?

Would he?

What did Hello? mean, with a little heart?

Hello, remember me? Hello, long time no see, but I still —

Did she? And even if she did, should she tell him?

If she didn't put her address, he couldn't answer. If she put her address she'd start looking out for letters. And if he didn't write —

Of course, he could always send one to 33 Curlew Gardens, might already have posted it, in which case it wouldn't arrive here, forwarded on, until at least a day later. So she needn't think about looking on the mat until the 15th or 16th, by which time anything could have happened.

Oh, yeah?

Like what?

Well, like —

She cast her mind's eye round the wine bar,

drew a blank. So far, anyway. So far, she'd been chatted up in light-hearted fashion by an estate agent, until his girlfriend arrived, and by the guy from the wine wholesalers, leaning his clipboard on the bar, and giving her the eye while they waited for Sandra, who soon put a stop to that. 'Want to come into the office, Jon? Janice, make us a cup of coffee, will you?' That was it, unless you counted the bearded bloke called Derek who vaguely reminded her of someone, and who told her he was a freelance graphic designer, whatever that was. He leaned rather heavily upon the bar until his wife showed up. Other than that — solicitors came and solicitors went, and likewise accountants, and not one of them had the smouldering, sinewy, all-dissolving *presence* which Eric —

She'd almost said his name aloud, and almost doing so — just almost doing so — put her in a spin.

No. She leaned back in the chair, in her sweater from Gap, which was new, and bought with her first week's wages, and refused to succumb. She'd come down to London to get away, remember? To find something new, something different. She'd made a good start.

Right, then.

No spins. No casting yearning glances at the past, with its rain-soaked night of passion.

And she leaned forward again, and with her pen wrote, inside the card:

Dear Steve,

Remember me? I do miss you and Cloud

Nine, and everything, and I hope you're getting on OK. It's good here, and I'm glad I came. Why don't you come and visit one day?

Lots of love — Janice

There. Written without a second thought, and safe as houses. And she addressed and stuck down the envelope and felt much better.

* * *

But it was a pity, she thought later, dropping the card into the postbox on the way to work, that not a single person she'd met so far had proved of real interest. Not lasting, I-want-to-get-to-know-you-better, I-wonder-what-this-might-lead-to interest.

Except, of course —

And at this thought Janice stopped, and stood for a moment quite taken aback, and then, pulling herself together, walked briskly on.

* * *

William spent the morning looking through the catalogues of salesrooms and auctioneers, with an open diary. He'd marked in Guildford already, which he and Buffy had yet to go to; now he entered Chichester, and, in early March, a house sale in Ippenham, a fair. He looked through the Phillips and Sotheby catalogues, circled a couple of things in each, wondered whether Janice might like to go to an auction, just for the experience. He made a cup of coffee, looked through the new programme of the National Theatre, just arrived, considered an evening of dramatised Proust, and was just about to whistle up Danny for a spot of shopping when it started to rain. They'd go after lunch, then. He made another coffee, and took it to the bookshelves. Was there anything else in the wine department which Janice might find useful? He ran his fingers over the spines, found himself, after a little while, straying towards the art shelves, taking down Matisse once more, and turning the pages, as the rain fell faster, and the sky darkened. He switched on a light.

Girls or young women?

Not for a moment would he call these creatures girls. They leaned back on ottomans, half naked, with their arms behind their heads; they sat at dressing tables, languid and long limbed; they unfolded themselves beside a folding screen, draped in vermilion and lemon and blue — oh, those singing colours.

He could not begin to place here any girl, or young woman, or woman, that he had ever known. Certainly Janice, with her easy stride, and roll-ups, and kind of — innocence? — did not belong here.

But they were . . . they were —

They must be something I never knew I wanted, he thought, settling into the armchair, just as the telephone rang. He got up to answer it. Danny followed.

'Hello?'

'That girl,' said Claire. 'Your lodger. Is she there?'

'She's not, as it happens. Hello, darling. How are you?'

'Fine, thanks. Could you ask her to give me a ring? She said she might like to do some baby-sitting.'

'Did she really? I'll be happy to baby-sit for you, any time — I'd love it. You have only to ask.'

'Yes. Well. If she's not free, perhaps. Anyway, could you ask her?'

'Yes, yes, of course.'

'Thanks. 'Bye.'

And that was that, and it was almost lunch-time. He left Janice a note on the hall table, and went down to open a tin.

* * *

Valentine's Day. The wine bar was packed. A single red rose in an opaline vase on every table, floating candles, a Valentine's Special — a spritzer, blood red with kirsch, and Sandra in something very short, and very low. Janice, from the moment she arrived, was rushed off her feet, which was just how she wanted it, since there had, of course, been no card on the mat that morning, and she had been unable to suppress the sudden plummet of disappointment, even though she'd known all along, hadn't she?

By now, she knew quite a few of the regulars, and chatted cheerfully away as she uncorked chilled Chardonnay, filled ice buckets, let champagne corks go whizzing across the room. This was all right. She refilled the bowls of olives, the dips and crudités, she nipped in and out of the marble-topped tables with a snow-white napkin over her arm and felt quite the business. Someone let off a party popper; Sandra, behind the bar, was flirting with Jonty, who was helping out; a couple were kissing with abandon on one of the banquettes, and here was the door opening again, and here was Derek, the graphic designer, with his sad little wife, all dressed up.

For a moment, watching them cast around for a table, and find one, and settle in, she thought they looked familiar, as she had thought before, the first time he came in. She went to take their order.

'Don't I know you from somewhere?' she asked them, and at once regretted it, as Derek's eyes lit up at this age-old opening line, and his wife began to shrink.

'Well, well, I've been trying to place you ever since we met,' he began. 'Do you recognise this young lady, Jenny?' But fortunately, just as he started to explore the limitless dead-end possibilities, the door opened once again and in came Claire Harriman, looking less like Mary, and with her — well, it must be him — her nice-looking husband.

'Excuse me just one moment,' said Janice, and, leaving Derek and Jenny with the wine list, she went to say hello.

'Janice.' Claire greeted her with a warm smile. 'I wondered if this was one of your nights. Let me introduce you — '

'Jeremy Lewis,' said the nice tall husband, and shook her hand. 'I've heard about you. You're staying with William.'

'I am, it's great.' And she pulled out their chairs, and took their coats.

'Did my father leave you a message?' asked Claire, handing her a very good silk scarf. She watched Janice tuck it into the sleeve of her coat, as Sandra had shown her was the thing to do. 'About baby-sitting?' she added, sitting down.

'Great balls of fire,' said Janice, embarrassed. He had, indeed he had. 'Sorry. I've been a bit preoccupied. But yeah, sure. When were you thinking of?'

'Oh, there were a couple of dates,' said Claire. 'Let's not bother about it now, you're so busy.' And she turned back to Jeremy, who was scanning the wine list. 'What shall we have?'

It wasn't until much later in the evening that Janice, helping everyone get drunk, getting a bit drunk herself, had a chance just to stand behind the bar and hazily observe proceedings. She observed the couple on the banquette stagger out, helpless with laughter and desire, and considered how pleasant this must be. She observed a row brewing between Derek and Jenny, and remembered where, incredibly, she had seen them before. In the Dog Museum, in the pouring rain the previous autumn. They had turned up with their child, a round-faced boy, just as she was leaving. It had been half-term, a filthy day, and they had been almost the only visitors. God, how weird. Well — she wasn't going to remind them. But thinking about that day, and about her life then, she felt a sudden wave of nostalgic longing for it all: places and people she knew by heart; all the old bats in the rainswept hills and valleys, the bicycling and dog-walking and cake-making, and Steve, and even her parents, who weren't really all that bad, just boring, like all parents were.

And yet, she thought, leaning on the bar and watching Sandra make a fool of herself, I wouldn't have missed coming down here for the world. She helped herself to a couple of olives, and took an order from a young man swaying like a tree in the wind on Leinthall Ridge. She wanted to tell him he had had enough, but it was none of her business, and anyway, what the hell. It was Valentine's Day, for God's sake: someone had to enjoy themselves. She was enjoying herself, in a funny kind of way, more than she'd thought she would, anyway. And she lit up a proper cigarette, for once, offered by the inebriate young man, and watched him walk back with incredible care to his table, where sat another young man. Which made her think of Steve, again, and wonder what he was doing tonight. Not much call for Valentine's parties, up in Cloud Nine of a February night. He'd be down the pub with everyone, as she would have been, had she stayed.

It was growing incredibly noisy and smoky and loud. Janice poured herself another glass while Sandra, sitting on somebody's lap, leaned back and roared with unbecoming laughter. She observed, beholding the throng once more, that Claire and Jeremy also knew Derek and Jenny, and were avoiding them. There had been a waving of the wine list by Derek, and a cheery

'How's school?' from Jenny, and then — after the little nod of acknowledgement, the smiles — a definite retreat. Well, you would retreat from Derek, wouldn't you? Hard to say quite why, but you would. No reason why a freelance graphic designer should be boring, but —

Claire and Jeremy were in conversation. Janice leaned on the bar and enjoyed her cigarette and glass of wine, and watched them. They didn't, Claire had told her, get out very much, with their three young children. She had made it clear, both to Janice and William, that life, with three young children, was a fearful strain. So you'd think that now they were off the leash they'd be —

Well, perhaps this was what marriage and three kids and overwork did for you. God, he looked knackered. It must be awful, being a barrister. But he also had a sweet, kind sort of look, and as he listened to Claire, and yawned, she wondered that they were not holding hands, or . . . well, laughing, or something. Perhaps one of the children was ill, or had failed an exam, or perhaps they'd discovered dry rot in the cellar, or whatever it was that gave people with mortgages sleepless nights. Or perhaps —

Smoke drifted here and there through the crowded room. The roses on the tables had opened in the warmth, and their scent was everywhere, mingling with the wine, and cigarettes; Billie Holiday, through the sound system, was unbearably husky and alone.

Claire looked up. She glanced towards the bar, and rested her eyes upon Janice, who was leaning upon it, with her cropped dark hair and her drink and smouldering cigarette held between her slender fingers. For a moment their eyes met. For a moment her smile was full of warmth and friendship. And then, as if recollecting herself — for Claire, Janice knew, was a terrible snob, and unlikely to allow herself to indulge in familiarity with her father's lodger, and anyway was a difficult, complicated person — then she returned her gaze to her husband, and took his hand, and he, with a little start of pleasure, leaned forward and kissed her cheek.

⋆ ⋆ ⋆

Valentine's Day. It came. It went. There was nothing but bills on the mat for Buffy, and for an instant she felt quite sick with disappointment. And straightening up, with her National Trust reminder for renewal, and the quarterly service charges from the landlord, she leaned against the wall in a sudden little spasm of giddiness.

Dear, dear, this wasn't right. She made her way cautiously back to the kitchen and sank on to her chair, her head in her hands. After a little while, everything stopped spinning, and with a few sips of tea she felt that wonderful rush of warmth and wellness which can follow a nasty turn. She slit open the National Trust envelope, looked through the booklet offering soaps and scarves and bird-life tea towels which accompanied the bill and gradually recovered herself.

But she only had one slice of toast, no room anywhere for another crumb, and as she washed up the breakfast things and thought about the day ahead — the getting across town to the Angel, the walk down to Camden Passage, the setting up of the stall, and the morning sitting out there, in the February cold and wet — it all felt almost daunting. Even though she was seeing William, even though this was the highlight of the week — she was tired, she was terribly tired.

But why? Was it all the getting up in the night, the trouble spent getting back to sleep afterwards? Was she doing too much? No more than she had ever done. Then was it, perhaps, something psychological?

Buffy had never had much time for the psychological. The closest she had come to interest, or insight, was with poor Matthew, whose suffering so tore at William's heart. Who knew what would become of that poor boy in the end, but at least, at Christmas, she'd had the good sense to wake William up to things, urge him to seek a review. Still, that hadn't taken much. Any fool could have seen things weren't right.

Buffy put away the toast rack. She put away the marmalade, and the butter back in the fridge. She considered her state of mind, which had, she knew, developed, as it were, a new strain, a new cast, since Christmas and New Year, when she had felt so happy. The nine o'clock news came on, and passed her by. She went into the sitting room, where sun was struggling through the rain. It lit the watery windowpane, the shoots in the window box, where the crocuses were just in bud; it filtered through the bright yellow poster for the Mary Ward concert, and fell upon her desk, where a pile of yellow concert fliers were waiting to be delivered. She always put them through her neighbours' letterboxes, and in the local shops, and the church, and she always took them to the stall. The Angel, after all, was not far from Bloomsbury, and people came, people liked to be told about musical events, it cheered them up.

But oh Lord, thought Buffy, putting them into an envelope, putting them into her bag, even the thought of the concert, the soaring Parry and the rousing Masefield and Kipling, somehow did not cheer her now.

⋆ ⋆ ⋆

'Hello, old thing.' William was in fine fettle, already setting up the stall, which she noticed had a different cloth upon it, a faded crimson damask, which set everything off a treat. He kissed her on both cheeks; he gestured to Danny, sniffing round other people's stalls, wearing a scarlet ribbon. 'That'll brighten up the punters, catch the mood.' He felt in a carrier bag on his folding chair, pulled out a pot of paper-white narcissi, and set it in the middle of the trestle. 'There. Springtime. Valentines. Love's young dream.'

'Where did you get that cloth?' asked Buffy, setting down her bag.

'Found it at the back of the press in the spare room. Woke up in the middle of the night and thought: I know just the thing. Change from all that black — it sets off silver so nicely, but today — ' He was rummaging in his cardboard boxes, taking out newspaper-wrapped packages, peeling off layers. 'What do you think of this?'

Buffy beheld a teapot, pale cream with fluted sides, wide spout and slender handle. Cabbage roses smothered it; the handle and the handle on the lid were dusty gold. 'Very nice,' she said, and it was. She lifted it and turned it over, clasping the lid until she saw he'd already taped it securely. 'Staffordshire. I thought so.'

'Did you really? That was clever.' William put his glasses on, and peered at the mark. 'It's about 1880. What do you think?'

'A good hundred,' said Buffy, on automatic now, getting into the swing again. It just went to show: you should never succumb. Moods. Tiredness. Out and about — that was the thing; getting on.

'Just what I thought,' said William. 'Shall we try one-twenty?'

'Why not?' And she set it down and waited for the next unwrapping. That, on good days, was one of the stall's delights. It wasn't just the shared days out, the sales in barns and country houses. It was the finding things individually, bringing them to show one another; the poking about on wet afternoons in little shops and salesrooms. Sometimes it was she who found something, poking about in the Chiswick Oxfam shop, the jumble sale, the West London auction rooms. Often there was nothing at all: there had, for instance, been nothing at all for a fortnight in Notting Hill, but sometimes —

'Now then,' said William, unwrapping something else. 'These I fell for.'

Traffic on the Essex Road was building up; people were running for the bus; the man in the Turkish antiques shop by the green was shaking out a kilim in the sun. The world felt normal and ordinary again, the morning's moment of distress, the dizzy spell and weakness, quite forgotten. After all, she had known William for years and years; friendship was what counted, in the end. It was simply silly to think of something more, it spoiled everything.

'There,' he said, and stood back for the effect.

Two white china doves lay side by side. Their feathery wings were folded, their heads tucked into their breasts, their eyes gently closed in sleep.

She picked one up. It was hollow: half a dove, in fact, the tail swept up into a smooth white fan, the body quite at rest.

'Jelly moulds,' said William. 'Nineteen thirties jelly moulds. Worth quite a bit.' He watched her set down again the one she had picked up. 'Especially today, don't you think?' And carefully, with his beautiful fingers, in the leather winter gloves she had always been so fond of, he moved the two birds close together, so that their sleeping heads could rest together tenderly, lovingly, as if for a lifetime.

* * *

'You've gone awfully quiet, old girl,' William said later. 'Everything all right?'

'Fine,' said Buffy. 'Absolutely fine.'

The Staffordshire teapot had been sold, knocked down to £75, to someone they'd thought was a dealer but had given the benefit of the doubt. Those darling doves had gone to a retired couple who still, in retirement, held hands as they walked away. Buffy watched them, then busied herself with the rearrangement of her rug. And so the whole wretched Valentine's Day went by, and then it was over, and a good thing too.

* * *

William and Janice walked up the hill to the hospital. The morning was brighter, lighter, the air fresh: again, despite the cold, you could sense just a hint of spring.

'It's very good of you to come,' said William, tugging Danny out of a doorway. He had said this several times.

'It's fine,' said Janice, as she had kept saying. 'Honestly.'

'I mean, of course it would have been much nicer for you to have met at home,' he went on, 'and I very much hope he'll come for Sunday lunch or something, soon, but I can never be completely sure if it unsettles him. At least we know he feels safe here.'

They had come to the open gates; he stopped, put a hand on her arm as a car turned in. Then they went through.

Danny, on familiar territory, trotted briskly ahead on the lead, making for the grass alongside the tarmac path. William drew him back. 'You'll have to wait a bit, old chap, same as usual.'

Janice, gloved hands in her jacket pockets, looked about her. She'd never been to a loony bin before. Was that what this was? She imagined, when the weather got warmer, the patients would be out and about, doing gardening therapy, or painting therapy, or playing ball games — was that the sort of thing they got up to? Now there were only the lawns, the huge dark firs, with a scattering of cones on the grass beneath, and a gardener working in the flower-beds, where bulbs were pushing up. Oh, and there was a squirrel, leaping towards the fir cones. Danny saw it too, gave a sudden yelp of excitement, and it was up on the trunk in a flash, round it and gone, just like that. Again, for a minute, she was tugged back to Shropshire, and loads of old squirrels, everywhere in the woods, and the sheep up in the hills, suddenly looming at you round a bush or a boulder, or scattered like stones on the slopes, with a crow or two flapping across the valley.

'Here we are,' said William.

Plate-glass doors were before them, one or two visitors coming out, one or two going in. She glimpsed a white coat, a nurse, an endless corridor, stretching away beyond the reception area; she heard, in the distance, the sudden blare of an ambulance. And for the first time, as William bent to clip Danny's lead to the hook on the wall, with the dish of water beneath, she felt a rush of nerves. What really went on in here? What the hell did she know about mental illness?

How ill was Matthew, and did she, really, even want to meet him?

'All right?' asked William, straightening up.

'Yeah, sure.'

He stepped aside as a doctor came out with a sheaf of notes; an anxious-looking woman was with him and they stood and conferred a few paces away, by a bench beneath a window, their voices low.

William was beside her again, his hand on her shoulder. 'You'll be all right,' he said. 'We needn't stay long, if you don't want to.'

She glanced up at him, saw the warmth in his eyes, considered for the umpteenth time the decades that lay between them.

Then he was ushering her through, as the automatic doors slid back, and she smelt that smell which distinguishes all hospitals, which she could recall from visiting Albert Page two years back, after a fall had put him briefly into Shrewsbury Hospital: disinfectant, flowers, school meals and cleaning fluid, and somewhere forbidden cigarettes. God, she could do with one now.

The Friends Coffee Shop was busy and bright; the flower shop likewise, full of greenhouse tulips and early daffs in buckets. The corridor running endlessly ahead was lined with paintings; a porter was wheeling an old girl along in a hospital chair; the phone on the reception desk was ringing, and was picked up. So far, so familiar; so far she might be in any old hospital.

Then she heard it. Then she saw it.

A man in his forties — fifties? — was coming

down the corridor towards them. His hair was the texture of fibreglass or something — lifeless and faded and dry, neither white nor a proper colour, and his mouth was open, fixed like that, like he was dead: a gaping black hole in a face the colour of tallow, quite without expression. He was walking with a stiff, strange gait, and every now and then an arm was flung out, or a hand was flung across his face, or his head jerked wildly, as if yanked by a string. And from the gaping, deathlike hole of a mouth came intermittent shouts, or cries, very loud, as if he were right out in the open, out on the hills or something, in some lost age, lost place, calling across from hillside to hillside, a madman abandoned to die out there, among stones and sheep and circling birds.

She felt herself go pale.

'It's all right,' said William steadily, and he put his hand beneath her elbow and led her along the corridor, with its still lifes and landscapes and London scenes.

They came to a crossroads, as it were: more corridors, running to right and left, signs up for wards, for clinics and departments.

'This way,' said William, and they turned to the right. A nurse pushed open a double door, and Janice glimpsed a little group, in a circle, sitting in silence. Then the door swung to.

'Are you all right?' he asked her.

'Yeah, sure. Terrific.'

'Nearly there. I know it's distressing when you first come here.'

'I need a cigarette, to be honest.'

'Ah.' William smiled. 'You'll be in good company, then.'

'Will they — ' She hesitated. How should she put it?

'Will they be like the poor chap we just saw? No.'

They walked on in silence. William asked himself: Why am I doing this? Why on earth am I bringing this poor girl here? Whatever was I thinking of?

Janice thought: if Claire made me think of Mary Harriman, what about Matthew? For a second she had a wild glimpse of Ernie, shuffling into the kitchen at the Dog Museum, in his grubby old jacket and holey socks, laughing and cadging a fag. She felt a rush of affection: what a strange old thing he was. Wispy as a dandelion clock, but sharp as a ferret. No flies on Ernie, though when you saw him out and about in town he looked . . . well, he looked pretty barmy, didn't he?

'Don't make that face,' she heard her mother say suddenly, as she sat at the kitchen table, being annoying at seven or eight. 'If the wind changes, you'll get stuck like that.'

If the wind had blown a bit harder, a bit longer, over the Shropshire hills, Ernie, let's face it, could have been that poor bloody sod they'd just seen, his mouth stuck open, yelling from the back of some dreadful dark cave of the mind, treading the barren wastes of the world, stony and dry.

And Sophie —

'Here we are,' said William.

And she came back to earth with a bump, as they entered the open doorway of a ward with the usual stuff — beds, lockers, nurses' desk, flowers in horrible vases.

A girl — a young woman — of nineteen or twenty was sitting quite still on the side of her bed. Her hair was scraped up in a knot on the top of her head; bright pink mules hung on bare feet; she was wearing a pink flowery dressing gown over a white nightshirt. Her skin was pasty and pale. The left-hand sleeve of the dressing gown was drawn up, and she was gazing intently at her arm, fingering a long line of . . . clusters of —

Christ.

'We'll find him in the day room,' said William, his arm around her, and she made to accompany him, but her legs were like jelly.

Christ. Did people really —

The top half of the door to the day room was of glass, and plate-glass doors lay beyond it, leading to the grounds. As they approached, this area of the ward was therefore full of light. And looking back, much later, Janice could remember of these moments — this turning point in the whole occasion, in the whole of her time in London — a sudden flood of light, of whiteness: from the walls of the ward, from the sudden striking through the cloud of the February sun, illuminating the winter grass, the great dark trees, the faces of those who sat smoking and thinking — of what? — around the leaping colours of the television screen, with its images of another world, a million miles away. The horrible sights of that screaming mouth, that burned-up, gouged-out arm, were still within her; she knew she was shocked, and shaking, and perhaps — looking back — more open to anything, more vulnerable, than she had ever been in her life. But around her, in this place of broken souls, there was now, all at once, this light, this radiance, as she stepped with William across the threshold of the day room, and a man who looked just like him, but decades younger, turned from his chair and saw them, and with an incredible beauty slowly smiled.

16

'Foot-and-mouth,' said Buffy. She was trembling with distress. 'Foot-and-mouth — look at this.' She flung the newspaper down on to the stall, where William was setting out a ring of eggcups.

'I know,' he said. 'It's ghastly.'

'It's unspeakable. Do stop fiddling about. Do you realise what's been going on all this time?' She dropped her bag on her folding chair and stood there, twisting the ends of her woollen scarf this way and that.

William glanced at the paper. Buffy, of course, took the *Guardian*, while he still clung to *The Times*, changed as it was from its days of grandeur. Still, in the coverage of this catastrophe there wasn't that much to choose between them.

'Gone are the days,' said Buffy, twisting her scarf. 'Gone are the days when a farmer lambed his ewes, and drove them to the local market, and sold them locally, and had them . . . well, slaughtered, in a local abattoir. Now they go up and down the country. They're sent off to Europe, they're sent to the ends of the earth. Do you realise that a lamb born in Northumberland can end up in *Beirut*?'

William unscrewed the Thermos.

'And we're importing so much — why do we need to *import*? Why do our sheep have to make horrible journeys while other meat comes in?

Infected meat in the food chain, and this is the result. Now we're having to slaughter fit, healthy livestock — those pyres, those dreadful pyres, have you seen them on the news? I can't bear it, William, I simply can't bear it.'

William took her bag off the folding chair and set it down. He put a hand on her arm, and indicated the coffee.

'My father,' he said, 'was never without his hip flask. Very wise. If I had one now, I'd add a little nip to this. You look as if you need it, dear. Do sit down.'

'A little nip?' She gestured wildly at the plastic coffee cup, and almost sent it flying. 'You think one can feel better about a thing like this with a little *nip*? Honestly, William, sometimes I despair.'

It was still early, not many people about, and Buffy's outrage was beginning to carry across the covered stalls. One or two heads were turning; William coughed. He pulled the chair out farther, patted her arm again.

'Do not,' said Buffy, 'pat me. Please do not.' She sank on to the folding chair, and shook her head.

'Poor Buffy,' said William. 'How you feel things.'

'Please don't tell me you don't feel things.'

'More the ones close to home,' he said. 'I fear that that's the truth of it. I don't have your wider vision. I wish I had.'

'How can you have spent your entire career in the heart of the country's most powerful institution, and not have a sense of the wider world?' Buffy, a little calmer, sipped her hot coffee and felt it do her good. 'No, don't answer. In the answer to that lie all this country's problems.'

'It isn't *quite* like that.'

'It's not far off it,' said Buffy. 'The blinkered civil servant.' She picked up the paper, revealing beneath it the pile of Winton dinner plates which had remained unsold last week. William, she noticed, had knocked the price down. Probably wise. Until spring came, this was a quiet season. In spring, with everyone perking up, you could charge almost anything. She finished her coffee, held out the cup for more. A biting wind was playing around her ankles. She should be wearing her boots — how foolish to think, with a gleam of sunshine, that she'd be all right in these old K flatties.

She folded the paper, with its heartbreaking photographs of soft-faced lambs, and maps of fearful journeys, and put it in her bag. Danny, beneath the trestle, poked his head out, draped in crimson damask. She bent to stroke his ears. 'Hello, old boy, how's things?'

Other stallholders were arriving, parking for five minutes on the double yellows, heaving their boxes out before the warden came sauntering along. Normal life in London. Not so normal in the countryside, with its sealed-off gates and footpaths, and disinfected straw in every gateway.

'Oh, dear,' she said aloud. 'Oh, dear.' And then, because this could not go on all morning, she turned to William and reminded him about the concert at Mary Ward, in three weeks' time. 'I gave you a flier last week,' she said. 'Remember?'

'Indeed you did,' said William, who had loyally put it up in his drawing-room window, though he knew, let's face it, that no one in Dulwich was going to trek up to Bloomsbury just to hear the old dears warble away. He'd been to these concerts, often. He knew what they were like.

Then he was struck by a thought. Something gentle, for Matthew to start with. Somewhere where people knew him. Buffy knew him well enough.

'I might bring Matthew,' he said, pouring his own second cup. 'I might bring Matthew and Janice. I was going to tell you — they've met.'

'Oh?'

'I took her up to the hospital.'

'Oh.'

'Bit of a risk, plunging her in at the deep end, but actually — ' He stopped, remembering that rare, meltingly beautiful smile, and the way in which Janice, entirely out of her element, had stepped into the day room, with its smoke and blaring daytime television, smiling back, and as William introduced them had taken Matthew's hand, and knelt down beside him, and said: 'It's really good to meet you.'

'Actually she coped with it perfectly well?' said Buffy, and leaned forward to rearrange a pair of art deco vases. Plaster parrots. She had never liked them.

'She did,' said William. 'I mean, there were patients who disturbed her, I think — you can see some very sad sights in there, of course. But with Matthew — they seemed to hit it off, somehow. We went for a little walk in the grounds with Danny, had a bit of lunch, then we saw him into his OT class and said goodbye.'

'Very nice,' said Buffy. 'And what are they getting up to in OT these days? Basket weaving?'

'No,' said William, wondering at her tone. She could be quite sharp, old Buffy, especially when something had upset her. Foot-and-mouth — of course it was dreadful, but —

'They're painting at the moment,' he said. 'It makes me itch to pick up a brush.'

'Pick one up, then,' said Buffy. 'There's nothing to stop you.'

A woman was approaching the stall, her eye, quite clearly, drawn to the pair of parrots. Buffy fixed her with an uncompromising gaze. '*Good* morning,' she said brightly.

* * *

'I've had an idea,' Ernie told the girls. 'Bit of an inspiration.' It was Saturday lunch-time; they were gathered in the kitchen. Outside it was the usual filthy wet weather, but dogs were dogs, and needed walking, and he'd done his stint — been gouged out of doors by Mary just after ten, hammering on his window with one of Father's walking sticks, shouting and carrying on.

'Wake up, you old idler! Bestir yourself!'

'All right, all right, no need to shout.'

He came to the door and peered out. What a sight she was.

'What sort of time do you call this?' she demanded.

'Time for a bit of peace and quiet.' He stood his ground, the door open just a few inches. Have her in here and there'd be no stopping her, banging about with a mop and pail, hauling out his sleeping bag. 'I wasn't asleep,' he told her. 'I was working.'

She snorted. 'Working on what?'

'You wait and see.'

'Those dogs have been waiting since I don't know when. Come on, out you come, get your boots on.' She turned the stick upside down; he eyed the crook.

'You keep that thing away.'

He closed the door; he pulled his boots on, fetched down his waterproofs. Then he went out to the pens. Behind the wire the dogs leapt and scrabbled, barking joyously.

'Here I am, my darlings,' he told them, as Mary snapped open the padlocks. He bent to embrace them, kissing wiry coats. 'Off we go, then, off we go.'

And off they all went in the wet, noses down, tails beating, legs cocked at every corner.

'Mind out the way of that car! Flossie! Mind out the way!'

He bent to hold on to scruffs and collars, he tugged in the ones on the leads. Estate cars and Land Rovers slowed: he smiled and nodded, until they had gone. Then he shouted after them.

'Think you own the place! Have us all killed, you will!'

It had happened, once, to Jessie, a bright

young springer: she'd slipped out of the pen in the days before the padlocks, and raced off, leaping the front gate and racing down to the bend just as —

It didn't bear thinking about.

He got them all over the stile, and into the rough empty pasture. Lambs'd be out soon, that'd be good, but it stopped them walking here. Make the most of it now. He squelched across, head down, the rain dripping off his waterproof hat, while they all enjoyed themselves.

Now it was lunch-time. Mary let him in. He'd done his stint of cheese and crackers: no man could live on blimming cheese and crackers. Time for a bit of hot soup. Time for a nice pork chop. That'd be the day. He settled himself at the table and waited, while she stirred.

'Where's Sophes?'

'She'll be down.'

He tried to picture her, doing things upstairs. He only ever went up there to have a bath, and that wasn't often: too blimming cold in that bathroom, too blimming draughty. When they were kids, of course, they'd all been up there together, put to bed at six by Mother, lights out, curtains drawn.

'And I don't want to hear a sound.'

All that giggling, after she'd gone. Them were the days.

Something settled itself on his feet beneath the table. He bent down to peer, saw the hen, kept quiet. He could have the egg for supper, if Mary didn't twig. He drummed his fingers on the table.

'Smells good.'

Mary sniffed. She went to the bottom of the stairs and shouted.

When Sophie came down, he told them.

* * *

The woman who bought the parrots was writing a book.

'I'm something of an expert on art deco,' she told them. 'Something of a collector.'

She tried to beat them down, but William would have none of it.

'Sorry, my dear,' he told her, with a winning smile, 'but I can't let anyone ruin me, not even you. Do tell me more about this book you're writing, it sound fascinating.'

When she had gone, he entered the sum in his book, and tucked her cheque away.

'Now then,' he said to Buffy, 'where were we?'

'I can't remember.'

The market was livening up a bit now, all the stalls set up and people wandering down past the Pizza Express on Upper Street, and the little Afghan café round the corner. But oh, how cold it was.

'Yes you can,' said William. 'I'm sure we were talking about something important.' He put his hands together, musingly. How clever and interesting he looked, thought Buffy, especially in that scarf. He *was* clever and interesting, even if he did have blind spots. She gave a small involuntary sigh.

'Oh, dear,' he said at once. 'What a sad sound.

What is it, Buffy dear? Foot-and-mouth? Or something else?'

And the look he gave her was so tender and kind that she quite dissolved.

'William,' she began, with infinite caution.

'Got it!' he said suddenly. 'We were talking about Matthew and Janice. You know, I think she's really rather special. She's sensible and down to earth, but she's also much more sensitive than I'd given her credit for. And principled. Did I tell you she's a vegan?'

Buffy got to her feet. 'Yes,' she said. 'You did. More than once, if I remember rightly. I'm going to have a little look round, if you don't mind holding the fort.'

And she moved back her folding chair and stepped past him. Danny, beneath the table, was at once on the alert, and made to follow her, but William put down a restraining hand.

'Stay there, old boy,' he murmured. 'Stay put for now. I'm sorry,' he said to Buffy. 'I must be a crashing bore.'

But she couldn't answer him, and made her way with care among the stalls, until she had left the covered part of the market behind, and was walking with some difficulty along the crowded passage by the pub. Antique teddy bears gazed glassily at her from the tiny shop on the corner. One had particular character and distinction. For a dreadful moment she wanted nothing more than to hold him in her arms and weep into his comforting old fur.

* * *

'See?' said Ernie, warming to his theme. 'This could run and run.'

The table had been cleared of soup plates; he had been out to the trailer and come back, everything clutched to his chest in plastic carrier bags. He set it all up, propping against teapot and tin and jam jar, a proper exhibition, if you like, now that he'd mounted them on card. They sat there gazing: from Labrador Ned to little Pip; from grey-hound to Jack Russell, from Flossie, so old, but still so precious, to Benjy, so playful and bright. There was nothing like a boxer puppy, couldn't beat it for character. Mind you . . . Sophie leaned forward, and fingered the nose of a soulful young sheepdog. Was that Flash or Gerry? She tried to think.

'Mind,' said Ernie. 'Don't get crumbs on it.'

'I haven't got any crumbs,' said Sophie, withdrawing her finger. She looked again. 'Isn't that a lovely face?'

'What's that in your hair?' asked Mary suddenly. She leaned across and peered. 'When did you get that?'

Sophie's hand flew to the Great Dane. He was here at last, and how could she not wear him, now he was home?

'He wasn't very dear,' she said, and at once saw Mother, standing there with her rolling pin. 'Don't you lie to me, young lady!'

'Frippery,' said Mary. 'Endless frippery!' She banged on the table and everything leapt. 'We haven't the money, we haven't the funds.'

'Steady,' said Ernie, rescuing a collie-cross about to slip to the floor. He propped it up again. It was one of his best, though he said it himself. 'I don't want no arguing, I don't want no sniping. There's a body of work here, and I want some serious suggestions.'

Silence fell. He sat there, turning over the egg in his pocket.

'You're the one with the head for business,' he told Mary. 'Here I am, with a bold proposal, and all you can do is complain.'

'Tell us again what you had in mind,' said Sophie timidly.

'Concentrate, this time.' Blimey, how he needed a cig. Not a shred of baccy left, and not a penny till Monday. 'It's no good just dreaming and saying how pretty they are — we all know that, that's the point. The point is to reach a wider market. Make some serious money.'

'Serious money,' said Sophie, lingeringly.

'We need a business plan,' said Mary, averting her eyes from the Great Dane prancing through Sophie's pudding-basin hair.

'Now you're talking.'

'We need proper marketing.'

'We've always needed that.'

'We need a patron.'

'My plan,' he said again, watching Sophie's mind begin to wander already, 'is to start with a good show in town. Where, that's the thing. Teashop? Cinema? Town hall?'

'What about down in the parish? Parish hall would do nicely, they'll put up anything.'

Ernie regarded Sophie with scorn. 'In town, I said. Where people go. Then, when they see it, they pick up the leaflets.'

'The Perfect Present,' said Mary thoughtfully.

'Your Dog in Your Dining Room,' said Ernie. 'Commissions Undertaken.' He could see it all: the opening of the gate on to the gravel drive; the greeting at the door, the offer of coffee or tea. Admiring looks at the portfolio beneath his arm, the bounding up, the instant bonding. Shown into the drawing room, settled into a corner beside high windows on to a lawn. Out come the paints and brushes, down sits Rover, gazing up adoringly. The long contented hours. The mahogany door is quietly opened. '*May* I have a look?' Footsteps across the carpet, the small intake of breath. 'Oh, Mr *Harriman* — ' His name is made, his name is on everyone's lips, he's charging — what? Fifty? A hundred? Put up the prices and people respect you, never let people think you're cheap.

'With You for Evermore,' he said aloud. 'Your Lasting Memory.'

'I know,' said Sophie, all at once. 'I know just the place.'

* * *

Buffy walked blindly up Camden Passage, past the Camden Head, where wonderful smells of hot lunch were wafting forth and bursts of cheerful laughter sounded. She passed the stalls of lace and linen, the maps and period postcards, period kitchen things. She passed without a glance the humbler offerings on mats set out on the ground — she knew those tins and trinkets, those plastic toys — and she marched past the grand glass-plated fronts of the real antique shops, with their fathomless interiors and fathomless prices. In the window of Beck's, that darling toyshop, the little Hornby train ran round and round, as it had done in all the years that she and William had had their stall here. They knew this place by heart, knew every shopfront and most of the dealers. In their time they'd had countless lunches in the Camden Head, pottered about among the shops and stalls, and bought things. They'd introduced Danny to Poppy, the West Highland who sat in her basket on Beck's counter, dear old girl; they'd browsed in the Angel Bookshop, after packing up the stall.

Happy days. Ordinary, contented days.

Buffy turned now into the second covered area, crammed with stalls of paper-knives, paper-weights, silly reproduction signs. Perhaps, if you were in the mood, they might raise a smile. She was not in the mood. She came into Pierrepoint Arcade, and walked along it, cold, and fighting misery. Tables were set out on the flagstones, outside tiny shops. Most of the arcade was china, and most she knew by heart. She slowed, her eye caught by a pretty green-and-gold tea set; automatically, she made a guess at the pottery, and date. She stopped, and stood at the window. It was crammed.

Inside was a space perhaps ten by six. A tiny heater burned in the corner; the owner was nowhere to be seen. Must have popped out to the loo — yes, there was the sign on the door: Back in a Tick. Could mean anything. Buffy pressed her face to the glass and peered. A comfy low chair with a cushion stood by the table, where rested an open book. There wasn't an inch of space uncovered: the tables, the walls, the mounted shelves were filled to the last inch.

And oh, how *warm* it looked, with that bright little flame, glinting on gravy boat and soup bowl. The cardigan hung on the back of the chair; what a nice chintz cushion. She could just see herself in there. With an inch more room, she could see William, too —

No, she couldn't. He was too tall, they'd need the same space all over again, to fit the two of them, and anyway —

'Excuse me.'

Someone was trying to get by her, as someone else came up the narrow passage. She pressed herself against the door, and a tall young woman strode past, in jeans and jacket.

Was that her? Surely not. Surely she wouldn't have come up here without warning; surely, if William had arranged it, he would have told her.

Buffy gazed after her. No — this girl was fair, and the Shropshire lass was dark, she remembered that. She breathed a sigh, and leaned against the door frame. It started to rain. She began to cry.

This was dreadful. Weeping in the open, on a Saturday morning. Going to pieces, in the middle of the day. What had become of her, where would all this lead?

She fumbled in her pocket, found a hankie. There. She blew her nose. There, that was better.

'My father,' she heard William say, in his

kindly, beautiful voice, 'was never without his hip flask.'

She had snapped his head off, it was awful. And oh, how she could do with a little nip.

She made herself grow calmer. She would not let this happen. She wiped her eyes, and she knew that no one had noticed, for, let's face it, who would? She was out in the press of a busy Saturday, people getting on with their lives, looking at old china, not at old bats like her. And she turned from the door, and walked slowly on, seeing in her mind's eye — oh, it was dreadful, dreadful — a poor frightened ewe, stumbling up the ramp of a huge dark lorry with all her companions, shouted at, pressed up against other heaving sides, hearing the door slam, and the bolts pushed to; feeling the engine start up, and the long, long journey begin.

17

William was out, with Danny. Janice was in. She took herself down from her blue-and-white room at the top of the house, past the family photographs, into the hall. It was mid-afternoon, and she'd done her lunch-time shift; in a couple of hours she'd be back for the evening. Now — the place was hers. She could hear, in the quietness, the tick from the kitchen clock downstairs.

'From my grandfather's schoolroom, I believe,' said William, winding it up each Sunday evening. He ran a finger over the mahogany casing, pushed the door to, and touched the pendulum. Off it went, steady and true; back went the big brass key on the top. 'There. I'd like to say it kept perfect time, but it's slow, like me. Getting old.' He took off his glasses, he gave her his smile. 'Now then, what shall we have for supper?'

She could hear, now, the carriage clock on the drawing-room mantelpiece, the little whirr of wheels, like an intake of breath, just before it began to chime. One, two, three notes into the stillness. The door was ajar; she went in.

Was it taking a liberty? Would he mind? He'd told her to make herself at home. She let the door swing to; she stood there, drinking it in, the size of it, the largest room she had ever been in, remembering her feelings the day she'd arrived, and they'd sat taking tea by the fire: that this was somewhere in which you could grow and expand, let your mind roam, feel at peace. The carriage clock ticked softly; she walked from end to end.

The winter afternoon was dull and cold; nothing in the sky today held the promise of spring; in the gardens at front and back the snowdrops were over, and although the beds and cracks in the flagstones were speared by bulbs they were still tight and only inches high, not a bud visible: the frost had seen to that. Yet this room was filled with light: pale, even, but everywhere, from the immense high windows at back and front, and she walked up and down between them, over the creaking floor, smelling the ash from last night's fire, observing the patina on book jacket, china, desk and oak cupboard and piano, where photographs of the family were crammed, and needed dusting, and where Matthew, before his illness, had used to play. She stopped in front of it.

There they all were.

There were William and Eve on their wedding day, he in tails, she in a lily-white dress, with her veil thrown back and her hand tucked into the crook of his arm, and the two of them, you could see it, truly in love. 'That rare state of being' — was that how William would describe it? Something like that. They stood beneath that old stone arch, in a flood of sunlight, and . . . well, there they were, and it must have been —

Here were the children: Eve with her newborn baby Claire, bending over that wide-eyed face, the long snowy fall of shawl, the little fist. Here was Claire at two or three, squinting cheerfully into the sun, in a square-cut fringe and candy-striped sundress, buttoned on the shoulder, clutching a bear. Janice paused: was he upstairs, with all the other things left behind? No, she was sure not — he must have gone: into a new home, three children, married life. Then, a year or two later, came the baby brother, sleeping in his canopied pram beneath the trees, with Claire, on sandalled tiptoe, peering in.

And there, thereafter, were the two of them, always together, or almost: on the beach, with their buckets and spades; coming down the little slide in the garden, her arms round his waist; in a studio portrait, side by side and laughing — two healthy, contented, loved and well-dressed children, prepared for well-balanced, purposeful lives.

And here was Matthew, in a frame by himself, in his new school uniform. Janice picked it up.

What could you know from the face of a child, of what might lie ahead? He was open faced, though not in Claire's square-jawed, frank, determined mould. He smiled — and he looked, already, a little like William, you could see that at once, in his height, the easy way he carried himself, his charm. And was there, in those smiling eyes, beneath the clear brow, the tousled head of fair hair, a shadow? He was thin: that was noticeable, but that was all.

She put the photograph back; she picked up another, and another: Matthew at eight, with his violin; Matthew at twelve or thirteen, at the piano — this piano; at fifteen or sixteen, with his violin again, here, in the middle of the family drawing room, before his music stand, his chin resting lightly upon the instrument, extraordinary fingers on the keys, the bow drawn back in his long right hand, his eyes, for a moment, raised from the music, entirely intent, absorbed, lost to the world.

Janice carried the photograph to the window, and stood so the light, wintry and dull as it was, could fall upon it. She breathed upon the glass, which needed cleaning; she rubbed at it, and as the vapour cleared, Matthew looked back at her, and through and beyond her: a gifted and completely beautiful boy, for whom, at that moment, no human being mattered at all.

The phone was ringing. Somewhere the phone was ringing, and had been for ages, she realised, coming to with a start, and hurrying out to the hall, the photograph in her hand. She put it down on the hall table, and picked up the receiver.

'Hello?'

'Janice?' said Claire. 'Is that you?'

* * *

William threw a stick, and then another. Danny, each time, came scampering back, over the muddy stretch of grass, on to the path where he was pacing about. Winter afternoon, a weekday, an overcast sky — few people out and about in the park, and how wise they were, thought William, feeling the cold, clapping gloved hands together. He nodded to one or two other dog-walkers, known by sight for a long time now: the fey-looking woman with her Afghan, the old chap with his sharp-faced black-and-tan mongrel, lifting a leg in the empty rose beds, whistled away.

'Not getting any warmer.'

'Fearful, isn't it?' He bent to retrieve Danny's stick, and held it high. Danny watched, eager and waiting.

'Go on, off you go!' And he hurled it as far as he could, not bad for someone of his age, though he said so himself: life in the old boy yet. Danny raced off, and he walked on, beating his arms, keeping the circulation going.

Far above, London gulls were wheeling, sharp-eyed and hungry, over the leafless trees. Across the park a gardener had lit a bonfire: the last of the debris of leaves and pruning and fallen branches before spring came, if it ever came, burning into the afternoon, smoke into smoky cloud. And what did this remind him of, this dark plume rising?

Foot-and-mouth! Look at these pictures, William — have you been watching it on the news? Those pyres, those dreadful pyres — I just can't bear it.

Poor old Buffy: how she took things to heart. Had he imagined it, or had she, away from the stall, been weeping about it all? She wouldn't look at him when she came back.

'I'm sorry.' She sank heavily into her chair. 'I'm dreadfully out of sorts for some reason — please don't take any notice.'

He patted her arm. 'It's my fault — I talk

about myself too much.'

'No, no, please don't say that. Let's just forget it, I'll be fine tomorrow.'

One or two punters came and went: they sold a Creamware jug, and a couple of Victorian tiles. Quite a good price for the tiles. But somehow — after all these years of friendship, the easy chat, the never having to think about a thing, just rubbing along so nicely — somehow all that was gone, today.

The rain fell harder; everything felt dismal.

'Let's call it a day,' he said at last. 'Let's go and have lunch.'

But the Camden Head was packed, and neither of them could face it: all that loud laughter, all those wet clothes.

'I'll treat you to Frederick's,' he said, as they came out into the wet. 'Come on, it'll do us both good.'

But Frederick's was booked solid, and at that point Buffy said: 'I'm fit for nothing anyway, William, I wouldn't enjoy it.' And she put up her umbrella and nothing he could say would dissuade her. He saw her to the bus stop, he saw her on to the bus, Danny tucked inside his coat, and she lifted a hand at the streaming window, but oh, so bleakly — not at all like spirited old Buffy.

'I'll phone you tonight,' he mouthed as the bus pulled away, but he didn't know whether she had seen. He went back to the car, parked in Duncan Terrace, the boxes piled up in the back, and a ticket on the windscreen. Raindrops clung prettily to the plastic envelope; he pulled it off, threw it into the glove compartment, and drove home feeling grim.

Janice was out; Mrs T. had been and gone, and though the house was clean it was also cold and empty. He put on the heating, had a hot bath, lit the fire. Restored, he phoned Buffy that evening, glass in hand.

'I'm fine,' she said, but she didn't sound it. 'Think no more about it, William, I'm having an early night.' And she hung up quite quickly, and that was that.

Oh, dear. He couldn't, as Mrs T. would say — so often — he couldn't make it out.

Oh, dear — and just when everything had been looking up.

And now —

Danny was running back again, stick clamped between his dachshund jaws. They were bred for hunting, of course; they were fierce, even ferocious working dogs by nature. For a moment, bending to take the stick — and that was enough now, it was simply too bloody cold to stay out a moment longer — he found himself thinking of the Dog Museum, with its great range of the canine: from stuffed to (presumably) working, to flat out by the fire. What a strange business it was. He clipped on Danny's lead, made his way to the gates.

There was nothing he could do about Buffy, not at the moment. And she'd rally, she always did. No — the next thing was Matthew, the meeting with Fisher at last: tomorrow as ever was.

Action. Teatime. He looked at his watch.

Janice would still be at home, before her evening shift. He'd light the fire, put the kettle on, call her down.

'Come on, Danny. Homeward bound.' He tugged on the lead, walked faster.

But when he reached the house, he knew straight away that it was empty — no light at the top-floor window, in Claire's old room, and the silence in the unlit hall was palpable. He switched on the lamp, saw the note by the phone:

Gone to see Claire, then straight to work. Janice.

* * *

'Come in,' said Claire. 'You must be frozen.'

'I'm OK.' She wiped her feet on the mat and entered the roomy hall. Through living with William she had, even in this short time, grown to have a sense of the well-heeled London life, but in his house everything was worn, faded, had been lived in, unreplaced, for donkey's years. The place gathered itself around you: you could sink in, settle down, get on. Here, where there were three children, coats were neat upon the coatrack, shoes in the rack below; the well-brushed stairs ran up to a sparkling landing window, hung with heavy curtains, looped back with silky ropes and tassels. Bloody hell.

She tucked her hat and gloves into her pockets; she let Claire take jacket and scarf and hang them up; she followed her into the kitchen, which was huge. Acres of classy vinyl, patterned in terracotta tiles; gleaming Rayburn, clean tea towels on the rail; long family table laid with that wipe-clean fabric but in a pattern which looked like antique wallpaper; more shining windows on to well-planted window boxes and the garden. There, at least, were signs that things had got a bit out of hand: no one, in this winter's weather, could maintain the perfect garden.

'Do sit down.' Claire was putting the kettle on. She leaned against the Rayburn rail as Janice pulled out a chair, and smiled at her. 'It's very nice of you to come.'

'That's OK.'

'I just thought — if you do come and baby-sit, it would be nice to get to know one another.'

'Yeah.'

'And for you to get a feel of the house, and meet the children.'

'Yeah,' said Janice again. 'Sure.'

There was silence. The kettle came to life. Janice felt for her tin, which wasn't there. Just as well — who would dare to light up in a house like this? She found herself looking round for signs of animal life: a dog basket, a dish, put down for the cat. Even a hamster cage would do it. Even a cockatiel. She looked at the shelf of cookbooks, the labelled boxes of Lego and felt tips and Warhammer elves.

'What time do the kids get back?'

The slightest furrow creased Claire's intelligent brow. 'Just after four. They don't come back by themselves — I'm on a rota.'

'Oh.' She watched the careful rinsing of the pot, over a spotless white sink; the taking out of tea bags from a tin. Rather like William's tin:

black and Chinese red — perhaps he had given it to her. Bit different from the caddy in the Dog Museum.

What was it with that frown, then?

'Did I say something stupid?' she asked. 'I don't really know much about kids.'

Again, that infinitesimal furrow, as Claire took expensive-looking mugs from hooks.

'I just have a thing about that word.'

'What word?'

'Kids.'

'Eh?'

'It's rather — I don't know — rather denigrating, somehow. It makes me think of *Time Out* special issues: Kidstuff. Where to Take the Kids. As if they were just a class of being. All those shrieking TV programmes — Kids! Everything so *cheerful*.'

'What do you call them, then?'

'Children,' said Claire, and took milk from the fridge. 'A proper word. Like childhood. You can't have *kid*hood.'

'You're just like your dad,' said Janice. 'I suppose I should call him your father.'

'I think you should, and I'm not at all like him.' She brought everything over, set it all down. 'Do you take sugar?'

'No. Nor milk,' Janice added, as Claire's hand moved towards a green-and-white jug which also put her in mind of William. 'I'm vegan, didn't he tell you?'

Claire sat, and looked at her.

'No, he didn't. We don't talk all that often, and anyway he's getting forgetful. How very principled of you. Would you like a slice of lemon?'

'If you've got it.'

'Of course.' And she rose, and took one from the vegetable rack, and sliced it into a cobalt-blue saucer with a thin gold rim. 'Here.'

'Thanks.'

And Claire poured the tea, and Janice dropped in a slice of lemon, and Claire asked, sitting back in her chair and observing her across the table, 'How long have you been a vegan?'

'Since I was a kid,' said Janice, giving what she knew was a winning, ironic little lift of an eyebrow, and the set of Claire's features, so uncannily like those of her fearsome distant cousin, dissolved all at once into a smile full of warmth and humour.

'I suppose I do need taking down a peg or two,' she said, and then, after a moment, sipping her tea: 'I certainly need something.'

'How do you mean?'

There was a pause. There was a look — as if she were on the brink of something momentous. Then Claire shook her head, and waved a hand. 'Never mind.' She put down her mug, and the subject, whatever it may have been, was clearly closed. 'How are you getting on here? You seem to have settled in very well.'

'Yeah,' said Janice. 'I suppose I have. William — I mean your dad — I mean your father — he's been great. I really like him. And I was lucky to get the wine-bar job.'

'How did you get it?'

She snapped her fingers. 'Just like that.'

Claire smiled. 'How clever of you. And what else have you been doing?'

'Oh, you know — going to a few museums and stuff.' She described the outings to Greenwich, the Dulwich Picture Gallery. She felt Claire's eyes intent upon her. She looked down at her expensive mug of black tea, with its slice of lemon.

'And?' Claire prompted.

The lemon was floating, meditatively, from rim to rim. Janice, watching it, held the memory and image of Matthew within her, as she had done for days, not telling anyone, as if to talk about him would break a spell. But not to mention the visit — if Claire found out afterwards, she'd wonder, wouldn't she? Think it strange.

'We went to see your brother,' she said, and heard herself, for the first time, sound awkward.

'Oh.' There was a little pause. 'And how was that?'

'It was . . . I was a bit freaked out by the hospital. But Matthew — I liked him. I felt . . . OK with him, I suppose.'

'Good,' said Claire, but when Janice looked up she was frowning again.

'Do you mind me going to see him?' she asked, and remembered, all at once, the glance along the sunlit upper landing, in William's house, towards her brother's old room, a glance full of sadness, quickly erased.

'No,' said Claire, lifting her mug to her lips. 'No, of course not.'

Was she telling the truth? Was it a bit of a

threat, a bit of an intrusion, having this stranger land in your midst, and start stirring things up?

Was that what she was doing?

'You were very close, weren't you?' she said. 'When you were young.'

Claire looked at her, and Janice felt herself begin to blush. There she had been, nosing about in the empty house, looking at family photographs without so much as a by-your-leave. Claire must realise — it must look dreadful.

'I mean,' she said, flounderingly, 'I mean that's what I imagine. I'm an only child, I don't know what it's like, I suppose . . . ' Her voice trailed away.

'Are you?' asked Claire, a sister and mother of three. 'I've always thought only children are so interesting, I must say. Such a complex relationship with one's parents, so many inner resources.' She smiled, in full child-psychology mode, and Janice felt her blush begin to fade, the conversation steered, quite deliberately, away from the source of her embarrassment. 'You become so independent, I imagine. I certainly sense that about you.'

'Yeah, well. Yeah, I suppose so.'

'But your parents must miss you. Is this the first time you've lived away from home?'

'Yeah, yeah it is. Time I gave them another ring, I suppose.'

And where had Matthew got to in all this? Was it safe to mention him again?

'Do you mind me asking — ' she began. 'About Matthew. I mean, like — ' She didn't know how to go on.

For a moment Claire did not respond; for a moment, in the silence, Janice felt aware once more of something quite unfathomable. Then the rain began to fall again, and Claire said slowly, 'He's been ill for a very long time. You do realise that.'

'Yes,' said Janice, as the rain sank into the untended garden.

'And is unlikely to recover,' said Claire, with great deliberation.

'Is that — ' Despite the lemon tea, her mouth felt dry. 'I mean — is that definite?'

'I wouldn't say anything in mental health was *definite*. But — ' She spread her hands. 'He's schizophrenic. My father must have told you.'

'No,' said Janice. 'Not exactly.' And she felt something within her shift, like the plates of the earth or something.

* * *

The sky darkened, the rain fell harder, the children — as she must think of them — were dropped off from the school run.

'This is Janice,' said Claire, when they had hung up wet coats and bags and come trooping into the kitchen. 'She's staying with Grandpa.'

'Like, the lodger,' said Janice, getting to her feet. 'Hi.'

'Hi.'

'Piers, Hugo, Geraldine,' said Claire, and they each shook hands. They were bright looking, nice looking. She expected them all to go off and collapse in front of the telly, like normal kids after school, but they sat round the table and waited, as Claire made tea.

'Have you brought Danny?' asked Geraldine, looking around.

' 'Fraid not. He's good, isn't he?'

'He's wicked,' said Hugo. 'Remember the skidding? Whee!' And he made a sweeping gesture.

'Skidding?'

They started to describe it; Claire came over with sandwiches and drinks.

'Janice is going to do some baby-sitting,' she told them.

'We've got a baby-sitter,' said Geraldine, taking her beaker.

'We don't need a baby-sitter,' said Piers, reaching for a sandwich. 'Not being rude or anything.' He was tall and lanky and had a blurred, tired look which put Janice in mind of his father, last seen in the wine bar on Valentine's Day. 'I can baby-sit,' he said.

'Are you fourteen?' asked Janice. 'It's illegal if you're not fourteen.'

Piers shrugged, and was silent.

'Why do we need another baby-sitter?' asked Geraldine.

Janice looked at her watch. Why did they? 'I'd better be off in a minute.'

* * *

'Please come again,' said Claire, in the hall, as she pulled on her jacket and scarf. 'We'd love to have you. I'll phone.'

'Yeah. Sure. Thanks for the tea.'

'It's a pleasure.' She put out a hand, and rested it for a moment on Janice's arm. 'You mustn't be upset about Matthew. It's sad, but it's how things are. My father should have told you. He can be very thoughtless.'

'He wants to have him home,' said Janice, with a flash of how this might be. 'He often talks about it.'

Claire shook her head. 'I think that's extremely unlikely.' And then voices rose in the kitchen, and she pulled open the front door, saying: 'I'd better get on.'

Outside, it was dark, and chucking it down. 'Do let me lend you an umbrella.'

'It's OK,' said Janice, 'I'll make a dash for it. 'Bye.'

And she went out into the rain, silvered in the lamplight, feeling Claire's watchful gaze upon her, until the door slowly closed, and she began to run.

18

Janice sat drinking tea and smoking, at the table in the kitchen with its red-checked cloth. It was mid-afternoon; she was waiting for William to return from his hospital visit.

'I should be home by teatime,' he had said, buttoning his coat in the hall, adjusting the sea-green scarf before the mirror. 'That is if Fisher is prompt — you can never tell, these days.' Beside him, Danny was looking up brightly, full of anticipation. 'Sorry, old chap — not today.' He turned to Janice, waiting at the foot of the stairs. 'Sure you won't come?'

'I'll keep the home fires burning,' said Janice, stretching out a hand to Danny, who at once came trotting over. 'I'll give him a walk, and be here when you get back. I might bake a cake, if that's OK.'

'Very OK,' said William. 'Entirely satisfactory.' He turned up his collar, pulled on his gloves, reached for his umbrella from its stand. 'Well, now — wish me luck.'

'Good luck.' And she came over, Danny trotting back again, and he bent to kiss her: once, twice, as Londoners did, she kept noticing, and she felt the dry brush of his well-shaven skin against hers, and the warmth of his lips on her cheek.

'There.' He squeezed her hand with soft worn leather. 'I'm off.' And he strode to the door, and she held Danny back, feeling almost choked.

'I'm sure it'll be fine,' she said.

'You haven't told me about Claire.' He turned, suddenly, his fingers on the latch.

'Not much to tell.' He'd been in bed by the time she got home from the wine bar; today Mrs T. had been banging about until lunch-time, had only just gone, and his mind was all on Matthew. 'I might do some baby-sitting one day.'

'You met the children?' His face lit up.

'I did, they're great.' She looked at him, standing there, hovering, really, putting off the moment. 'Go on,' she said gently. 'You'll be late.'

And he nodded, and opened the door. She caught a glimpse of the tight buds on the magnolia, just in leaf, felt the cold come into the unheated hall, and then he was gone, and she buried her face in Danny's chestnut neck, noticing grey hairs.

'Come on.'

Down in the kitchen, she let him out into the garden, opened the cupboard doors. She shook raisins into a blue-and-white striped bowl, cracked eggs into another. Cornish Ware, William had told her, worth quite a bit these days. She'd seen bowls like this on Albert Page's dresser, cracked and yellow with age, like him. How was he getting on without her, poor old git?

She turned on the oven, put half a packet of organic soya spread to warm in a Creamware bowl within it, and opened more cupboard doors until she'd found a baking tin. She greased it, shook wholemeal flour over it, watched Danny, in the garden, sniffing and cocking a leg, looking up as a magpie suddenly arrived, landing on the wall and giving that hoarse cak-ak-cak she'd know anywhere, had heard all her life in the Shropshire woods and hills. He cocked his glossy head, and lifted his tail, his eye wicked and bright. Cak-ak-ak-cak, across the London garden, soaked by the endless rain into mud: no one but Danny had been out there for weeks.

One for sorrow.

Janice took out the Creamware bowl and beat brown sugar into the softened soya spread. She beat the eggs with a fork into a foaming froth, stirred them in with a wooden spoon, beat in wholemeal flour and raisins, and finely grated lemon and orange peel. But for the eggs it was vegan; she wouldn't eat it, she'd keep it for William, in a tin wrapped up in greaseproof paper, something he could have by the fire when he felt like it; something to take to the china stall and share with his old friend Buffy, whom she was waiting to meet. She spooned it all into the baking tin, put it in the oven, set the timer. Right: that was that. She washed up the bowls, partly because the largest was too big to go in the machine, and partly because, though it made her feel like the Harriman cousins, she wasn't used to dishwashers — not at home, nor at Cloud Nine, come to that. She wasn't used to a lot of things she'd met down here, but then that was the point of coming, wasn't it? To open up her life.

Cak-ak-ak-cak. Bright eyed, watchful, still there. Janice put the kettle on, and leaned on the sink and watched the bird and dog and fitful sun and cloud. Shropshire things, if you just made a list of them: she might have been in the kitchen in Cloud Nine, looking out over the hills at magpie and starling and blackbird, and the dogs of the visitors, hoping for biscuits. And she had a sudden memory of the morning during the storms of last November, of cycling up on Leinthall Ridge, finding a tree down and hauling boughs out of the way across the road, watched by a beady-eyed crow, and a couple of magpies. Two for joy — old wives' stuff, the kind of thing her gran was always saying, or one of the cousins, or Albert, but it had cheered her up, and that very day she'd met Eric.

Well. So much for that.

And now —

One for sorrow. What a harsh cry. And now he was up and away, on a sudden gust of wind, over to a tree in a neighbouring garden, where she could still hear him, and Danny, too, looking up and barking.

The kettle switched itself off; the kitchen, which had smelled of Flash, now filled with the smell of baking. Janice made tea in a blue-and-white Cornish Ware mug; she let Danny in again, sat down with her tin at the table. Would William mind if she smoked? Just one. And she rolled up and lit up, as Danny settled into his basket — she wasn't going to take him out, sorry, she'd done enough dog-walking to last a lifetime, and it was warm in here, and she needed to think.

And she thought about Claire, and yesterday afternoon: the intensity of that gaze, across that table, in that perfectly appointed kitchen.

I suppose I do need taking down a peg or two. I certainly need something . . .

And what is that? wondered Janice, inhaling Golden Virginia. What is it with this immaculate house and everything just right, but not right at all?

She thought about Matthew, as she had thought about him for days; of the silence when one tried to find out more.

You do realise he is very ill . . . he's schizophrenic . . . my father should have told you . . .

I couldn't have gone today, thought Janice now, drinking her milkless tea. Should she have done? Been a support for William, going off all alone to a meeting he dreaded? She knew that he did — she could tell; he must do. But she couldn't have faced that place again, without having some hope —

Of what?

And is unlikely to recover . . .

If William knew that —

How did Claire know that?

And she closed her eyes, and relived once again that moment of illumination, entire and complete and unlike anything else, when a man with a face like a sleeping angel had slowly turned, and seen her, and dissolved her with his smile.

* * *

William sat across the desk. Matthew's consultant pulled a file from a heap, and opened it. The room was cramped, the file was bulging. William read, upside down, snatched details of his son's confinéd life — the phrase came upon him, even as his eyes skimmed over the dosages of drugs, the reports and observations, his own impassioned letter.

My son's confinéd life —

The music of Shakespeare, or Donne. He pictured a winter garden, a man alone, in a hat and black buttoned coat, pacing up and down and writing, to ease his own distress.

'Well?' asked Fisher. He was of an age and type which William, from the quite different milieu of his Treasury days, knew well: over sixty, living a life of driven intensity, saved by a powerful mind from complete exhaustion. He thought it was Fisher who had signed the papers sectioning Matthew, all those years ago — confining him, indeed, lest he murder his own father.

'Well?'

William looked at shrewd pale eyes behind newly fashionable wire-rimmed spectacles.

He said, with difficulty: 'I'm very wound up. I've lost my concentration. Please forgive me. What were you saying?'

Fisher took off his glasses and leaned forward in his cushioned plastic chair. The shadow of a wing fell briefly upon William's letter, as a magpie flew past the window.

The sorrow of my son's confinéd life —

Fisher leaned on the desk, and pressed long, sixty-year-old fingers to his lips. His gaze met William's; William's eyes filled with tears.

'Forgive me,' he murmured again, and cleared his throat.

'You have been through a very great deal,' said Fisher, watching him. 'I understand your feelings — they are entirely natural.'

'But things have been getting much better,' said William, feeling for his handkerchief. 'Much.'

'You mean with Matthew?'

'Not exactly. I mean . . . well, yes, in some ways. I have sensed potential, I have allowed myself to hope. I have wanted to — ' he gestured, blew his nose. 'Have wanted to bestir myself — breathe some new life into the whole thing. Oh, dear.' He put his handkerchief back in his pocket, coughed experimentally. Yes: he was steady again.

'At Christmas — ' began William, and explained a little about Buffy, an old friend with clear views, who had made her feelings about Matthew plain. Drugged to the eyeballs, if Fisher would forgive him. Turning into a zombie: Fisher would understand that this was only one person's view. But then — and he explained a little about the arrival of his lodger, a bright, original young woman who was livening up the household, who had put a spring in his step, lessened his loneliness, made him feel —

'Young again?' asked Fisher drily.

'And what is wrong with that?' asked William, recovering his spirit a little, now that his tongue had loosened.

'Nothing at all. It all sounds — ' But he left the sentence unfinished, and lifted William's letter from the file, and ran his eyes over its distinctive hand once more, turning the pages.

'I brought Janice here,' said William. 'Last week. I introduced them.'

'And?' Fisher laid down the letter.

And William described the encounter: the radiant smile, the walk in the grounds, the way in which Janice and Matthew — curiously, quite unexpectedly — had seemed at ease with one another. It was something he could not account for, but it lifted his spirits.

'And you are proposing? Your wish is?'

William closed his eyes. There stole upon his inner eye a scene: Matthew in the drawing room, before his music stand. Violin and bow were in his hands; the one met the other, hesitantly, in a little scale. A smile played over his lips; Janice, perched on the piano stool, watched intently, swinging a foot. The scale rose and fell, and rose again. William, in his chair with Danny, leaned back and listened, feeling the old days begin anew.

He opened his eyes, saw Fisher's cool, clear-sighted gaze upon him. He asked carefully, 'What is the best we can hope for?'

Fisher's long fingertips were pressed together as if in prayer — did anyone but a doctor or priest ever make such a gesture?

'We can adjust his medication,' he said slowly. 'It's true he has been heavily sedated for perhaps too long. They're pretty much a sledge-hammer, the traditional drugs — Stelazine, that's what Matthew's been on, I think.' And he looked down at the file again. 'Yes. Well — we can ease him off that, we can try him on one of the new-generation pills. Respiradone.' He made a note.

'What does that do?' asked William. My darling boy, he thought, pumped through with all of this. My darling clever boy.

'Respiradone is still a sedative. But it's gentler, it's one of a group we call atypicals — ' Fisher reached behind him, pulled down a pharmacopoeia from the shelf, flicked through the index, found the page. 'We'll try it,' he said, still reading. 'We'll give it a go.'

'And will there be — ' William tried to imagine it. 'Side effects? Withdrawal symptoms?'

'Probably.' Fisher closed the book. 'Almost certainly, I should think. But in time he might do much better. We'll have to see.'

'And if he does well?' asked William, with a little flare of hope.

'Then you could try a longer visit home, see how he responds. Is that what you would like?'

'It is,' he said fervently. 'I feel so certain that this is what he needs: familiar surroundings, stimulation, love . . . '

Fisher made another note in the file, and closed it. 'Of course,' he said carefully, 'there are those of a younger generation than I who'd throw all these drugs out of the window. They wouldn't even give Matthew this diagnosis. 'Schizophrenia' — they say it's a label, an all-purpose, meaningless term. Psychosis can take many forms, have many causes. They'd look for a psychosocial model — they'd try to treat him with therapy. Cognitive behavioural therapy

— have you heard of that at all?'

William had not. He recalled, with a horrible intensity, the night he tried never to think of: Matthew's unrecognisable hatred, and rage, the smashing, splintering glass and furniture, the upraised candlestick become a murder weapon.

Something had had to be done. Something had had to knock him out.

But now —

But why —

'It's all *your* fault,' he heard Claire say bitterly. 'Because *you* never notice anything — '

'Oh, dear,' he said aloud. 'Oh, God.'

Fisher put a hand across the desk. 'We can only try. If he picks up, we might try all sorts of things. But please — don't expect too much. Disappointment is hard to bear as one grows older.'

William looked at him, but there was no elaboration, and slowly he got to his feet.

'Thank you,' he said, as he had been saying for years. 'You've been very kind.'

And then they shook hands, and he opened the door on to the waiting area, the Tuesday clinic — oh, such a blessedly ordinary phrase — with its understated turmoil, its sea of troubled lives.

* * *

It was growing dark. William walked down the road, towards his home, where lamps were lit: in the hall, with its tattered apricot silk; in the drawing room, where firelight flickered. He quickened his step, beat the umbrella against his coat. God, it was cold.

The iron gate squeaked at his touch, and was stiff: something else that needed attending to, as soon as spring arrived. He closed it, climbed the stone steps, unlocked the door.

The house was warm, and the smell of baking wafted up from the lower depths. A fruitcake, with a hint of citrus. Heaven. He was about to call out, to whistle, to say he was back, but then he didn't want to — he wanted only to savour the moment, and he quietly closed the door and stood there, letting it all wash over him: a proper home, a proper tea, a place for Matthew to return to, now he was going to recover. For he would, he would.

The sorrow of my son's confinéd life / Is washed away, for he is well again . . .

The phrasing had run through his head during the entire long walk home, musical and haunting.

And what rhymes with life? he asked himself, leaning against the door in a flood of weary happiness, seeing her walk up the stairs, and smile, and come to greet him.

⋆ ⋆ ⋆

They stood in the middle of Healing Arts, and strange scents wafted over them. Ernie started to cough.

'Blimey. It's like a sweet shop.'

'Ssh,' said Sophie, tugging at his sleeve. 'Come along here. Come and say hello.'

Portfolio beneath his arm, he shuffled across

to the counter, temporarily unattended. Baskets of soap wrapped in Cellophane stood next to jars of prettily coloured balls of bath oil.

'Thirty-five pence, for one of them? How much are them soaps?'

They were £2.60 each.

'Blimming rip-off. And what's a tea tree, when it's at home?'

'*Ssh!*'

There were little heaps of leaflets. He picked one up. It was pale green, and written in calligraphy, with a leafy border. He peered. There was a name, with a lot of letters after it. There was a photograph, of an intense-looking woman past her prime.

Are you suffering from tension, anxiety and stress?
Is insomnia ruining your life?
Are you a victim of compulsive habits?
I am a qualified Masseuse, Hypnotherapist and Counsellor.
I have many years of successful experience in treating phobias, depression, smoking, relationship problems and back complaints.
Unlock your hidden energy. Learn the secrets of an ancient healing force.
Restore your body's natural balance and rid yourself of toxins.
Private consultations and group work.
Your life is in my hands.

Ernie snorted. He picked up another, in raspberry pink. It offered a course in one-to-one life-focusing, in tranquil surroundings. Where was that, then? He peered at the address. That was old Ford's place, wasn't it? Who'd he sold up to, after all these years? Must've been someone with a bob or two, to do up that old ruin. He picked up another leaflet.

If you'd like to improve your ability to stay grounded and centred, to purify your working space and keep your energy clear, I may be able to help . . .

Sophie was gazing at the cards of hair slides and earrings. Her square, bitten fingers strayed towards a pair of dangling trout.

'*Good* morning!'

They both started.

'How are you, Sophie?' The woman behind the counter was bright and smiling. She wore a nice soft jumper in royal blue, with a scarf loosely knotted at the neck, and a cheerful lipstick. Ernie perked up. The last time he'd been in here they'd been served half-heartedly by a wan-looking girl whose grey-complexioned child slept in a pushchair. And not so much stock in here, neither: half-empty shelves. Under new management, that must be it. Rip-off. Profit. Just what he needed.

'This is my brother,' said Sophie, pushing him forward. 'Ernie. He's an artist.'

'How do you do?' she said kindly. 'I'm Daphne.'

'Pleased to meet you.'

'And what can we do for you today? I see you have your eye on those trout, Sophie. Aren't they pretty?'

'She's an old trout herself,' said Ernie. 'Heh, heh, heh.'

Mary would have swiped him good and proper, shop or no shop, but Sophie just gave him her look.

'We was wondering — ' she began, and he put his portfolio on the counter with a flourish. Leaflets fluttered to the floor and a lucky magnetic ladybird dropped from the side of a jar and fell among the Cellophaned baskets. Daphne retrieved it. Sophie bent for the papers, and muddled them up. Customers stepped aside.

'Oh, dear.' Daphne lifted the portfolio in her manicured hands and leaflets swirled this way and that in the passage of air. Sophie's hand went to her mouth: he could feel her thinking, We should never have come.

'Like she says,' he began, with some authority. 'I'm an artist, and that there's my work. And some leaflets. We was thinking about a show.'

People were queuing. People began to cough. Daphne stood the portfolio behind the counter and looked firmly past them. They took themselves into a corner, and waited.

'Never give up,' said Ernie. 'That's my motto.'

* * *

'Well, now,' said Daphne, some while later. 'Well, now. These are rather — '

They were in her office; her part-time assistant had arrived, panting, and was now at the till. Ernie had unzipped the portfolio, and spread his work out on the desk. It smelled like a sweet shop in here, too: bunches of dried stuff hanging over his head and boxes of sickly soap and shampoo in every corner. Crystals were hung in the lancet window: it had started to rain. He stood next to Sophie, watching Daphne consider his portraits, one by one. Quality, that was the thing. It always told.

Daphne propped up a noble-headed Labrador in profile: that was Ned. She paused over Alfie the Westie, and Benjy the boxer-cross; she turned over Flossie and Pip, with their faithful eyes, and then turned back to them. He'd put in six profiles and six full-on — sock 'em with the lot.

'And them's the leaflets,' he said, pointing.

Daphne picked one up. Here was where quality told, as well: look at that hand and you'd know you were with a professional. He'd spent hours on it, writing it all out, taking account of the girls' suggestions.

Your Closest Friend Will Never Leave You.

There. Couldn't beat it. He'd pasted on Ned, gazing loyally, soulfully, upwards; he'd taken the sheet into CopyFast and done a hundred: 4p a throw. Nearly broke him. Still: there they were, and he was proud of them. Put that holistic beeswax in the shade, said Mary, and he knew she was right. Balance. Toxins. Crystals. Load of old cobblers. Dogs were the thing. Dogs had meaning. A dog would put you right.

'What do you think?' asked Sophie timidly. He gave her a look. Never ask. Let them come to you, like an animal. Make 'em wait.

'Well,' said Daphne again. 'Of course, it's not our usual thing at all, but actually — ' She ran a finger along Ned's nose and Ernie knew he'd done it. 'I had a dog like this once,' she began, and he knew they were in at the kill.

* * *

'See?' he said to Sophie, as they made their way back through the close. 'What did I tell you?'

Fifty leaflets were on the counter, and Ned was on the wall, next to an astrology chart, and a poster of Britain's Butterflies. Most of them he hadn't seen for years.

'No,' said Sophie. 'I told *you*. It was me what thought of it.'

Rain was swirling over the lawns, the bells of the cathedral struck the hour. Lovely.

'Clever old you,' said Ernie. 'What a team we make.'

She flushed with pleasure.

Out in the street, outside the newsagent's, there were huge great numbers on billboards. In the window of Radio Rentals the lunchtime news was on, on a dozen screens. They stopped to look. This was the only time they ever saw the telly: might as well make the most of it. And they stood in the rain, and watched the man talk to them, as the fire behind him burned up carcass after carcass, and stiff legs pointed to the sky.

'It's bad,' said Sophie, her eyes widening. 'It's very bad.'

'It hasn't got to here,' said Ernie. He thought of their father, up every morning at six for the milking, taking his cap off the peg in the passage, pulling his boots on, walking off with his lamp to the farms in all weathers. He thought of the three of them, pressing in to watch on summer evenings: the smell of it all — a proper, animal smell. The munching on feed, the swish of the tails, the stream of the milk in the pail, his father's hands running down teats, the farm cat slipping in.

Foot-and-mouth. They'd had it before, but this was —

'Come on,' he said to Sophie, and tugged her away from the sight of it all, the cruel wicked sight of them hoofs, them lolling heads, them heaped-up, beautiful creatures.

IV

Home

19

'Everything's uncomfortable,' said Buffy. 'Everything's an effort.'

The surgery was packed: she'd been waiting for forty minutes beyond her appointment, leafing through the kind of magazines she only ever read in here, or at the dentist. Bright women beamed in their awful houses; there were long ghastly articles about sex.

'Well, now,' said the doctor, kindly. 'You're not *quite* as young as you were.'

'I haven't come to be told that,' Buffy said sharply. 'I know exactly how old I am, thank you. What I want is a diagnosis. Something's not right.'

He was new, he was a fool. They were all fools. No one knew anything any more.

He sat back and looked at her. 'Go on.'

So she went on. She told him about getting up in the night, and the giddy spells, three now, and her ever-expanding waistline. She told him how exhausted she felt, even just doing the shopping. She said there was nothing she wanted to eat, anyway; she'd lost her appetite. She said she would never eat meat again as long as she lived, and she started to say why, and began to cry.

'And I've got a pain,' she sobbed. 'That's new. It comes and goes, but it's there.'

'Where?'

She pointed. Her tummy felt like a football.

'Let's have a look.'

And she blew her nose on a man-size tissue from the box on his desk, and lay on the couch while he felt all over her.

'Here?' he asked, prodding and poking. 'Here?'

'What is it?' asked Buffy, when he had finished. 'What have I got?' She swung her legs off with enormous difficulty. Oh, how nice it would be to tuck down with a hot-water bottle and never have to do anything again.

The doctor was writing on her notes, in an illegible hand. She peered.

'It's probably nothing at all,' he said, turning them over. 'But perhaps we had better be sure.' He put down his pen, and smiled at her.

She tried to smile back: after all, she'd met worse, and at least he was thorough.

'I'm going to get you an appointment at the West London,' he said lightly. 'Just, as I say, to be sure.'

'With what department?' asked Buffy, but she wasn't a fool. She knew, she knew.

* * *

Out of sight? What of that?
See the Bird — reach it!
Curve by Curve — Sweep by Sweep —
Round the Steep Air —
Danger! What is that to Her?

Janice lay on the blue-and-white quilt in her bedroom, revisiting Emily Dickinson. Smoke from her roll-up drifted through the open window into the cold March air, clouds drifted over a hesitant sun, she heard the beat of wings.

Curve by Curve — Sweep by Sweep —
Round the Steep Air —

She said the words aloud, felt herself climb with them, swept on through soaring currents, feeling the rush, the rise, the dizzying descent, the whirling up once more, into —

Into what danger, what treacherous place?

She put the book down. The last time she had read this verse was up in Cloud Nine on a gusty, rainy afternoon, with the place to herself, the rain beginning to die away at last, the sun to break through. It glistened on the wet glass door, which was all at once pushed open.

Had she been in danger then? She supposed she had been; she supposed she might have gone into free fall, picked up and taken to airy heights like that, then dropped like a plummeting stone. And thinking this she remembered all at once the stiff, gaping man in the corridor of the hospital, his mouth wide open as if to shriek the shrieks of madness, into echoing hill and stony valley.

Wild, unreachable places.

Janice drew on her cigarette once more, and laid it to rest in the ashtray by the bed. She let the image of Matthew's face swim before her again, sink into her again, as it had done ever since she first saw him, coming and going, leaving and returning, as if to the right place.

She picked up the book again, hearing, from the magnolia, the blackbird's sudden rush of song.

> Danger! What is that to Her?
> Better 'tis to fail — there —
> Than debate — here —
> Blue is Blue — the World through —

Was that beautiful, or what?

She closed her eyes, let them rest on the blueness of calm and distant hills, and safety.

★ ★ ★

Buffy, after her visit to the doctor, took herself home. She went slowly down the surgery steps to the windy street, beneath the pollarded plane trees to the main road, where buses roared past and people did their shopping, and had their hair done, and lived their lives. She turned into the corner of her own street, and after some moments found herself at her own front door.

She felt in her bag for her keys and could not find them. Very carefully, she searched again, and there they were. She turned both latches, went into the communal hall. In the dimness, the atmosphere of closed doors, and everyone out, was almost palpable. She stood there, taking breaths. Then she climbed the stairs, pressing the time switch on the wall to turn the light on, feeling the wornness, where everyone had pressed it, going up, going down, year after year after year.

She let herself into the flat, the silence. After a moment or two, the light on the stairs went out.

⋆ ⋆ ⋆

Ernie, in his pyjamas, put the kettle on the gas ring and looked out on the back field. It was March, it was spring, there were ewes and lambs out there — they'd woken him up with their racket, but he didn't care, just so long as they were safe. There were buds in the hawthorn hedge, the first hint of leaves on the trees. And about time too. He pulled on his jacket and went outside for a pee, round the back of the trailer. Good for the grass, and more natural: he got sick of using that smelly old Elsan all winter. Time to get out and about. Time for pastures new. And he smelled the cold spring air, and listened to the lambs, and banged his foot on the hollow gas canister, and swore. A hen beneath the trailer cocked her head. They liked it under there: nice and dark, bit of peace and quiet.

'Hello, old girl. Got a nice egg for my breakfast?' He rubbed his sore foot, bent down to feel beneath her in the mud. Not a dicky bird. Ha.

'Not much use, are you?' He straightened up, turned, and peed an arc, over the rotting fence and into the field. There — life in the old boy yet. He turned back, saw the brown hen watching. 'Wasn't bad, was it?' he asked her, and shuffled back inside.

The gas was flickering feebly. Another blimming thing to think about, another blimming thing to buy. Them canisters cost a fortune. He stood there listening to the weak putt-putt of the flame.

'Go on, give us a cuppa at least.'

The kettle was small and lightweight, like him. Like his old black wireless: he'd had them both for donkey's years, however many that was. And now, looking out at the lambs, waiting for his early-morning cuppa, he put the wireless on, fiddling with the coat-hanger aerial and dial until he heard the eight o'clock pips, and set it back on the table and listened, shaking his head.

The kettle, at last, approached the boil, just before the flame went out. He made his tea, he opened his tin, he sat smoking and drinking and watching the lambs, the butting and wriggling, and skipping about, as the clouds rolled back and the day broke properly. The wireless murmured beside him: that John Humphrys, talking about the crisis to that Nick Brown. What did any of them know, stuck in London? What was that Janice Harper doing, stuck down there?

The lambs, as lambs did — he knew, he'd been with them all his life — suddenly all took off, all together, haring round the field, up and down, round and round the trunk of the holm oak, just in bud. Look at them, look at that, what a sight for sore eyes. On the wireless, they were talking about emergency measures, and experts. If they sent any of them experts up here, if they started any of that culling up here —

Someone was throwing stones at the door.

He got up, opened up, saw Sophie at the bottom of the steps in her gumboots. Dogs were

following, dogs were barking in the pens.
'Action stations,' said Sophie. 'She says are you up.'
'I don't need no chivvying,' said Ernie crossly. 'What's she on about?'
'She says we've got to walk them while we can.'
'We can't,' he said flatly. 'Haven't you heard the news? No one's going out anywhere. Not now.'
'She says we've got to. She says we're not an infected area.'
'She'll have to whistle. We can't.'
He looked down at the sea of eager faces, beating tails.
'Sorry,' he told them. 'Not today.'
Sophie, in her pinafore and gumboots, shifted from foot to foot.
'But how are we going to manage?' she asked him. 'What are we going to do?'

* * *

Janice walked into the hospital grounds. Daffodils blew in the flower-beds, a girl sat on the bench outside the main entrance, talking on her mobile. Her hair was lank, and her wrists were bandaged. She wore leopard-print mules and a big black cardigan. 'I'm going mad in here,' she said.

Janice went through the sliding doors, and took herself down into Matthew's ward, looking neither to left nor right. If the wilderness man was haunting the hills and corridors she did not wish to see him. She did not wish to encounter slashed wrists, or infected sores from cigarette burns, or to hear, from behind a screen, the sounds of some poor bastard throwing up his overdose. Sorry, can't handle that. So how come you think you can cope with Matthew? a part of herself enquired, and this she could not answer, except by being here.

She found the ward, and told the staff nurse who she had come to see, and that she was a friend, and had been before, with Matthew's father. 'I remember,' said the nurse, who wore a badge that said Eileen.

'How is he?'

'Up and down. We've changed his medication — did you know?'

'Oh, yes,' she said, remembering the conversations with William: his happiness, his hope, his taking of her hand. 'I'll go and find him,' she said, and turned to cross the floor to the light-filled day room, and saw a tall, stooping man walking slowly towards the nurses' desk, and was about to step aside when she thought he reminded her of someone she liked a lot, and realised who it was.

She stopped. 'Hello, Matthew.'

He inclined his head towards her, gave a hesitant smile. She sensed in it everything he had been brought up to be: well mannered, careful with other people's feelings, kind.

'Have we met?' he asked, with painful slowness.

'Yeah,' she said, and took his hand. 'I'm Janice, remember? I came here with your dad.

We had lunch together.'

'Of course,' said Matthew. 'Of course we did. I remember now.' And his eyes moved away, and he withdrew his hand, and walked slowly to the nurses' desk. 'What day is it today?'

'It's Thursday,' said Eileen. 'All day. Are you going to talk to your visitor?'

'Visitor?' He looked round.

'Me,' said Janice. 'Would you like to go for a walk?'

He looked at her, and through and beyond her. She felt his remoteness, his utter apartness, his long, slow flailing about inside, like a stranded creature.

'I'm here,' she said. 'There's no hurry.' And she went over, and took his hand again, and led him towards the light.

'You know where the coats are?' called Eileen, and picked up the ringing phone.

'Where are they?' asked Janice, and his eyes roamed around the ward.

There was a pause.

'In there, I believe.' He gestured at a door, as if moving under water.

Slow though his speech was, he had, she realised, spoken more in the last few minutes than during the whole of previous visit.

Inside the cloakroom, she watched him move among the hooks, finding, at last, his own long winter coat. He took it down, handed it to her. She held it open for him, helped his beautiful hands slip into each sleeve.

'Great,' she said. 'That's brilliant. Right, we're off.'

And they went back through the ward, and through the blaring day room, and out into the grounds, which smelled of earth after rain, and fir. She slipped her hand through his arm; he looked down at her, from his father's height.

'I remember you,' he said. 'You've been here before.'

'Yes.'

'What day is it today?'

The cold spring wind stirred the boughs of the fir tree, the shadows of massive clouds moved over the grass.

'It's Thursday,' said Janice, and leaned her head against his shoulder. 'All day,' she added, watching a London blackbird rise and fall on the wind.

* * *

'Buffy!' said William. 'How are things?'

'Fine,' said Buffy. 'I was just about to phone you. Are you coming to the concert?'

'I am indeed. We all are.'

'All?' She reached to turn down the television.

'If there are tickets left. Is it a sell-out? Might we hope for three returns?'

He sounded positively buoyant.

'Three?' she asked him.

'I'm bringing Matthew. Do him good. And Janice — high time you two met.'

'Ah,' said Buffy. 'Well. I'll have them put on the door. Or did you want me to send them?'

'Send them? Can't you bring them to the stall?'

'The thing is — ' Buffy began, and did not know how to proceed. 'The thing is — ' she tried again, and felt the icy coldness which had taken root somewhere in her lower spine, ever since the visit to the surgery, begin to seep into every part of her. 'I've got to have a little check-up,' she said firmly. 'That's why I was about to ring — it's on Wednesday, as it happens. So I'm afraid I can't do the stall this week. I'm so sorry.'

'Check-up?' William was on the alert at once. 'What kind of check-up?'

'Only a little one.'

'For — ' He hesitated. 'Don't want to pry, dear, but — '

'Women's things,' said Buffy. 'Nothing you need give a thought to.'

'Ah.' She could sense his relief. What babes men were. What fools. Even William. Even after Eve.

'So I'll see you at the concert,' she said cheerfully. 'I'm so glad you can all come.'

'So am I,' said William. 'Matthew's first outing for ages. All thanks to you, Buffy, dear. New pills. You were perfectly right.'

'I'm so pleased.' And she moved the receiver to her other ear, since this, like everything else, was heavier than it used to be, and listened, as William went on.

* * *

'Good,' he said, replacing the receiver. 'Very good.' He finished his whisky, poured another. Just a little nip more. 'A nippity nip,' he said aloud, moving the last of the ice around the glass. The curtains were drawn, the fire was lit, and Danny was snoring before it. He looked at his watch, turned on the Channel 4 news. Good chap, Jon Snow, always liked him — met him, once, at some do. He settled back into his chair.

There were over a thousand cases. Over a thousand. In Northumberland, in Cumbria, in Devon — in Devon they were almost under siege. Couldn't go anywhere, couldn't move a lamb.

'This is quite dreadful,' said William aloud, beginning to see what Buffy was on about. There were cases in Scotland, pyres in the Welsh borders. Herefordshire. Shropshire.

And how were the cousins coping with all this? He might give them a ring. As you were — he might drop them a line. 'They've never had a phone,' said Janice. 'Never had a washing machine. Nor telly.'

Well, they'd be spared the close-ups of dying lambs. Or perhaps there were sights like this all around them.

The phone was ringing: he picked it up, as the feature finally ended, and the advertisements began.

'Hello?'

'Is Janice there?'

'Hello, darling,' said William, realising that the second whisky, on an empty stomach, had perhaps been a mistake. 'All this foot-and-mouth,' he said. 'Isn't it frightful? Have you been watching the news?'

Claire gave an exasperated sigh. 'No,' she said

shortly. 'I haven't. This coverage has got completely out of hand, the whole business is absurd. They're getting compensation, aren't they? What are they fussing about?'

'Oh, dear,' said William, feeling the chasm yawn open once more, but wider still.

'I was asking if Janice was there.'

'So you were. No, she isn't. She's working tonight. Shall I give her a message?'

'You could say I rang. I'll try her again.'

'How are the children?' asked William. 'Have I told you about the concert? One of Buffy's things — Matthew's coming. I'm so pleased. I don't suppose you'd like to join us? I can't remember the programme — ' He felt among his papers. 'Parry, I think.'

After a moment, he realised he was talking to thin air.

* * *

'Hello, Janice.'

'Oh. Hello.'

Early in the week, Sandra's night off, and the wine bar pretty quiet. Janice, once she had served the one or two regulars, and polished up and put away the lunch-time glasses, had settled herself on the stool behind the bar with a glass of house red, her tin and her thoughts, which were many. Now she slid off, and prepared for action.

'I'm disturbing you,' said Claire.

'No you're not. What can I get you?'

'What are you drinking?'

'Plonk.'

'I'll have a glass of that.' Claire heaved herself up on a stool, and took out her purse. 'And what about you? Can I get you another?'

'I'm fine for now, thanks.' She turned to reach up for a glass, and filled it; she set it before Claire, and passed her the little bowl of olives, dressed with lemon and dill. 'That's two pounds fifty,' she said, and took Claire's fiver, gave her the change, and sat down again.

'Cheers,' said Claire, raising her glass.

'Cheers.' Janice took out her tin and set to work, teasing out strands. Nice to be able to afford a decent roll-up these days. She thought of poor old Ernie, eking out every shred. 'Not often you can get out on your own, is it?' she asked Claire, his distant cousin — how incredible was that? — and finished off, running the tip of her tongue along the paper. 'Who's looking after the kids? I mean the children,' she added, with a little smile, and reached for her lighter.

'Jeremy,' said Claire, smiling back, watching her. 'I've been at home all day — I just thought I'd have a breather, come and see how you were getting on.'

'That's nice.' Janice lit up, inhaled, took up her glass again, met Claire's intense dark eyes.

'And we must make a date,' said Claire. 'For you to come and baby-sit, when you've got time.'

'Yeah. Sure.'

Claire opened her bag again, and took out her diary. She leafed through its packed weeks, checking off aloud the picking up and dropping off of children, the after-school maths, the music lessons, swimming lessons, Geraldine's dance class, Jeremy's court appearances, people in for drinks. There were theatre tickets, secured with paper-clips, there were dinner dates, with sitters already booked.

This is Matthew's sister, Janice thought, as pages turned, and Claire went on and on. This was the little girl peering into the pram on tiptoe, smiling into the sun, clasping Matthew round the waist on the garden slide, leaning on the piano, watching him play.

She had kissed his cheek when they said goodbye, back on the ward from the windy grounds, hearing the bang of the trolleys for lunch, feeling the dryness of his skin beneath her lips.

'Nice to see you,' said Matthew, as he must have said many, many times in the past, saying goodbye, goodbye, see you soon, kissing his friends, his parents' friends, his sister.

'I'll see you at the concert,' she said.

'What day is that?'

'Saturday,' she told him, as she had told him twice before, walking beneath the towering fir trees, seeing squirrels leap. 'We'll come and pick you up.'

He nodded, smiled, turned away. Did she imagine it, or was he steadier in his walk since the first time they'd met, making his way along the ward to the tables with more certainty?

'How about the nineteenth?' asked Claire at last. 'That's the Thursday after Easter. We're going out to supper.'

'Yeah, maybe,' said Janice. 'I'll have to check here first.'

'Well, just let me know.' And she stuffed the diary back in her bag. 'The children would love to have you.'

Would they really? Why was that?

'Anyway.' Claire raised her glass again. 'How are you?'

'Fine.' Janice drew on her roll-up. 'Fine, thanks.' She hesitated, feeling Claire's gaze so intent upon her. 'I went to see Matthew yesterday,' she said, though she didn't want to, and she heard his name echoing, over and over again, as if in a chamber, with a grey-green sea at its entrance, rushing in, pulling back, drawing everything in its wake.

Claire frowned. 'Oh? How was he?'

'I think a bit better,' said Janice, and with every word she spoke sensed unease and disturbance and danger, though whether to her, or to Matthew, or Claire, she could not tell.

* * *

It's dark, it's raining, Claire is walking home. The Village is behind her, with its lit-up shops, and pubs, and shut-up library. She turns into her street, full of family houses, as the rain drums faster upon her umbrella, and drips from each sharp point. She takes out her keys, unlocks the door of her home, where her daughter and younger son are sleeping, and her husband and elder son are watching the news, Piers's dark head upon his father's shoulder, slaughter and death before them.

'Is that you?' calls Jeremy, hearing her footsteps in the hall.

'Yes, it's me,' says Claire, hanging up her wet mac, and she walks past the open sitting-room door and into the kitchen, so warm and welcoming, the heart of the family house, and puts the umbrella to dry before the Rayburn.

'It's me,' she says again.

The kitchen curtains are undrawn, the table lamp is lit, its reflection gleaming in the dark wet glass, and she leans to pull the curtains to, and catches sight of herself, whoever that might be.

20

Spring rain: more spring rain, splashing off the buds of London plane and hornbeam, soaking into the well-kept garden of Queen Square, the flower-beds of daffodils and tulips, the lawn and shrubbery. It's seven o'clock on a Saturday evening, and outside the confines of the square bus and taxi swish in the wet along Southampton Row, up to the Aldwych, and over Waterloo Bridge to the South Bank, to theatre, theatre bar and concert hall. Here in Queen Square the audience is arriving for the concert at the Mary Ward, shaking out umbrellas on the steps; pushing open the heavy front door on to the cramped but well-lit hall, with its pleasing black-and-white tiles; crowding into the lavatories, making the ascent up the broad shallow stairs with some difficulty, for it's a hell of a climb, quite frankly, when you're getting on.

But the concert is on the first floor, in rooms that are lovely and spacious. Tall rainswept windows overlook the square, and the atmosphere tonight is lively, with tables laid with light refreshments, programmes, jugs of spring flowers. Through the double doors the chairs are arranged in a sweeping semicircle, with notices of future events — the summer concert, summer party, summer trip to Bruges — on every one.

'Marvellous,' says William, ushering Janice and Matthew. 'Splendid. Let me get you a drink.'

He is a good head taller than anyone in the room, except for Matthew, and each, in different ways, attracts quick glances. William has always attracted glances, all his life, and never less than here, among the Over-Sixties, with his silver hair, his well-cut, well-worn clothes, his courtesy and charm, that smile. This evening he is wearing a Marie Curie paper daffodil in his buttonhole: it looks, on William, fresh and alive.

'Now then.' He scans the bottles of red and white, the elderflower, the orange juice, smiles at these good people offering all this, and Rosemary Barker, uncorking chilled Blue Nun, feels the evening's brightness fall, in particular, on her. 'What will you have?'

'I'll have the elderflower,' says Janice, holding Matthew's hand. Matthew, because of his medication, has not touched alcohol for years; she knows this, feels how cold his hand is in hers, sees one or two people look at him, and look away, as she asks him: 'Is the elderflower OK?' and he nods, with a vague, sweet smile which turns her over.

Matthew is his father's son. He is tall, and well made, and, as she took in the first moment she beheld him, beautiful. But the years of his illness, his drugs, his long confinement, have dulled the thick hair, dulled the eyes which once swept over Bach and Chopin; there is an invalid pallor to the skin on good Harriman cheekbones, a pinch to the Harriman nose. His circulation is poor, and his movements slow, and the long, slender fingers which ran over Beethoven and Schubert, which lifted violin and bow as if they were a part of him, now rest in hers cold and passive. And, after all these years, he is set apart: seeing him in a crowded room, on the crowded pavement, even out of the corner of an eye, you think at once — something's not right. Looking more closely, you know it. The beauty is damaged, the stone of the angel eroded.

But we will restore it, thinks William, passing drinks. We'll have you back in the world again. He raises his glass of Blue Nun. 'Cheers. Well done all round.' He moves them away from the crush at the table, and looks around, feeling extraordinarily happy. The first outing: they've done it, and here he is again, back with the old dears and looking forward to it.

The choir have been changing, behind the scenes. Now they emerge, one or two, in their concert clothes, and mingle.

'Buffy!' calls William. 'Over here!'

And she looks round, looking good, he observes, in her smart black skirt and fuchsia silk shirt and silver earrings, and sees him, and she feels oh, so many, many things as she moves through the crowd to this little knot of three.

'Buffy. You're looking marvellous.' He bends to kiss her, once, twice — as Londoners do, Janice notices again; he takes her hand, turns to his son. 'Matthew, you remember Buffy. We had the most marvellous Christmas.'

'Of course,' murmurs Matthew, as she reaches up to kiss him.

'Lovely to see you here,' she says brightly. 'Really lovely.'

'And this,' says William with joyful emphasis,

'is Janice Harper. Janice — my dear old friend Buffy Henderson. At last I've got you two together.'

'How do you do,' says Buffy, extending her hand, with its silver rings, which had once been Mother's, and its liver spots and wrinkles.

'I'm fine, thanks,' says Janice, clasping it in her strong young fingers. 'Great to meet you.'

'We're so looking forward to this,' says William, as the piano strikes up in the concert room, just a few scales, to tune up, and put them all in the mood.

'Me too,' says Buffy.

And she watches Matthew all at once raise his head, as the accompanist runs up and down the keyboard, and sees William and Janice both notice too, and exchange quite radiant smiles.

'We'd better go through,' she says, and turns away, going to line up with the altos, clearing her throat.

Janice is watching Matthew, so tall among the crowd, so close to her but so set apart. A frown plays over his features; she feels in his hand a tremor of movement, like an enquiry. Then he relinquishes his grip, and moves towards the double doors, slow but intent, listening. The scales run on, the choir is assembled, the audience is moving through.

'Give me those.' William is taking their glasses, smoothly depositing them on the long table, reappearing. They are ushered to their seats, and he raises his programme to Buffy in encouragement. The scales die away, there is a general settling, coughs, a hush. Within it, you can hear for a moment the patter of rain. Then Michael, the young conductor, makes his appearance, and bows; the first full chords of Parry's *Sirens* resound in a mighty opening, and with the choir's audible intake of breath the concert has begun.

Music and rain and upraised voices: for a moment, his programme resting on his long crossed legs, William feels a current of joyous excitement run through him, no less powerful than if he were in the stalls at the Festival Hall with Eve.

'Where the bright Seraphim, in burning row, / Their loud, uplifted angel trumpets blow . . . '

What stirring stuff it is, and what a good sound: dear things, how keen they are.

'Oh, may we soon again renew that song, / And keep in tune with Heaven, and keep in tune with / Heaven . . . '

Buffy is singing her heart out, silver earrings catching the light as she turns the pages, head uplifted. Dear girl. And he settles back, and glances at Matthew, to see what he is making of it all, now they are here at last.

Matthew is very still. He seems to listen as if from a great distance — to the first rumble of thunder, or the first fall of rain on the sea. It is, thinks Janice, sitting next to him, her upper arm touching, just, his upper arm, as if he were under water, and she sees again in her mind's eye a sea-filled chamber, his name resounding with each rush and retreat of the waves.

She is conscious of William's glance: she turns, and smiles at him, and he locks her gaze in the intensity of his joy — at seeing his son, from however far away, respond, once again, to music.

'To live with Him, and sing in endless morn of light . . . '

Janice watches the long musician's finger lift from his lap — just a little, almost imperceptibly — in hesitant response. And although she has never heard music like this in her life, and finds it incredible, really, that she should even be here, used as she is to hanging out at gigs down the pub, she finds herself quite swept up in it all: the stirring song, the turning pages, the sight of them all, singing their hearts out on a cold wet night in spring, the trees dripping in the square beyond the windows as the rain falls on and on.

The first song is over: she finds herself clapping alone, looks round, sees William's kindly gaze. Oh, right, not till the interval, then. And they're off with another, and Matthew inclines his head.

* * *

'We're doing some rather marvellous songs in the second half,' says Buffy, in the interval. She settles herself on the row in front, turning in her chair to face them. 'Masefield,' she tells them. 'Masefield and Kipling and Whitman — lovely rousing songs, we've really enjoyed them.'

'Kipling,' says William, shifting his legs in the space between the rows, which isn't big enough. 'Haven't looked at him for years. Who reads him now, I wonder?'

'No one,' says Buffy. 'Certainly not me. But I think there's a new biography — did you see it in the papers?'

'Possibly.' He tries to remember.

'Dreadfully sad about his son,' she goes on. 'I think that's what they were saying. Kipling sent him off to the front, to make a man of him, and he was killed and Kipling could never accept it, tried for years to think he was missing, and would come back. It almost broke his heart . . . ' She stops, her voice trailing away, then quickly recovers. 'Goodness, what am I thinking of, talking about such sad things? How are you enjoying it all?'

'Very much,' said William.

'It's great,' says Janice. She has dimly heard of Kipling, though Steve, in Cloud Nine conversations, never mentioned him, but she wonders that Buffy should, indeed, choose on this very evening to talk about sons, and death, and heartbreak. She touches Matthew's hand: he is gazing towards the window. 'You liked it, didn't you?' she asks him, and he slowly turns his head, and slowly nods, and a smile lifts his mouth for a moment and is gone again, as a cloud moves over the sun. She lets her hand rest on his, and he does not move it away.

She feels Buffy watching the two of them.

'Have you been singing with the choir for long?' she asks her, taking in the ageing face, bright clothes and sharp, bright gaze.

'Oh, for years,' says Buffy briskly. 'When you get to my age, you've been doing everything for years.'

'Oh, come, come,' says William gallantly, and then, to Janice, 'You really must come to the stall one day — we've certainly had that for ever, haven't we, Buffy, dear?'

'We have. How did you get on on Wednesday?'

'Rather well, if I remember rightly. Those teacups went.'

'The Marguerite? I knew they would. Remember *I* found those.'

'I remember perfectly well. And how did you get on with your little test?'

'I'm waiting for the results,' says Buffy. 'Nothing to worry about.' And then there is the sound of a handbell, and people are coming back to their seats, and she rises — with some difficulty, Janice notices — and says, 'Right. Back to business. We end with Tennyson.'

'Tennyson?' William picks up his programme. 'What Tennyson?'

' 'Crossing the Bar.' Very beautiful. And affecting, it must be said.'

And she pats William's arm, and makes her way back to her place, second row from the back. There is, once again, the settling, reassembling, clearing of throats, and then Michael is back, and bowing again, and they're off.

Buffy, in her place in the altos, sings the Masefield with vigour. It swings, it rouses, it takes her away on its tall ships, billowing sails and great winds sweeping the crew to sunlit islands. Marvellous, she can hear William say, and looks up to see him nodding in time, loving it all. He meets her eye, he smiles, and she sings on, lifted from Masefield's ships to Kipling's white road running, running, down through the grassy hills.

Everything's all right, she tells herself. Everything's all right. And she knows that as long as nobody knows, that as long as she can keep going, and being bright, she'll manage. She just doesn't want to tell a soul, that's all. All around her, voices are raised in joyful unison — how that white road runs, and how the white foam rolls across the sands!

And then there is a pause, and they turn to the last song, and the piano is sounding a pure and haunting note, as the Tennyson begins.

Sunset and evening star,
And one clear call for me!
And may there be no moaning of the bar,
When I put out to sea . . .
Twilight and evening bell,
And after that the dark!
And may there be no sadness of farewell,
When I embark . . .

Buffy, in the altos, in the place she has occupied for years and years, as she has done everything now, everything in her life familiar, and properly done, and interesting — yes, life at its best is *interesting* — feels herself borne now upon a great wave of mournful, tender sound, as if someone else is singing for her, so that she can look out across the room to where, among the audience, sits Janice Harper, who seems, on the face of it, a perfectly pleasant young woman; and Matthew, entirely filled with the beauty of the music — she can see this, it is just as William had hoped; and William himself, gazing across at her, absorbed, intent, tears glinting, knowing nothing of what she will, quite soon, have to tell him.

⋆ ⋆ ⋆

It's Mary's and Sophie's turn: they heave their bags round the shops.

'Will you come and have a look-see?' asks Sophie, when the last Savers tin of beans, and Savers Swiss Roll and custard, have been stuffed into the bag with the broken zip. She shifts the weight from one hand to the other; Mary grunts.

'Might as well.'

They make their way to the cathedral, hearing from within, as they cross the precinct, the sudden, unexpected sounds of treble voices, soaring exquisitely. Beneath her coat, and cardigan, and nylon jumper, Sophie feels the prickle of hairs rise all up the back of her neck, and along her arm.

'Choir practice?' she wonders. 'On a Saturday morning?'

'Must be a wedding later,' says Mary, and they stand outside the great west door and listen: to the muted swell of the organ, those pure, sweet voices rising ethereally, and the crooning of a pair of pigeons from a lofty medieval niche.

'Love Divine, all loves excelling . . . '

Sophie is transported: some cloudy, half-dreamed place where bluebirds play in the balmy air awaits her, she can feel it, and she stands on the old stone flags with her bulging bags of

Lo-Cost dog food, murmuring, 'A wedding . . .'

'Oh, don't be so daft,' snaps Mary, and as the last strains fade she pulls at her sleeve and drags her into the cloisters.

'No harm in listening,' says Sophie, mulishly. 'No harm in a bit of music.'

'Puts a lot of nonsense in your head.' Mary sets down the bags for a moment. 'There's quite enough of that in there already.'

Sophie does not reply; she puffs along half-empty cloisters. It's mid-morning, it's almost Easter, there should be lots of people, lots of tourists looking round and buying things. Postcards, cathedral tea towels, bookmarks with lovely prayers on. They should be coming down to Healing Arts, snapping up Ernie's pictures. Instead —

'Gone ever so quiet,' she says.

'What d'you expect?' Mary's eyes are like bright black coals. 'Remember Oswestry, in '67?'

But Sophie has never had a head for facts and figures. That was what had done for her at school, the facts and figures: she hadn't had Ernie's gift with Art, she hadn't had Mary's quick, sharp way with sums. She shakes her head, as she has shaken it all her life. Mary gives a snort.

They come out into the alley. As always, even from here, you can smell the wafts of scent from Healing Arts — the gift-wrapped natural soaps, the natural creams and natural massage oils. And all those little bottles. Aromatherapy — isn't that a lovely word? Just to hear it makes you feel better.

Mary is wrinkling her nose. They pass the second-hand bookshop, and Cloisters Gallery, its window filled with oils in heavy frames.

'How about in there?' Sophie had thought suddenly, when they came to set up Ernie's exhibition. 'Would that be better?'

'That's posh,' he said, shifting his portfolio to under his other arm.

'Healing Arts is posh.'

'There's posh and posh,' said Ernie. 'Trust me.' And he marched up to Daphne's polished door and set his shoulder to it. Ting! In they went, and there was Daphne, smiling, with a space on the wall all cleared. Sophie hadn't seen him look so happy for years.

And it's all my idea, she told herself, following him inside. Got something right for once.

Now she is following Mary: inside the shop they set down their bags behind a window display of natural sponges from the depths of the seabed — that's what it says on the card. Pearly little balls of natural bath oils are strewn among them; there are tall glass jars of soap, with round glass stoppers. There are Easter chicks. There's a seahorse!

She tugs at Mary's arm, but Mary is looking fiercely around the empty shop, and coughing. For a moment Sophie wonders whether the bunches of dried herbs and flowers will bring on an early bout of her hayfever. It makes her savage, all red and streaming, and never enough handkerchiefs.

'Well? Where are they?'

Mary is building up to something, Sophie can

tell, and sensing this she feels as anxious as she has ever done, all knotted up and fearful, as if she has — she feels a dreadful flush — as if she has wet the bed, and Mother is coming up the stairs.

You naughty girl —

Made to stand in the corner, the wet sheet over her head. Not for long, but long enough. And all that washing.

'They're over there,' she says, as helpfully as she can. And she points to the wall on the left, from where the British Butterflies have been removed, and the Wild Flowers. Now, in their place, are Ernie's paintings. 'Look.' She points again, to Ned's noble head, and Flossie's loving gaze, but Mary slaps her hand down.

'No need to point. No need, ever, to point.' Goodness, how like Mother she can sound.

'Isn't it nice?' she whispers.

Mary is marching over, beetle-eyed. She stands full square and glares at every picture.

'Sophie! How nice to see you, dear.' And here is Daphne, coming out from the back with a box of pretty things. She sets it on the counter. Mary swings round.

'Are you in charge?'

Daphne — even she, nice and kind and always smiling — is taken aback. Sophie watches, twisting her fingers in their holey green gloves.

'I am,' says Daphne, staying behind the counter. 'Daphne Clark,' she adds. 'How do you do?' She looks across at Sophie, and back at Mary, wonderingly. 'Have we met?'

'We have not,' says Mary. 'Last time I was in

here there was some pasty young girl at the till, with an undernourished baby. Born out of wedlock, no doubt.'

'Kirsty,' says Daphne faintly. 'That was a long time ago. And you are — ?'

'Mary Harriman.' She nods violently at the paintings. 'The artist's sister.'

'And my sister,' says Sophie weakly, explaining. 'My brother. We're all related, see.'

Mary gives her a withering look. 'What I want to know,' she demands of Daphne, 'is where's all the red dots?'

Daphne gestures at the empty shop floor, with its baskets of sponges — more sponges! There must be a glut. Sophie, escaping, pictures a slender dark-haired boy diving down to the seabed, knife in hand, and bubbles streaming upward. Oh, those little Ladybird books! How she used to —

'I'm afraid it's been rather quiet,' Daphne is saying carefully. 'The crisis is hitting all of us, I'm afraid.'

'There's no foot-and-mouth in the city centre,' says Mary.

'No cows in the cloisters,' says Sophie under her breath, and claps her hand to her mouth, seeing just that: a dear old cow called Buttercup, munching on that nice trim grass, listening to the bells.

'It's a knock-on effect,' says Daphne, quiet but firm.

Mary glances at them both. 'Frivolity!' she snaps at Sophie. 'Frivolity in the midst of penury!' She swings back to Daphne. 'We need the money,' she says. 'We've got mouths to feed.' She gestures at the paintings, beneath their lettered sign. Daphne had been doubtful about the sign, but Ernie had insisted.

Your Faithful Friend — With You For Ever — Commissions Undertaken.

'This is our livelihood,' Mary says with finality. 'Foot-and-mouth or no. I don't care what you have to do to sell them, but' — and she marches across to the counter, waving — 'sell them you must.' Her wild hands send a counter basket flying. Shell-shaped soaps tumble to the floor, Easter chicks are everywhere. 'Frippery!' shouts Mary. Her eyes rake the racks of healing oils. 'Holistic beeswax! Whisky and aspirin and an early night! That'll soon put you right. All this quackery — '

Sophie is awash with fear: she hasn't seen Mary so overheated for years. Whatever has got into her?

'Now, look — ' says Daphne, and her own voice is beginning to rise.

Just then, the door tings open. Everyone swings round. A young man comes in, wiping his feet on the mat. His bicycle is leaning up against the window, his skin fresh and healthy, his earring catching the light.

'Hi,' he says, sounding lovely and cheerful and normal, and closes the door behind him.

Mary is beside him in a trice. 'Here,' she tells him, seizing his hand, and marching him across to the exhibition. Shell-shaped soaps crumble beneath her feet. 'You buy one of these.'

* * *

Later, after Daphne has threatened to call the police, and has taken every picture off the wall, after Sophie has swept up every soap crumb, picked up every trampled Easter chick, and said, over and over again, that she's sorry, they heave their bags out of the shop and make their way in dreadful silence back through the cloisters.

'Do you think you're coming down with something?' Sophie ventures, taking all her courage in her hands.

'If I am,' snaps Mary, 'I'll know where not to go to find a cure.' She gives a violent sniff, and quickens her pace.

Sophie trails miserably after her. The choir-boys have finished their practice and are streaming out of the west door, in mufti, as Father would have said, ragging about before the afternoon wedding. How beautiful that will be, how happy. She starts to cry, very softly. Mary is on to her at once.

'No snivelling! Pull your silly socks up!'

Mother to the life.

They make their way through town to the market bus stop. Tom's trailer is selling soup and hot dogs, just as usual, but there isn't much of a queue, and the silence from the market is eerie. No shouts, no bleating or lowing, no clang of pens. No farmers. It's all shut up, just a few bits of straw blowing like ghosts across the carpark, and no one, in the queue at the bus stop, is talking of anything else.

* * *

Ernie is out in the huts. Blimming heck, it's like an ice house. Some of the newspaper stuffed in the gaps in the boards has been blown out by winter winds, and there's draughts everywhere. The concrete floor is sound, give or take a few cracks, but even he can smell damp, and no wonder. Rain getting in all winter, floods and storm and pestilence. Could have brought the whole lot down. He tramps about, inspecting. Spiders scuttle away, there are cobwebs everywhere. Time for a good spring clean, time for a good stiff brush, and mops and buckets. Might even do the trailer, before Mary starts going on: have a good sweep-out, beat a few rugs, wash the windows. The windows in here — blimming heck.

But despite the general dilapidation, he feels, as he shuffles from stall to stall, a swell of pride. Look at that Eskimo, look at them scales on that fish, them straining huskies. Shackleton would have been proud to have had a team like that, Scott would have shaken his hand.

I am going outside, and may be gone some time . . .

Them were the days: proper men, proper heroes. Expeditions, rations, ice picks; disappearing into the snowy wastes and no blimming mobile phone.

Hello? Hello, Darren, I'm in the toilet . . .

Ernie has actually heard someone say this once, down the pub: he snorts at the memory. End of civilisation. Bring back National Service

— that'd sort 'em out. Go off on an expedition, and don't come back.

The cold spring wind blows through, newspaper dances over the floor, and there's something else — a whisk, a scampering. He stops, and his eyes dart everywhere. Well, what do you expect? Shut up all winter, cracks and gaps. So long as it's only mice — if it's rats, he'll set the dogs on them.

He strides across to Africa, feeling masterful. Look at that waterfall, look at that poor drowning girl. What were her parents thinking of, leaving her like that? Missionaries, Bibles, preaching to the natives — what about their own little daughter? 'Course, Livingstone had had no children, nor Stanley neither, not that that made them what everyone nowadays would say it made them, nothing like that. Proper men, proper heroes, doing what they thought was right. Fever and swamps and quinine. Borne on stretchers, lips all cracked; snakes dropping down from the trees in lethal silence. 'Onward Christian Soldiers' and 'I Did It All For Thee'. Sun beating down on a simple wooden cross.

Ernie, walking from scene to scene, deep in thought, grows more thoughtful still.

Heroes.

Not just places, and themes, but a real sense of history in here.

He stands before the Swiss Alps, the sunset peeling away from the back, lets his hand stray over the noble head of the St Bernard, feels it all too soft to the touch, and watches sawdust stream to the heaps of polystyrene snow, from where the mice have gnawed. Right behind them furry ears. Dreadful. He bends to look, sees a blimming great hole, pokes about, hears squeaking, pulls out his fingers, sharpish. Blimming heck, right inside the head. Well, what can you expect, with no protection? Should have polythene sheeting wrapped round everything, all winter; should have poison down, and mouse traps.

And walking along to the hunt, and finding even old Foxy full of holes, and moth throughout the hunting coat, he feels a wave of mingled grief and shame.

Can't even afford a roll of polythene sheeting.

Can't even run to a flipping mouse trap.

Here he is, sixty-eight, the curator of a fine museum — unique, probably, nothing like it nowhere — falling to pieces before his very eyes.

Here he is, an artist to his fingertips, an exhibition in town, acclaim just round the corner, and all these works of art in here are on the brink of ruin.

Venice in Peril. Restoration. Trust funds.

What is to be done?

He lights up, though he knows he shouldn't, not in here, but a man has to have something. Ah, that's better. And he paces about, smoking, thinking furiously — always thinks better with a cig in his mouth, always has done — hearing drips, and scuttling, smelling the damp, the mice, the spiders; hearing, from outside, the wind in the trees, the birds, them darling little lambs, still safe, thank God; hearing the whines and sighs of them poor old penned-up dogs, and the wild triumphant cackle of a laying hen.

Something for lunch, then.

That was something.

Got it!

Heroes of yesteryear.

(*Dogs of Yesteryear*?)

No — heroes always pulls them in. He ticks them all off on his fingers, yellow with baccy stains, chapped and cracked with the cold.

Shackleton. Scott. Livingstone. Wellington. Nelson — must have had a dog, bound to, they'd never set sail without a good old sea dog for the rats. Who else? Hillary — must have had dogs at the base camp. Himalayan mountain dogs? Or is it Pyrenean? Look it up in the library, next time they're in town. He looks at his watch — Dad's watch, a proper heirloom. Mary had Mother's. How're they getting on in town today? All them red dots — that's what'll pay for this bold new venture.

Capital. Investment. Restoration funds.

Who else?

Lindbergh. No — he'd never have taken a dog up there.

I know that I shall meet my death, / somewhere in the clouds above. / Those that I fight I do not hate, / those that I guard I do not love . . .

Keats. Blimming marvellous, had to learn it by heart at school, had to recite it: he could remember it now, standing up and trembling.

Should've gone to Oxford. Should've gone to the Royal College, that was certain.

Not Lindbergh, then.

Who?

Where'd they keep that *Pears Cyclopaedia*? Indoors somewhere. Must be there.

Ernie props open the door of the hut with a brick, to let the spring wind blow some fresh air in there properly. The dogs, at his reappearance, are at once alert, getting stiffly to their feet — in the pens; outside the back door; and here comes Pipsqueak, down the trailer steps from his snooze on the mat. He bends to pat him, feeling the faintest warmth from the April sun on his rough little coat.

'Good boy, good boy.' He feels in his pocket, but there's only crumbs. 'Stocks are low,' he tells him, straightening up. 'They'll be back soon.' And he shuffles down to the gate, Pip at his heels, and leans on it, looking along the lane.

Blimey, it's quiet. Not a car, not a walker striding out across the fields and into the hills with a rucksack, not even a bicycle. Be good to see that Janice, wheeling along on her bike with them panniers bulging, fresh faced and cheerful, ringing that bell.

Hello, Ernie!

Got any baccy?

Might have.

Striding into the house with the bags, putting the tins out, cheering them all up.

London. What's she getting up to there, then? Still, can't be worse than here. Shut down, that's what it is. Whole blimming countryside.

He leans on the gate, hearing the restless dogs in the pens begin to bark, feeling the press of the house dogs all around him, waiting for the gate to open, and the walk begin.

'Not today,' he tells them, as he's told them all, every day for weeks, letting them out only to run about the yard, then back. Nothing for it, Mary can shout as much as she likes, he's not going to walk forty dogs across them fields and get shot at. Because they would shoot, he knows it, any farmer would, seeing his sheep all shot in the head and heaped up in a ditch, watching his herd all driven away and that filthy choking smoke, them hooves sticking up, them crumpled horns —

Finches flit into the hedgerows, buzzards wheel over the hills. At least the birds are safe.

Close your eyes, hear the fowls of the air and the bleating sheep, hear that hen on her nest, and you'd think all was just as always. But it isn't, it isn't, and leaning on the gate, his eyes wide open, smelling, on the April wind, the distant pyres, and the disinfectant on that straw, outside all the farms where Dad long ago went milking, he feels another great wave of sorrow. Them farmers will be ruined; them lovely animals, sick ones and healthy, will have lost their lives; and he and the girls, out here in the sticks, with barely a farthing in the tin, and no prospects of visitors, are, like the farmers, up against it.

His cig has gone out in the wind; he drops and crushes it beneath his leaking shoe.

Blimming dreadful. Blimming terrifying.

Still.

And as he rallies — for he, an artist and curator, has never been without ideas, and has been rallying all his life — he sees a magpie, its beak stuffed full of hay, land on the telephone wire, and cock its glossy head.

Quite right, says Ernie aloud. You get on with that nest.

One for sorrow.

Don't be so blimming morbid.

And he turns and goes into the house, on the search for a nice cup of tea, and the *Pears Cyclopaedia*, where Mother used to look up all their ailments. Not that she ever gave them anything for them, not that they ever saw the doctor, not that he can remember. Only with the measles. And the mumps, come to think of it, he'd had a bad time with them mumps. Still — lived to tell the tale. Rallied.

All is not lost, he tells Pip and the rest of them, putting the kettle on, looking along the shelf. There's an exhibition, after all; them pictures will save us all.

⋆ ⋆ ⋆

It's half past one, and he's out in the trailer, door propped open, nice boiled egg for his lunch inside him, couple of bits of toast, nice strong cup, and he's sitting at the table leafing through the *Pears*. It's so old it's coming to bits, the pages mildewed, but still — heroes are heroes, and they're still in here. Douglas Bader. There was a fellow. Just to hear the words Hurricane and Spitfire makes Ernie go all goosey. Dogfights — ha. Battle of Britain. Up in the cloudy skies facing old Jerry, Biggles jacket and goggles and hand on the joystick, ready to die. Dad said when Bader woke up, after they'd taken his legs off, he could still feel his toes at the end of the bed, waggling away through all that pain.

Like the hens — chop their heads off, as Dad did, wring their necks, like Mother used to, and they'd get up and run across the yard. One flew over the fence, once, squawking demented, like. When he was little, he used to think it was funny. Now — wring a hen's neck? Wring Martha's? One-eyed old Jemima? Kill them? Doesn't even bear thinking about, though Mary does it, and he — a blush creeps up his neck — will eat it. Nice bird on the table, nothing like it. Gravy and roast potatoes and he'll have a leg, ta very much. Once they're dead, it's different: can't explain, just is. So long as he's had nothing to do with it, so long as he doesn't know who it is.

Now then. Churchill. His Finest Hour. *We shall fight on the beaches . . .* He'd have had a dog, bound to. Give him a bulldog? No — bit too obvious, bit too in your face. Probably had Labradors, down at Chartwell, flopping down beside him while he and Clemmie had tea on the lawn. He can see it now, the shadows of great trees lengthening as the sun goes down —

Right, then, who else?

Thing about encyclopaedias is you get distracted, looking through; you go off at a tangent. Ernie finds himself running his finger down columns and stopping. Crustacean. Damocles. Kuala Lumpur — you'd never know that was a city. And he pictures a great Antipodean mammal, swinging slowly in the heat from tree to tree.

His cig has gone out in the saucer. He picks it up, lights up with the last of the matches, hears sounds at the gate and looks up. They're back. Wait till he tells them. And how much have they made to date? How many red dots? How many commissions?

This is it, he tells Pipsqueak, snoozing at his feet, and he pushes his chair back and goes to greet them, completely rallied now, until they turn from closing the gate behind them, and pick up their bags, and he sees their faces.

⋆ ⋆ ⋆

Easter. Wild April skies, rain sweeping over the hills and then a flood of sunlight. Church bells: up in her bedroom, Sophie sits and sobs. Then the broody hen in her coop beneath the back kitchen window hatches two chicks on Easter Monday and Ernie yells up to her to come and take a look. Mary comes out beside her, face like thunder, but as they all bend to the battered old box, the chicken wire and hay, and hear the tiny peep beneath the wings, everything else is forgotten.

'Could be worse,' says Ernie, straightening up, looking at the vast light sky, the oak in bud and the lambs, racing around the field. 'Could be worse.' He goes to let the dogs out and they pour through the yard to the gate. 'Back here!' he yells at them. 'Get back here, you hounds!'

In early evening, taking Nellie and Pip and Benjy out just for a little run, on leads, for a mile or so down the lane, he meets old John Dickson, in the Land Rover, pulling up at the straw-strewn gateway to Broxwood Hall, where Dad, all his life, went milking. Ernie nods, touches his hat, tugs the dogs on to the verge. Dickson is looking grim. He winds down the window, leans out.

'Evening,' says Ernie.

'There's four new cases been found,' Dickson tells him. 'Up at Llanrhos. That's it, now. We're in for it now.'

Ernie feels something inside him move and turn over, in some dark, terrible place.

'That's bad,' he says at last. 'That's very bad.'

Dickson nods. He slowly gets down, and slowly walks in his gumboots through the heaps of wet straw, and opens his gate. Then he gets back in the Land Rover, and slams the door.

'I'll do the gate, behind you,' says Ernie, but Dickson shakes his head.

'Best get on home with those dogs. Best stay there.' And he turns and bumps in, and brakes and gets out and walks slowly back again, and heaves the gate on to its latch. He gestures at the straw all round it. 'This was a precaution,' he says grimly.

And he walks back, gets in, bumps away up the track to the farmhouse, between fields where young lambs are racing to the calling ewes, as the last of the sun slips down, and night approaches.

* * *

They're there at dawn. Ernie wakes, and hears them: the shouts, the panting dogs, the bleating.

Beside him, Pip is at once alert. He sits up in his sleeping bag and pulls the curtain. There they are: striding over the field in ghostly white clothing, masked, and carrying guns. The sheep stream away through the gates held open: into the next field, and the next. The first rays of sun break the rolling clouds; the gates, one by one, swing to; and then the first shots are fired.

Ernie slumps down on his lumpy pillow, and wraps his arms round Pip, and howls.

21

'Well, now, Miss Henderson,' says the consultant, and pulls Buffy's file towards him. 'Let's have a look.'

The consulting room is small and unadorned. Buffy is sick with fear. She sits on the edge of her chair and clasps her handbag so tightly that the little gold fastening digs into her palm. The pain is almost a relief.

The consultant is turning pages. He pulls out an envelope, slips out a print-out, slips it back again. He is about forty-five, she supposes, grey beginning to show here and there, designer glasses on a rather clever-looking nose. Well — to be a consultant at forty-five, you'd have to be brilliant. That's something: at least she is in the best possible hands.

'You've had a scan,' he murmurs. 'Two scans. And blood tests. Mmm.' He closes the file and looks at her. 'And how are you feeling? Generally?'

'Really quite well.' Buffy feels sweat seep into her leather bag. 'Rather tired, of course, but when you get to my age — ' She utters a little laugh, gives up, and meets his gaze. 'Tell me,' she says, summoning every last drop of courage from every last cell. 'Tell me the worst.'

'Your blood count is very low,' he says gently. 'We're going to have to get lots of iron into you as soon as possible. And the scans — the truth is, we don't quite know. It could be just a horrid old lump that needs to come out, and that's the end of it.'

'Like fibroids,' says Buffy, her breath very shallow and fast. 'That sort of thing?'

'Exactly. Exactly that sort of thing.' He rubs his chin for a moment, and smiles at her — a smile she will remember later as being almost as lovely as William's, but not quite. Nothing could ever be quite like his. 'Or it could be something else,' he says carefully, and the words she has known she will have to hear come to her now as if spoken in an echo chamber, sounding over and over again: something else, something else, something else —

He reaches across the desk, and takes her hand.

* * *

'And how did you get on?' asks William, phoning next morning. 'The results of that little test — everything all right?'

It's spring — proper spring: the daffodils bright in her window boxes, the scent of the pheasant's-eye narcissi drifting in where the window is open at the top. Buffy, even at the height of her campaigning, has never been aware of the natural world with more intensity. She takes a long deep breath.

'I've got to have an op,' she tells William. 'Rather a big one.'

* * *

The phone is ringing: Janice, running down the stairs and late for work, picks it up in the hall. Through the open door to the drawing room she sees William, sitting in his chair by the phone in there, with Danny on his lap, stroking him, over and over again.

'Hello?'

'Good morning, Janice, it's Claire.'

'Oh, hi.' She gives William a little wave, and he raises his hand. Not looking quite himself today, she notices.

'Just ringing to check about tomorrow.'

Tomorrow. Oh, God. She looks at the calendar on the wall, inked in here and there in William's distinctive hand. Buffy's concert. Dentist. Phillips sale. What's happening tomorrow?

'Remember you said you would baby-sit,' says Claire. 'The Thursday after Easter, remember?'

'Oh, yeah. Sure. What time did you want me?'

'Could you be here by six-thirty? Jeremy's in court, unfortunately, so I'm going to have to pick him up. We're having dinner with friends in Blackheath — we'll try not to be back too late. I know you're working the next day.'

'OK, fine, thanks.' Janice looks at her watch. She must go. 'See you then.'

'Look forward to it,' says Claire, and hangs up, without asking for William, or how he might be, but then she never does.

So she asks him herself, from the door — 'You OK?'

He nods, turns to look at her. God, he's gone pale.

'What is it? What's up?' Matthew, she thinks

suddenly, and crosses the room in a couple of strides. 'Tell me.'

'Poor old Buffy's not too good.'

How papery and pale is the liver-spotted skin on the hand, stroking Danny's chestnut coat, on and on and on.

'Why? What's happened?'

'Got to have an op,' says William, quietly. 'Poor old thing.'

'An op?' No one she knows ever uses this term — it makes the business of going into hospital sound like nothing, really. Which she supposes is the point.

'Exploratory. Probably nothing to worry about. Still — these things are never nice.' Then William gives himself a little shake, and visibly rallies. 'Go on, Danny, down you get.' And he slips him to the floor, and gets to his feet, and smiles, looking more like William. 'You must go. And I must get on — things to organise. You're here for supper?'

'No, I'm working, remember,' says Janice, bending to give Danny a pat. 'And I'm out tomorrow, as well,' she adds, straightening up. 'That was Claire on the phone. I'm baby-sitting.'

'Are you, now?' He gives her a little kiss. 'You're very honoured, I must say.'

* * *

When she has gone, racing off down the steps and clanging the gate, he takes himself slowly down to the kitchen, lets Danny out to the garden, and makes a very good pot of coffee. A spring breeze is stirring the willow tree, where he and Eve used to sit and have tea, on distant summer days. There is now, as so often, rain in the air. He watches Danny nosing about among the daffodils; hears Edith Horsley, three doors down, open her back door and call her cat. Another old thing on her own. He pours his good strong coffee into his good Portmeirion Botanical mug, carries it back up the stairs, and sets it on his open desk. Then, from the drinks cupboard, he takes his father's hip flask, sniffing the leather case, unscrewing the silver top, sniffing again. Nothing like it. And he crosses the room and pours into his Botanical mug a good big nip. And another. He screws the silver top back on.

Do not, he hears Buffy say wildly, waving the paper, with its dreadful headlines, *do not, at a time like this, talk to me about little nips*.

Dear Buffy, how she felt things. He must stand by her now, though the thought of hospitals —

He sits at his overflowing desk, his father's desk, letting coffee and brandy reach just the right spot, and pull him back together for the tasks that lie ahead, seeing Eve's darling thin face on the pillow, feeling her weightless hand in his, Eve barely Eve, her voice a thread.

* * *

It's dark, it's raining; Janice runs down the street, and up the soaking steps to Claire's front door. She knocks and waits.

Rain splashes on to the bay tree in its tub; the

door is opened; Piers observes her wetness coolly.

'Come in.' He steps aside, and Janice wipes her boots about a hundred times on the fitted coconut matting.

'Thanks.' She pulls her hat off, pulls off her gloves. They need wringing out. So does she.

'Janice! Oh, you poor thing. Why is it always raining when you come to see us?' Claire takes the wet things at once. 'I'll put these on the Rayburn rail — do you want to bring your jacket in there, too? We can hang it on the airer.'

Piers slips away and Janice follows her, into the shining warm kitchen, with its halogen lighting and floor fit to eat off and glass-fronted cupboards painted in matt Shaker green. Claire is unhooking the rope on the airing rack, letting it down gently. 'There we are. Now, if you give me your jacket — '

'I feel like a drowned rat.'

All Janice really wants is to strip off and get into a hot bath, with clouds of steam wafting through William's comfortable bathroom and the radio on and the prospect of supper by the fire. Instead, she's got to flipping baby-sit. She runs her hands through her wet hair.

'Come and warm up by the Rayburn.' And Claire moves the wet gloves and tea towels along the rail. Janice stands with her back to it. God, that's better. For a second she closes her eyes. All she needs now is about twenty-five dogs snoozing away at her feet, and a mug of Mary's stand-your-spoon-up tea. She gives a little smile.

'What are you thinking about?'

'Your cousins, to tell you the truth.' And Janice opens her eyes in time to see Claire's quick little frown.

'I haven't seen them since I was small,' she says. 'I can't really remember them at all. Anyway — ' She looks at her watch. 'I must be off. Now then — the children are all fed and watered, and once they're in bed you must make yourself at home. I've left our friends' number by the phone. The boys are doing their homework, I hope, and Geraldine has had her bath. She'll want a story. Light out for her after that, and lights out for the boys by half past eight. Oh, hello, darling.'

'I don't want you to go out,' says Geraldine, in cream pyjamas and soft blue dressing gown.

'I like those pyjamas,' says Janice, wheeling into action. 'I wish I had a pair like that.'

'We got them in a sale,' says Geraldine, brightening reluctantly.

'Did you? That was clever. I don't suppose you'd like to show me your room, would you? I bet it's really nice.'

Flashes of gratitude across the kitchen. The baby-sitting evening has begun.

* * *

By nine, the house is quiet.

* * *

It's dark, it's raining, a key turns in the lock. Janice half asleep in front of *Question Time*, come to with a start: they're back. She looks at her digital watch, pulsing away: not quite eleven, not too bad. God, how the rain's pelting down — will they run her home?

Footsteps in the hall. She turns to do her baby-sitting stuff: Hi, had a good time? They've been really good —

The door swings open.

Janice looks round, sees a tall, half-drowned man walking slowly into the room, like a sleepwalker, his skin white, his soaking hair plastered to his head, his eyes like stones.

For a moment she is so shocked she cannot speak or move.

Then —

'Matthew — '

She finds she is on her feet; he turns and sees her.

'Hello, Matthew. God, you gave me a fright, I didn't know you had a key — '

As if he's just popped in from next door or something, not walked out of a ward, out of a hospital, in and out of the traffic on a dark wet night, mile after drowning mile till he comes to his sister's house. Looking around for her now, in this perfect family sitting room.

Jesus.

'They're out,' she says. 'I thought you were them. I'm baby-sitting — '

Matthew is staring at her, those fathomless dark eyes like depthless mountain pools, wherein you might fall, and plunge, and never be seen again.

'It's me,' she says, and knows for the first time

what it means to hear your own voice shake. 'It's Janice, you remember me — ' She takes a step towards him, holding out her hand, keeping her voice as low and as calm as she can, as if she were talking to a frightened animal. 'It's OK, darling.'

Has she ever used this word to anyone?

'I'm here.' She says it again. 'Darling Matthew, I'm here, I'm here, everything's OK.'

Matthew looks down at her blankly. Once more, she can feel how utterly enclosed he is: shut away, miles away, in some far distant place; a ship far out at sea, where sky and water meet and dissolve, where a ship might slip silently over the rim of the world, and disappear.

'You remember me,' she says gently, stroking the long musician's fingers, over and over again. 'I've been to visit you in hospital, we went to a concert together, you and me and your dad — '

And at last, like the movement of water, like the first incoming wave of the returning tide, a smile breaks his frozen gaze, and he begins to quicken — she can feel it, the coming to life again.

'I think I remember,' he says slowly, smiling down at her. 'I think I remember that.'

Rainwater from his soaking clothes is in patches at his feet; she leads him over to the leaping pale flames of the coal-gas fire, and they stand before it.

'This is Claire's house,' he says, as she helps him off with his dark wet coat.

'Yes.' She lays the coat on a chair. 'I'm baby-sitting,' she says again, returning to his side. 'They'll be back soon.'

He looks around the room, at sofa and books and papers and box of toys; at the television, where farmers in the *Question Time* studio are shouting. He frowns; she switches it off, and now the only sounds are the puttering fire, and the rain, falling on and on.

'I've come to see Claire,' says Matthew slowly. 'Where is she? Where have they taken her?'

Janice holds his hand again, a little warmer now, though his face is still deathly pale.

'She's with Jeremy, no one's taken her anywhere, they're out having supper with friends.'

He shakes his head, and although he is calmer now, and warmer, and although, in his returning smile, she has seen him step back towards the world, she can sense, too, the way in which illness is coursing through him, flooding in, flooding out, draining and exhausting. He takes his hand away, rubs at his face, frowns.

'Who am I?' he asks her, from miles and miles away. 'Tell me who I am.'

'You're Matthew,' says Janice, almost in tears, as a key turns in the lock. 'You're Matthew Harriman, Eve and William's son. Claire's brother.'

And then there are voices in the hall, and Claire, all at once, is in the doorway. She sees him, goes white, and in two steps has crossed the room and taken him in her arms.

* * *

An ambulance moves down the street, its blue light flashing; curtains are pulled back at upstairs windows. Jeremy, who has called it, gets up and goes quietly out to the hall. Janice, at the window of the sitting room, watches it come to a halt, and the men jump out in the wet.

Claire is sitting by the fire, holding Matthew's hand. He is calmer now, but with every move he makes — every frown, each glance, each sudden start — Janice senses illness at the gates.

She hears the front door opened, the rushing fall of rain.

'Do you want me to go with him?' she asks, as the men climb up the steps, and speak to Jeremy in low voices.

Claire shakes her head. She looks much older.

'I'll follow in the car, I'll see him back on to the ward. If you don't mind waiting until I get back — then one of us can run you home.'

'If it stops raining, I'll walk — ' But Claire is getting to her feet, saying, 'No, no, you wait here,' and anyway Janice can't think that far ahead, can't really think about anything except Matthew, white-faced, exhausted, leaning back in his chair as if he might never move again, as if he has come home.

Then the men are in the doorway, and Jeremy is saying gently: 'Matthew — ' and he looks up, goes paler still, then bows his head, and lets them take him.

* * *

They've gone.

* * *

The rain is easing off. In the gleaming warm kitchen, Jeremy makes tea, and Janice lights up, watching him, her hands still shaking. She has seen him, as the ambulance doors swing to, run down the steps in the rain to where Claire is unlocking the car again. She has watched him ask: Are you sure you don't want me with you? And seen Claire shaking her head, insistent, getting in quickly, flashing the ambulance driver: All right. Let's go.

Now Jeremy is leaning against the Rayburn rail, weary, his eyes for a moment beginning to close. Smoke drifts across the kitchen, and he coughs.

'Sorry,' says Janice. 'I'll put it out.'

'No, no, it's fine.' He smiles at her, and the smile becomes a yawn. 'I'm sure you need it, after all this. At times like this, I wish I smoked myself.' He turns, and picks up the teapot. 'How do you like it?'

'Black, please. Are there often times likes this?'

'I wouldn't say often, no.' He brings a mug across, goes back to fetch his own, stirring in sugar. 'Not for a long time, in fact.'

'Do you mind me asking — how come he had a key?'

Christ, how sad that sounds. As if he must never have one, as if it's out of the question. And she thinks of him, in that ambulance, staring out of the smoked-glass window, rain streaming down it as they pick up speed. His sister is behind them: his sister, whom he has walked long, dark miles to see, is sending him back where he belongs.

Is this it, then? Is this how it has to be?

Jeremy is pulling out a chair. 'Claire gave him that key years ago,' he says, sitting down. 'Not long after we moved here. I think she wanted him to feel a part of things. I did wonder if it was wise. But he's never actually used it like this before — suddenly turning up. I'd quite forgotten he had it, to tell you the truth.' He waves away smoke, apologetically, and Janice stubs out at once.

'Sorry,' she says again.

'Please. It just makes me cough, that's all — ' He drinks his tea. 'That's better. I haven't offered you anything stronger, I'm afraid. Would you — '

'No, no, I'm fine. I think I'd better just keep steady with this.' She clasps the mug; they smile at one another, two people who've just been through something quite out of the run of things, and who'll never, because of this, need to break the ice. Not that there's much ice to break with Jeremy: he's a good, kind man through and through, she can feel it. And yet —

There's something in this well-run house that absolutely isn't right.

Somewhere near by, a clock is striking midnight. Must be St Matthew's, on the common. 'I go there once in a blue moon,' William said once. 'Buffy and I went at Christmas. I suppose, come to think of it, we might have taken Matthew; he might have enjoyed the carols. But he was so ill, then, so withdrawn — '

Not like now, then, thinks Janice, and sees him again, climbing into the ambulance, as if it were something inevitable, the doors closing behind him, the blue light turning in the rain. Just as he was beginning to get better, she could feel it. And she sits there drinking her tea and thinking: of Matthew out in the hospital grounds, on windy spring days, so gentle and quiet; turning to say, with that slow, sweet smile, I do remember you. She thinks of him at the concert, lifting his finger at the sound of the piano, listening, listening, coming back to life.

And then there is tonight: Matthew unhinged, barely reachable, falling into his sister's arms.

Jeremy drinks his tea. She wants to ask him . . . oh, lots of things, but they'll have to wait.

'You go to bed,' she says, as he yawns again. 'I'll wait for Claire.'

'Are you sure? You've had such an unnerving time — '

'So have you.'

He shrugs — not dismissively, but in resignation. 'It's part of our lives. I don't mean nocturnal visits, just — ' He spreads his hands. 'Just the whole thing.'

'Can you tell me — ' she begins cautiously, but he's too tired to pick it up, to say more, or explain.

He just says: 'It's worse for Claire. It must be, though she never really talks — ' And then he gets up, looking drawn. 'I'm so sorry, it's just that I have to be up at six.' He touches her shoulder. 'Thanks for holding the fort. You were great. Not everyone could have done that.'

'Oh, I don't know,' says Janice, but she knows it's true. Somehow, frightened though she was, she had known what to do, had felt the connection between her and Matthew run strong and straight and true. Somehow, she understands him: it's as simple as that.

'I'm off. Tell Claire she can wake me if she needs to.'

And he leaves her, climbing the stairs to the bathroom, and then to bed. After a little while, the house is quiet again.

* * *

It's half past two in the morning. A key turns in the lock. Janice has fallen asleep at the table: she wakes with a start. It's stopped raining; it's the dead of night. For a moment she can't think why she's here. Then it all comes flooding back.

She gets to her feet as Claire comes into the kitchen. She's strained and white: a different person.

'How is he?' Janice's voice is thick with sleep; she clears her throat. 'What happened?'

Claire drops her keys on the table, sinks into a chair. God, she looks tired.

'They've sedated him: nothing too drastic. I saw him back on to the ward, I talked to the night staff. He'll be OK.'

'Will he? Did he mind being back?'

'By the time we got there I think he'd had

enough. We'll see — ' She rests her chin in her hands.

'You must be wiped out.'

'Sort of.' Claire gives a little smile, looks up at her. 'You too, I should think. You're still here, you're still awake. I thought Jeremy might have offered you the spare room.'

'I wanted to wait up. He's gone to bed — he says you can wake him if you want.'

Claire shakes her head. She doesn't say: He's got to be up at six, I'll let him sleep. She just says: 'What's the point?'

Comfort, perhaps? thinks Janice. The warmth of human kindness? But she says only: 'Shall I make you something? Tea? Coffee?'

'Coffee,' says Claire, with a long sigh, and her hands go over her mouth and her eyes close. She sits there, immobile, lost in thought, and Janice, putting the kettle on, spooning coffee into the cafetière, can feel how deep this is, how enclosed Claire is — like Matthew, in a way.

How strange.

'Just going to the loo,' she says quietly, and if Claire hears her she does not respond. When Janice comes back, she's still there like that: has she fallen asleep?

'Claire?' Janice sets coffee things before her. 'You all right?'

Claire's eyes open, and she gives her little smile — coming back, like Matthew, though from somewhere — yes? — closer to home.

'You're very good. Thanks.' And she gives herself a little shake, comes to, watches Janice pour strong black coffee into a deep blue mug.

Out in the garden, rain drips from tree and shrub. Janice sits down on the settle. There's a silence. There is, all at once, the soft hollow hoot of an owl. Claire listens. It comes again. She shuts her eyes, her hand goes to her mouth once more, as if, as if —

'What is it?' asks Janice, watching her. 'What is it?'

'Nothing.'

Janice knows this isn't true. She waits. The owl calls again, soft and low and haunting. Claire begins soundlessly to cry.

'Hey — ' Janice reaches across the table, touches her hand. Claire shakes her head. Tears spill from behind closed lids. Janice sits waiting, observing, behind those closed lids, a terrible struggle, as Claire wipes the tears away, away, over and over, with her strong, square-tipped, capable fingers which are, Janice sees now, bitten down to the quick.

At last she is calm. She opens her eyes, feels for a handkerchief tucked up her sleeve, blows her nose, tries a smile.

'We get quite a few owls round here,' she says unsteadily, tucking the handkerchief back, picking up her coffee. 'Sometimes you'd hardly know you were in London.'

'Yeah,' says Janice, remembering. 'I heard one the night I arrived. At the back of the house, I think, but I could still hear it.'

She talks on, wanting to be comforting, and normal, while Claire recovers. 'It made me think of Shropshire — you hear them all the time in the woods.'

But Claire isn't really listening to this.

'Even when Matthew and I were little,' she says slowly, her hands round the deep blue mug. 'We used to lie awake and listen to them. We used to give them names.'

'What sort of names?'

'Oh, I can't remember them all. Merlin was one, I think. And in winter once or twice we used to see them, sitting in the trees. So beautiful. So mysterious — '

Janice, turning her tobacco tin in her hands, listens to this different woman, talking of her childhood. She sees them both: brother and sister, up against the window on a frosty night, the sky a midnight blue, pricked with stars over walled town gardens, a London owl on a leafless London plane tree, silhouette just visible —

Look!

She smiles, feeling Claire's eyes upon her now.

'They came year after year,' Claire says slowly. 'The sound of them always takes me back.'

Janice is rolling up. Without thinking, she says, 'Did you share a room, then?', although she knows, of course she knows, that Matthew and Claire each had their own room, right at the top of the house, for she, after all, is living in one of them, is she not? She's living in Claire's blue-and-white room, with its white-painted shelves, and the bedside rug with the blue-and-white animals, going round and round the perfect childhood, by the bed set beneath the casement window, curtained with pandas, barred for safety, against the long, long drop.

There's a pause: she looks up.

And Claire says, very quietly and deliberately, 'No, no, we didn't. Not officially, that is.' And she holds her in a long and burning gaze, which says, unmistakably: Look at me. Look at me. Understand.

Janice can feel her heart begin to pound.

And then there is a long, long silence.

* * *

No, please no.

* * *

She cannot look at Claire. When at last she does, she feels a blush, deeper than any she has ever felt, begin to rise, and spread, until it is flooding through every part of her. She turns away, can hardly breathe, turns back. Their eyes meet again.

* * *

Claire says at last: 'There are things you can't tell anyone, ever.'

* * *

'Why are you telling me, then?' Janice asks at last.

'Because — ' Claire is burning, burning. 'Because I hardly know you. Because I must tell someone.'

Her eyes drop, to the beautiful deep blue mug,

with its thin gold ring, like a wedding ring, enclosing everything.

The church clock chimes the half-hour. Janice thinks: I was in one world, half an hour ago, and now I'm in another. Then the owl calls again, and she thinks: That sound will mark my life. Not in the way it's marked Claire's but it'll be there. Always.

She picks up the roll-up. Claire watches.

'Do you mind?'

Claire shakes her head. Janice lights up. Even though she's been smoking all evening, she feels the nicotine like a hit.

'And Jeremy?' she asks, wondering about his life, his kindness, his terrible fatigue. 'You've never told him. About . . . you and Matthew.'

It is terrible to say these words. Saying them fills the room, the world.

'No,' says Claire. 'I haven't. I never will.'

'Don't you think he might understand?'

Claire is silent. Then she says: 'He loves me. He loves me and the children. We're very lucky.' There is a twisted little smile. 'With three children, you can blot out a hell of a lot.'

'But not for ever.'

'No.' The mug in her hands is held so tight.

'And if you were to tell him — '

'I can't. I'm not prepared to take the risk. And anyway — ' There is another silence. 'That time belongs to Matthew and me. We were everything to each other — it's precious, it's ours.' She is trembling now. 'But I had to tell you.'

'Why?' asks Janice, filled with the enormities of the night's disclosure, and deception. 'Why?'

'Because . . . because I thought you were falling in love with Matthew.' Claire waits, crimson. 'I could feel it. Is it true?'

'Yes,' says Janice, who has carried his name, his melancholy, his musicality and his extraordinary smile within her, since the first moment they met. 'Yes, I'm afraid it is.'

* * *

They sit in silence. Rain drips from the trees.

* * *

'What are you trying to tell me?' asks Janice. 'That because . . . because you and he — is that what made him ill? Is that why he broke down?' She can hear her voice rising, as if she has something to avenge. 'You said he was schizophrenic — '

Claire flinches. 'That was the diagnosis. When he went into hospital. No one has ever said anything different. And I don't know if there's any connection. I think it would have happened anyway.'

'Why? Why should it?'

She makes a gesture, huge and full of questions. 'No one knows. It happens, more often to young men. Matthew was at the classic age. You read all the literature — I used to read it. Is it genetic? Is it reactive? Do you treat it with drugs, with therapy? What brings it on, when it strikes? All my life I've blamed my parents — so wrapped up in one another, so in love, that they never saw what was coming. And it's true that they didn't notice much. They certainly had no idea — ' She stops. 'But perhaps I was just thrashing about, casting all the blame on them, when really . . . Perhaps when Matthew left home, all the guilt caught up with him, perhaps it did trigger something that was lying in wait — ' She covers her face, rocking. 'It nearly killed me when he broke down. And now — I don't know, I don't know, I don't know.'

* * *

'And what are you saying?' asks Janice again, as the milk float hums down the street, and tyres swish in the wet. It stops: there is the chink of bottles. Such blessed, ordinary sounds: things to remind you, after a long, terrible night of illness, that you are still alive.

'You're warning me off,' she says slowly. 'Why? Because he's so ill? Because he can never recover? Or — ' She cannot meet Claire's eyes. 'Because you still love him yourself?'

There is another silence. It goes on and on.

'I can't answer that,' says Claire, her voice breaking, and upstairs, deep within the bedroom of her married life, an alarm begins to ring.

* * *

It's almost dawn: out in the street, where water is gurgling along the gutters, the faintest light breaks the darkness, and the stars in the rained-out sky are pale. Puddles are everywhere, shining in the light from the sodium lamps, and from one or two porch lights, left on all night.

Janice stands in the middle of the wet pavement. It feels as if she will never move again. She hears Claire's revelations; sees Matthew's beloved, haunted face.

Where is she? Where have they taken her? Tell me who I am . . .

She starts to cry, and then she starts to run, sobbing aloud, racing along the wet pavements, past curtained houses with who knows what dreams and desires and suffering within, through the silent, shut-up Village, and down the well-kept streets to William's street, and William's beautiful, cherished, roomy family house. She leans against the wet railings, gasping.

Dawn is breaking; the birds are starting up. She hears the whistle of an early train and then, as it dies away, the blackbird's liquid, glorious, full-throated stream of song.

She takes out her keys, and climbs the steps to the porch, where trailing wisteria is just in leaf, and the milk bottles have been rinsed and set out. She unlocks the door, very quietly, closes it behind her, quieter still, but Danny, down in the bowels of the earth, is at once awake, and gives a sudden bark behind the closed kitchen door.

Sssh, she whispers to the empty hall. Sssh, go back to sleep.

And slowly, carefully, to avoid the creaking treads, she climbs up the staircase, right to the top of the house.

22

William drives Buffy to hospital. Her little case is packed, and rests on the back seat; she sits beside him, clasping her handbag, dreadfully still. For once, it's a beautiful day.

'As soon as you're better,' says William, slowing down at a zebra crossing, 'we'll go to the sales. I've got the catalogue, I've had a look. There's a lovely old place in Gloucestershire, sounds a dream: everything must go before they sell up. I'll pack up a hamper — ' He changes gear, drives on. 'You'll love it.'

'And when is this?' asks Buffy, as they swish past shops, and shoppers, and normal life.

'Middle of June. After the election. Just right.'

'The countryside is closed,' she says, envisioning an avenue, rustling trees, peaceful parkland, safely grazing sheep. Not any more. 'Remember? Just because it's not on the front page every day doesn't mean it's stopped happening. There were twelve new cases yesterday, didn't you hear? And anyway — ' She tightens her grip on the handbag. 'I don't know if I'll be quite up to sales by the middle of June.'

'We'll see.' He turns to glance at her. God, what a white little Buffy. He gives her a pat, drives on. 'We'll see how we go.'

And Buffy, filled with fear and apprehension as she is; facing facts, as she has made herself do; is, with the prospect of a sale, and tea in a tent, infinitesimally comforted.

Then they come to the hospital gates, and William starts talking about parking, and she shuts her eyes, and braces herself for it all.

* * *

He settles her into the ward, carrying her case in, looking for Sister.

'Not Sister,' murmurs Buffy. 'Admissions clerk.'

'Ah.' He's forgotten all this, or perhaps it's changed. He strides down the ward, and heads turn.

'We'll soon have her right again,' says the student nurse who finally, finally, shows her to her bed.

'Of course you will,' says William, and pats Buffy's arm.

'Almost worse for relatives, I think,' the girl goes on wisely, all of eighteen, with a stud in her nose. 'Especially husbands.' She gives them both a special smile.

'Well, we're not actually — ' William begins, and sees Buffy's sudden, quite unexpected blush, and gallantly, automatically, courtesy and kindness in his every cell, adds sweetly, 'Would that it were so.'

'Don't be foolish, William,' Buffy says briskly, through her blush, and the student nurse looks from one to the other and says, 'Oh, dear. Trust me.'

'Now then,' says Buffy, when she has gone, and looks about her.

She's in a bay of four beds. Two are occupied, one has curtains round it. I'm going, she thinks, in a sudden access of dread. I shall leave, now, I'm not going to have this op, I'll just have to die at home.

'Dear Buffy,' says William, watching her. 'How brave you are.'

She shakes her head. 'Not really.'

'Yes, really. Now — is there anything else I can do? Shall I leave you to unpack, and then come back to say goodbye? Would that be the thing?'

'Yes,' says Buffy. 'I think it would.'

'I'll have a little wander, bring back some tea.'

'Before there's that ghastly Nil by Mouth sign up,' says Buffy, and he frowns, and then remembers, and takes himself down to the Friends Shop, and Flowers, where he buys a huge bunch of dreamy pink-and-white lisianthus, realising, as he pays for them, that they are just what Eve would have loved. In fact, they're probably just what he bought her, when he took her in to Barts. Or perhaps it was roses. Yes, perhaps it was.

Someone is talking to him.

'I beg your pardon?'

'I said here's your change,' says the girl, and he comes to with a start, and takes it, and goes back up to the ward with two teas and the flowers in Cellophane.

Buffy has unpacked, but not undressed. She's sitting in the bedside chair, Ackroyd's *London* on the locker, dressing gown on the end of the bed. Her eyes are closed and she looks drawn and old — for a moment he sees her as a stranger would, and everything that makes her Buffy vanishes.

'Here we are,' he says cheerfully, and she opens her eyes, sees the pink-and-white flowers, is Buffy again.

'Heavenly. Heavenly. Thank you.'

'Is there a vase?' He goes to look for one, is sent to the sluice, finds something made of weightless tin, which he assumes is not a urinal. How strange it is, he thinks, taking it back, to be in a mainstream hospital. He's so used to visiting Matthew, week after week, year after year, but that's different, at least on Matthew's ward. He's accustomed to being patient, to thinking about the life of the mind, trying to guess at the life of Matthew's mind, talking to consultants about drugs and occupational therapy. All this — the curtained beds, the Nil by Mouth, the prospect of dreadful operations — it feels more real, more frightening, now. He's frightened for Buffy, suddenly: truly afraid.

'Here we are,' he says again, and takes out his pocket knife, to slice through the tape on the Cellophane.

'I've forgotten something,' says Buffy, watching. She gets to her feet, with difficulty. 'While you were gone, I realised.'

'What's that?' He crumples the Cellophane, starts to arrange the flowers. That vase. He shakes his head.

'Just some little things of Mother's,' says Buffy, helping with the flowers. 'It sounds so silly, but suddenly I want them with me. I put them out, on my desk — her scent bottle, and her little bell, that might be useful. How could I have forgotten them?'

'I'm sure there's a bell here,' says William, and finds it, a buzzer encased in cream plastic, at the end of a long, cream, medical-looking tube. Horrid.

'I'd rather have Mother's,' says Buffy, eyeing it.

'Of course you would. Don't worry, I'll go and get it. And the scent bottle — anything else?'

'No, I don't think so. There's no rush. Just . . . when you can.'

'I'll bring them in after the op. Give me the keys, and I'll pop in, as soon as they say I can visit. Or would you like me to go back there now?'

'No, no. I can look forward to having them. When I wake up. If I do.'

'Of course you will,' William says quickly. 'Don't be silly.' And he takes her hand.

'Oh, William,' says Buffy, on the verge of crumpling. 'I'm so sorry.'

'Sorry? What do you have to be sorry for?'

'It's just — ' She hesitates. 'You're being so good and kind. And I know it must be awful for you, I know it must bring it all back.' Her lips are trembling. 'Poor Eve.'

'Nonsense.' He grips her hand. 'You mustn't think about it, don't give it a thought. It's you we're concentrating on now.' He leans forward, kisses the top of her head. Her hair comb is put in all wonky, he notices. 'Now then.' He straightens up again, and taps his pocket. 'What would you say to a little nip?'

* * *

It's late: the afternoon sun is streaming through the gap in the blue-and-white curtains, with their pandas, contentedly chewing bamboo. Janice stretches, turns over, sees the clock, remembers.

Should she be at work? She shuts her eyes. It's . . . Friday? Yes. She lies there for a while, coming to, feeling the darkness of those night-time hours, that conversation, lying within her like a stain, a shadow, something she'll have to live with.

After a while, she gets up, goes downstairs, not looking at Matthew's old room, phones Sandra. She's ill, she says, she's sorry. And she won't be coming back. Yeah, she'll work out her notice if she has to, but she's leaving London. Soon.

She puts down the phone, feels the quietness all around her. Where's William? Where's Danny?

Down in the kitchen, she finds William's note, and Danny in his basket, tail beginning to thump at once. She fondles his ears, lets him out, reads the note.

Taking Buffy to hospital — the West London. Back for supper. You were late last night — ? Lots of love, Wm PS If you would give Danny just a little run . . .

Janice makes a mug of milkless tea, and carries it up to the bathroom. She runs the deepest bath of her life, pouring in the very last of Eve's bath oil. 'Sorry,' she says aloud, as the room is filled with the scent of roses.

She peels off her nightshirt, she sinks beneath the waves.

Emerges, gasping, hair dripping into her eyes; wipes her face; lies back, drinking tea, and thinking, thinking.

⋆ ⋆ ⋆

William, emerging from the hospital, swings the car round to go home. It's just after four: he'll miss the rush hour. He turns on Radio 3, hears something that sounds like Harrison Birtwhistle, and turns it off again. Right, off we go.

This time tomorrow, Buffy will be coming round. God Willing. What a long wait.

'I'll have visitors afterwards,' she told him, as they said goodbye. 'Over-Sixties bods, Dorothy and so on. When I'm feeling up to it. I don't want anyone now. Just you.'

He squeezes her hand. 'Chin up.'

She lifts it bravely, like Little Grey Rabbit, captured by the stoats. Or was it weasels? Weasels, he thinks, and thinking of Buffy, all alone in a long, long frightening night, he pulls up at the traffic lights and turns left. He'll go to the flat now, get Mother's things, something to comfort her, while she waits. And he drives back to her street, parks in a Residents Parking Only bay, leaving a note: Doctor on call. Well — it's worth a try.

Inside, he presses the time switch, climbs up the stairs. God, you need to be pretty fit for this. Poor old Buffy — how will she manage, when she comes out? He unlocks her door, through which, over the years, he has carted in many a box of china, and carted it out again. Now then. Where did she say?

Inside her windowless little hall, he puts the lamp on; he opens the sitting-room door. The afternoons are getting longer, but still, it's not Summer Time yet, and dusk is falling. And it's cold in here. The sitting room is full of shadow, and she has half drawn the curtains, so the room has a strangely suspended atmosphere — between night and day, light and dark, here and there.

Not nice, being in someone else's empty place: he doesn't like it — especially at this dusk-filled hour, especially with Buffy ill. He makes his way to the desk, sees the soft gleam of the glass-and-silver scent bottle, the little silver bell. And something else: the whiteness of a letter, propped up against the walnut letter rack. Something she's forgotten to post — well, he can do that. Is there a stamp? He puts on his glasses, has a look, sees his own name, his own address. He picks it up.

Darkness is gathering quickly now. He puts on the desk lamp, picks up her paper-knife, remembers buying it for her, years and years ago. He hesitates. Should he read this now? Is that what she intended? Or was it meant for —

He slits it open, unfolds it — rather good paper — and sits at the desk, the heart of her campaigning: all those leaflets and posters, all those envelopes.

Dearest William,

This letter is for you to read in case I don't

come back. I hope I will: there seems, all at once, to be so much to live for, but — you never know. I want to tell you something I have never been able to tell you, all these years. I hope you won't think me too foolish, or carried away . . .

The clock on the mantelpiece is ticking softly into the empty room. He turns the page.

It's this: that I have always loved you — I know that now. Even when darling Eve was alive, even though I was so terribly fond of her — such a good friend, and didn't we all have such lovely times together? All those outings, all those happy years on the stall.

Anyway — that's all such a long time ago. I'm really talking about now, about how much you mean to me.

I've never written such words to anyone.

William leans back in Buffy's chair: an old swivel, upholstered in bottle-green moquette — a man's chair, he realises, probably her father's. He's never sat in it before. He looks around the room, observing with enormous tenderness its antique rose paper, and shelves of china, the worn old sofa and ancient television — so many things just like his things, going back decades, impossible to part with.

There's another page.

You have been an endless strength to me. You have made me laugh, you've been wonderful

company, always — and didn't we have a heavenly Christmas? You're generous and clever and kind, and, well — I just have to say it, even if it's from the other side:
I love you.
Buffy

Darkness has fallen. Between the half-drawn curtains the window-box daffodils are ghostly against the pane.

William puts down the letter, with its declaration. How has he not seen, not known?

'Oh, Buffy,' he says aloud, into her empty flat, so filled with her presence, her absence.

And does he love her? Does he feel the same?

Well. He cannot imagine life without her.

And he gathers up the empty scent bottle, the little silver bell, the letter, brushing it with his lips, and prepares to go to her.

* * *

The room is cleared; her things are packed away. Janice tugs up the zipper on her bag and drops it on the floor; she takes a long look round. That's it. That's done, then. Good. And she stands looking out of the open window, on to the garden far below, where the magnolia, amidst the mossy flags, still damp from the long night of rain, is in full white waxy bud, ready to burst open, any day now. Beyond, the long street stretches, filled with spring, the fresh, sharp limes, the bulbs in bed and window box, the distant tops of plane and chestnut in the park. A train is approaching the station, slowing down; it brakes, doors slam, and the whistle blows; then it is moving off again, up the track to the London she has hardly got to know; up to the mainline stations, the Intercity trains.

She'll be on one, soon.

She goes to the desk, sits down with the notebook and pen from her shoulder bag.

Dear William —

What can she possibly say?

She thinks of the last time she wrote to him — not the domestic little notes they've got used to leaving for one another, but the letter she struggled to write, months ago, up in her bedroom in Curlew Gardens, snow and silence everywhere in the winter fields, the telly blaring away downstairs. *Dear Mr Harriman —*

She was a different person, then.

She reaches for her tobacco tin, rolls up, sits smoking, thinking, picks up her pen and tries again.

Dear William —

She pictures him, coming into the empty house, calling her name, seeing the envelope on the hall table, picking it up, frowning, taking it through to the drawing room, reading it by the unlit fire. She sees his face. She sees herself, hunched up in the corner of an Intercity carriage, speeding up to Shrewsbury between the lifeless fields, away, away, leaving him, leaving Matthew —

She thinks: I can't do this.

In the silence of the house she hears all at once a sound on the stairs, and turns, quickly, towards the bedroom door. It's not quite closed: there's a scrabbling, then it's pushed open, and a chestnut nose pokes through.

'Danny — '

He trots in, looks up at her, beats his tail.

'Oh, Danny — ' She bends down, scoops him up against her pounding heart, buries her face in his coat, carries him round and round the room, weeping and holding him close.

⋆ ⋆ ⋆

Dusk approaches. Danny is on her bed, curled up on the blue-and-white bedspread like a cat, but keeping a half-open eye upon her, as dogs do.

The letter is abandoned.

For the hundredth time Janice goes over the previous night: sees Claire's burning gaze, and Matthew's deathly pallor. He's taken himself out of the hospital; an ambulance has taken him back. Is this to be the pattern of his life for ever?

Oh, Matthew —

Matthew is far out at sea and drifting, drowning. She has glimpsed his desperate efforts to return, old drugs ebbing out of him, new drugs streaming in; she has watched him struggle to remember what day it is, where he is, who he might be; lifting his head at the first great chords on the piano; walking through the soaking night; — and is she to abandon him now?

Janice gets up. She's suddenly very hungry — she's spent hours up here, sleeping, writing, thinking, wondering what to do.

'Come on,' she says to Danny, and he's off the bed in a trice, nosing through the door, off down the stairs. He stops at the turn, to look back up at her. But Janice, on the dusky landing, is suddenly still.

Here, a few paces away, is Matthew's room, which she has never entered.

* * *

She enters it now. Quietly she turns the handle, and steps inside.

* * *

The bed is covered with an Indian cotton spread; the rug beside it is an old cotton durrie, striped in blue and green. There's a desk, a chair, an armchair. Everything's very plain.

Some of the things which furnish the room of Claire's childhood, and of her adolescence, are in here, too: more things, in fact, for Matthew, after all, has no new home. There's nowhere he can take the books, or school photographs — everyone lined up in blazers, squinting; the cricket team, with him — she looks, and finds him, yes, that's him, down in the deep, miles away in the long summer grass, waiting for the catch. Where can he put the heaps of music, except in the piano stool downstairs, or up here, where they lie on the bookshelves, gathering dust?

There's his violin.

It rests in its case on top of a long, low

bookshelf: she crosses the room, sees the thick film of dust all over it, reaches out a finger, draws it back. This is his. He's the one who must clean it up, open it up one day.

The whole room smells of dust; the air is musty, shut up and still. She goes to the window, opens up the casement to the fading light, feels the fresh, rained-through evening spring air on her face, lets it enter the room. She leans out, and looks down on the walled back garden, where the willow is stirring, just a little, in the breeze. She looks beyond — to garden upon garden, set here and there with tall trees, chestnut and sycamore, plane and mountain ash. One or two people are out, snipping things in the dusk; she sees a cat leaping softly up on to an ivy-covered wall, she hears the birds of London gardens, settling for the night; she hears, all at once, in the distance, the low, breathy hoot of an owl, as dusk descends, very suddenly now, and then it's dark.

⋆ ⋆ ⋆

Buffy's bed is empty when he gets back. Must be in the loo, unless they're doing some ghastly test. Surely not, not at this time of day. She won't be having supper — just as well, to judge by what he saw on the trolleys. He sets her little things on the locker, beneath the pink-and-white lisianthus, just opening now in the central heating, and paces about, nods to one or two other patients, goes over to the plate-glass window of the bay and looks out.

West London spread beneath him, fourteen floors below. Darkness and fairytale strings of lights, tiny lines of traffic, moon coming up. If they weren't in here, with the prospect of tomorrow, it could look rather romantic. He feels the letter in his inside pocket, next to his heart. Well. Here's a thing.

Where has she got to? Better have another look.

And he leaves the glittering panorama of the city at evening, and goes back into the main ward, looking up and down.

Someone is coming along from the bathroom, in a pale blue woolly dressing gown, and mules; a towel is draped over her arm, she's clutching a flowery sponge bag. Her grey hair is up in a knot, and she's pale, but walking determinedly, giving a faint little smile to one of the nurses, looking about her, trying, he can tell, to get her bearings: which bay was it? And his heart turns over: how brave and strong she is, how independent, after all these years alone.

'Here we are,' he says, walking down the ward towards her. 'Here we are.'

'William!' Her face alight with happiness. 'What are you doing here?'

'Thought I'd pop back,' he says, his hand beneath her elbow, guiding her back to her bed. 'Thought it might be nice for you to have your things tonight.'

'Oh, it would.' She sees them, on the locker, beneath those lovely flowers: the glass-and-silver bottle of scent, the little silver bell. She has had them beside her for years and years. She puts down her towel and sponge bag.

'Is that from the National Trust?' asks William.

'It is, as it happens. I couldn't resist. Oh, thank you so much, I can't tell you how much better it makes me feel to have these things in here.'

And then she suddenly stops, and remembers. She'd left the bell and the bottle on her desk because she was preoccupied — with writing that letter, trying to get it right, sealing it at last, and leaving it for him, just in case —

She doesn't know where to look.

'William?' she says, because she has to know, she'll never ever sleep tonight if she has to worry about all this, as well as whatever hell lies in store tomorrow.

'Yes?' He's picked up the little bell, and he shakes it, gently: what a sweet, old-fashioned sound. Perhaps they could start collecting these. He shakes it again.

'I wrote you a letter,' says Buffy, feeling herself go pink. 'I wrote you a letter, but I didn't mean you to read it, not yet. I must have been terribly flustered when I left the flat — ' She's terribly flustered now; this is dreadful. She looks up at him, sees that smile, feels weak. 'Did you get it?' she whispers.

He puts down the bell; taps his pocket.

Then he draws her close to him, folding her in his arms.

* * *

She's not going to leave. She can't. Not yet, not until she's seen him again, tried again, found out what hope there might be. She realises, unpacking her stuff, putting it back in the drawers, that this is how William must have felt for years: going on and on, hoping and hoping, against all the odds. Well. Well — if you don't have hope, you'll die. And down in the kitchen she eats two bowls of cereal, whistles up Danny, clips on his lead. 'Come on. Let's have a run before supper.'

It's cold again, it threatens rain again, but she doesn't care: she must get out, go walking. Danny is thrilled. He trots along the pavement, sniffing and lifting his leg at every third railing. She tugs at his lead. 'Come on!' God, but it's different from walking the Shropshire lot.

And how are they? she wonders, turning her collar up, turning the corner of the street. How are they coping with the crisis, poor old bats? God, it must be hard; she had better write.

She walks briskly on, tugging at Danny — get a move on, get some proper exercise. The wind is beginning to blow: she feels it, cutting across the park. There's a moon, rinsed clear as glass after all that rain, rising, rising, high above the trees.

* * *

'Hello? Anyone at home?' He closes the door behind him, smells something delicious, feels a great wave of contentment. He hangs up his coat, looks in the mirror, gives a little wink. 'Hello?' he calls again, making his creaking descent to the bowels of the earth. 'I'm back.'

'So it seems,' says Janice, stirring at the stove. 'Hi. How's Buffy?'

'Bearing up well.'

He gives her a little kiss, looks for the corkscrew, finds it.

'Yes?' He waves it at her.

'Yes, please,' says Janice, taking the pan off the heat.

'And what is that?' he asks her, peering.

'Mushroom and courgette sauce, to go with spaghetti. Is that OK?'

'Very OK.' He has a look in the wine rack, uncorks a bottle of red. What a very satisfactory sound it makes: never fails to cheer one, after all these years.

They sit drinking together, while Danny snoozes.

'Manage to take him out? Well done. Well, well — ' He raises his glass. 'Cheers. Quite a day. What with one thing and another.'

She looks at him: he's much less strained and anxious. 'How do you mean?'

'Oh — ' He gives a little wave. 'We'll talk about it later — all in the fullness of time.'

'Is she going to be OK?'

And then a shadow does cross his face again.

'Let us hope. One can only hope and pray.'

'What time is the op?'

'Half past ten — they said I could phone in the evening.' He lifts his glass again. 'God, that's good.' He looks at her, looks again: rather pale, rather drawn about the gills. 'And what about you?' he asks her. 'You were *very* late.'

'Yeah,' says Janice. She reaches for her tobacco

tin — he's got used to it now, he doesn't mind. 'We stayed up talking,' she says, and feels a blush begin to rise.

He raises an eyebrow. 'Did you, now? What about?'

'Oh — ' She gazes down, teasing the strands of tobacco.

This isn't right — she knows it. Matthew is his son, he walked out of hospital, all that way through the rain and traffic. He might have been killed. How can she keep this from him?

She takes a breath. She'll say it, she'll keep it as cool as she can. There was a bit of a do last night, to tell you the truth. With Matthew —

And then she thinks: But he's safe, he's safe now. William's got Buffy to worry about, with everything else. I'll tell him — I will, if Claire doesn't. But not now. Not yet.

And she rolls up, runs her tongue along the Rizla paper, reaches for her lighter, saying: 'Oh, this and that. But you're right, it was too late. I'm having an early night.'

'Very wise,' says William, waving smoke away. 'I think I'll do the same.'

⋆ ⋆ ⋆

It's morning. William wakes early, as is his habit. He lies for a moment, coming to, listening to the birds, as is his wont. It's spring, but it's still dark: how they go on, in spite of this. Something's happening today: for a moment he can't remember what. Then he does. He looks at his clock; half past seven, three hours to go. She's probably been awake for hours; they wake you at the crack of dawn in hospital, it's brutal. He can remember Eve, who rarely complained, saying how hard it was, when you'd hardly slept all night —

He shuts his eyes. 'Oh, darling.'

Then he gets up. He pulls on his dressing gown, has a look in the mirror, picks up Eve's photograph, which has stood there in its leather frame on the chest of drawers for years and years. Taken . . . when? He can't remember — probably when the children were still at home, growing up, but still here: there's only the hint of white in her hair, she still looks young — but then she always did, almost to the end. He picks it up. What a sweet smile — you could tell Eve anything. No wonder Claire went to pieces when Piers was born. You need your mother then, of course you do.

He holds the photograph out before him, brings it close again, kisses the glass. 'You don't mind, do you?' And then he puts it back, goes to the window, draws the curtain, sees the daylight begin to break through, and the last star fade.

* * *

It's morning: Janice sleeps on and on.

When she wakes at last, she lies there, looking at the sun behind the panda curtains, thinking: something is happening today.

What's that?

Buffy.

Yes, but something else.
Matthew. She's going to see him again.

★ ★ ★

It's almost nine: breakfast over, the paper looked at, Danny getting hopeful. Bang of the letterbox: ah. And what do we have today?

William climbs up the stairs to the hall and peers along it. Bills. And a square of white. He walks along the polished tiles — God, one day Mrs T. will have them all in hospital — and bends to the mat.

A Shropshire postmark, but the writing isn't the wild hand in which he remembers Mary addressing him last autumn. It's a good hand, a clear, artistic hand. Well, now. He takes it to his desk, picks up his paper-knife. Outside the window, he notices the blue tits flitting back and forth across the garden, beaks stuffed with bits of moss. Lovely, must be the ones he fed all winter. Now then. And he takes the letter out.

Dear Cousin William,

This is your cousin Ernest writing. I am truly sorry to trouble you after all these years, but we is on the brink of ruin . . .

★ ★ ★

He's asleep. They've put him in a side room, on his own, near the nurses' desk. His door is half open, and the curtains on the window into the ward are half drawn back: they can keep an eye;

he won't walk out again.

'I'm a friend,' she says to Eileen, on duty again. 'Remember?'

Eileen nods. 'That's good. He needs a friend.'

She tiptoes in, she blinks. It's the middle of the morning, and the sun is bright outside, but in here it's all dim and quiet. Not in a soothing way — in an institutional way. Coarse grey curtains, pale vinyl floor, pale bedspread — everything colourless, lifeless, in this poky little room.

He's breathing heavily, lying on his side, facing the door. He's so long limbed and tall — his feet beneath the bedspread are right up against the end rail. She takes off her jacket, and sits down in the plastic bedside chair.

'Matthew?'

No answer. God, how pale he is. She leans forward, strokes the dry hair which once was springy, strokes his sunken face, takes his hand, and lifts it to her lips. Then she sits there, holding his hand in hers, watching the slow rise and fall of his chest, saying his name now and then, waiting.

* * *

Another nurse comes in, and checks his pulse.

'How long will he sleep?' asks Janice.

'He should wake up soon. It should be wearing off.'

* * *

A houseman looks in. 'Are you a relative?'

'No,' says Janice. 'No, I'm a friend.'

He nods, like Eileen.

'Talk to me,' says Janice, looking at him straight. 'Tell me the score.'

He smiles. He's young. The white coat suits him. She feels he will tell her the truth.

'He's been very ill for a very long time,' he says, not sitting down.

'And?'

'Until last night we were getting hopeful. I think they were going to call his father in, make plans. The new medication — it does seem to be waking him up.'

'And now — after last night?'

'He'll be OK. I think he was having a bit of a bad reaction — all those substances, swirling about — ' He's nice, she thinks; he's human. Probably taken a substance or two himself, in his time. 'If we get the dose right now, he'll be happier, I hope. And he's musical, isn't he? That might pull him through.' He looks at her, sitting there, holding Matthew's hand. 'And are you . . . how shall I put this? Are you intending to stick around?'

Janice looks back. 'How shall I put this?' she says. 'Give it to me straight. What are the chances?'

'Of — ' But he knows, he knows what she means. He sits on the chair by the basin. 'Of normal life.'

'Yes.'

'How long have you known him?'

'Not that long.'

'But . . . you care for him.'

'Yeah.' Her grip on Matthew's hand tightens; she turns to look at his sleeping face, all the night's trauma smoothed away. How beautiful his eyebrows are. 'Yes,' she says. 'I do.'

'In that case,' says the houseman, 'I should think his own chances are somewhat better than those of a hell of a lot of other people in here. And as for the two of you — no one could pretend it would be easy. But you're pretty young, aren't you? If that doesn't sound too personal.'

'We're talking personal,' says Janice. 'That's exactly what we're talking.'

He smiles, then his pager goes off. 'Excuse me.'

Janice sits there, stroking Matthew's hand, listening as the houseman talks to another ward. Yes, he's on his way. Hang on a tick. And he switches it off, gets up from the plastic chair.

'I don't know,' he says, looking at the two of them. 'You can only give it a go, can't you? If that's what you both want — give it a try. Why not? If it doesn't work — well, as I say. You're young.' He smiles again, slipping the pager back in his pocket. 'A doctor speaks, for what that's worth.' He goes to the door. 'I think he's pretty lucky,' he says. 'If that's not too personal.'

They smile at one another. Out in the ward, the coffee is coming round.

'Can I ask you something?' Janice says, as he pulls the door wide, and the sun comes in. 'How much do you know — ' She swallows. 'About his background. His family.'

He turns back to look at her. 'Not a great deal.

I'm new. Whatever Fisher knows will be on file. Why? Is it important?'
'I don't know.'

* * *

The sun comes through the open door. There's a patch of it on the grey vinyl floor, and on Matthew's pillow. Janice drinks her coffee, and goes on sitting there. Matthew stirs, gives a long, sleepy sigh.
'I'm here,' she says, and puts down her polystyrene cup and gets up, leans over him, kisses him gently, on the forehead. Then on his lips. 'Here I am.'
He opens his eyes, he sees her: she can feel him swimming up to the surface, breaking through.

* * *

William writes back by return.

Dear Ernest,
How good to hear from you. We have been thinking of you all so much: what a dreadful business this all is, and of course you must be feeling the pinch. Janice Harper, the nice young woman whom Mary recommended, has told me so much about the Museum, and all your good work. I hope you will accept this small enclosure, just — as it were — to keep the wolf from the door. Soon, I hope to come up for a visit. I have a dear friend who's rather

under the weather — in hospital, in fact. As soon as she's right, I might bring her up for a little spring break —

You fool, William, he hears Buffy say, at her briskest. There's no such thing as a little spring break any more, that's the point. The countryside is closed, can't you understand?

But didn't they open the fells, at Easter? No, perhaps not. Everyone wanted them to, but —

He crosses that out, with a long, elegant sweep of the pen.

As soon as everything has settled down, and you're back in business, we'll be up. I might bring my son, who's making great progress, I'm pleased to say. A family reunion — wouldn't that be fun?

It would be, it would be marvellous, after all these years. And he puts down his pen, and thinks about them all, all together again, with everyone on the mend, and getting on.

But first — first there is Buffy. It's half past eleven — she'll be in theatre now.

He sits there, watching the slender gold hands of the carriage clock on the mantelpiece creep slowly round.

* * *

It takes for ever to get him out of bed, on his feet, down to the toilet with a nurse, who takes him through. By now, the mid-morning sun is pouring in through the windows of the main ward, and the grounds are full of spring light and shade.

'How about it?' she says, when he comes back. 'Fancy a little turn?'

'Might do him good,' says the nurse. 'Give him a bit of an appetite for lunch.'

'Matthew?'

He looks down at her from his great stooping height, bends his head in polite enquiry.

'Shall we go outside for a little while? Get some fresh air?'

He nods. 'Yes. I'd like that.'

She feels a little rush of happiness.

Outside, the squirrels are everywhere, bounding over the grass, leaping among the firs. Janice puts her arm round Matthew, ushers him slowly to a bench. They sit in the sun, her arm round his shoulders, watching, letting the warmth sink in.

'You do remember me,' she says at last. She looks at him, gently turns his head towards her, so he has to meet her eyes. He does.

'Yes,' he says, with a slow half-smile.

'What's my name?' she asks him, and then there is a long, long pause.

'That I don't know,' he says at last.

'It's Janice.'

'Yes, yes, of course. I remember now. You looked after me once.'

'And when was that?' she asks him, filled with emotion.

'When I was drowning,' he says slowly. 'I do remember that.'

23

'You see?' Ernie is triumphant. 'You see? Blood is thicker than water, family is all.' He waves the cheque before them. Mary snatches it from him. 'Give that to me.'

'No fear.' He makes a grab.

'You'll tear it,' says Sophie. She puts her hand to her mouth.

'Now look,' says Ernie, banging the table, as Mary waves the cheque aloft. 'What we have here is a hundred pounds. For all of us. But made out to *me* — I'm the one what wrote.'

'*Who* wrote,' says Mary, tucking it into her pinafore pocket.

'I wrote. You know I did.'

'No, you old fool, I'm talking grammar.'

'Grammar? Grammar, when we is on the brink? Them dogs — ' He gestures towards the open window, the endless barking. 'Them dogs is on emergency rations, no walks, no exercise — '

'It's out of our hands,' says Mary, slamming the kettle on. 'A crisis is a crisis, it's not just us.'

'I know that. We all know that. But we're talking grub, not walkies. Not one visitor. Not one. No income. And *you* — ' He glares at her. '*You* was the one what ruined my show. That would've brought us a bob or two, that would have kept us going. More than that — ' He waves his arms about, thinking of it all — the fame, the acclaim, money in the bank and a diary of appointments. 'You and your temper. You and your rages. Now give me that cheque.'

'No.'

'Oh, please,' whimpers Sophie, backed up against the door to the stairs. 'Please, please, please don't argue — '

But Ernie's blood is up. 'I had a dream,' he tells Mary. 'A proper steady life, a proper income. You've gone and ruined all that. I had another. History. Heroes. Visitors in droves — ' He's spluttering now, gasping for a cig, but there's no cigs now, not a penny for baccy nor papers — nothing. 'That blimming Janice,' he says all at once. 'What did you want to go and send her off to London for? Nothing's been right since she went.'

And he turns on his holey heel and makes for the door.

'Yes, go!' shouts Mary. 'Get out and stay out!'

'You menopausal old hag!'

Sophie is sobbing. Mary is beside herself. She picks up the rolling pin, and Sophie shrieks.

But Ernie has scarpered, banging the back door so it's almost off its hinges, hobbling across the yard, where hens fly up in astonishment, feathers everywhere.

'Go on!' he shouts at them. 'Out of my way! No blimming use anyway, no blimming eggs — '

It's true. Even the hens have stopped doing their stuff. They flutter up on to the fence and sit there, croaking, while the dogs go mad.

'Useless old birds. Put you in the pot, that'll learn you.'

And he stumps up the rotting steps, missing a fall by a whisker.

'I'll be back!' he yells across the yard.

'You haven't got a bank account!' shouts Mary, from deep within the house.

He slams the trailer door.

Pipsqueak is on his filthy old sleeping bag, snug in a patch of sun. He jerks up at the violent sound of the door, and begins to tremble.

'It's not you,' Ernie tells him, slumping on to the bunk. He's shaking all over. 'It's not you, old chap.' He strokes him with a shaking hand. They sit there together for a long time. Ernie's head is bowed. 'I dunno,' he says, over and over again. 'Blimming women. I dunno.'

After a while he spots something. Under the table, right in the corner. Baccy! A little bit of baccy in a screw of gold paper — what's that doing there? Must've dropped it, painting. Forget about everything when you're painting, that's half the joy. He gets up, shuffles over, bends down carefully so as not to bang his head, fumbles about. Got it! He comes out backwards, gets up, and bangs his head.

Never mind, never mind, there's hope yet. And he rubs his head, and unscrews the paper, and yes, there's enough for a couple of cigs.

He puts the kettle on, scrabbles about in the table drawer, with its filthy old stained spoons and marbles and bits of wire and useless blimming tin opener. Must be a packet of papers somewhere, must be.

The kettle begins to sing. He finds two torn papers, right at the back.

'Things is looking up,' he tells Pip, but Pip has gone back to sleep, twitching.

Ten minutes later, Ernie is sitting at the table, drinking weak sugarless tea and smoking. Ah. That's better. That's much better. The wireless is on, posh people talking about the European papers. Europe! What do they know?

'The French believe Britain is having a collective nervous breakdown . . . '

Ernie draws in an enormous evil breath of tobacco smoke, and looks out over the empty fields. No sheep. No lambs. Filthy, disgusting black smoke, rising from beyond the trees. Them pyres have been burning for weeks. No visitors. Mary off her rocker.

'Too blimming right,' he murmurs, drinking his horrible tea. 'Too blimming right.'

* * *

Buffy is getting better. She is sitting up and taking notice, nibbling at fruit. The Over-Sixties sent an entire *basket*. And she's had the results back from the lab. This was the moment she dreaded: the drawing of curtains round the bed, the consultant sitting down beside her, quiet and grave. But instead —

'It's benign!' she tells William, propped up against the pillows, using a mobile phone for the first time. That nice little student nurse has lent it to her.

'What's that?' God, what a line. 'Speak up.'

'I said it's benign,' says Buffy, as loud as she can without making a spectacle of herself.

'Everything's all right. They've taken it all out, and I'm clear. No chemo, no radiotherapy — '

'No tricks, no unpleasant bending,' says William, and she starts to laugh, then stops, as the stitches tear. Goodness, how sore she is. But still — who cares? What's a few painkillers, compared with —

'This is marvellous,' says William. 'Splendid. I'm coming over.' And she can hear his relief, his complete light-heartedness. She feels just the same. 'What would you like me to bring?'

'No grapes,' says Buffy, who never wants to look at a grape again. 'Nothing. Just you.'

'I'm on my way.'

* * *

'And now,' he says, sitting at her bedside, holding her hand. The scent of the roses he has brought her fills the bay: two dozen, long stemmed, cream and pink — the very best he could find.

'Look at them,' says Buffy happily. 'Just a dream.'

'And look at you,' says William, stroking her hand. It's thin and white, like her now — she must have lost half a stone at least. There's a nasty little bruise from the drip. But still — she's here, she's perking up. 'Now,' he says again, leaning forward and kissing her. 'Convalescence. We must find just the right place.'

'People don't convalesce any more,' says Buffy, stroking his face. Even this is an effort, and she leans back against the pillows again. She's on the mend, but the stuffing's taken out of her, no doubt about it. Except when she thinks about William, and William and her — then she's a helium balloon, floating o'er hill and dale . . . She brings herself back down to earth. 'There's no such thing as convalescence,' she tells him. 'People don't even use the word any more. You're ill, you go into hospital, you die, or you're out in the twinkling of an eye and expected to get on with it. I'm coming out on Tuesday.'

'Tuesday? You only came in here — ' He counts.

'Five days ago. I know. But they need the bed. And they say I should be up and about. They say it's good for me.'

He shakes his head. 'Well, you can't go back to the flat. Isn't there some nice little place? Tempting meals? Fluffy towels? A garden?'

Eve had died in hospital — he hadn't had time even to think of such a place. And Matthew — well, that's a different kettle of fish altogether.

'By the way, I must tell you,' he says, patting her hand, but carefully, avoiding the bruise. 'Matthew seems to be turning the corner.'

'Really? Oh, William, that's marvellous. Tell me.'

'All thanks to you,' he says. 'Well, in the beginning. You woke me up, got me going. They've taken him off those fearful horse pills, put him on something much lighter. He's coming to, talking more. Much more. Quite lucid, sometimes. I saw him yesterday. And he and Janice — '

'He and Janice what?' asks Buffy, looking at him intently,

'Well, I don't know. But she's often down there, at the hospital. And she wants to bring him home. For a visit, I mean.'

'Very nice,' says Buffy. 'You'll enjoy that.'

'I tell you what,' he says, and everything is clear to him now — of course, this is what they must do, he always knew he should hold on to the spare room, in spite of all Claire's fuss. 'You must come home to me. I'll look after you. I'd love it.'

'Are you sure?' What a heavenly thought.

'Certain. And Janice is the most marvellous cook, you know, there'll be lots of little meals on trays.'

'It does sound . . . well, William, it sounds quite perfect. If you're sure.'

'Certain,' he says again. 'Good, that's settled. And we'll have a little party, once you're up to it. Have Matthew there. And Claire and the family. A celebration.'

'How is Claire?' she asks him, exhausted by the very thought of all this. She'll have to be careful, she mustn't let him get carried away.

'Not really sure,' he replies. 'Haven't heard from her for a bit.'

'That makes a change.'

'Well — one day we'll sort it all out.'

'She's not about to announce a divorce, do you think?'

He's horrified. 'Oh, no, no, no, no, I'm sure

not. Jeremy's the most marvellous chap.'

'But are they happy?' asks Buffy, and this he cannot answer.

'No,' he says at last. 'No, I don't think they are. I don't see how she could be as she is, if they were. But still — I do hope they'll stick it out.'

'Why? Why, if they're not happy?'

'Well — you know. The children. All that.' He shakes his head again. The very idea. 'We don't go in for divorce,' he says. 'We're a monogamous lot, the Harrimans. When we get married, that is,' he adds, thinking of the mad old cousins. No one could possibly marry them. And he tells her about Ernie, and the cheque. 'Might take you up there, one day. Would you like that? Once all this business is over, once everything's opened up again. Little spring break — or perhaps in the summer,' he adds quickly.

'I'd love it,' says Buffy, and she would, once everything's opened up. But, oh, those poor, poor animals — do they really have to die? 'It's not even as if foot-and-mouth kills them,' she says. 'The sheep can get better, certainly. Even the cows, sometimes. It's all about yield, and profit, it's awful.'

'That sounds like my old Buffy,' says William, leaning forward and kissing her cheek. 'You *are* on the mend.'

She holds his hand to her cheek. 'Thanks to you. *We're* happy, aren't we?'

'Very,' he says, and it's true. He wakes up in the morning and he feels — contented. Especially now they've had the results.

'Shall I tell you something?' says Buffy, as a

trolley comes rattling along. Coffee? She peers. No, library books. She hasn't touched the Ackroyd. Now she can really enjoy it at last.

'What's that?' he asks her tenderly. 'Anything — you can tell me anything.'

Is that true? Will that always be true? She hesitates.

'Do you know,' she says, 'that for ages I thought . . . I thought — ' She feels herself go pink again.

'Thought what? Go on, my darling, what did you think?'

'I thought you were falling in love with Janice,' she says, and is scarlet now.

'Ah.' He looks at her over his spectacles; he takes them off, releasing her hand, and wiping them on his handkerchief.

'And were you?' she asks him, fearful now.

'She made me feel young,' he says at last. 'She cheered up the house, no doubt about it. Still does. But — ' He puts his spectacles back on, dissolves her with his smile. 'It would hardly have been suitable, and anyway — ' He leans forward, kisses her tenderly on the mouth. 'You and I are going to have a very nice life together.'

'Kiss me again,' whispers Buffy, and he does.

* * *

'And you're really, really sure I can come and stay?' she asks him, over a hospital lunch. He's been down to the Friends Shop, brought up a shrimp salad sandwich and coffee which he has while she struggles with something in a compartmented dish. 'I'd better eat it,' she says, poking it about. 'It's vegetarian, I must have ordered it.' The prospect of tempting little meals on trays, of being looked after in that lovely house —

But all those stairs —

'You're sure it won't be too much for you?'

'Of course not.' He pokes a shrimp back into the lettuce. Rather good.

'And where — ' She hesitates. 'Where will I stay?'

'In the spare room, of course.' He looks at her over the top of his specs. 'At least for now.'

* * *

It's June. Buffy is up and about again. Still having naps in the afternoons, still having breakfast in bed, brought up by William or Janice, but so much better. Soon she'll be back on the stall, which William, all this time, has kept going. Sometimes, in the mornings, they go for a little potter about in the south London auction rooms.

'I say, William, do come and have a look at this.' She picks up an octagonal bowl, patterned in green and white, with a thin gold base. They peer at the trademark. 'Oh. For a moment I thought it was Worcester.'

'Could be,' says William, pushing his spectacles up his nose. 'Worth getting anyway, don't you think? Terribly pretty.'

He goes back that evening and bids, comes

home with the bowl, and six Masonware dinner plates.

'What do you think?'

'Lovely,' says Buffy. 'How clever you are.'

It's just like the old days, but better. He kisses her. It gets better every day.

* * *

One hot Sunday, Matthew comes home. Just for the day: that's how they'll take it — one day at a time.

William goes to fetch him, taking Danny. Buffy and Janice prepare the lunch. Janice carries the garden table out of the shed and sets it up beneath the willow tree. Long strands brush her face as she goes to and fro from the house, carrying folding chairs, a green-check tablecloth, silver and glasses, white china, green linen napkins. All William's lovely old things. She's nervous and happy, cutting a spray of palest pink Albertine roses from the ramblers on the wall, pricking her finger, running water into an antique vase and setting it out on the garden table. There. Perfect.

Buffy observes all this, and keeps her counsel. They hear the slam of car doors at the front. Janice goes racing up the stairs.

In the hall, she stops, takes a deep breath, steadies herself and looks in the mirror. She runs her hands through her hair, brushes a willow leaf away. Here they are, coming up the steps. Here's William's key in the lock, here's Danny, nosing in at the first chance, here's Matthew —

She stands there, dead still, as the door swings wide, watching him walk slowly through, his father behind him, patient and unhurried, and he, so tall and so beloved, coming into the cool of the hall, patterned in emerald and violet light, seeing her, holding her in his gaze, flooding her with his smile of recognition.

She walks towards him; he takes her hand.

* * *

'Well, now,' says William, under the rustling willow tree. 'Isn't this perfect?'

He uncorks a bottle of 1995 Pouilly Fuissé, glistening with cold; he unscrews a bottle of elderflower, icy to the touch. He fills their glasses, one by one. Everyone raises them, Matthew too.

'Cheers.'

'Cheers.'

'And all we want now,' he says, over chilled mint-and-cucumber soup, 'is for Claire to be here. With all the family.'

Nobody answers him.

* * *

Even under the willow, it's dreadfully hot. After lunch, they all go up to the drawing room, where the huge tall windows are open and the air is cool.

'Oh, that's better.' Buffy sinks on to the sofa, William sinks into his chair. 'I'll make the coffee,' says Janice. 'Matthew? Would you like coffee?'

Matthew is standing at the front window, looking out on to the front garden, where the magnolia is leafy and full, and the afternoon sun on the flags is dappled by its shade. He's very still.

'Matthew?' She goes up and stands beside him, slips her hand in his. 'Are you all right?'

He nods, he turns and looks down at her. 'Just thinking,' he says, in his beautiful low voice, so much steadier now, so much clearer.

'What about?'

'Different things. Many different things.' He shakes his head, he turns back and looks around the room: at his father, long legs stretched out in the old armchair; at Buffy, surrounded by cushions, watching him intently; at the piano, with its crowded family photographs, of him and his parents, him and his violin, him and Claire, him and Claire, him and Claire.

Janice can hardly breathe.

His gaze moves away; it lights upon the violin case, which she has brought down, and dusted, and polished but not opened. It's resting on the piano stool, and the leafy sunlight dances over it.

'That's mine,' he says slowly.

'Yes.'

He drops her hand, walks across to it, runs a finger over the polished wood. The stillness in the room is palpable.

'This is mine,' he repeats. 'One day I might play this again.'

'Do you want to play it now?' asks William gently, from across the room.

Matthew looks at him. It's a long, slow look

whose meaning Janice can't begin to guess at. Then he bends down, and slips the brass hooks on the case. It takes him for ever to do this. Nobody offers to help. He lifts the lid, he looks down, at bow and violin, resting there, as they have rested for years.

Out in the garden, the breeze is stirring the leaves of the magnolia; blue tits flit back and forth to the nest in the wall; somebody's cat pads softly across the flags.

Summer in London. A train goes rattling past.

Matthew bends down, and slips the bow out from the lid. He runs it through his long musician's fingers. He lifts out the violin, and blows off a film of dust, takes out the duster from the bottom of the case and runs it over the body. He lets it fall to the floor.

Then he stands up straight, and tucks the violin beneath his chin, stops, readjusts himself, settles. He lifts the bow, draws it slowly across, tunes up, adjusting the keys. Everything is hesitant, everything takes for ever.

Janice walks over to the piano stool and sinks upon it, filled with such feelings as she has never known.

William's eyes fill with tears. Buffy observes this, and swallows.

Everything in the huge, airy room is concentrated into this moment, upon this man.

He begins to play.

24

Late June. The Sunday paper flops on to the mat. Buffy, in her dressing gown, goes to pick it up.

She bends down — goodness, how difficult this still is; perhaps she should be having physio.

'Or yoga,' Janice has been saying. 'Yoga would do you a power of good.'

'I'm much too old for yoga.'

''Course you're not.' Janice is radiant these days. She thinks anyone can do anything.

Buffy gets up slowly, dropping half the paper. God, what a weight, it's absurd, no one needs all these sections. At the hall table, she puts it together again, as best she can, smoothes the front page, looks at the headlines.

Needless slaughter of up to two million animals.

'I knew it,' she says aloud, trembling with fury. 'I knew it all along.'

* * *

Late June, very hot, and in London the pock of Wimbledon, back and forth, back and forth, hour after hour. In the country, some of the lanes are open again, and some of the footpaths.

Ernie and the dogs go walking, hour after hour. Sometimes Mary does it, sometimes Sophie. They're talking to one another again, things is looking up.

But still. They have barely a farthing. A hundred pounds is a hundred pounds, and in the end he let her cash it, but where does it get you nowadays? What they need is capital. Investment. Serious money.

Sitting in the trailer with the door and windows open, the breeze blowing in and the breeze blowing out again, listening to the hens, scratching across the yard in the sun, seeing the dogs flat out beneath the trees, he picks up his pen, and writes another letter.

* * *

'A family reunion,' William says to Claire, holding the letter in his hand. He reads it out to her, sitting at the phone in the drawing room, having a lunchtime snifter, windows open, blue tits darting about. 'Do come, darling, it would do you so much good. A little break. Bring the children. Bring Jeremy.'

'I'll see,' says Claire.

'We haven't seen you for months.'

'We're very busy. Jeremy's always in court.'

'Yes, but still — ' He's determined not to give up. So much has happened, and she's been outside it all. 'Buffy's staying here,' he tells her.

'Buffy? Whatever for?'

'She's been very ill. She's convalescing.' He takes a deep breath. 'If you would only come here, darling, I could tell you things. I don't like to give you all the news and never see you.'

'What news? What are you talking about?'

'Never mind,' he says wearily, damned if he's going to talk about wedding plans over the phone. What's wrong with the girl, what's wrong? He has one last go. 'And Matthew's much better,' he tells her. 'Or perhaps you know. They've changed his drugs, he's turned the corner.'

There is a silence.

'Hello?'

'I don't suppose Janice told you,' Claire says slowly at last.

'Told me what?'

'That he absconded from hospital. In the spring, when she was baby-sitting. He absconded and walked out all the way here. He was off his head.'

William is so shocked he cannot speak. At last he says: 'And why did nobody tell me? Why?'

'What was the point? You'd only have got in a flap. I took him back. I rang the next day and he was all right.' There's another pause. 'What do you mean when you say he's getting better?'

'He's happier,' says William. 'He's much more alert. He's started to play again. He's been home several times now. And he and Janice — ' He hesitates.

'What? What about him and Janice?'

'I think they're in love,' says William slowly. 'I know it all seems . . . well, improbable. But I think they are.'

There's a huge, dark silence — even from here he can feel how huge and dark and strange it is.

'Darling? Claire, darling — '

Then the phone clicks dead.

* * *

'You didn't tell me,' he says quietly to Janice later, when Buffy is having her nap. They're clearing up in the kitchen, after lunch.

'Tell you what?' But she knows, as soon as she looks at him. 'You mean about Matthew. Leaving the hospital. Claire's been talking to you.'

'Inasmuch as she ever talks to me,' he says. 'Inasmuch as she ever says a word. She did tell me that.' He opens a cupboard, puts away the pepper and salt, turns back to her. 'Please,' he says carefully. 'Don't ever do that again. Don't hide things from me. Not about Matthew, not things like that. I'm his father, I have a right to know.'

'I know,' says Janice, feeling her cheeks begin to burn. 'I know. I'm sorry.'

She takes out her tin. He pulls out a chair, and sits down opposite her.

'Something is terribly wrong with Claire,' he says. 'I've got to face it. Do you have any idea what it is?'

'No,' says Janice, on fire all over, twisting and twisting the paper in her fingers. 'No, I don't.'

* * *

It's evening. The sun is setting over south London gardens, glancing off greenhouses and sinking into the green-gold depths of lily ponds, filtering through the trees. Buffy is soaking it up after supper, lifting her face to its warmth.

'I'm better,' she announces. 'I can feel it,

through and through.'
'Marvellous. Dear Buffy.'
William, in the garden chair beside her, pats her hand. Janice is visiting Matthew; they have the place to themselves.
'I want to ask you something,' he tells her, slipping his Panama down a little, shielding his eyes.
'Ask on.'
'Janice and Matthew. What do you think?'
'You mean in the long term?'
'Yes.'
They sit there holding hands.
'I'm not sure,' says Buffy, 'and that's the truth. What do you think, William?'
'Oh, I don't know.' He shakes his head. If it weren't for Buffy, how old all this would make him feel. 'It's a hell of a thing,' he says. 'Let's face it. Hell of a thing for a young girl like that — young woman, rather.'
'It is.'
'On the one hand . . . well, it's wonderful. All these years of emptiness, and now, the prospect of . . . well, the prospect of some kind of future, at last. Look at how much better he is, playing again, taking part in conversations. And the way they look at one another — it makes me feel happy, I can't help it.'
'I know.'
'But am I being irresponsible?' he wonders, reaching for his glass. 'Do you know what Claire told me, this afternoon?'
'No.'
He tells her. Buffy is shocked.

'Oh, dear.'

'Of course, that's some weeks ago now,' he says, swirling the last of the ice. 'Matthew's clearly been going from strength to strength since then. But Janice didn't tell me. I had to confront her, I'm afraid, give her a little talking to.'

'Quite right.'

'And Claire — ' His sigh breaks the spell of the summer evening. 'Oh dear oh dear, that poor girl. She went so quiet when I talked about Janice and Matthew. I think she hung up on me, to tell you the truth.' He drains his glass. Thank God for whisky. 'What is to be done?'

'Nothing,' says Buffy. 'I hate to see you upset by her, year after year. She's a married woman, William, let her get on with it.'

There's a silence. On this perfect golden evening, he can feel their first little rift. So can she.

'Oh, darling — ' She turns to him. 'Lift up that Panama. Look at me.'

He does both these things.

'That's better. Do I sound terribly harsh? I know I can't possibly know what it's like, not really. When you have children, I'm sure you must *ache* — '

The rift begins to close. He squeezes her hand. 'I'm afraid it's true.'

'So what do you want to do?' she asks him. 'Should we invite her to supper? Invite both of them? Or do you think you should go and see her? Have it out, once and for all. It might clear the air, dear, it really might.'

'It might,' says William, but the prospect terrifies him. 'I'm afraid I've always been a bit of a dodger,' he says. 'When it comes to unpleasantness. Not very good at having things out, when it comes down to it. Oh, dear.' He lifts her hand, rests it upon his heart. 'What an old fool you must think me. How brave you were, writing me that letter.'

'I thought I was going to die.' How far away it all seems now. The way she feels tonight, she could go on for ever.

She tells William this. He lifts her hand and kisses it.

'I'd never have woken up,' he says. 'If you hadn't written to me. That's what I mean — I don't see things. That's what Claire has been saying for years.'

Buffy kisses his hand, so wrinkled and papery, but still, underneath, so strong. 'You see quite enough. You're a dear, loyal father: no one could wish for better.'

He shakes his head, but he's comforted. How good love is.

'How good love is,' he says, thinking of Buffy, thinking of darling Eve, whom he can sense there, somehow, out in their garden on a summer night, understanding everything. It's getting dusky now, but still it's warm.

'Indeed,' says Buffy, thinking of William, thinking of Janice and Matthew, so strange but, at least for the moment, so happy. 'She's a strong young thing,' she says, knowing she's understood at once. 'We'll just have to wait and see.'

'I suppose we can pick up the pieces.'

'If we need to.'
'Quite.'
The sun is slipping away, the dusk is deepening. Two soft hollow notes sound from within the trees.
'Those owls,' says William. 'They come back year after year.'

* * *

A golden summer evening. Out in the hospital grounds the long, deep shadows of the firs are splashed with light. People are out and about, walking slowly, sitting on benches outside open doors. There's a little game of croquet; someone is laughing; swallows swoop low.
Matthew holds Janice in his arms. 'You're bringing me back to life,' he tells her. 'You're making me well again.'
'Me and the pills,' she says, looking up at him. Tall as she is, she has to do so. His eyes are clearer; they hold such tenderness now that she can hardly breathe.
'Mostly you,' he says quietly. 'I think it's mostly you.'

* * *

A warm summer night. They've all been out to the park in the afternoon, and played cricket. Hugo is going to be good, no doubt about it. Jeremy tells him, and he flushes with pleasure. 'Almost as good as Piers,' says Jeremy, taking out the stumps. Piers is in the first eleven now: he's often away on Saturdays. This is the first time they've played as a family for ages. Geraldine has run like the wind, though her batting, Hugo tells her, is pretty pathetic still.

'Shut up.'

'That's enough.' Claire comes in from the deep, where she likes to be.

'You don't *have* to always be fielder,' says Piers, as she walks up, back to them all.

'I don't mind. It gives me time to think.'

'And what do you think about?' asks Jeremy lightly, dropping the ball in the bag.

'The thoughts of a mother of three.'

Now it's time to go home. Other families are doing the same, walking towards the gates, their shadows long on the grass behind them. Some of them they know.

'There's Martin,' says Piers, and raises his hand to a plumpish boy, walking between his parents.

'He's a nerd,' says Hugo.

'He's OK.'

Martin's parents are waving to Jeremy and Claire. Pleasantries are exchanged at the gates.

'Isn't it funny,' says Derek, rubbing his beard. 'That we all knew that Shropshire girl.'

'What Shropshire girl?' asks Martin, as Claire goes on ahead.

'You remember. From the Dog Museum. She fetched up at Drake's, in the Village.'

'That Dog Museum was wicked,' says Martin.

'Oh, I *wish* we had a dog,' says Geraldine.

At home, next door come over for drinks. It goes on for ever, as the sun slips down. The children get peckish, then grumpy. Crisps won't do it for ever. The air is full of the smell of barbecues. Next door go back to theirs. Sausages come over the fence; the children perk up, while Jeremy sizzles away.

'How can you put away *more*?' he asks them, turning the kebabs Claire made that morning, thick with marinade.

'Easy.' They burn their tongues on mushrooms, shrieking, and come back for more.

At last it's time for baths and bed. At last, after the tucking up of Geraldine, as the boys settle down before the bedroom computer, Jeremy and Claire are alone. They wash up, they clear up, at last they sit down. Jeremy has brought out the map of France; they sit at the garden table, tracing the route they'll take in late July. They've rented the house before, a couple of years ago; now Geraldine's older the journey won't be quite so bad. And once they're there —

Once they're there, it'll all be non-stop, just like here, though with another family they can share the load a bit.

'Time we went off on our own,' says Jeremy, leaning back, letting the last of the sun sink in. 'Time we did our own thing, don't you think?'

'Mmm.'

He lets his arm rest lightly across her shoulders. There is no answering gesture, no turn of the head. He's used to this. He's had to get used to this.

'Claire? Was that William on the phone? At lunch-time?'

'Yes.' She smoothes the map out, her hand running over the Loire, the Auvergne, the Cevennes. All those beautiful places, he thinks, watching that hand, with its bitten-down nails. She lifts it now, to gnaw; gently he pulls it back. She shakes him off.

'Stop it.'

He lets his arm fall from her shoulders; he lets his eye fall upon Paris, and Chartres. That view of Chartres from the plain; that blue. They went there before the children were born. It wasn't quite right, even then, though then he had not dared to think this.

'How was he?' he asks, as the birds settle down in the trees. 'William?'

'Oh — all right. Buffy's living there, apparently.'

'Buffy?' He's always had a soft spot for her. 'How come?'

Claire explains, and begins to fold up the map.

'Well, how nice for them both. How cheering. We should have them to supper. And is Janice still there? Or has she gone back to Shropshire?'

'She's still there,' says Claire, and now the map is folded. 'Coffee?'

'In a minute. Stay here for a moment.' What a week it's been. What a year. How long is it since they sat out here like this?

'And Matthew?' he asks her, and feels the blinds come down. 'How is he getting on?'

'Fine. Much better, apparently — but then we've been here before.'

'I don't remember you ever saying he was much better before.'

'No. Well, they've changed his medication. I'm sure I've told you that.'

'Perhaps.' And perhaps she has, and perhaps he wasn't paying attention, after the usual day. The briefs on his desk in their bedroom make two piles now: somehow he must get through things before France. He thinks of it all: the heat, the long afternoons upstairs, the shutters pulled to, the children out with the other lot, and he and Claire —

He knows what it will be like.

'Darling?' he says now, and draws her to him again. 'Do I not listen enough? When you try to tell me things? Are there things you want to tell me?'

'No,' says Claire. 'No, there aren't, everything's fine.' Briefly she rests her head on his shoulder; then she gets up. 'I'll make the coffee,' she says, and goes inside.

This is our life, thinks Jeremy, gazing out over the garden. This is how things are. He hears the coffee beans grinding fiercely; the smell of them wafts out through the open kitchen window. When it stops, he can hear the owl they've heard all summer, calling from somewhere nearby. It's almost as if he belongs here, he thinks, listening to that slow, sad cry.

It's gone very quiet in the kitchen. After a minute, he gets up, goes to the window, looks in. Claire is just standing there, very still, as the kettle begins to fill the room with a dreamy cloud of steam. He's shocked at her unutterable sadness: he can feel it, even from here.

'Darling — '

She looks at him, her dark eyes enormous in the shady room.

'I'm sorry,' she says, her eyes brimming, now. 'I'm so sorry.'

'What for?' And now he could go in, he could take her in his arms, he could take her upstairs and tell her, over and over again, that he loves her, that he will always love her —

He doesn't. He's done that before, though not for a very long time, and sometimes he's felt as if he were saying these things to himself, that nothing — nothing he can ever say or do — will truly bring her to him.

So he waits: for her to make the move.

'What are you sorry for?' he asks her quietly.

And this is a defining moment in their marriage: he can feel it — a turning point, the possibility of naked truth between them.

Then Claire turns, and takes the kettle off the hob, and says through her tears: 'Nothing. Nothing. Forget it.'

Scalding water pours into the pot. He stands there in silence, unable to move. Claire puts everything on a tray.

'But I will say this,' she says to the empty air. 'My life would be nothing without you all.'

25

A family reunion. William has booked them all into a nice little inn, outside Oswestry, for they can't, of course, stay at the Museum overnight. But they can, of course, spend the afternoon there.

The car speeds up the motorway, William and Buffy in the front, Matthew and Janice in the back. His arm is round her shoulder, she leans against him. This is the longest time he's been out of hospital for years. Danny is in his basket, tucked beside her. The smell of summer grass blows in at the window, as they turn off the motorway, off the bypass. They drive down the lanes with their towering hedges. Danny sits up, and presses his nose to the glass, his ears streaming back in the wind. They look through the gates. Most of the fields are empty.

'Dreadful,' says Buffy sadly. 'Dreadful. There should be sheep, sleeping under the trees, there should be cows, munching away — '

'I've told you,' says Janice from the back. 'If we were all vegan there'd be no need — '

She can hear herself going on; just as she did to them all in London; just as she used to do with her parents, and with Steve. Tomorrow she'll see them all again. And they'll all meet Matthew — she feels a little twist of nerves, but they'll manage, William will see them all through.

'That's enough,' he says now, slowing at a crossroads. 'If we were all vegan, the country would have not a single sheep nor cow. And how would you like that?' he asks Buffy, watching a lorry rumble past. It says Sun Valley Chickens, all over it; crates of white feathery birds are piled high within, he knows it, and hopes she hasn't seen.

'I wouldn't like it at all,' says Buffy, who's seen it perfectly clearly. 'No, of course I wouldn't. But . . . oh, dear.' And she looks out of the window, wondering what's for the best. I shall start a campaign, she thinks, as soon as I'm properly fit. I shall take out a sub to Compassion in World Farming. I shall send money to donkeys, in the Far East.

'We're almost there.' Janice is suddenly hugely excited. She turns to Matthew. 'Can you remember them at all? From when you were little?'

He shakes his head. 'Perhaps when I see them I will.'

Here's the sign: The Dog Museum, painted on wood in black and white, tied up in a hawthorn hedge. Here's the house, and there are the huts beyond it, and here, at the gate, a million dogs are waiting in the sun.

'Well, well, well,' says William, braking. And then is frankly speechless. He hoots; they wait.

Ernie and Mary and Sophie come slowly down the yard, in ancient sunhats.

'Get back, you hounds!' shouts Ernie, and tips his hat and lets the gate swing wide. In bumps the car, and a million dogs mill round it, barking madly.

* * *

They sit at the kitchen table, drinking tea. Sophie's hand is fluttering over her hair slide. It took her for ever to choose which one. In the end, she chose the bluebirds.

'Bit more normal than them cockatoos,' Ernie says in the morning, when he sees her. 'You look batty as a fruitcake in them cockatoos.'

'I don't want another penny spent in that shop,' says Mary, banging out jam tarts. 'I hope that's clear.'

Sophie says nothing. Never to go in there again — she twists her handkerchief.

'If we play our cards right,' says Ernie, 'we can buy the whole place up.'

Mary sniffs.

'I'm not talking extortion,' he tells her, dipping a filthy finger in the jam. She slaps it away. 'I'm not talking blackmail or bailiffs. Just investment. He must be rolling, old William. Treasury pension, roomy family house — '

As soon as he sees the car, he knows he's right.

And here they all are, sitting round, proper family, just as it should be. And that Janice, back again at last. He gives her a wink.

'Got any baccy?'

'I have, as it happens.' She passes the tin across, and he opens up happily. Ah, that's more like it. He looks across at Matthew. Something not quite right there, and no mistake. Still, if that's what makes her happy. And he lights up, feeling better than he has for months.

'I do like that hair slide,' says Buffy to Sophie,

and she flushes with pleasure.

'Ta very much.'

Mary glares at her. Sophie takes no notice.

'I like your combs,' she says to Buffy, admiring the tortoiseshell.

'How kind of you.'

They smile at one another, in perfect understanding.

'Now then,' says William, finishing his ghastly tea, Danny on his lap and a hundred dogs at his feet. Dear, dear, dear, what a set-up. 'I'm longing to see round.'

Ernie needs no second bidding.

'Right, then.' He gets to his feet. 'Follow me.'

* * *

Inside the huts, William and Buffy and Janice and Matthew walk from booth to booth, from moth-eaten Labrador to mouse-filled St Bernard, with his panting felt tongue and little keg. Janice has seen it all before, of course, and tried to describe it, but no description could ever, ever —

'But this is magnificent,' says William. 'This is artistry.'

Buffy gazes at the shining fish, the huskies, the Northern Lights.

'This is unique. We must preserve it.' Her mind is racing. The Museum of Childhood, perhaps, in Bethnal Green. A grant? There must be a grant, for something like this.

Ernie is bursting with happiness and pride. 'What I have in mind now,' he tells William, when at last they've done the rounds, 'is a series of exhibitions. Now, if you'd like to step into my trailer — '

'Are you sure they'll want to do that, Ernie?' asks Janice, but he takes no notice. He's on a high, on a roll, the world is his oyster now.

* * *

Inside the smelly old trailer, he shows them it all, everything he's done since the Healing Arts fiasco. Portraits of Pipsqueak, and Nelly and Spot, portraits of Tilly and Ben. They're all taped up on the walls.

'Fantastic,' says William, and means it.

'It makes me long for a brush,' he tells him, and Ernie picks up his tin box of paints and flourishes them.

'No need to spend a fortune. I've managed with these. Mind you,' he adds quickly, 'sable would be nice. Can't beat a good sable.'

'Indeed,' murmurs William, as Danny comes bouncing up the steps.

'Ah,' says Ernie, picking him up. 'Now you're a nice little chap. Why don't I do your portrait?'

'There's a thought,' says William. He can see it now.

* * *

The sun is slipping down. A million dogs are eating from a million tin dishes: in the pens, in the yard, outside the back door.

'But where did they all come from?' asks

William. ‘How did it all begin?’

‘Little by little,’ says Mary, patting a greyhound. ‘It’s an endless task, a life’s work. But worth all the sacrifice, worth all the effort.’

‘I’m sure.’ He’s completely baffled. ‘But how on earth can you feed them all? It must put you to dreadful expense.’

‘Ah,’ says Ernie, Pipsqueak in his arms, ‘now if you’d like to come back to the house, perhaps we can have a little talk. Man to man,’ he adds, and everyone melts away.

⋆ ⋆ ⋆

It’s early evening. Everyone’s happy. William, inside the house, has listened. He’s looked at the business plan. Well — why not? It is, after all, unique. And as the others troop in at last, and Mary, uniquely, fetches a bottle from the snug, and some really rather good little glasses, he takes out his cheque book, takes out his beautiful old fountain pen, unscrews it, and writes an enormous cheque.

‘I’ve made it out to you,’ he says to Ernie, waving it to dry. ‘Is that right?’

‘It is,’ says Ernie, who has opened an account with a pound, just yesterday. ‘It is indeed.’ And nobody says a thing. It will, after all, be to everyone’s benefit.

⋆ ⋆ ⋆

It’s dusk. They’re all outside, sitting on hard chairs with their drinks in the long, long grass leading up to the field gate. Bats flit about, the hens are making their way into the hen-house — 'Before that wicked old fox comes along,' says Ernie — and the sky is streaked with gold.

Matthew and Janice are holding hands. 'I think I do remember this,' he says, looking around at it all.

'We remember you,' says Sophie. 'You and Claire. Dear little things, you was.'

The sun dissolves at the edge of the farthest field, and then is gone. More bats, and then, all at once, through the dusk, they hear an owl, calling from deep within the woods.

Janice's hand in Matthew's tightens. His expression, in the dusk, is unreadable. The owl calls again: those two hollow notes, timeless, mysterious, achingly sad.

'I wish Claire was here,' says William quietly. 'It isn't right, without her.'

He looks at Janice, and she looks back: such a long, long, searching gaze he gives her; she has to turn away.

William is no fool. He knows she's keeping something back. Does he know what it is? Does he guess?

The owl is calling, the scent of summer grass is everywhere, the darkness is almost upon them now.

Could anyone, ever, guess that?